JOURNEY TO ECSTASY

He took her in his arms, gathering her so close she could feel his breath upon her face. As he spoke, he lowered his lips to brush against hers ever so lightly, ever so tantalizingly. "No one can protect you," he gently warned. "I want to devour you . . . I want to take you to places you've never been before. I want to strip you naked and cover your flesh with kisses. And I want to hear you pray that no one will rescue you."

Dani moaned, knew she should resist . . . knew she did not want to. Her arms clung to him, and he effortlessly, gently lowered her to the ground . . .

LOVE AND SPLENDOR

PATRICIA HAGAN

AVON
PUBLISHERS OF BARD, CAMELOT, DISCUS AND FLARE BOOKS

AVON BOOKS
A division of
The Hearst Corporation
105 Madison Avenue
New York, New York 10016

First Avon Printing: October 1987

For Bettie . . . and the summer of '84

Chapter One

Paris, 1891

DANI Coltrane gathered her white ermine wrap tighter about her bare shoulders. She had learned long ago that late summer evenings in France could be quite cool, and she had anticipated the chill, just as she had expected that her escort, Perrine Ribaudt, would draw her outside to the seclusion of the terrace behind the Paris Opéra.

It was intermission, and she stood waiting for him to return with champagne.

Rainbow streams of light spilled through the stained-glass panes of the building's arched windows. Combined with the silver bath of the full moon above, Dani stood in a rainbow hue. The billowing skirt of her delicate pink gown of watered silk seemed to come alive and breathe, rippling with thousands of glittering sheens and shimmers. Her chestnut hair, caught and held high in cascades of curls by tiny circlets of diamonds and pearls, shimmered like melted gold.

She was the personification of beauty. She had inherited her mother's delicate loveliness, her father's charm and wit. But as she stood bathed in the magical radiance, she was the mirror of intense, smoldering agitation.

Each time Perrine maneuvered her into a situation where he could once again attempt to persuade her to accept his proposal of marriage, she became angry with herself for allowing such a predicament. Kind and handsome though he might be, she had no intentions of marrying him or any of the other would-be suitors who called at the mansion where she lived with her father and stepmother. Love, and marriage, she felt, meant manipulation, subservience, relinquishment of her own will to another human being, and, by god, she had learned her lesson. Never again would she allow herself to be controlled or directed by anyone.

She walked to the edge of the terrace and gazed thoughtfully toward the Etoile, at the western end of the Champs-Elysées, with its twelve avenues of light radiating out from what appeared to be the center of a giant star. In the center of that star stood the colossal Arc de Triomphe, 164 feet high, more than twice the size of the Arch of Constantine in Rome. It had been planned by Napoleon to honor his victorious army.

Turning, she could see the glow of the Place de la Concorde, but nothing to suggest it was once the notorious Place de la Guillotine, splashed with the blood of Louis XVI, Marie Antoinette, Lavoisier, and other victims of the Revolution.

Lost in a realm of historical scenes before her, Dani allowed herself to be carried back in time to reflect once more upon those painful, miserable years of her earlier life, when she had allowed herself to be entirely manipulated by her Aunt Alaina . . .

She recalled the story of how her father, Travis Coltrane, renowned Union cavalry officer and hero of the War between the States, had married, at war's end, the beautiful and spirited Kitty Wright, who had borne him a son. They had settled on her inherited farmland in North Carolina. Then, several years later, she had been abducted by an old enemy. Travis had traveled across the country to the deserts of the west in search, only to be told she was dead. Attempting to escape his deep, gnawing grief, he had accepted a job as a Federal Marshal and an assignment in Kentucky to quell the violence of the newly formed Ku Klux Klan.

Dani knew there was much she had not been told and realized that what Aunt Alaina had told her had been her personal interpretation of events back then.

She also knew that her aunt had been romantically involved with her father for a time, but it was her mother, Marilee Barbeau, whom he'd eventually married. Alaina had never forgiven him, had probably hated him with the last breath she drew.

Dani sighed, shook her head with pity. Such hatred had to eat upon the heart like a gnawing cancer. How else could her aunt have been so cruel as to create the breach between father and daughter?

When her mother died giving birth to her, her father had already discovered his beloved Kitty was not dead but suffering from amnesia. They were subsequently reunited, and then Alaina had set out to destroy the relationship between Dani and her father and Kitty.

She had succeeded.

Alaina persuaded Dani to come and live with her permanently. Her father had resisted such a move, but the situation in the household, due to Alaina's constant interference, and Dani's subsequent intolerable behavior, became unbearable to everyone.

At first, Dani had lived at the Barbeau estate in Kentucky. When Alaina married Count Claude deBonnett, they had moved to Monaco, in the south of France, to live in the deBonnett château. Dani had no memories of a happy marriage between the two, for it was no secret Alaina had married the Count only for his money.

Alaina had also taken young Gavin Mason with her to France, the son of the only other man she had ever loved—Stewart Mason. Stewart, Dani was to learn, was another reason her aunt so vehemently hated her father. Stewart had been a leader in the Klan and, in a gun battle, her father had shot and killed him. Alaina adopted his son, and, through the years, Gavin and Alaina succeeded in making Dani quite miserable.

Seeking love, Dani turned to the church. She felt all alone in the world. There was no way of knowing then that letters she wrote through the years to her father, and those he wrote to her seeking a reconciliation, were intercepted by Alaina and destroyed.

When the Count was killed in a duel, massive gambling debts left Alaina in dire financial straits. Gavin had proposed marriage to Dani, wanting, she knew, to claim whatever she might one day inherit from her father.

She had turned her back on Gavin's proposals and her aunt's pleas and joined a strict cloister isolated in the Maritime Alps. Placing her earthly past soundly behind her, Dani looked to a future of absolute servitude to the church.

Then, a sudden, unexpected, and forbidden visit from her half brother, Colt, awakened her to reality. She learned that her father was living in Paris and had divided up his fortune between her and Colt. Not knowing about the money, Dani also had no way of knowing that Gavin Mason had blackmailed a servant girl to pose as Dani and go to America to claim her share.

The terrible tale had unfolded as Colt miserably recounted how Briana, the servant girl posing as Dani, had made him believe he had seduced her. Overwhelmed by guilt to think he had bedded his own sister, he had signed over everything he had to her and gone away in shame. It was only later, when he returned, that he learned the family ranch had been sold.

Colt followed Briana and Gavin to France, where Briana told him of the entire scheme. She had never wanted to be involved, had been blackmailed because of her sick brother, whom she had to support.

Eventually Colt, aided by his father, had tracked Mason to the Greek island of Santorini, where they recovered the swindled money . . . and found Mason murdered by one of his own men.

Alaina, it was discovered, had died after plunging from a window of the deBonnett château to the jutting rocks below while attempting to murder Gavin Mason's mistress in a jealous rage.

After much contemplation, Dani realized she did not truly wish to be a nun. She left the convent and moved to Paris to get to know the family she had been denied—all because she had allowed herself to be manipulated.

Dani felt a warm glow now to think of the happy times shared with her father and stepmother during the past year. Travis Coltrane was every bit as wonderful as she'd hoped he might be, and Kitty was more like a sister than a stepmother. In fact, it had been Kitty who had helped her come to understand how so many people had been hurt by her inability to make her own decisions, by allowing someone else to interfere in her life.

Kitty, Dani had admiringly come to realize, was an independent spirit, yet she was able to love a man while maintaining her own identity.

Dani wanted to be just like her.

It was also Kitty who had helped her to see that she owed it to herself to live her life to the fullest. There was a fortune already bequeathed to her by her father, and she had the money to do anything she wanted.

And the one thing she wanted above all else was independence . . . to make up for all those lost years.

The sound of Perrine's voice calling her name sharply snatched her from the grasping cobwebs of the past. She turned to face him.

Perrine Ribaudt was not only handsome, with dark, curling hair and laughing brown eyes, he was also intelligent. Educated at Oxford in England, he spoke flawless English with only a touch of a French accent. However, if he had not, there would have been no language barrier, for Dani spoke perfect French.

They had met at a reception at the embassy. Perrine was being groomed for an ambassador's post and came from a wealthy, influential family. Dani found him to be enjoyable company and had accepted his invitations to attend various social functions. All she had wanted was a friendship, but then, after they had been keeping company only a few months, he had proposed. She had refused, but he was undaunted and continued his attempts to persuade her to say yes.

He held out a glass of sparkling champagne and smiled fondly, dark eyes glowing with his love for her. "I'm sorry to have kept you waiting, my dear, but the hall was crowded."

She took the champagne, wishing to hear the silvery tinkle of the bells signaling the beginning of the last half of the performance. If she stayed in Perrine's company, unchaperoned, for very long, she knew what would happen.

She did not have long to wait for the inevitable.

He was staring at her intently; suddenly, it was as though he could not bear the moment any longer. He flung his glass to one side, into the shadows, and then, to her astonishment, took hers and did likewise. With one, swift movement, he crushed her against his chest, and his hungry lips began to nuzzle her face as he moaned, "Dani, oh, Dani, my cherished, my love. Why do you torture me so? Don't you realize I must have you for my wife?"

She pressed her hands against his chest and pushed with all her might, but she was helpless against his strength. Twisting her head from side to side, she protested angrily. "Perrine, stop it! If you don't, I'll scream. I swear I will—"

"No!" He covered her lips with his own—warm, demanding, possessive. His hands moved across her back to press her yet closer.

Dani continued to struggle against him, beating upon his chest with tiny fists. Then, slowly, insidiously, like an unseen enemy, she began to feel the first stirrings of the betrayal of her own body. She knew she did not love Perrine, yet her loins grew hot with the warmth of desire. She had never known a man that way, but the impulsive wave of yearning screamed to not be denied. Silently, she demanded her heart, her body, her mind, to turn away, not yield to this clawing, nagging beast that was turning her blood to the hot, flowing lava of lust.

She melted against him, but only for one, brief instant. It was as though, in that final moment, when acquiescence seemed imminent, that a bolt of awareness shuddered through her body, flashing the warning that to yield meant to be manipulated . . . made to do something not of her own volition.

Instinctively, Dani stiffened in his arms. She could admit to herself she had desires, wanted to be taken to untold heights of passion and pleasure, but only when *she* wished to be taken there. Never would she allow herself to be seduced!

Perrine felt her resistance, knew he was defeated. His arms dropped from the embrace, and he looked sadly down at her in the silver glow of moonlight. "Dani, my love. What can I do to prove how much I love you?" he whispered miserably. "You're breaking my heart. You—"

Dani pressed fingertips of silence to his lips. "I don't love you, Perrine," she told him. "I like you. A lot. But I don't love you. I'll never love you . . . never marry you." Her eyes searched his for some sign of understanding, acceptance, but he merely continued to stare at her, crushed.

She drew in her breath sharply and turned away.

At once, she felt his hands on her shoulders and cringed at his touch. He chose not to notice. "Dani, I've told you before—I'll make you love me. We were meant for each other—"

She whirled about, just as the bells rang their signal. "You just want a wife, Perrine," she cried, frustrated, for there seemed to be no way to get through to him. "You have a career. You want a wife to go with it. You think that's what life is all about."

He blinked, confused. "Isn't it? Isn't that what you want, Dani? To marry? Have a husband? A home? Children? A lovely social life?"

She held her breath against the fury churning within. Finally, when she felt in control, she said, "Why do I have to have a husband? Children? Why can't I have a career and a lovely social life of my own? Why do I have to live for other people?"

He looked at her incredulously, as though he had never really seen her before. "You—you don't want marriage? A family?" He shook his head, sure he had not heard correctly. "Why—why, what kind of career is there for a woman except a family?"

Her lips parted to speak but then she shook her head and laughed softly, sadly. "Don't you see, Perrine? I seek that answer myself."

He gave her a look of both bewilderment and anger but turned to lead her back inside.

Together, they walked among the magnificent and ornate Second Empire architecture, the lavish decor of classical statues and sculptural groups. They passed through the Italian loggia with its roofed gallery, open and supported by great white marble columns.

They began their ascent of the grand staircase of gleaming marble steps, the balustrades carved of the finest onyx. Lining each side were the resplendent soldiers of the Garde Républicaine, in their fabulous full-dress uniforms of scarlet and white, gold helmets gleaming in the light of dazzling crystal chandeliers, sabers drawn.

All about were the elegant costumes of the Paris elite, and to Dani, it was a fairy-tale world. Entranced by the opulent surroundings, she was oblivious to Perrine's pouting, as well as the admiring glances of those who saw her and acknowledged silently that she was easily the most beautiful woman in attendance at the sumptuous showplace.

They found their seats. Dani turned her full attention to the performance, ignoring Perrine's now and then sideways glances of perplexity. He made no effort to hold her hand as he had done earlier. While she would have liked his friendship, she knew, sadly, that their relationship would end after this night. He wanted total possession, and the thought of such a fate filled her with cold dread and muted anger.

He took her home in silence. They reached the sidewalk that led through the ornate wrought-iron gates. Glittering lanterns of brass and glass adorned the surrounding brick wall. Ahead loomed the imposing two-story mansion, its windows smiling a warm, illuminated invitation to enter.

"Would you like to come in for a brandy?" Dani politely offered. "I'm sure my father is still up and would enjoy your company."

He shook his head, gazed pensively toward the house for a moment, then gave her a wretched look as he said, "I do love you, Dani. Believe that. But I can't go on like this. Seeing you. Being with you. All the while aching because I'm afraid there's no hope . . ." He shook his head, sighed. "I'm afraid I'm not the sort to just keep hanging on and wishing. It's useless and frustrating . . . and painful," he added with a shudder.

Dani nodded. "I understand, Perrine. I'm just not ready for marriage to you or any man. Maybe I never will be."

He stiffened. In the mellow glow of light, anger shone in his eyes. "Then you're trifling with me," he accused.

His voice had risen, and in proportion, so did Dani's ire. How dare he make such an insinuation? Good Lord, did all men think merely because a woman accepted an invitation that they were a candidate for the position of wife?

"I resent your implications," she said sharply. "I asked for nothing more from you than your friendship. If you consider that 'trifling,' then you're sadly mistaken."

She lifted her skirts and turned to swish angrily through the open gates.

At once, Perrine contritely called, "Dani, wait. I didn't mean it. I just love you so, and . . ."

His voice faded amid the furious roaring in her ears as she hurried on up the sidewalk, up the stairs, and past the waiting doorman, a bewildered expression on his face.

She entered the circular foyer, with its marble floor, the walls papered in pale green satin with designs of ivy in a darker shade of velvet.

Standing patiently, she allowed Cletus, the butler, to take her white fur wrap, then she moved toward the burgundy-carpeted stairs that curved upward to the second-floor landing. To either side stood a pair of carved wood and gilded pedestals, supporting a pair of bronze and ormolu candelabra.

When she reached the landing, she turned toward the left, to her quarters, but suddenly Kitty cheerily called out to her from the direction of the other wing.

"Dani, good evening. Didn't you invite Perrine in for a nightcap?"

Dani felt a rush of need and turned to look at Kitty, peering from a doorway, wrapped in an emerald dressing gown that complemented her lovely eyes. Her hair, the shade of a brilliant summer sunset, tumbled softly about her shoulders.

Dani's eyes were imploring as she miserably whispered, "May I come in and talk to you, if it won't disturb Poppa?"

At once aware something was wrong, Kitty beckoned to her. "He's at the embassy, getting ready to leave for Panama tomorrow. Come in and have a glass of wine."

As always, Dani was impressed by the beauty of Kitty's parlor. Since moving to Paris, Kitty had become passionately involved in the study of interior design, as well as art, and as a result, the Coltrane mansion was a showplace of taste and culture. An invitation to visit and view was a prize coveted by the social and government aristocrats of Paris.

Dani was especially fond of the magnificent and imposing Chippendale mahogany secretary bookcase that stood just inside the door, with a beautifully carved swan-neck pediment and its unusual ogee bracket feet. Kitty had said it dated from 1775.

Beside it sat a George I period chair in walnut on elegant cabriole supports which were decorated with shell-carved knees that terminated in ball-and-claw feet.

To the side of the secretary, on the wall covered in yellow watered silk, hung a fabulous pair of carved wood and gilded two-branch girandoles, decorated with birds, torches, and wheat-sheafs, and hung with crystal drops.

Kitty had crossed the room to where she kept her evening bottle of wine on a Chinese altar table with two secret compartments. It was one of her favorite pieces, and she watched, smiling with pleasure, as Dani admired her other pieces . . . fruits of long hours of laborious searching in out-of-the-way French antique shops.

She poured them each a glass of rosé, then served Dani before gesturing to her newest addition to the room. "A treasure," she explained proudly as they stood before the painting of a young man and woman embracing as they sat together in a wooden swing, suspended by ropes from an overhanging branch. "I was at a tea last week given in honor of the new German ambassador, and it was such a lovely afternoon, I decided to walk home. Along the way, I discovered a tiny little shop on the Rue Jussieu, and the owner was not learned enough to know the works of Pierre-Auguste Cot. He died in 1883, and his paintings are becoming more valuable each year."

Dani was appropriately impressed. Thanks to Kitty's influence, she had herself been studying art for the past year, and she could well appreciate the works of Cot.

Kitty motioned her to join her on the Hepplewhite sofa.

Dani nodded in acknowledgment of the 1786 piece. Kitty had discovered this treasure, covered in blue velvet, with graceful curves and light, slender woodwork, along the Rue Bonaparte. "You are a wonder," she said. "I'm afraid I've much to learn."

"You grew up surrounded by art treasures," Kitty was quick to remind her. "I've heard that once upon a time the deBonnett family possessed one of the most valuable collections of art in France."

Dani laughed ruefully. " 'Once upon a time' is right. I recall when we first went to live at the château, the halls were lined with paintings, but as the Count's fortune diminished due to his compulsion for gambling, so did the enviable collection of art. By the time he was killed in that duel, the halls were bare."

Kitty sighed. "Such a waste. But come, enjoy our wine, and I'll tell you all about your father's trip." She went on to explain how Ferdinand de Lesseps, the noted French engineer who had built the Suez Canal, had organized a joint-stock company to cut a canal across the Isthmus of Panama, but the venture had turned out to be costly and difficult. Two years ago, the company had collapsed, and large numbers of shareholders had been stripped of their savings. Consequently, demands were being made for a parliamentary investigation, and Travis had been asked by his government to go to Panama and view the situation in preparation for the hearings, because the interests of many American investors were also involved.

Dani listened, but halfheartedly, for she was still quite peeved over Perrine's remarks.

Finally, Kitty dared to probe. "Something is wrong, Dani. Do you want to talk about it?"

Dani felt a warm rush of gratitude and poured out all that had happened and her feelings about it.

Kitty listened quietly, patiently, nodding now and then until Dani had finished. Then she said, in what she hoped was not too stern a voice, "I know you want to be in control of your own life, dear, but are you sure you aren't confusing the struggle for independence with obstinacy?"

Dani blinked, not understanding. "Obstinacy? Why on earth would you think that?"

"I know it has to be very difficult to learn to make your own decisions when your every thought was manipulated by your aunt Alaina, but just because you're now determined to think for yourself, don't close your heart to love."

"I don't understand what you're trying to say, Kitty."

Kitty sighed, stood, and began to pace about. Dear Lord, she was not this girl's mother, had not raised her, had only come to know her, actually, this past year. She realized there was a thin line between advice and interference, yet Kitty had never been one to mince words when she felt strongly about something, so she decided to plunge ahead. "Don't turn your back on the possibility you might truly love Perrine, Dani," she said. "You may be so determined to be independent that you might be willing to deny that love."

A furious shake of her head sent chestnut curls flying about her face. "I don't love Perrine, Kitty," Dani said firmly, fiercely.

It was Kitty's turn to be baffled. "But you seem so upset—"

"Yes," Dani was quick to admit, "upset and angry, because he dared to insinuate I was trifling with him. Since when is a woman obligated to marry a man merely because she accepts his company socially? Since when does it mean I'm looking for a husband because I enjoy going out with men?"

Suddenly, Kitty burst into uncontrollable laughter, sinking down on the sofa once again and covering her face with her hands as her body continued to convulse with amusement.

Just as Dani, somewhat miffed by Kitty's behavior, was about to demand an explanation, Kitty reached out and clasped both her hands tightly. "Oh, Dani, you're the echo of my own indignance when I was your age. I didn't mean to laugh, but it just brought back so many memories.

"You aren't wrong to feel as you do," she went on. "You don't owe a man anything except honesty, and not even that if you're disposed to answer only to yourself. You certainly owe Perrine nothing. Not even an explanation as to your feelings."

Dani was filled with gratitude but felt the need to confide further. "I can't help but feel a little bit guilty, because I did hurt him, and—"

"No!" Kitty cried sharply. "You are never responsible for what another person feels, only what *you* feel. Remember that you are never accountable for another person's reactions to your feelings and beliefs."

She paused to give her a hug. "I love you so much, Dani. You're the daughter I never had but always wanted, and I want you to be happy."

Dani grinned from her heart. "I know, and I'm so grateful for a friend like you."

They shared a second glass of wine, and Kitty once more renewed her urging that Dani travel. "Spend some of your money, see the world, experience all life has to offer."

Dani assured her she had thought about it but then declared, "The truth is, I don't want to behave like a giddy-headed debutante, or rich society girl, flitting all over the world with no purpose except having fun. I want a goal. A challenge. A career. I want independence . . . a life of my own without having to depend on anyone else."

Eyes glowing with the warmth inside, sired by the wine and the love she felt for her stepdaughter, Kitty leaned to embrace her once more as she whispered huskily, "Then do it, Dani, darling. If that's your dream, then go out and find it."

Chapter Two

Dani was awakened just before seven by Lurline, her personal maid.

Sunlight rushed into the room as Lurline opened the white brocade drapes. *"Bonjour, mademoiselle.* Your father would like you to join him on the terrace for breakfast."

Dani stretched, yawned, smiled with delight. "Wonderful. I was hoping to see him before he had to leave."

"Shall I draw your bath?" Lurline offered.

"Please." Dani sat up, stretched once again. She loved the large bed, loved everything about this room. While Kitty had urged her to make the final choices of decor, she had certainly guided her all the way, and the results were, she felt, quite lovely.

The canopy gracefully draping above the bed was of the finest handmade Belgian lace. Nearby was a superb Louis XV bombé commode in kingwood, with gilded bronze mounts of the highest quality. Each morning, in season, a bouquet of fresh flowers from Kitty's pampered gardens was placed on it.

Dani and Kitty had found the Queen Anne bureau bookcase at an estate auction only a few months ago. Enriched by ornamentation of hand-molded brass, it opened to reveal a leather writing surface and numerous shelves and pigeonholes within.

At one end of the room was a white Bechstein piano and a Regency loveseat covered in imported Spanish velvet with a hand-embroidered design of swans and geese.

There was hand-rubbed mahogany molding around the walls, with rich beechwood paneling below and wallpaper of Flemish design above.

Dani's favorite in the room, however, was the wall opposite her bed, which displayed paintings from France, England, and Austria, representing four centuries of European landscape.

Dani bathed. Then, with Lurline's help, brushed her hair back into a chignon, which was the quickest style. She adorned the coif with a scarf of chiffon the same lavender as her dress.

She looked among the many crystal atomizers which were displayed on a gilt-edged mirror tray on her dressing table, and selected the one her father had brought her from a trip to Austria in the spring. She misted herself lavishly, then rose to scrutinize herself in the large, oval mirror above the table.

Lurline, hovering nearby, pressed her hands together in delight. "Oh, mademoiselle, you are lovely, as always, like a breath of fresh air on a spring morning."

Dani thanked her for such a dramatic compliment and continued to stare at her reflection thoughtfully. She had but one photograph of her mother, and that was in the tiny gold locket she wore about her neck. Her grandfather Barbeau had given it to her when she was a child, and it was her most cherished possession. But back in Kentucky, in the short time she lived there before Aunt Alaina married and they moved away, she had spent long hours standing before the huge life-size painting of her mother which had hung in the parlor, memorizing every detail.

Her mother, she recalled, had been tall, as was she. Her hair was also chestnut, and her eyes, brown. Yet, she could also see a part of her father in the reflection before her, in the thick lashes, the curve of her jaw.

Men said she was beautiful. She wondered if she truly was, then laughed to herself with a touch of vanity and decided maybe she was attractive after all.

There was a knock on the door, and Lurline hurried to respond.

She returned with a dozen long-stemmed red roses cradled in her arms and, smiling knowingly, declared, "They are from Monsieur Perrine Ribaudt. Shall I read the card?"

Dani's retort was sharp, almost angry. "No! I'll read it later. I'm late for breakfast."

With a swish of her skirts, she moved by Lurline, who stared after her in bewilderment.

Glass doors opened from the dining room onto a sprawling terrace of marble. Overhead, the roof was camouflaged by a canopy of entwining vines and fragrant jasmine blossoms. Beyond the terrace, streams of buttery-gold sunshine made their way through leafy trees to tease and tantalize the bubbling diamonds birthed by the ornate fountain, situated amid Kitty's prize lilies.

A narrow, shrub-lined path led from the fountain into the beauteous interior of the gardens. Melodious song rose from the variety of birds attracted to the meticulously cared-for landscaping. Butterflies of every kind and color flitted among the numerous flowers, oblivious to the humming of civilization just beyond the thick, protective hedge lining the busy Rue de Bordeaux.

The mansion afforded the Coltranes by the government was conveniently, and attractively, situated on a knoll which bestowed a splendrous view of the Porte de la Tournelle to the northeast.

Dani loved the scene before her but most of all, she reflected with a gentle skip of her heart, she loved the man seated at the round glass table on the terrace.

Maturity of years had not robbed Travis Coltrane of his build or stature. He was still ramrod straight and tall, with broad shoulders, and firm, corded muscles in his arms and thighs. His steel-gray eyes glowed with the mysterious fires of a man keenly intelligent, attuned to adversary and admirer alike. And the touch of silver at his temples merely added to his allure.

Travis Coltrane was still a strikingly handsome man, who turned the appreciative eye of every woman he passed. And he was her father, Dani thought with glowing pride.

She hurried onto the terrace and went to stand behind him, wrapping her arms around him in a fond embrace. Bestowing a kiss on the top of his head, she said, "Bonjour, Poppa."

Travis reached up to wrap his fingers around her wrist in a returning embrace. "Poppa, indeed," he scoffed. "That sounds like one of those old men wool-gathering in front of the Square du Vert-Galant. Do I remind you of them?"

She shook her head merrily. "Of course not." She gave a mock sigh. "Very well, then—bonjour, Father!"

"That's more like it." Then softly, fondly, he murmured, "Good morning, lovely daughter." He was warmly grateful for the closeness spawned between them in the past year.

She sat down next to him, waving away his offer of the silver tray of warm, flaky croissants, glistening with butter. "I must watch my figure"—she saucily quoted Kitty's fond saying—"so the men will watch me."

Travis raised a teasing eyebrow. "Like young Perrine Ribaudt? I hear roses arrived first thing this morning."

Dani made a face. "I'm afraid roses won't smoothe over his accusation that I'm trifling with him merely because I won't marry him."

Gone was the twinkle in his eye, and Travis's voice took on a serious note as he covered her hand with his. "Kitty told me about your conversation last night, Dani, and I agree with you he had no right to make such an insinuation. Would you like for me to speak with him?"

She shook her head. "I'm not going to think about it anymore," she announced. "If he wants to be ridiculous, then, sad though it be, I can live without his friendship."

Travis nodded his approval. "Good girl," he said, then added with fondness, "but I can't blame him for trying. You are lovely, Dani, just like your mother. You have the same charm and grace, though I suspect sometimes you inherited a bit of vinegar from your 'Poppa.' " He winked.

"Well, that's just fine and dandy if I did," she said. "I just wish I'd inherited it sooner, like years ago, when Aunt Alaina started her evil. . . ."

She allowed her voice to trail off, deciding not to bring up such an unpleasant subject. They had already spent long hours talking about it, when she had first come to Paris to live. They had decided it best, then, to get it all out in the open, discuss it, then put it away and try to forget. Yet, here she was, allowing the ugliness to surface once more.

She attempted to change the subject abruptly and asked, "Will you be away long? The ballet opens at the Théâtre National de l'Opéra in just three weeks, and Kitty and I are looking forward to having you escort us and make us the envy of every woman in Paris."

Travis apologetically explained that in all likelihood he would be away much longer than three weeks, perhaps a month or more. "I'm leaving by train this afternoon for Cherbourg, and the ship leaves from there. Quite frankly," he added, pouring himself another cup of tea, "I dread the trip. I wish Kitty were going with me."

"Oh, do take her, please," Dani said quickly, realizing her presence was probably preventing Kitty from going. "I'll be just fine here alone, really. The two of you could have a nice vacation together."

Travis shook his head and assured her she was certainly not the reason Kitty was staying behind. "The climate down there isn't that appealing, and neither is the political atmosphere at this time. Besides that, she wants to be here for the ballet, as well as to start new classes at the Sorbonne.''

Dani remembered Kitty having mentioned taking a course there, had even thought about attending with her. She found the history of the college fascinating. Located off the little square called Place de la Sorbonne, the name of the university was taken from Robert de Sorbon, who founded it in 1253. Near the main entrance the Church of the Sorbonne was situated, and it was there that Cardinal Richelieu was entombed. As a powerful cardinal and head of the Sorbonne, he decreed that the faculty should owe allegiance neither to Paris nor to France, only to the Council of the Sorbonne. This had permitted teachers wide freedom, which accounted for the independent spirit of the university.

Suddenly Travis flashed her a probing gaze and bluntly asked, ''Why don't you take Kitty's advice and do some traveling yourself? You're young. Intelligent. Beautiful. Financially independent. Why are you doing nothing with your life?''

Dani was at once hurt by his words. ''I don't call learning to know and love my family doing nothing with my life.''

Travis immediately apologized. ''I'm sorry. I didn't mean to be so critical.'' His eyes searched hers then with affection, and he said, ''I think we do know each other now, Dani, as well as love each other, so perhaps it's time you experienced other things in life, met new people, educated yourself by learning more about the world around you.''

She nodded thoughtfully. ''Perhaps you're right.''

He reached into the pocket of his coat and brought out a long white envelope and held it out to her. It was addressed to him, in care of the embassy, and had been opened. ''Perhaps you can start by making one last trip to Monaco.''

She blinked, puzzled, took the envelope and withdrew the folded letter inside. As she scanned the pages, Travis explained, "As you know, when Alaina died, she was nearly destitute. The Count had lost the family fortune due to his gambling compulsion. Alaina had begun to sell off her jewels and the valuable furnishings. That was what motivated her to back Gavin Mason's scheme to take your money and Colt's in a swindle that almost worked."

Dani closed her eyes in painful remembrance. "I really don't want to go back over all that. It makes me think of the convent, and all that happened, and how I nearly lost you forever."

He murmured in agreement, then continued. "Well, I made a trip down there to close out her estate, what there was of it, and that's when I discovered I could hang on to the château for you by paying the delinquent taxes."

"I never wanted it," Dani reminded him quietly.

"True. You said so at the time. But I also pointed out that when Alaina moved to France, she took what was left of value from the Barbeau estate in Kentucky. I figured the château represented all that was left of your mother and her family, and you had it coming to you."

Dani shook her head. "I still don't want it. I never want to go there again. I certainly don't intend to live there."

"That letter," Travis said, "is from a lawyer in Toulon who says he has a buyer for the property. You will see that the amount offered is not that great, but it will add a nice sum to your bank account."

Dani laid the letter aside as Kitty walked onto the terrace. "Then sell it," she said simply. "As I've said before, it only holds sad memories for me, and I never want to go back there."

Kitty bade them good morning, then Dani told her about the letter.

"I'll get a letter off to the lawyer before I leave and tell him you'll accept the offer," Travis said.

Dani shrugged. "Fine. I'll be glad to know it's sold and gone."

Kitty had been listening thoughtfully. Then she said, "Dani, let's go down there."

Dani shook her head. "Why on earth would I want to, Kitty? To stir up old memories of what it was like having Aunt Alaina dictate my every thought, word, and deed . . . or how miserable it was to grow up with a lecherous little monster like Gavin? No, thank you. I've lost nothing in Monaco and have no reason to return."

"I disagree," Travis declared.

Dani turned to stare at him incredulously.

He and Kitty exchanged understanding smiles, and then he turned to Dani and said, "I know why she thinks you should go, kitten. There are still some things in the house, things that might have belonged to your mother's family that you might possibly like to keep. I don't know what might be there, since at Alaina's death I instructed the attorney to seal up the château and to let us know if anyone was interested in buying it. You don't know what's stored there."

Dani really did not want to go, yet she knew they were probably right, that there might be some articles there of sentimental value, things no one else would want. Anything of any real worth had no doubt been sold by Alaina before her death.

"Well?" Kitty prompted, a hopeful smile spreading across her lovely face. "Just say the word, and I'll begin making arrangements for the trip. We'll go by carriage so we can bring things back."

Dani was still not convinced it was the right thing to do. Still, a change would be nice. Maybe it would whet her appetite for taking Kitty's advice and traveling.

Just then Cletus, the butler, appeared in the doorway of the terrace.

Kitty acknowledged his presence. "Yes, Cletus. What is it?"

He nodded to Dani. "Monsieur Perrine Ribaudt to see you, mademoiselle."

Dani felt the nerves in her jaw tighten, her spine stiffen. How dare he just come to the door, uninvited, so early in the day, especially after insulting her the night before?

"Tell him I do not wish to see him," she curtly directed Cletus.

Then she looked first to her father, then to Kitty, and announced, "Maybe I do need to get away for a while. We'll leave for Monaco as soon as we can be ready."

Kitty clapped her hands with delight.

Travis grinned his approval.

Dani, strangely enough, felt a warm elation starting to build within. She would face the memories and perhaps by so doing leave them permanently behind . . . and walk with head up, into the future . . . to make her own decisions, her own destiny.

Chapter Three

Dani and Kitty left Paris a week after Travis's departure for Panama. He had insisted they go by train, for the road south was rugged, narrow, and wound precariously through the French Alps. By carriage, the arduous journey would require several days, as well as a coachman and guard.

They had brought with them formal clothes, as Kitty had rushed a special message to a friend in Marseille, informing her that they would be passing through, and there would be time between trains for tea. The friend immediately responded with the insistent dispatch that they must spend at least two nights.

Kitty consulted with Dani over the invitation, pointing out they were really in no hurry. It was best to enjoy the trip along the way to get the most out of the entire journey. "You will love Rabina Altonderry," she had assured Dani. "I met her when she was in Paris shopping for the new home she and her husband built in Marseille. He is in counsel with the embassy, and the four of us were together at many socials.

"We share an admiration for the work of Van Gogh," Kitty continued. "Rabina was fortunate enough to find a lovely work of his known as "Le Père Tanguy," and that was *before* he died. Can you imagine what it must be worth now?"

They reached Marseille in the morning, after a comfortable night in the spacious compartment they had reserved. Dani had been awake since first light to sit and stare out in wonder at the breathtaking scenery that rolled by the window. She had always thought it lovely, the countryside so lush with exotic vegetation—orange, eucalyptus, lemon, olive, and pink laurel filling the air with their perfume. Palms and cactus lent a tropical atmosphere.

Marseille, Dani knew, was one of France's largest seaports. She had never seen the *calanques,* the cobalt-blue miniature fjords of Cassis but heard they offered magnificent views. She longed, also, to see the Château d'If, from which Dumas's legendary Count of Monte Cristo made his escape, as well as the tiny, jewellike crescent beaches of nearby Cavalaire, Le Lavandou, and Pampelone, with their stretches of clean, white, sparkling sand.

They stepped from the train, the warm summer sun kissing their faces in greeting, and were met by a coachman, resplendent in a purple satin coat with white lapels, tight white riding pants, and knee-high boots of glistening black leather. He removed his jaunty white cap with an immaculate white-gloved hand and bowed in gracious greeting. "Madame and Mademoiselle Coltrane. I am Alphonse, coachman for Madame Altonderry, and as soon as I have loaded your trunks, I shall take you to Derryateau. Come with me now to the carriage, please."

When he turned away, Dani and Kitty exchanged amused glances, and Kitty giggled and whispered, "Derryateau, indeed! Although I know from all Rabina told me, and what I've heard in Paris circles, that they built one of the most splendorous estates in all of Europe, I still find the name amusing."

Dani whispered back, "It sounds like a dairy."

They were still laughing when they reached the waiting carriage but then fell silent . . . awed by what awaited. The carriage was painted purple, the wheels, gold. The seats inside were covered in purple and gold velvet. There were six magnificent white horses to lead the way, each decorated with purple and gold harnesses. Each was covered elegantly in a gold and purple brocade blanket.

Dani blinked. "The lady likes purple, and I had to wear a *red* dress today, of all things. I'll look like a riding nightmare."

"And my yellow doesn't look too appetizing next to all the gold," Kitty murmured. "But you must admit it is elegant."

"There is," Dani said, with a mock-haughty air, "a very fine line between elegance . . . and ostentation."

Again, they laughed together, and it was a good feeling, Dani silently acknowledged. Yet, once more, she was struck with a twinge of painful remorse to think how much she had missed during all those precious growing-up years. Life with Kitty for a stepmother would have been a blessing each and every day. There would have been good times . . . happy times . . . and lots of wonderful memories.

She shook away the shadows. No need, she reminded herself, to become locked in the grayness. There was far too much sunshine ahead.

At last, Alphonse returned with a porter pulling a trunk cart. They were loaded and ready to leave, and Dani was almost trembling with excitement. To Kitty, she confided gleefully, "Oh, I am so glad you wanted to accept the invitation. I think it's going to be such fun."

Kitty agreed that they were in for a delightful stay, then said, "I neglected to tell you about Carista, Rabina's daughter. She's about your age, I think. I only met her once, when she was visiting on a holiday from school in Switzerland."

"A new friend," Dani acknowledged. "That's nice."

Kitty's brow knitted in a touch of doubt. "I *hope* it will be nice. My first, and only, impression of Carista was that she is a very spoiled, snobbish girl. A pity, because otherwise she would be a real beauty."

Dani was disappointed to hear that. Kitty was not the sort to criticize without cause . . . and rarely did so, anyway. Well, Dani decided, surely she could stand the company of anyone for just two days.

All other thoughts but the sight before her vanished from Dani's mind as the carriage approached Derryateau.

Kitty nodded in quiet acknowledgment of all the fabled reports of the showplace. "Twenty acres, one hundred twenty rooms overlooking the Mediterranean. Within those walls are Hispano-Moorish tiles from Spain, frescoes from Florence, a gold-relief ceiling fashioned after Venice's Accademia and reinterpreted in a sunburst design, and a one-hundred-foot castle tower for an unimpeded panorama of sea and sky." She drew a long breath and let it out slowly, reverently. "A real fantasy come to life."

Dani was momentarily awed, and it was a full minute before she could swallow and then ask, "Where did the money come from? I never knew such a palace existed outside the royal families."

"I understand that both Rabina and Laudlum come from old European money. Laudlum owns several Greek ships. Rabina has interests in several diamond minds in Africa."

The carriage turned from a narrow road onto a wide, sweeping driveway that was neatly packed in cobbled stones. To each side, there lay a carefully manicured border of flowering hibiscus shrubs. The lawn was a sweeping sea of green velvet, dotted here and there with stone-lined squares of rose, lilac, and gardenia gardens.

The drive was circular, surrounding a towering fountain fashioned of fat cherubs entwined together amid a cascade of sparkling waters flowing from the top.

The carriage slowed to a stop and immediately a servant wearing a uniform of purple and gold appeared to help them alight.

Hovering to one side was a young woman wearing a simple dress of white cotton. The neckline was high; the

long sleeves slightly puffed at the shoulders, tapering to
points at her wrists. An apron of purple poplin protected
the long, straight skirt. Her dark hair was brushed back
from her face and secured in a severe bun. A tiny cap of
white cotton and lace was perched on top of her head.

She came forward to introduce herself as Francine, their
hostess for the southeast wing of the second floor, which
would be their quarters during their stay. She informed
them that Madame Altonderry would expect them to join
her for lunch at half past noon. Meanwhile, they were to
be shown to their suites so they might freshen themselves.

High, arched double doors of cypress, adorned with
hand-carved, high-relief gilded cherubs, were opened by
uniformed butlers.

They entered the entrance hall, blinking against the
glimmer of the gold-inlaid ceiling above and six giant
crystal chandeliers vying for attention amid the glitter and
sheen. A handwoven rug of red, blue, and purple velvet
lay in the middle of the foyer. Bronze sculptures were
displayed against the tiled walls.

Dani would have liked to have seen the salon completely but only caught a glimpse of the lofty sunburst
ceiling as they turned toward the wide, winding stairway
and its impressive hand-rubbed mahogany banisters. The
steps were covered in a stitched brocade of white roses
amid a background of green.

On the second floor, Francine beckoned them to follow
her to the left. Here, Dani decided, it looked like a separate house entirely, for the way to the southeast wing
was marked by a miniature version of the double, cherub-
adorned doors downstairs.

As if by invisible signal, a butler appeared seemingly
from out of nowhere to open the doors for their entrance.
The marble hallway was illumined by miniature crystal
chandeliers along the way, and the walls were covered in
rare silk needlework Venetian panels.

Midway down the hall, Francine stopped before yet more double doors set on each side. She gestured to the left for Dani; the right, for Kitty. Then she proceeded to explain that there would be a butler, two chambermaids, a housekeeper, and a *coiffeuse* on call at all times. Should they desire anything, from a hot tub of water to food, at any hour, they had only to pull the gold velvet bellcord in their quarters, and service would be immediate.

Francine curtsied, smiled. "Welcome to Derryateau. I hope your stay will be pleasant. Your trunks will be brought to your suites shortly."

Dani walked through her quarters as she waited for her luggage to be delivered and was quite impressed. There was a parlor, a dining nook overlooking a sweeping view of the glimmering sea, and two enormous bedrooms, each with a room containing bath and toilette, and spacious dressing area.

She selected the bedroom with the widest windows, the view magnificent from the little marble table where she would take her morning tea.

Her trunks arrived, and so did her personal chambermaid, Corine, who was young, extremely talkative, and, Dani soon discovered, somewhat impertinent concerning her employers.

Dani was smoothing out the skirt of the pale blue chintz she planned to wear for lunch when Corine squealed with delight as she withdrew an emerald velvet gown from the trunk. "Oh, you should wear this tonight. Look at the bodice. Why, it is encrusted with pearls and rubies. It is exquisite. Of course"—she sniffed in disdain—"Mademoiselle Carista would be as green as this dress."

Dani took the garment from her with loving care. She'd had it made expressly to go with her father's Christmas present—a necklace of emeralds and diamonds with matching earrings. Prudently ignoring the chambermaid's sarcastic reference to her mistress, she inquired, "Is there a special occasion tonight other than a formal dinner?"

Corine was only too eager to share the gossip with her. "Oh, yes. It was planned before you and Madame Coltrane sent word of your visit. You see"—she lowered her voice to an excited whisper—"Mademoiselle Carista is hoping to announce her engagement. The man she wants to marry is visiting from Paris, and has been for almost a month now."

Dani wanted to dismiss such a personal subject. "Well, I hope her wishes come true then." She laid the dress aside. If this was to be Carista Altonderry's special night, she would certainly not try to be the belle of the ball and steal her rightful attention.

Corine continued to gossip as they unpacked what Dani felt would be needed during their brief stay. Dani listened, not really caring.

"He is from Russia," Corine said of the man Carista Altonderry hoped to marry. "And quite handsome. Every woman he meets falls madly in love with him, but so far, no one has captured his heart. Of course, Mademoiselle Carista is just conceited and arrogant enough to think *she* will be the chosen one."

"Well," Dani interjected, "perhaps she will be. If he has been here almost a month, there must be more than casual interest on his part."

Corine's laugh was derisive. "Ha! Then where does he go when he leaves here every morning? He tells no one of his comings and goings. There is a rumor that he sees other women."

Dani shrugged. "Then that would appear to be Mademoiselle Carista's error in judgment for offering him the hospitality of her home." What she did not say, for she felt it would be an impropriety to converse in such a manner with a servant, was that it sounded as though perhaps her Russian suitor was a fortune hunter, seeking out the wealthiest young woman available before choosing a wife. She had not met him, already disliked him, and for the first time thought they should have just continued on their way to Monaco without visiting people who were strangers to her. Then she instantly admonished herself for the selfish thought. Kitty was entitled to visit her friends, and she would just bide her own time and be as pleasant as possible during their brief visit.

Corine rattled on while she finished unpacking, then Dani dismissed her, asking that she return one hour prior to lunch to draw her bath.

She settled in front of the window to enjoy the view and savor the precious moments of solitude.

Dani was glad to be here, to be traveling, and, she vowed firmly, she was going to be independent and travel alone in the future. She was not a little girl, and she did not care for the conventions and decorum of the day. Never again would she be influenced by ritual, tradition, or the like. The only hegemony she would allow was *her own.*

All too soon, it seemed, Corine returned, immediately conveying more gossip. "It surely looks as though Mademoiselle Carista expects her monsieur from Russia to agree to the announcement of their betrothal tonight. I overheard her and her mother arguing, because she is sending out special messengers with invitations for a champagne reception." She shook her head in disgust. "It is not proper. No one, but *no one,* extends, or accepts, an invitation at such a late hour.

"But," she went on with a resigned sigh, "the mademoiselle shall have her way, as always."

Dani agreed, silently, that to invite people to a gala, only hours ahead of time, was unthinkable. It seemed to her, though once more she was not about to voice her opinion to Corine, that Carista Altonderry, whom she had not yet even met, was attempting to apply pressure to her Russian sweetheart.

A smile touched Dani's lips. The evening just might be entertaining, after all. Certainly different. While she did not want her hostess embarrassed, it would be interesting to see who won the battle of wits, and *hearts.*

* * *

When Dani left her suite, Kitty was just emerging from hers. She would have liked to have had time to tell her of the tense atmosphere that would surely be in evidence during the lunch hour but could not do so with Francine near, leading the way downstairs.

They went down a hallway on the first floor, which led to the rear of the house. Double doors of rainbow stained glass led to a sweeping terrace which overlooked the azure sea. On each side were thick banks of fragrant lilacs and white and yellow tuberoses. Large china pots overflowing with pansies and petunias had been placed beneath in a border.

The day was lovely, with a clear blue sky and a soft, sweet breeze blowing in from the waters.

Rabina Altonderry rose from an oblong glass and white wrought-iron table to greet them. She was medium height, thin, and while her face was not beautiful, there was a quiet, warm charm about her. Thick-fringed eyes of a hazel color smiled out to Dani. Her dark hair was swept up into a chignon and fastened with a pearl clip, and she wore a simple yet lovely dress of light blue silk. The skirt was covered with a long, dainty apron of pure white lace.

She came forward to clasp hands with Kitty, bestowing a kiss on each cheek. "I am so happy that you accepted my invitation. It has been too long since we've seen each other."

She turned to Dani, held out her hand, as Kitty made the introductions. "Welcome to my home, child. You are as beautiful as your father described you in his last letter."

Dani felt her cheeks warm, but not with embarrassment, for she was not flustered by compliments. The feeling was sired by the love she felt for her father, to think he would write of her in such a way.

Rabina invited them to be seated and, at once, wine was poured into their long-stemmed crystal glasses. She explained pleasantly, "I save this wine for special occasions, special friends. It is Burgundy, and comes from Beaune.''

Dani glanced at the two empty places at the table, but made no comment. Kitty, however, curiously inquired, ''Are we to be joined by Laudlum and Carista later?''

Dani noticed that Rabina's face shaded momentarily with perplexity. Her smile was slightly forced as she airily explained, ''Oh, Laudlum has been in Barcelona for the past three weeks on business. I expect him home today, however, as Carista has a houseguest, and we've planned a little soirée for tonight.''

Soirée, indeed, Dani echoed silently, suppressing a grimace.

''She should be along soon. I suppose they are out riding, or something.'' She turned the conversation to a query about the social scene in Paris.

Dani listened in polite silence, and they were almost through with their meal when a young woman suddenly stormed onto the terrace, then stopped abruptly to allow her insolent gaze to flick rudely over Kitty and Dani.

Rabina swallowed, cleared her throat. She was somewhat shaken by her daughter's lack of manners. ''Carista,'' she managed to say, ''do sit down. I want you to meet our guests, Madame Kitty Coltrane and her stepdaughter, Dani.''

Dani offered a smile which was not returned.

Carista grudgingly took her seat, shrugging away the servant who stepped up to graciously hold her chair.

Long tresses of honey-gold hung loosely about her bare shoulders. She was wearing a tight-fitting satin blouse, the bodice cut low to display large breasts and much cleavage. The riding pants she wore were also tight, molded to long, curving legs and made of black suede. Knee-high boots jangled with dainty little silver spurs.

Her lips were painted bright red and were full, pouting. Her cheeks were flushed with tiny dots of anger, and her eyes were stormy.

Rabina's hand trembled as she reached for her glass, taking a needed sip of wine before daring to inquire, "And where is our guest? Is he—"

"Why, right here, of course!" Carista sharply interrupted to gesture insolently toward Kitty and Dani. "Here are our guests, Mother. Everyone will be delighted to meet the Coltranes of Paris at our party tonight."

Rabina shook her head in bewilderment.

Kitty and Dani exchanged puzzled looks. Only Dani felt she just might know the reason behind Carista Altonderry's bizarre behavior.

Rabina leaned to touch her daughter's hand gently. "We can talk later, dear. Let us enjoy a pleasant lunch."

Carista, Dani thought, would be quite beautiful were it not for the pinched and unpleasant look to her face that was one of permanence, not birthed temporarily by her present mood. It seemed that nothing in Carista's life was ever to her entire liking, and everyone with whom she came in contact should be on guard, lest they evoke her disfavor.

Tension was as thick as the vines of the vineyard on the western slope, as Rabina and Kitty attempted normal conversation in the midst of Carista's apparent brooding rage. Something was obviously wrong, but no one dared to inquire. Dani was curious but, after an unprovoked glare from Carista, decided she really did not care about the haughty girl's problems. If her mysterious Russian had refused to be intimidated into a betrothal he did not want, then good for him, Dani declared to herself.

Suddenly, Carista leaped to her feet so quickly that her glass of wine tipped over. She threw down her napkin and turned hate-filled eyes upon her mother. "You can cancel the party tonight. Drakar has been called back to Paris. He won't be here, and I won't attend without him."

Cautiously, Rabina said, "Darling, it's unfortunate Drakar has to leave so suddenly, and I *know* how disappointed you must be, but I am sure you will agree that it would be improper not to go on with our plans. After all, Kitty and Dani are our guests, too, and we certainly want our friends to meet them."

Rabina patted her hand. "Perhaps you would like to go and lie down for a while. You'll feel better later."

Carista jerked away from her touch and blistered her with a glare. "What do you know?" she screamed.

Rabina stood, her own ire rising. Clutching the table for support, she met her daughter's defiant eyes. "You will apologize to our guests, and then you will leave us and go to your room."

Carista wadded her napkin, flung it to the table, then screamed, "I owe no apology. I owe nothing to *bourgeoises!*"

Rabina gasped.

Dani and Kitty stiffened.

Carista turned and ran from the terrace and disappeared inside.

Rabina sank back into her chair, took a deep breath, and then turned tearful eyes to Dani and Kitty. "I am so sorry. So dreadfully sorry. What can I say?"

Kitty attempted humor to help reduce the tension. "I might not like being called 'middle class,' Rabina, but there are worse things in life."

Dani said nothing.

Rabina shook her head, reached for the little silver bell beside her plate, and gave it a shake. At once, a maid appeared. Rabina gestured to the mess Carista had made and ordered it cleaned. Then she poured herself another glass of wine.

As she did so, Kitty offered, "We are a bit tired from the journey, Rabina, so perhaps we should go to our suites, and if you wish to cancel your plans for tonight, please do not consider us in your decision. It makes no difference to us, really."

"No!" Rabina's retort was sharp, final. "We will go ahead with the party. I tried to tell Carista she was rushing things, but . . ." Her voice trailed off, and her eyes widened ever so slightly with the realization that there was no need to confide shameful family gossip to friends as important and influential as the Coltranes.

Quickly, she countered with a forced smile. "You know how impetuous young girls can be, wanting to show off their beaux. Carista will be fine, and I promise you that Laudlum will see that she apologizes for her despicable behavior."

Later, when they were alone, Dani related to Kitty what Corine had told her earlier.

"Well, I'm not surprised," Kitty said. "Had I known Drakar was involved, I would have expected this."

Dani blinked in surprise. "You know this Russian?"

Kitty nodded, laughing softly. "I know *of* him. He has quite a reputation where the ladies are concerned. Oh, I can easily see why they chase after him the way they do. He's handsome, charming, well educated—speaks five languages fluently, I've heard. He reminds me of your father in a way, except that your father was not wealthy when I met him. Drakar is said to be very rich.

"I met him at several gallery opening parties," she continued, eyes narrowing in thoughtful remembrance. "He was always quite pleasant, but there was just this aura about him, mysterious, somehow, as though he were not quite what he seemed."

Suddenly, Kitty shook her head. "It doesn't matter. I feel sorry for Carista, but she should have known better. She doesn't seem to be a likable sort of girl, anyway."

Dani shared her feelings about Carista, and she really couldn't care less about this Drakar, whoever he was. The whole situation merely reaffirmed her stand where men, in general, were concerned—let them get a hold on a woman's heart and next they would control her mind and spirit.

Carista was a fool.

Dani would never allow such a thing to happen to her.

She owned her heart, and her mind, and her spirit . . . and by god, it was going to stay that way!

Chapter Four

RABINA'S party had been successful, considering that Carista had locked herself in her suite and refused to come out. Even her father's incessant pounding on her door, with threats of every violence imaginable, short of absolute mayhem, had not dissuaded her from self-imposed exile. Explanations of sudden illness were made to the guests, and if there was gossip and speculation due to the mysterious absence of Carista's houseguest, it was not apparent.

Dani and Kitty had a delightful evening, despite mild feelings of discomfort due to the tension in the household. They met many new people, danced the night away, and enjoyed so many glasses of sparkling champagne that they were light-headed and giggling before night's end.

They decided to leave on the morning train for Monaco, rather than stay over to the next day as was originally planned. Their presence, they feared, would only add to Rabina's discomfort over Carista's abhorrent behavior.

They spent the night at a small hotel in Monaco, and the next morning they made arrangements for two horses so they could ride to the château. Dani thought it would be nice after the long train ride to stretch their bodies a bit rather than take another carriage. Their luggage would follow.

The wind snapped hungrily at their faces as they rounded a curve in the road, and then both reined their mounts to a sudden, silent halt. Ahead, nestled beneath jutting rocks, sat the stark deBonnett château. Its walls of gray stone seemed to blend with the misty morning, the clouds of fog parting now and then, making the structure appear to sway, and move . . . and live.

Kitty gasped. "What a cheerless place! Why, I'm surprised anyone would want to buy it, much less pay the price you'll be getting."

Dani had to admit she had also been surprised when she had learned of the selling price. "Maybe the land is worth something. They might be planning to just tear it down."

The grape arbor to one side was thick and overgrown with weeds amid the runaway vines. The entire yard was one chaotic display of overgrown grass and nondescript vegetation.

Dani shook her head dolefully. "It doesn't take a place long to fall apart when no one cares, does it?" She nodded to the gate, hanging by its hinges.

Kitty agreed, staring up at the yellowed, dirt-crusted windows.

They walked their horses the rest of the way, then dismounted at the gate. Kitty wanted to explore the yard, but there was nothing to see, for the little gardens Alaina had preened through the years were lost amid the weeds.

Dani attempted to show her around. Pointing to a small stone cottage on a nearby rise, she told her that that had been the caretaker's cottage, where Briana had lived.

Kitty frowned. She had been told Briana's motivation for being part of Gavin Mason's scheme to get his hands on Colt and Dani's inheritance, knew that she should feel sympathy for the way she'd had to literally sell her soul to get medical help for her ailing younger brother. Still, the young woman's name evoked unpleasant memories.

The château was built on a smooth plateau that dropped sharply, abruptly, with a sheer fall to the dangerous, jutting rocks below. The churning waters, whipped by the winds of the sea, today covered the rocks with clinging foam.

They made their way to the rear where Dani stood staring without expression at the first arched window to the south, on the second floor. There was a small balcony just outside.

"They said she fell from her bedroom window." She turned her gaze downward, to the hungrily foaming waters licking at the fingers of rocks below. "They found her down there somewhere."

Kitty shivered at the image, and turned back toward the pathway that would lead them to the front of the château once more. She knew it had to have been a terrible place for a little girl to grow up, especially with a wicked aunt like Alaina Barbeau. She was glad Dani would never have cause to return to this house once they left.

Dani took from her purse a key Travis had given her and led the way up the steps to the front door. With a turn, and a loud, grating squeak, the door swung open.

They were met by shadowed darkness, and when Dani stepped inside, she gasped, startled, at the feel of sticky cobwebs against her face. Slapping them away, she irritably cried, "Let's get the shutters open, and the windows. I don't care how damp and cold it is outside, I want some fresh air and light in this—this *tomb*."

They rushed around the first floor, Kitty having to feel her way, not being used to the setting. Then, when there was light spilling through the grimy windows, she looked about and was relieved to see it had not been ransacked. There were a few pieces of furniture left, some bric-a-brac. She could not tell yet if they were of any value.

"It looks as though we'll find a few things," she called to Dani. "Not much, but something . . ." Her voice trailed off at the sound of Dani's footsteps on the stairs to the second floor.

A few moments later Dani returned, smiling broadly as she met Kitty in the foyer. "It looks as though my room has hardly been touched. Even most of my clothes are still there.

"Strange," she continued. "When I left the convent, I wanted to go straight to Paris. I refused to come here, couldn't stand the thought of coming back to this house of hate and coldness. Surprisingly, it doesn't bother me as much now as I thought it would."

Kitty hurried across the marble foyer, oblivious to the grit and dirt crackling beneath her shoes. Putting her arms around Dani, she hugged her. "I'm so glad to hear you say that. I was praying I wouldn't regret suggesting your coming back."

Dani returned the embrace, assured her she did not, and added, "I'm glad you're with me. I think we're going to have fun these next few days."

Chapter Five

B Y the time Dani and Kitty had been in Monaco for a
week, they were both convinced that the trip had been
worthwhile. Alaina might have disposed of most of the
truly valuable furnishings and objets d'art, but they had
still been able to find a few items of sentimental significance to Dani. They spent time in Monte Carlo, enjoying
the glittering night life and trying their luck at the famous
Casino.

One day, they went to the rocky incline that stretched
above the small vineyard to the north of the château. It
was the site of the family graveyard. The path upward
was steep, rocky, overgrown with weeds. The view, as
Dani remembered, was awesome in its splendor, and they
were so taken by it that they were almost oblivious to the
gloom surrounding the decaying burial ground.

In the center was a large common marker, on which
was carved "DEBONNETT." Surrounding it were smaller,
less significant tombstones. They walked among these until they found one marked "CLAUDE" and, beside it, a
small wooden cross, obviously furnished by the under-
taker who had been given the task of burying her, on
which was crudely scrawled "ALAINA."

Kitty drew in her breath in a contemplative draw, let it
out slowly. "How sad to be remembered in life but forgotten in death, don't you think?"

Dani nodded. She would much prefer to move through her own life quietly touching those about her and then have them remember her with kindness when she was gone.

"I don't want you to hate her, Dani."

Dani turned to stare at her in wonder. "You can't expect me to love her."

"No. It's just better that you try not to feel anything at all." She knelt beside the grave and absently pulled a few weeds from around the paltry marker, tossing them to one side before continuing in a voice edged with pain.

"I've told you a little bit about my own past, about the people who hurt me so deeply. For a long time, I hated them, too, and then I found that the memories didn't hurt so much if I just pretended those people, and the things they did to me, just never existed at all. I could almost pretend it was just a terrible nightmare."

She paused to shake her head and emit a bitter laugh. "I suppose there are those who would say I was just not facing reality, but why should I? I couldn't undo the past, what had happened to me, so why should I dwell on it?"

Standing once more, she gestured to the raw mound of dirt and rocks that was Alaina Barbeau deBonnett's grave. "If she had been able to pretend that Travis had never existed, that he had never chosen her sister over her, then we would not be standing here now. But she never forgave him, never stopped trying to get her revenge."

Dani understood the wisdom of what she was saying. It was truly time to turn her back, to pretend none of it ever happened. She whispered, "Let's go now. I have everything I came for."

They were walking back down the path, and Kitty was talking about Colt's visit to the château to find Briana, when Dani suddenly stopped and cried excitedly, "The wine cellar! We haven't thought about going down there to look around. There might be something there, if just a few bottles of wine!"

Kitty agreed, though she admitted she did not relish the idea of going down there. "Colt said the steps were so long and deep that they seemed to go right into the bowels of the earth."

Dani had gone down there only a few times as a child, and only then because Alaina made her, for some reason she could not now remember. "We'll need torches," she said.

Once they had their torches, they went to the wooden hatch on the side of the château, and straining and pulling together, they managed to open it with a loud, grating squeak. At once, they were hit full in the face with a blast of sour, stagnant, dusty air.

"Are you sure you want to go down there?" Kitty asked doubtfully.

Dani said she was, then added teasingly, "It's your fault, you know. You're the one who's gotten me all enthused about treasure-hunting. Though I don't know what on earth I'll ever do with all the things we're sending back. Maybe I should open an antique shop. My own little *magasin d'antiquités* . . ."

She had been laughing, but the laughter faded, along with her voice, as she turned slowly to stare at Kitty.

Kitty was staring back . . . and she was not laughing. The idea of opening an antique shop was not impractical or frivolous.

"I can run it for you while you travel all over Europe on buying trips," Kitty said.

"And it's the proper excuse to travel," Dani chimed in. "Not that I need one, but it will give me something to do, a purpose."

They hugged each other happily, then Dani pulled back to urge, "Come on. Maybe we'll find something truly wonderful down there."

When they reached the cellar, they realized quickly that it was empty. Even the hundreds of slots for wine bottles were empty.

Dani was disappointed. "I guess it was asking too much that vandals not find their way down here. There was no lock on the hatch, and everyone would have known the château certainly had a cellar for storing wine."

Kitty held up her torch, the light eerily dancing on the walls carved out of the stone innards of the earth. "Let's take a look around now that we're here. We might find an old box of dishes or something stashed in a corner. If there was room for Gavin Mason to store Coltrane gold down here, then there is certainly room for a few old forgotten boxes or barrels."

They picked their way among small stones, clods of dirt, a few bits of broken wine bottles. Dani moved toward the deep shadows beneath the stairs, saw nothing, turned away, then hesitated. *Had* she seen nothing? She went back, held out her flickering torch, and carefully looked about.

Then she saw it—the strange-looking iron ring hanging from the rock wall. Slowly, cautiously, she reached out to touch it, felt the chill of the metal against her fingertips and shivered slightly.

Kitty called hopefully, "See anything?"

"A ring in the wall."

Kitty hurried to join her, quickly examined the ring, then began to run her fingers along the wall. "It could be—" she began excitedly, then cried, "It is! A hidden door. I feel the lines in the stone. Here. Help me pull."

They laid aside their torches carefully, propping them so the flames would not go out, then, mustering all their strength, they grasped the rusting ring and pulled.

There came the scraping sound of ancient stone against stone and then the door slowly opened; once again, they were assailed by the smell of thick, dead air.

Dani grabbed up her torch eagerly and stepped inside the cavity without trepidation. At once, her eyes feasted upon the sight of the square wooden box propped against a far wall. It was the size of a small tabletop, perhaps a foot thick. "Oh, it has to be valuable!" she exclaimed. "It wouldn't be hidden here if it weren't."

Kitty was more cautious. "Let's get it upstairs, where we can open it properly and see exactly what you've found."

The box was not heavy, and they were able to maneuver it up the stairs with a minimum of strain. Once inside the house, it became obvious that tools would be needed to pry it open. Dani remembered seeing a few implements in the caretaker's shed, and she quickly ran to get them.

As she worked at the boards, Kitty warned, "Not too hasty. You don't want to damage anything inside."

Once the outer boards were pried loose, however, they were dismayed to find yet another crate within. Working feverishly, anxiously, Dani soon had that one open as well, and they found much straw and packing inside.

"Paintings!" Kitty cried jubilantly. "Oh, let me see, Dani, let me see!"

Dani moved aside, knowing Kitty would be able to make a reasonable judgment should there be anything of value.

"Oh, I don't believe this!"

Dani was beside herself. "What? What? Kitty, if you don't tell me—"

Kitty looked at her with eyes that brimmed with joyful, excited tears. "Rousseau. I'd know his work anywhere. And here!" She held up another. "Daubigny."

In all, there were six works inside the crate, and as they spread them out, Kitty explained what she felt they had discovered. "Around 1850 or so, there was sort of a rebellion against studio painting. A group of young landscape painters, most of whom were also printmakers, formed a group that became known as the Barbizon school. Critics felt that the etchings of Théodore Rousseau, Jean-Baptiste-Camille Corot, and Charles-François Daubigny were very close to the spirit of the seventeenth-century Dutch landscapes."

She went on to say that while their find might not be truly valuable in terms of money at that point, they would be treasured by some collectors. "And," she pointed out with a broad smile, "just having these in your shop will give you a start. You'll make quite a name for yourself from the very beginning with treasures like these!"

Dani was beside herself with happiness. She knelt before the display to scrutinize their condition more closely. "It's amazing that they're so well preserved. I wonder how long they've been stored down there?"

"Didn't you say the Count was killed just a couple of years ago?" Kitty asked.

"Yes. In a duel. Some argument over a gambling debt. I never understood exactly what happened. Aunt Alaina wouldn't discuss it. But what does that have to do with these paintings?"

Kitty theorized that because of the well-preserved state of the paintings, they could not have been hidden for longer than six or seven years. "The Count had to have been the one to hide them. Otherwise, Alaina would have had them appraised and sold along with the other things she was forced to dispose of."

There was one painting smaller than the rest, and Dani lifted it up for closer inspection. "This one seems different."

Kitty joined her in scrutiny, shook her head. "It isn't the work of any artist I've ever studied. It isn't even well done, but I can see that the subject matter must be beautiful—some sort of palace."

Dani fingered the wooden frame around the painting. It was crude, unfinished wood, but she found it elegant, somehow, in its simplicity. "I like the frame better than the painting."

"Well, the mystery surrounding these will make a wonderful story for the art circles in Paris."

Dani gathered up the paintings, headed for the front door, then paused. "This is it. We've found everything there is to find here."

Kitty put her arm around her and gave her an affectionate hug. "I think you found much more than you came looking for, my dear . . . and also left a few things behind," she added pointedly.

It was true. Dani had at last put to rest the past.

Chapter Six

Carson City, Nevada

JOHN Travis Coltrane, called simply Colt by family and friends, sat on top of a grassy knoll overlooking the Coltrane ranch.

The air was sweet with the smell of fresh-cut hay, overshadowing the tinge of sourish aromas from the herd of cattle grazing toward the western horizon.

Beneath him lay a thick bed of pink and white clover, dancing in the desert-sired breeze.

He leaned back against the flaky bark of a huge cottonwood tree on this late summer evening, and contemplated his life.

The ranch and the silver mine were both doing well. It had been over a year since he had almost lost both.

A shudder moved through his tall, muscular body. What a fool he had been—but Gavin Mason had worked his scheme well. Briana, with the threat of medical aid for her sick brother being withdrawn, had performed well in her role as Dani. Once he thought he had bedded his own sister, all he had wanted to do was get the hell out, sign everything over to her as a penance. When he finally woke up and decided maybe the world hadn't come to an end after all, he had returned to discover that Mason had arranged for the sale of everything to Seth Hollowell, who owned adjacent land to the north. Seth was willing to sell it back once he heard Colt had been duped.

So he had gone to Europe, to France, to find Briana, the truth . . . and Coltrane money.

He had succeeded . . . but paid a dear price.

Branch Pope, his foreman, his best friend, had lost his life at the hands of one of Mason's men.

Eventually, after following a trail that led all the way to the Greek island of Santorini, the gold had been recovered. Mason and his men were dead.

He had been able to understand, and forgive, Briana's part in the scheme. He had even brought her back to America with him, along with her brother. For a time, they had lived happily, never thinking about the future, just enjoying each other and spending long, passionate hours savoring the wonders they discovered together in bed. Then, out of the blue, it seemed, they mutually realized, and decided, that while what they shared was good, it just wasn't enough to form the basis on which to build a lifetime, a marriage.

They had parted ways . . . and parted as friends. She had reluctantly accepted the money he insisted on giving her when she left to head east and find a new life.

Now and then he heard from her. She had a job as a governess to a wealthy family in Boston who allowed her brother to live with her. She had sent Colt back part of the money, saying she had considered it a loan.

Colt shook his head and smiled in fond remembrance. Briana was one hell of a woman, and one day she would make some man a fine wife . . . but not him.

Sometimes he wondered if he would ever get married and settle down. He liked women. No doubt about that. He enjoyed their company—in bed, and out. He never used them or abused them, always made sure when they parted that they left him happy, and satisfied. Relationships between a man and a woman, he believed, should be shared, not dominated by either.

He looked toward the two-story house. Actually, it should be called a mansion. Sweeping front porch, tall and stately pillars. Marble steps. It was a fine place. A place to be proud of. But he was a bachelor, and what did he need with a two-story, twelve-room mansion?

Silver and cattle. His father, Travis Coltrane, had built a wealthy empire and signed it all over to him and his half sister when he'd taken Kitty, his mother, and gone to Paris to live. Dani was there now with them; the ranch and silver mine was his to run as he saw fit.

So now, a year later, after getting it all back again, Colt felt things were going well. His new foreman, Bart Townsend, was a grizzled, leathery sort who knew how to keep a hundred hands under his thumb at all times. Colt did not have to do anything.

He was beginning to feel a bit useless.

. . . And also a little bit lonely.

Sometimes, on a Saturday night, when the hands would ride into town to raise hell and have fun, he and Bart would sit on the front porch, drink cold beers, and talk.

It was on these occasions that Bart invariably got around to how Colt ought to be thinking about taking a wife. "You need a woman all the time, not just when you got a yen. You need to start thinking about having young'uns. Boys to grow up and carry on the ranch. It ain't good you just seein' this 'un and that 'un, and never gettin' serious about none of 'em. More and more, lately, you just hang around the ranch."

Colt would become amused at Bart's nosing in his business and invariably would challenge him. "Then why don't you take your own advice and find yourself a good woman? Get married. I've told you I'd give you the land to build a house on."

As always, Bart would snort, mumble about how he was too old to have some woman around all the time, then change the subject.

Colt smiled. It was Saturday again. He was not planning on going into town with the hands. He'd wind up on the porch with Bart once more and hear the same lecture all over again.

It wasn't, he acknowledged, that he did not think about what it would be like to get married, to love someone, have someone to share his life. It might be nice, also, to fill up the spaces in his heart, and the big mansion, with children.

There was no shortage of candidates for a wife.

There was Melissa Waitley, comely daughter of Doc Waitley. She could have her pick of suitors, but she had let him know she placed him at the top of her list. Not a week went by that she didn't send him an invitation to Sunday dinner.

Then there was Arista Blankenship, the young schoolteacher. At least every two weeks she invited him to dinner, was always sending out cakes, pies, cookies.

He did not consider himself arrogant to acknowledge privately that every eligible woman in town had let him know, some subtly, some almost brazenly, that they would like to be considered for the position of Mrs. John Travis Coltrane.

Neither did Colt feel he was conceited to acknowledge his own worth. He was rich. He had followed in his father's footsteps and continued to keep the Coltrane holdings extremely successful. He also knew he was considered good-looking. Tall, muscular, with dark hair and eyes, he'd been told by enough women that he was attractive that he believed it himself.

So, he candidly asked himself, why couldn't he find a woman to marry?

But that, he reasoned, was not the question that bothered him, haunted him in quiet, contemplative times such as this.

The burning issue really was that Colt just did not trust women.

He had been burned too many times. Even Briana, whom he had fancied himself in love with for a time, had originally tricked him, deceived him. Maybe it left a bad taste in his mouth for all time.

Maybe, he mused with bitterness, he was just bored. Since returning from Europe there had been no excitement in his life. All he had done was more or less watch someone else tend to his business. Sure, there were ponies to be broken, records to be kept, decisions to be made, dozens of chores to take part in. But it wasn't what he wanted, not the way he wanted to spend his life, and it certainly did not make him eager to rise each morning and face a new day.

He needed, and wanted, something more. Only he could not figure out what.

In the distance, he saw a lone rider coming down the road, heading in. He knew it would be Bart, who had gone into town earlier to order supplies, check on mail, do a few other errands.

He got up from his solitary perch and made his way down the slope. By the time he reached the porch, Bart was reining up.

He gave Colt a broad grin, held out a small wicker basket. "Had to balance this just right, or the meringue might fall. Compliments of Miss Melissa Waitley."

Colt took the basket from him. He had expected something like this. Melissa always hung around the general store where either he or Bart did their Saturday shopping if they were in town.

Bart dismounted. "There's also fresh-baked cookies in the saddlebags, compliments of Miss Jessica Owens." He pretended to frown, as though in deep study. "Can't recall any gifts from her before. In fact, I can't even recall seeing her before. Comely little lass, though. Blond hair, big green eyes. Had Miss Melissa fuming, she did, when she walked right up and introduced herself and said she was told I was your foreman, and would I please bring you some treats and remind you that you promised to stop by her house for tea next time you was in town."

Colt also frowned as he tried to recall just who Jessica Owens was. He had stopped in to see the dentist last time he was in town, and there had been a young lady working for him as a nurse, and she *had* said something about maybe he could stop by for refreshments sometime so they could get acquainted, because she was new in town, and didn't know many people yet. But was her hair blond? For the life of him, he couldn't remember.

Then Bart tired of his teasing for the moment and handed him a packet of letters. "There's one from Paris," he pointed out.

That was the one Colt opened at once. He scanned the neatly written lines from his mother describing how she and Dani had just come back from Monaco, where they had cleared out the deBonnett château.

He read on about how Dani was planning to open up her own art and antique shop. His mother was going to run it while Dani traveled around Europe on buying jaunts.

She went on to wish that he was well and tell him once more how much she loved him, missed him, and hoped that soon they could make plans to come home for a visit.

Colt folded the letter, stuffed it in the pocket of his buckskin vest, and grew thoughtful. His father traveled, now Dani would also be traveling . . . and, suddenly, Colt knew exactly what he was going to do with his life.

He got to his feet, stretched, smiled, turned toward the house. There was much to be done.

Bart sat straight up. "Hey, where you goin'? It's not even good dark yet. We're gonna cook us some steaks, like always, have some beers. No need in being alone on Saturday night. Ol' Pete didn't go into town neither. I tol' him we'd be cookin' some grub soon, and he could join us."

Colt opened the screen door, then turned to give Bart one last, thoughtful look as he declared, "I'll be leaving Monday. I've got a lot to do before then."

"Leaving?" Bart was on his feet and hurrying across the porch, a baffled expression on his craggy face. "What're you talkin' about? We ain't got nowhere to go this time of year. It's time to get set for the winter, and—"

"Oh, there is somewhere for me to go, Bart," Colt said with a quiet smile. "Europe."

Bart at once bellowed, "Europe? What in thunderation for?"

Colt went on inside, called over his shoulder with nonchalance, as though he traveled abroad often. "Oh, my family's there. I miss them. I'd like to get to know my half sister better. I want to spend some of my hard-earned money. I just want to live."

He hurried up the stairs, Bart still calling to him, but he kept on going.

He had, he hoped, an appointment with his destiny.

Chapter Seven

CYRIL Arpel scrutinized his reflection in the vertical glass beside the front door of the Coltrane mansion. He decided he liked what he saw—a slender, well-proportioned young man of proper height. His dark hair had just the right amount of curl, enough to make him appealing in a little-boy way but with just the right amount of unruliness to be masculine.

He liked his face, also. Clean-shaven, his skin was smooth. Green eyes. A nice Roman nose. A hint of a cleft in his chin.

The gray pinstripe suit he wore gave him the successful aura he deserved, thanks to all the years of struggling to become one of the most respected art dealers in Europe.

He touched the maroon tie. It gave a nice touch, a little hint of roguishness to prevent him from appearing too austere. After all, he was one of Europe's most eligible bachelors, and he intended to stay that way for a long time. An almost perverse smile spread across his lips as he thought of the good times he had at some of the Continent's most exclusive, and best, bordellos. A wife would only tie him down, and he enjoyed a variety of women.

Of course, no one knew about Cyril's "other" life. On the surface, in public, he had a reputation for absolute decorum and refinement. Never would he dare for anyone to find out about his wild nights of passionate orgies. That was his secret. He intended to keep it that way.

He touched a white-gloved finger to the bell, took a deep breath, and waited. He, like everyone else in the upper echelon of Paris society, had heard about Mademoiselle Daniella Coltrane, daughter of the respected and wealthy American emissary Travis Coltrane, and her plans to open an art and antique shop in the Montmartre quarter on the Right Bank. And, like all the others who had heard the rumors about her having found a valuable collection of paintings in an inherited château in Monaco, Cyril was anxious to view them. However, he was not about to wait for the grand opening of the shop. Therefore, he had sent an imploring message to Madame Kitty Coltrane herself, requesting a private showing. He knew her well because of her interest in art, felt she would honor his request, had been delighted when she did.

The door opened, and Cyril held out his engraved calling card to the stiff-necked butler. He was motioned inside, left standing only momentarily in the glittering foyer before he was led to a flower-bedecked parlor where Madame Coltrane received him.

He pressed his lips to her extended hand, appreciative of her beauty, as well as that of the room itself. "I had heard you had a stunning home, madame, but I was not prepared for such absolute splendor."

He stared upward at the ceiling, frescoed with an allegorical composition. The entire room was resonant with French baroque grandeur. The floor was of rich *parquet de Versailles*. A Russian silver and onyx garniture adorned the mantel shelf.

But his attention was captured by a painting by Edouard Manet, which was set off by carved floral swags on the *faux-marbre* walls. He walked to it and, after a moment of reverent silence, spoke in almost a whisper. "That is "Olympia." He completed that in 1863. However did you come by it?"

Kitty smiled. It was always a pleasure to share her passion for art with someone. "It was a private sale. My husband heard about it in his travels. We went to Strasbourg to buy it."

A maid in crisp yellow cotton appeared with a silver tray on which were glasses of sparkling Burgundy. Cyril took one, then accepted Kitty's invitation to join her on the damask lounge before the window overlooking her beloved rose garden.

"You requested a private showing."

Cyril nodded with enthusiasm. "And I wish to thank you for allowing it. I suppose I do not have to tell you that the treasures you and your stepdaughter discovered in Monaco are the talk of Paris."

"Actually my stepdaughter found them. And, yes, we are aware of the interest. We're very excited over the opening of the shop."

"I can understand why. Tell me," he urged, "will she allow any of the Monaco paintings to be sold prior to the gallery opening?"

"I doubt it. I think she'd like to have them on display for a time, to generate even further interest in the shop. I doubt she'll offer them to be sold until sometime next year."

He flashed a wry smile. "You cannot blame a dealer for trying."

"Let me get Dani," Kitty suggested. "She's set up a little display area in the library, and I'm sure she'd like to meet you and show you the paintings herself. I've a late-afternoon tea to attend. Will you excuse me for going?"

Cyril politely rose. "Of course, and I'm sure I will enjoy your stepdaughter's company. Charm, no doubt, runs in the family," he added with a small bow.

Kitty demurely thanked him for his compliment, and was almost through the door when she suddenly whirled about. "You will be receiving an invitation soon. To give our friends a private showing prior to the public opening,

Travis and I are hosting a reception and ball in the Jardin des Tuileries. We do hope you will be able to come.''

Cyril knew in that moment that nothing would keep him away. A social event in the breathtaking gardens directly behind the spectacular Louvre Palace was not to be missed if one was fortunate enough to be invited. He also knew that a Coltrane affair was always lavish, always the high point of the social season.

When he was alone once more, Cyril discreetly moved about the room examining the splendid furnishings. He was wealthy in his own right, was not intimidated by such opulence but merely wanted to compare it with his own. Material things, he felt, were not truly important in life, but he happened to like them, intended to have the best of them.

He paused before a sculpture with a Carrara marble base, absently wondering where the beauty had been acquired.

He dared to run his fingertips down the delicate lines of the Allegrain, a woman with a water jug held almost sensuously against her breast.

There was, he grimly, silently, acknowledged, something he did not have . . . something he wanted, had to have, if he were to achieve total success in his life, his career.

In order to reach that coveted pinnacle that would acclaim him as the absolute connoisseur in Europe, perhaps even the world, *he had to make a discovery*!

He had to discover something truly valuable, rare, perhaps even priceless.

He had traveled extensively, lived for a time in many countries—Austria, Germany, Russia, even Italy and Greece. When something came along, he would know it.

Enviously, he thought of Mademoiselle Daniella Coltrane and *her* discovery. That had been a stroke of luck, had nothing to do with knowledge, perception, ingenuity. But had he, Cyril Arpel, discovered the hidden cache of valuable paintings, it would have, no doubt, launched him all the way to the moon in terms of being hailed by his peers.

"Monsieur Arpel. Bonjour."

He turned quickly at the sound of the sweetly soft voice, was at once struck speechless when he found himself looking at the most incredibly beautiful young woman he had ever seen.

Long, golden brown hair. Soft, cinnamon eyes, limpid in their loveliness and fringed with long, thick, curling lashes. Skin almost as alabaster-smooth and white as the sculpture he had just touched. A perfectly shaped nose, slightly, saucily tipped. Lips almost petulant, pink and moist.

She was wearing a gown of pink cotton, overlaid in delicate white lace. Her hair fell softly to perfect shoulders. He could see that the body beneath the dress was molded to perfection, and he almost gasped at the thought of such a sight.

Dani cocked her head to one side, slightly puzzled. The man had not spoken, merely stared as though in a trance. *"Monsieur?* You *are* Monsieur Arpel?" she added, a touch of doubt in her tone.

"Uh, yes." Cyril began to recover. God, she was beautiful. He had never been dumbstruck by the sight of a woman; he had seen thousands, bedded perhaps hundreds, but never had his lusty, hungry eyes feasted on such a sight as she.

He quickly crossed the room to bestow a kiss upon her fingertips. "Forgive me. You startled me. I dared to touch the Allegrain, and I felt like a naughty child when you caught me." He grinned affably, pretended anxiety. "You won't tell on me, will you?"

Dani laughed. At once, she could see that Cyril Arpel was a welcome change from the austere types she had met thus far in the art society of Paris. He had a mischievous twinkle in his eyes, and she found him handsome as well. "No, I won't tell. I admit I have to do the same when I'm around something I find attractive."

"You are very kind to allow me a private showing of your Monaco discovery. I feel quite honored."

Dani shrugged. While it had been a thrill to find something supposedly valuable, something that was giving her much publicity for the impending opening of her gallery, she could not share the enthusiasm of others. She just was not, she privately acknowledged, that intensely interested in art. Dancing, particularly ballet, was her true love. The gallery, the antique shop, that was something to while away the hours, give her a hobby, as it were, an interest.

She beckoned him to follow. "I am happy to oblige. My stepmother tells me that you are one of the most renowned art dealers in all of Europe. I will be interested to hear your interpretation and opinion of what we found in Monaco."

One of the most renowned dealers. Her words burned within him. Let me make a discovery of my own, and I'll be *the* most renowned, Cyril vowed silently, fiercely.

They entered the library, which, Cyril decided, was apparently furnished in the taste of Monsieur Coltrane, whom he knew to be, on the occasions he had been in his company, a rugged sort. Oh, he possessed all the social graces necessary for his important, respected position, but there was an air about him that hinted he would be much happier on the back of a horse, or some other unappealing activity, as far as Cyril was concerned.

At the far end of the room, amid the rows and rows of books arranged on hand-rubbed mahogany shelves, the paintings were displayed on easels.

Cyril began his inspection reluctantly. Suddenly, paintings, however valuable, were not on the top of his list of priorities. The captivating Daniella Coltrane *was*.

She gestured to the paintings. "Here they are. Take all the time you want."

Cyril moved forward. It was for moments such as these that he had studied so diligently, had learned how to view with close scrutiny.

Perhaps ten minutes passed in silence. Finally, Cyril announced that he especially liked the Rousseau and explained why. "He was able to show nature as a wild and undisciplined force, and it earned him the admiration of many of France's leading Romantic painters and writers.

"He did not exhibit regularly until 1831," he went on to explain. "Then in the forties he settled in the village of Barbizon, where he worked with the likes of Jean-François Millet and Charles-François Daubigny."

"They were known as the Barbizon school," Dani put in. "It was during the period when Rousseau produced tranquil pastorals such as this."

Cyril was impressed and said as much. Dani smiled. "I have my stepmother to thank for what little I know about art. I'm afraid it isn't exactly my forte."

"Oh, I rather think your forte would be just about anything you wanted it to be, my dear."

Letting his compliment pass without comment, she offered refreshment, hoping he was not in a hurry to leave.

Cyril was about to accept, also wanting to linger, when suddenly he realized he had been viewing five paintings, not six, as he'd heard had been discovered in Monaco. Almost accusingly, he asked, "Where is the other painting? Did you sell it?"

"No. I'm not selling any of them for the time being," she replied. "I didn't think you would be interested in seeing the other one. It can't be of any value."

He drew in his breath, let it out slowly. Lord, didn't these amateurs realize that it was the truly great paintings that slipped right by them, because they did not have the expertise, the knowledge, to know a valuable work of art when they saw it?

Somewhat exasperated, he implored, "May I see it, please? Allow me to be the judge."

Dani shrugged. Let him see for himself that it was worthless. She went and got it from where it was stored in a cabinet, then held it out to him. "See for yourself, monsieur."

"Oh, please call me Cyril," he murmured airily, taking the small framed canvas and walking to the window to view it in daylight.

Suddenly, creeping fingers of excitement began to work their way up his spine. He could feel his flesh start to tingle.

Was it possible that this was the missing Alexandrovsky painting?

For long, tense moments, he stared at the picture of the famed Alexandrovsky Palace, which was located in Russia, south of Saint Petersburg.

He could not afford to take any chances.

Cyril Arpel knew that if there was the remotest possibility that this was the painting sought by those closest to the Czar himself, then he had his discovery . . . the *find* that would establish him as the greatest connoisseur of art in the entire world.

Few, he thought excitedly, knew the secret behind the painting, for the scandal behind it had been discreetly dealt with. There was no way that Dani, or Kitty Coltrane, could have the slightest inkling of what was in their possession. Yet, he reminded himself anxiously, Dani had removed the painting from the collection.

Struggling to keep an edge from his voice, he inquired, "Do you know this scene?"

She shook her head. "No, but it looks like a very lovely palace somewhere."

He studied her eyes. There was no hint that she was hiding anything. She probably knew nothing, except that the painting was not the quality of the others, might take away from their true beauty.

"It is in Russia. About twenty-two kilometers from Saint Petersburg. I know it well, because I have lived and studied in Russia."

Dani's interest was aroused. "Tell me about it," she urged.

He began to explain: "Catherine the Great commissioned an Italian named Quarenghi in 1792 to build a palace for her grandson, who later became Alexander I. It was known as the Alexander Palace, later called the Alexandrovsky Palace.''

He paused to sneer at the painting, then said critically, ''This doesn't do it justice. Actually, it is an insult to the elegance of Alexandrovsky.''

Dani nodded, but murmured, ''I rather like it. There is something hauntingly beautiful about it, a uniqueness I can't describe, and—''

''I want to buy it!'' he interrupted, eyes wide and shining.

At once, Dani held out her hand for it, shook her head vehemently. ''No. It's not for sale. None of the paintings are for sale. I intend to use them for publicity, for display, for everyone to enjoy for a while, and then I will sell them, but not this one.''

Cyril felt a wave of panic, began to stammer. ''But—but my dear. You can see this is poor quality. It will only shadow the others.''

''Then I won't display it with them,'' she said matter-of-factly, still holding out her hand.

Cyril's fingers tightened around the frame, and he pressed it against his chest. ''It means something to me,'' he lied. ''Sentimental, you know. I will give you a good price.''

Dani sighed, slightly perturbed. ''It is not for sale.''

Cyril had to have the painting. He was one of only a few people who knew the secret, and he wasn't even supposed to know, *would not know,* were it not for eavesdropping on a conversation between the famed Russian goldsmith Peter Carl Fabergé, and one of his sons at the opening of their Odessa store one year before.

He had wandered away from the mingling, ogling crowds, as was his custom, and boldly gone beyond the gold velvet drapes separating the store proper from the workrooms. He wanted to see not what was offered to the general public but the creations that would be presented for private sale, to royalty.

He had found a tiny room where he marveled over a Chinese marriage cup, carved in mutton-fat jade and mounted in oxidized silver by Fabergé. The rim was engraved with a pattern of lines and dots, and the two handles were stylized jaguar heads, each revealing cabochon amethysts within open jaws formed of leaf motifs.

It was beautiful, and there was a countess in Lyon who would pay a fortune for it, he knew.

He was about to boldly seek out Carl Fabergé and make an offer for the piece. Then he heard voices, stood back to listen . . . and heard the conversation that revealed to him the secret of Alexandrovsky Palace and the painting he now held in his trembling hands!

Dani was losing her patience. The man was behaving strangely. "If you will give me the painting, I will put it away and have refreshments served," she stated evenly, almost coldly.

Cyril hated to hand it over to her but knew he had no choice. For the moment, her mind was set against selling it, and to continue to attempt to persuade her to change her mind would only risk arousing her suspicion as to why he wanted possession of it so badly.

Breathing in deeply, with nostrils flaring, he silently vowed that he would eventually have it . . . would stop at nothing to get it!

He forced a smile to dry, nervous lips. "Well, if you change your mind, please let me be the first to make an offer. Memories, you know," he added with a flippant shrug.

When they were back in the parlor once more, enjoying glasses of champagne, Cyril turned his attention to another matter—his infatuation with this stunningly beautiful creature. "Your stepmother tells me there is to be a grand social to celebrate the opening of your gallery and shop. I would be honored if you would allow me to escort you."

Dani groaned inwardly at the thought of the planned event. Oh, what a heated discussion that had been with her father and Kitty, when they approached her with the idea. Yes, she could see having a simple reception, but a ball? With an orchestra and all the trimmings? She had accused them both of wanting to put her on display, like a *debutante*, for god's sake. "Stop trying to plan my life for me," she had angrily protested. "Stop trying to find a husband for me! I don't want a husband! I don't want marriage. I don't want a debut into society. All I want is to be left alone to make my own decisions!"

It had not been a pleasant scene. Travis had become angry. Kitty seemed hurt. Dani had not apologized for her outburst, feeling she had a right to state her feelings. She had eventually given in to the idea of the ball, albeit reluctantly, but had no intention of being escorted, no intention of doing anything except play the role of new gallery owner, new shop owner.

Better a dilettante than a debutante, she had declared to herself.

Politely, she declined Cyril's offer. "That's very kind of you, but I will be so busy I would not be much company for you."

Reluctantly, he rose. "I thank you for your hospitality, for granting me a private showing, and should you change your mind about allowing me to be your escort, please let me know."

She walked with him to the door. He clasped her hand, raised it to his lips. "You are beautiful," he told her reverently. "I issue fair warning to all your other suitors that I intend to compete for your company."

Dani laughed with pleasure. "I should be honored, monsieur." She gave a small curtsy, said she would look forward to seeing him at the ball, then said good-bye.

Cyril took his hat from the butler, then made his way out and down the steps.

At the wrought-iron gate, he paused to gaze back at the mansion. Two treasures lay within—Dani Coltrane and the painting of the Alexandrovsky Palace.

He intended to possess both.

Chapter Eight

No expense had been too large, no detail too small, in planning for the spectacular celebration of the grand opening of the antique and art gallery of Mademoiselle Dani Coltrane.

Due to her father's political and social position, there was no problem in gaining permission to host the festivities in the famed Tuileries Gardens.

The gardens held a special place in Dani's heart, for she loved their symmetrical formality, yet found them anything but severe. Their openness and spacious views offered lightness, charm.

She did not, however, like to think of some of the grim history surrounding them. The dreaded guillotine had been erected near the gates in 1793, and records stated that for the next three years 1,343 people had been decapitated.

Dani liked to think that the flowers of the gardens bloomed especially for the memories of those poor dead souls. Marigolds lined the path to where the guillotine had stood, with chives in bloom forming pink bouquets. Baltic ivy draped a huge sundial, and, in a lively contrast of form and color, yarrow flaunted yellow blossoms above purple hibiscus and orange tiger lilies.

Little had been changed since André Le Nôtre laid out the gardens two hundred years before, in 1664. He had been born right in the garden, in the gardener's cottage, and had also died there.

Carrying out the line of his central *allée* beyond and
out into the country, a path traced straight along the
wooded hill to the west of the palace. It was on this hill-
top, 170 years later, in 1834, that the Arc de Triomphe
was erected, in celebration of Napoleon's victorious cam-
paigns of 1805.

At the eastern edge of the garden, Napoleon III had
erected a hothouse, which was called the Orangerie, and
a court for tennis—the Jeu de Paume.

The formal exit gate was flanked by two winged horses,
dating back to the seventeenth century, and gave a splendid view of the Place de la Concorde, the moat-skirted
octagon designed by Jacques Ange Gabriel in 1753.

Had inclement weather prevailed, the festivities could
have been moved on short notice into the palace. However, on the day of the event, conditions of nature could
not have been better. Though the air was cool with the
promise of fall, skies were clear and void of clouds. By
mid-afternoon, a brightly smiling sun had bestowed
warmth upon Paris . . . and the gardens.

Canopies of silk, in every color of the rainbow, and
mounted upon shining brass spears, dotted the lush, green
landscape. Each color designated a different fare, set out
upon tables covered in the finest lace over satin sheeting
the same shade of the canopy above.

A green canopy was the invitation for fruits—assorted
melon balls marinated in grape liqueur; succulent bananas
dipped in sugar, then fried and coated in coconut; apples
stewed thick and rich in a peppermint syrup; grapes
dusted in the most delicate powdered sugar; plump figs
soaked in honey; cherries and pineapple laced with
brandy.

Yellow silk displayed an array of egg and cheese
dishes. There were pots of simmering fondue for every
taste bud, with chunks of bread waiting to be dipped into
luscious cheese, egg, mushroom, or snail cream sauces.
For the sweet tooth, there were tiny squares of cake for
dipping into thick, rich chocolate.

After the *apéritif* tents, blue canopies offered first courses: *Bisque d'Ecrevisses* (crayfish bisque); *Jambon Persillé de Bourgogne* (parsleyed ham in aspic); *Fricassée de Petits-gris aux Croûtons* (fricassée of snails); and *Oeufs en Meurette* (baked eggs with bacon and croutons).

Bright red canopies heralded the delicious menu for second courses: *Gougeonnettes de Filets de Sole* (fried sole fingers); *Steak Bourguignon à la Moelle* (steak with beef marrow); *Bouribout aux Raisins* (ragout of duck and grapes); *Estouffade de Boeuf au Pommard aux Pâtes Fraîches* (beef stewed in red wine with fresh noodles); and *Cuisses de Grenouilles à la Comtoise* (frogs' legs in cream sauce).

As an added treat, it had been Dani's idea to invite chefs from a number of the culinary regions of France to present their regional specialties. From the Ile-de-France, the region surrounding Paris, there was the steak filet known as chateaubriand. Salmon was presented by the Loire Valley, as well as their famed meatballs made from pork and goose meat. Brittany heralded its specialties of lobster and fish, and the pancakes called *crêpes bretonnes*.

From Normandy, there were omelettes, excellent cheeses, and Rouen duck. The region of Champagne was celebrated for its trout stews, kidneys fried in champagne, and braised pike.

The Germanic influence was evident in the dishes prepared by the regional chefs of Alsace-Lorraine, such as *choucroute garnie* (sauerkraut garnished with ham, pork, sausages, and assorted vegetables.)

The chef from the Burgundy region used its renowned wines to cook fish balls, and Lyon featured sausages and *foie gras*.

Southeast of Cognac lay the region of Périgord, famed for its truffles, a subterranean fungus rooted from the ground by specially trained pigs and dogs. This delicacy, treasured by gourmets, was offered in abundance, for demand would be immense.

There was also a special canopy which provided only cheese, with breads and crackers for accompaniment. Tasty varieties such as Roquefort, Camembert, Brie, and Gruyère were laid out.

What was no doubt the favorite tented restaurant of all was the pink silk-roofed buffet of desserts: *Marquise au Chocolat à la Fine Champagne* (chocolate cake with Cognac); *Tarte Tatin à la Crème Chantilly* (apple tart with whipped cream); *Gâteau de Riz Crème Anglaise* (rice pudding with custard sauce); and *Crème Renversée Caramélisée* (caramelized cream custard).

The vineyards and wineries of the various regions were represented heartily—Cognac, Bordeaux, Burgundy, Rhine, Moselle. In addition, there was *génépi des Alpes* (alpine liqueur); *marc de Savoie* (grape brandy); and *mirabelle* (white plum brandy). Sparkling mineral water was provided as well.

Although Dani was still somewhat piqued by the thought of her father and stepmother using the ball as her social debut, she had found herself enthusiastically caught up in the excitement. Handwritten invitations in gold ink on blue parchment had gone out to over 1,500 people. Each and every recipient had accepted. It was, by public and private declaration, a gala not to be missed.

Dani rose early the morning of the festivities, declining breakfast and opting for only tea due to the excited churning within her. It was, she knew, going to be an event she would always remember. To her family, it might seem she was merely on display as a most eligible and rich young debutante, but she knew better. Opening the shop meant a firm statement of her own independence. The events surrounding it, no matter how lush and expensive, were merely of a business nature as far as she was concerned.

The most renowned *coiffeur* in Paris, Mimi Letrouse, arrived at the Coltrane mansion promptly at nine that morning to do first Kitty's hair, then Dani's.

Dani sat impatiently while Mimi painstakingly curled each tress of her autumn-gold hair with a heated iron. Then, each was twisted and pulled high up on her head, in layer after layer, every ringlet fastened with a specially designed heart-shaped clip of gold, set with tiny emeralds and edged in diamond chips. These had been a gift from her father from a trip to South Africa, and he'd had them especially made for her to wear on a very special occasion.

That occasion, Dani knew, was most definitely now.

When his wife made her way down the grand staircase, Travis Coltrane felt his heart quicken at the dazzling sight. She was still the most beautiful and exciting woman he had ever known. Dressed in a gown of purple satin, her lavender eyes glowed as though electrified beneath long, dusty lashes. Lush, firm breasts strained against the thickly beaded bodice. Ribbons of green satin umbrellaed down the skirt and were dotted with gleaming white pearls set in rosettes of lavender lace. At her slender throat were the elegant emeralds he had given her so long ago, set in gold filigree and interspersed with delicate rubies and tiny diamonds.

She reached the marbled foyer, and he gently brushed his lips to her forehead and murmured huskily, "You are lovely, and you drive me crazy . . ."

Kitty laughed, wickedly glancing at his white silk trousers and noting the slight bulge. "Travis, you always were insatiable."

Then, on silent cue, they stopped their whispered bantering to turn almost reverently to the stairs once more. Dani stood at the top, awesomely beautiful in her simplicity. Her gown was of gold lamé. Strapless, unadorned, it hugged every line of her body as it cascaded smoothly, like liquid fire, to the floor. With her cinnamon tresses afire with emeralds and diamonds, she wore no other jewelery. White gloves reached to her elbows. Her shoes were also gold.

Kitty felt her eyes fill with tears as she whispered, "Oh, Dani, my darling, you are truly beautiful . . ."

Travis went to clasp her hand as she reached the foyer, and he forced his voice around the emotional lump that had risen in his throat. "God, honey, if only your mother could see you . . ."

When the Coltranes arrived at the Tuileries Gardens, they gazed upon a seemingly endless sea of people amid a myriad of softly blowing canopies, the entire seascape drowning in flowers of every color and kind.

Dani caught her breath, held it, then let it out slowly to speak in a quivering voice. "I never dreamed it would be like this."

Travis smiled encouragingly. "It's all yours, my sweet. Enjoy every minute."

For the first hour of the gala, Dani was literally smothered by the swarm of well-wishers who pushed forward to congratulate her on the opening, and the fabulous party. She smiled, made appropriate comments, all the while feeling heady with the fragrance of the flowers, the delicious champagne, and the divine sound of music, from three orchestras, that filled the air.

When Cyril Arpel appeared suddenly to stand at her side, he did not leave. Dandily dressed in formal attire of red velvet and black satin, he had never felt more ebullient. After all, people were looking at *him* as he stood next to the ravishing Dani Coltrane, as though *he* were her escort.

Cyril hoped the attention would last all evening. Whenever Dani finished a conversation with someone, he would immediately start one of his own, if he considered the person important enough. Dani did not seem to mind, or notice, that, for all appearances, it looked as though they were together.

Finally, she turned to him almost in desperation and murmured, "My throat is so dry, and I haven't seen a waiter go by with champagne in ages. Please, would you get me some?''

He was quick to oblige. "Of course.'' Then he added hopefully, ''And as soon as you can politely remove yourself from this impromptu receiving line, perhaps we can slip away and have our dinner. The aroma of all those delicacies is making me ravenous.''

Dani laughed and confessed, ''Me too. We'll slip away soon.''

Cyril, she decided, was a dear—pleasant, charming, quick-witted. She found him to be extremely enjoyable company.

She was staring thoughtfully after him, momentarily oblivious to what was going on around her. Then, feeling her hand grasped gently, lifted, the touch of warm lips against her fingertips, she turned back to the moment at hand . . . and saw the tousled dark hair of the head bent before her.

The man straightened.

Dani suddenly found herself looking up into the most beautifully sensuous blue eyes imaginable, fringed by incredibly thick black lashes . . . and all a part of the most handsome man she had ever seen in her entire life. His complexion was dark, as though he spent many hours lounging in the sun on the beaches in the south of France.

He was tall, broad-shouldered, and wore a simple, but elegant, suit of maroon velvet. His shirt, ruffled and open at the throat, was of fine blue silk that complemented his fantastic eyes.

He continued to hold her hand as he gazed down at her. There was the play of a smile on his lips as he said finally, lazily, ''Miss Coltrane, you are even lovelier in person than in reputation.''

He had addressed her in flawless English. However, she noticed that while his voice had no trace of a French or American accent, there was a light touch of British

. . . but yet, there was another sound, one that she found intriguing, and pleasant to the ear.

As he continued to caress her fingertips and look at her in an almost intimate way, Dani felt a strange stirring within. Good Lord, she silently admonished herself, what was wrong with her? She had certainly been around men before, been held, and kissed, and caressed. She was certainly not the innocent little novice who had left the convent a year ago. She knew what it was like to feel warm rushes of longing.

But never like this . . .

She jerked her hand from his so abruptly that he smiled, as though he knew what she was feeling.

Dani commanded herself to remain coolly in control of herself, on the surface, at least. She was pleased with the unconstrained tone of her voice as she responded, "Monsieur, I do not believe we have met."

He pursed his lips thoughtfully for an instant, then said quietly, "I am known as Drakar."

Drakar. Where had she heard that name before? There was a familiar ring to it, yet she could not remember, knew only that had she ever met so strikingly handsome a man before, she would certainly remember him . . . as did every other woman who had ever had the pleasure, no doubt!

Without a word, or invitation, the tall stranger boldly took Dani's hand once more and whispered, "Come along. I want to get to know you better, and that is impossible in this mob."

Dani glanced wildly about, wondering fleetingly about the propriety of having a strange man spirit her away from her own party.

"Sir, I don't think this is proper," she protested, but her voice sounded unconvinced, even to her own ears.

He turned to give her a lopsided, devil-may-care grin. "Sorry if you're offended, Miss Coltrane, but I just don't take you for the sort of woman who frankly gives a damn about what's proper and what isn't.''

Dani gasped indignantly, pulled back. "I—I beg your pardon!'' she stammered, then hated herself for sounding so . . . so priggish!

At the feel of her resistance, Drakar stopped, turned, and looked down at her with eyes of icy challenge. "I merely want a chance to get to know you better, Miss Coltrane. I thought we might have a dance together at the little pavilion down by the river. If you find me offensive, then I will apologize.''

Suddenly, Dani knew that she *did* want to know him better. There was something wild and reckless about him—a spirit she found refreshing . . . and challenging. With a smile touched with arrogance, she coolly said, "Very well, sir. I doubt I have anything to fear with so many people around.''

Cinnamon eyes met sapphire eyes in challenge.

They had paused beneath an arched trellis thick with the free-flowering vine of blue wisteria. A waiter passed by. Drakar reached out and took two glasses of sparkling champagne, gave one to Dani, and they each took a sip, eyes continuing to lock as they stared at each other over the gilt-edged rims.

Finally, Drakar nodded his head ever so slightly and whispered, "If I wanted more from you than a dance, Miss Coltrane, we would be on the way to my apartment.''

Dani was surprised to feel only amusement at such a bold remark. If it had been any other man, she would probably react in anger, indignance, but already she was well aware that this Drakar, whoever he was, was unlike any man she had ever encountered before. She found him mysterious, handsome, and, oh, yes, extremely desirable. But more than that, she found him to be the first real challenge in a man she'd ever experienced. He was not fawning, obsequious. He was, she silently acknowledged, a *real* man.

"I find you quite insolent and presumptuous, sir. Do you really believe you have only to desire a woman, and she will respond to you so easily?"

He slowly finished his champagne before casually stating, "Desire must be mutual, my dear, in order for a man and woman to achieve reciprocal enjoyment . . . *and* satisfaction."

It was her turn to lift a mocking eyebrow. "And you think I desire you?" she asked.

Drakar did not hesitate to nod. "Oh, yes. I sense hunger in women, and I can see in your eyes that there is a famine for love inside you."

Dani felt herself bristling. He was becoming a bit too presumptuous, and needed to be put in his place. "Perhaps you sense your own famine, sir, and see in women what you want to see, because you, yourself, are starved for love."

His eyes twinkled with amusement. "No, you're wrong. I ignore the hunger in women for whom I have no desire. As I have already told you, desire must be mutual."

He tucked her hand in the crook of his arm, then smiled and winked. "We have plenty of time to talk about *our* desire. May we have that dance now?"

Dani had to laugh. How could she be angry when she was enjoying herself so much? The man was an enigma, but she was not intimidated. She found the carefree banter refreshing.

They walked to the end of the gardens and behind the large octangular pool, pausing to admire the floating lilies, so colorful and gay, then passed the fine statues of the Orangerie.

"Your stepmother tells me you have a wonderful gallery and antique shop planned," he said easily as they moved away from the partygoers and headed for the private wooden pavilion that had been constructed for dancing near the banks of the Seine. "I look forward to seeing it. Could I possibly persuade you to give me a private tour before you open to the public?''

Dani saw nothing wrong with his request. The same had been granted to Cyril, but then Cyril was a dealer, with shops in several countries. She could not help but wonder why this stranger, however charming and handsome he might be, would request a special, private showing.

"I will be opening the shop formally on Monday morning," she told him, then boldly asked, "Why do you want a private tour? And how is it that you know my stepmother? Are you friends?"

A shadow crossed his eyes, Dani thought, but she could not be sure.

"I met your parents at several embassy parties in the past," he explained. "You might say we are good acquaintances, casual friends. As for wanting a private showing, I'm like everyone else, I suppose—anxious and curious to see your new shop."

Dani nodded. "All right. I'll be happy to show you around the gallery Monday morning, say, a half hour before the doors officially open."

Drakar frowned. He wanted more than half an hour to view the art from Monaco. "Are you free tomorrow afternoon? I could take you to lunch, and then we could go to your shop."

Dani thought a moment. She had to admit she would like to see him again, but Sunday afternoon was to be a busy time, with so many last-minute details to be taken care of. Still, she was tempted to give in. "I don't know," she hedged. "I'd planned to work at the gallery tomorrow, and—"

"I would love to help you," he cut in to offer amiably, then, with a flirting wink, added, "In certain situations, a man can prove quite helpful."

To which Dani coquettishly countered, "It depends, sir, upon the situation."

Drakar nodded in conciliation, murmured, "Touché," then held out his arms to her, for they had reached the dance pavilion.

To the lilting music of Johann Strauss, he moved her through the gliding, elegant steps and slides of the waltz. Then, as the tempo became lighter, he easily led her into the rapid, whirling Viennese style of the dance.

Others on the floor, admiring the grace and beauty of the elegant couple, stepped aside to give them ample room for their gliding and dipping movements.

Dani found it hard to keep from gasping, for never had she thought she could keep up with such intricate steps, but the man was a marvel. He seemed to anticipate her reluctance in certain variances and was able to swiftly and easily maneuver her through them with style and grace. It was, she realized, as though they had danced together their entire lives.

Sapphire eyes held cinnamon eyes transfixed in a silent message of mutual desire.

Dani could not deny the pulsating emotion within. Never had she wanted a man more.

Yet, Dani felt no trepidation at the thought of being in the arms of such an obviously experienced man. No matter that she was a virgin. She knew, without a doubt, that he would lead her to untold wonders of joy with the same ease that he had led her through the intricacies of the Viennese waltz.

But would she ever allow it?

From the shadows, Cyril Arpel watched the couple as they moved together on the dance floor. From where he stood, he could even see the looks on their faces—so enraptured with each other, oblivious to everyone and everything around them.

Cyril angrily turned and tossed his glass of champagne into the Seine.

Damn Drakar!

Cyril's teeth ground together in anger. He should have known he would turn up, that he would, somehow, hear of the discovery of the cache of paintings. There were but a few people who even knew the secret. And Drakar was one of them.

Cyril knew he had an advantage over the Russian, because Drakar did not know that Cyril also knew the secret. And he was not about to let him discover the truth. He had never let anyone know of the conversation he had heard at the Fabergé shop. So now he would be free to continue his quest to get his hands on the Alexandrovsky Palace painting.

And nothing would stand in his way.

Chapter Nine

DANI, intrigued with Drakar and his aloof, yet casually flirting banter, allowed him to monopolize her time for over an hour. They danced till weary, then walked slowly along the path beside the Seine River, until the shadows of day began to lengthen in dusty gold umbras about them.

She forgot all about Cyril and her promise to have dinner with him. She was fascinated with Drakar, but found she was constantly on her guard lest he regard her as merely a capricious fluff, or worse, one of the women he was no doubt used to having fall under his charming spell. Not she, by god!

Inquisitive, she asked him questions about himself, noted at once his reluctance to answer, the dark shadow that clouded his eyes. He told her he was born in Russia, that his parents were dead. His father had been Russian; his mother, French.

She heard the chill in his voice as he spoke of his family, and, attempting to restore a cheerful air, commented, "So, your blue eyes came from your mother, no doubt. I wondered about that, when you said you were born in Russia."

He said nothing.

A glance told her the muscles in his jaw had tightened. So, he did not want to talk about his mother.

She changed the subject. "You speak fluent English."

Finally, a smile.

"I should. I studied at Oxford."

"So, what brings you to Paris?"

"Beautiful women," he murmured, squeezing her hand, which clasped his arm. "I'm with the most beautiful in all of Paris at this very moment."

She drew in her breath, hoped he could not hear the pounding of her heart. Other men had told her they found her lovely, and she had accepted the compliment graciously. Why, now, did she feel all fluttery inside?

Attempting to steer the conversation in another direction, she asked where he had lived in Russia.

Again, the chill in his voice.

"Saint Petersburg."

"Ah," she cried, delighted. "Then you no doubt have seen Russian ballet at its best."

He seemed relieved to speak of something besides himself and quickly said, "Oh, yes. Louis the Fourteenth might have founded professional ballet in Paris, when he issued the decree in the seventeenth century that gave birth to ballet as a theater art, but once the school of ballet opened in the royal palace in Saint Petersburg, less than seventy years later, Russia became the creative center."

Dani was enthralled, for she had found someone who seemed to love ballet as much as she. Drakar, she learned, had visited the Imperial Ballet School many times, and she was quite awed to hear him casually mention that he actually knew Mathilde Kschessinskaya.

"Why, she is the star ballerina of Marius Petipa, the principal ballet master and choreographer of the Imperial Ballet in Saint Petersburg!"

Drakar nodded.

"Tell me about her," Dani urged.

He shrugged. "She is considered the most fascinating and fashionable ballerina of our time. The jewels she wears on stage, and off, are real, and they belong to her.

She's radiant, coquettish, amusing, enchanting, vivacious—*like you* . . ." His voice trailed off suggestively.

Dani felt her cheeks grow warm. He was gazing at her so . . . so *hungrily!*

Quickly, perhaps too quickly, she mentioned that she had heard Mathilde Kschessinskaya had left Russia to go to Milan to master the difficult steps developed and taught only there so she could dance in Petipa's *Sleeping Beauty*. It had premiered with an Italian ballerina, Carlotta Brianza, Dani recalled, the year Mathilde had graduated from the Imperial Ballet School, earning her position as *prima ballerina assoluta* on the Maryinsky stage.

Drakar stared at her in wonder. "I am quite impressed with you, Miss Coltrane. It is rare that I encounter a woman with such extensive knowledge of ballet. Most only care about the costumes, the music, but you seem to take a very personal interest in the performers themselves. Have you studied ballet yourself?"

It was Dani's turn to be reluctant to discuss her past. "No," she murmured, "but I always wanted to."

"Well, one day you should visit Russia. If I am there, I would be most happy to escort you to the ballet, and if Mathilde is dancing, I will see to it that you have a personal introduction, and I will take you both to dinner, as well."

Dani smiled, thanked him, vaguely thought how nice it would be, doubted it would ever happen.

Looking toward the sinking sun, she realized they had been away from the festivities far too long. "We'd best be getting back," she said, then added, "It has been delightful talking with you."

"The pleasure is mutual, I assure you."

When they neared the crowds of people, Drakar spotted the young man he had seen hovering about Dani earlier. He drew back, wanting one last moment of privacy. "So, you will agree to give me a private showing tomorrow?" he asked.

Dani nodded. There was no harm. It was no inconvenience. She had to admit she would like to see him again. Yet, there was still something about him, some mysterious aura that she had been unable to probe beyond. "You never did tell me the real reason you're in Paris," she dared to point out.

The shadow returned. He struggled for a relaxed air. "Well, let's just say I like to travel, Miss Coltrane, and see everything, do everything. This year, Paris. Who knows? Next year it might be Greece, or Spain. One day, I plan to journey to your native country."

She sensed a falseness, somehow, to the lightness of his tone. Boldly, she asked, "But why? What do you do? Why are you so interested in art?"

Drakar felt a stiffness along his spine. The young woman was quite astute, but then it was not logical to think she had become so learned by being afraid to ask questions. With a touch of his own audaciousness, he declared, "What I do, Miss Coltrane, is spend my inheritance any way I like, while fending off fortune-hunting young ladies. I doubt I would have that problem, however, with someone of your obvious wealth.

"As for my interest in art," he went on, aware by the way she was staring at him that she was somewhat stunned by his candor. "Why not? I happen to find it fascinating, for the moment, that someone hid valuable works of art in a wine cellar in a château on the south coast of France. Perhaps, eventually, you will discover they were actually stolen. One never knows."

He looked at her in anticipation of indignant rebuke. Instead, she cocked her head to one side and blandly retorted, "No, one never knows, sir, which makes my possession of the paintings all the more intriguing. Why, think how much they will be worth when I do decide to sell them, after rumors such as the one you have just started spread all over Europe! Everyone will want to see them, to find out if they *are* stolen.

"However," she hastened to inform him, "I must spoil your fantasy. The paintings were hidden, no doubt, by my late stepfather who was, at the time of his death, terribly in debt due to his gambling compulsion. The paintings were obviously of some great sentimental value to him, or else he did not want to part with them if there was any way to avoid it, so he stashed them away to keep his debtors from taking them from him."

Drakar studied her thoughtfully. If he found what he was looking for, this lovely young woman might prove a formidable foe. She was not like other women he had known, for she was vastly intelligent, perceptive.

Finally, he said, "Then I thank you again, Miss Coltrane, for indulging my fantasies and allowing me to view the paintings before your opening."

He gave her a slight bow, grinned lazily. "Perhaps we may have another dance later in the evening. We seem to move so well together."

Dani said perhaps that would be possible, then turned and walked away.

Drakar watched her go. She was truly the most lovely creature he had ever met, not an ordinary woman, yet still a woman . . . *and not to be trusted*!

All he knew was that a cache of paintings had been discovered hidden in the wine cellar of a deceased man he had never even heard of. There was probably no connection with his quest. Yet, as he had done for the past ten years, he would leave no stone unturned, no rumor ignored. And one day, he would find what he was looking for. He was grateful that only a handful of people knew what that was. He had more freedom to search. After all, he had the word of honor of the Czar of Russia, Alexander III, that everything surrounding the scandal would be kept as confidential as humanly possible, and, for the past decade, Drakar had found no reason to believe otherwise.

He watched the young man hastily approaching Dani—Cyril Arpel. He had seen him at a few showings and socials in the past, and not just in Paris. There had been occasions in Rome, Vienna, Zurich. Only in his thirties, Arpel was already quite well known and respected as a connoisseur and dealer. He was no doubt smitten with Dani.

Drakar smiled.

What man would not be?

"Dani . . ."

She turned, and at once felt a wave of guilt. Cyril's expression was a mixture of anger and hurt.

"Have you eaten yet?" he asked.

She told him she had been walking with one of the guests. "The time got away from me, I'm afraid." She slipped her hand around his arm. "Shall we go and sample the food my stepmother has fretted over for weeks? I need to freshen up a bit, but I won't be long."

He walked with her to the entrance to the ladies' powder room, then said he would be outside waiting.

A few moments later, Dani was about to leave when she heard Drakar's name mentioned. She tarried before a mirror, pretended to fuss with her hair as she looked at the reflection of three young women, about her age, standing together to one side. She did not recognize any of them, but then, there were not that many people at her own party that she did know. Almost all were friends, or acquaintances, of Travis and Kitty.

"I don't care about his reputation," one of them was saying. "He is devastatingly handsome."

"Those eyes! That smile!" another chimed in. "And he's so intriguing. There's a mysterious air about him I find absolutely fascinating."

The third young woman sniffed in disdain, airily commented, "Russians are like that. Cold. Aloof. I don't find him intriguing or mysterious at all. It's certainly no mystery what he's after in a woman!"

The other two laughed. The one who had just spoken reddened and indignantly snapped, "Well, I don't intend to fawn after him the way you two do. He may be a collector of women, as they say, but *I* don't intend to be part of his collection!''

One of the others cattily cried, ''He doesn't want you for part of his collection, Cécile. That's why you hate him so. It's common gossip that you ran after him at Madame NePrix's tea dance last summer, and he ignored you pitifully.''

The girl named Cécile angrily whirled and rushed from the powder room in a flurry of satin and lace.

Dani remained in front of the mirror. She was enjoying the conversation. It did not bother her at all to hear such things about Drakar, because they did not affect her. She also thought he was handsome, fascinating, and so on . . . but she was in complete control of her emotions and would certainly not become part of his collection. She found it all quite amusing.

Then, just as she was turning to go once more, she froze where she stood as she heard the sympathetic proclamation of one of the young women: ''I feel so sorry for Carista Altonderry. What he did to her must have been terribly humiliating.''

Past the sudden roaring in her ears, Dani heard the unsympathetic response: ''That was her own fault. My maid is a second cousin to one of the stable hands at Derryateau, and he told her he heard from the household servants that Carista insisted Drakar agree to announce their engagement. He had no choice but to run.'' She giggled. ''Derryateau might be large, but when Carista starts chasing a man, even a palace isn't large enough!''

''I don't blame her for trying, though,'' the first young woman commented with a sigh. ''I hear that Drakar is rumored to be Europe's greatest pleasure to a woman . . .'' Then, a barely audible whisper, ''*In bed!*''

Her friend cried, aghast, ''Naneen! What a thing to say!''

Then they both convulsed in giggles.

Dani did not glance in their direction as they walked out together.

So, she thought with only mild concern, the man she had just met was the same one who had been visiting Carista Altonderry at Derryateau; who had, somewhat rudely, disappeared just before a party where he was to be one of the featured guests. Considered a womanizer by some, he was also reputedly a wealthy man. True, she found him a bit arrogant, mildly conceited, but decidedly attractive and intriguing. If Carista had been so lacking in control of her emotions as to allow him to draw her into his web of passion, giving herself over to his control and manipulation, then, by god, she had deserved the spider's bite.

She left the powder room and found Cyril waiting, looking somewhat impatient. "Again, I apologize," she told him as she took his arm. They began to walk toward the sea of canopies where food awaited. "You must be starving."

He looked down at her and flashed a warm smile. "Starving for your company, lovely lady. Only my heart needs nourishment."

Dani made no comment; she was not interested in flirtatious banter. Though Cyril was a dear, she doubted she could ever regard him as more than a treasured friend.

They took time to visit all the canopies to view the spectacular offerings of food. Cyril tried to take a small portion of each, wanting to sample everything, but all too soon his platter was filled.

"You'll just have to come back for seconds, and thirds, and fourths," Dani teased.

He nodded toward her own plate, barely filled with dainty portions. "Women!" he scoffed. "It is an absolute sin not to be piggish when you have a chance to eat these delicacies."

"Enjoy them today and suffer for weeks trying to lose the extra pounds."

He shook his head, lifted a frog's leg and took a bite, then sighed. "I don't care. It's worth every ounce!"

Just then Kitty called, "There you are. I've been looking all over for you two." In mock reproach, she turned to Cyril. "How dare you spirit her away from her own party, sir?"

Cyril knew she was teasing but still felt a wave of resentment. Stiffly, he informed her, "It was not me she was with, madame, to my sorrow, I might add."

Kitty looked to Dani curiously.

"I met the famous Drakar," Dani nonchalantly explained.

Kitty recalled the disgust Dani had felt over the situation at Derryateau concerning Drakar and decided she should have discussed inviting him with her, but there had been so much going on lately that she really had not thought about it.

"Travis said Drakar called on him at the embassy," she explained, "and said that he had heard about your finding the paintings in Monaco and expressed an interest in them. Travis has always gotten on well with him and enjoyed the times they had met at various socials, so, you know your father, always the genial host. He invited him to come today."

Cyril, frowning, asked, "What is his interest? He's no collector. From what I hear, he is nothing more than a— a *sybarite*!" he stammered, struggling to hold back his resentment.

Kitty gave him a strange look, decided he was obviously jealous. "I really don't know, Cyril, except that Travis did say something about Drakar hearing that one of the paintings was of a palace in Russia, and since that is his homeland, he wanted to view it."

Cyril felt a churning sensation in the pit of his stomach. His suspicion was correct. Drakar was hoping to find the Alexandrovsky Palace painting.

It was only with great effort that he affected a normal voice to ask, "And has he seen it?"

Both Kitty and Dani looked at him.

Cyril cursed himself for being so obvious. He must never let them know there was any connection between Drakar and the Alexandrovsky Palace. He attempted to steer the conversation away from the painting. With a chary expression, he smoothly stated, "I admit I wanted to be the only one honored with a private showing, and"—he gave Dani a fond look—"to share your company for the same."

Dani again ignored his flirting.

Kitty laughed. "Well, you may relax, Cyril. You are the only one she's granted the privilege to. Frankly, I forgot all about it, so he will just have to stand in line like everyone else at Monday's grand opening."

No, he doesn't, Dani mischievously thought to herself. *No, he doesn't, because I find him quite appealing and charming, and I think I am actually looking forward to breaking down that supercilious façade of his and getting to know the* real *Drakar!*

Kitty touched her arm in a gesture of apology. "You aren't upset because I invited him?"

"Of course not," Dani responded tartly. "He seems quite nice. We had a delightful time."

"Good." Kitty kissed her cheek, hugged her, stepped back. "Now you two go and enjoy yourselves. I want to see you having the time of your lives and dancing the night away."

Cyril was seething inside but managed to appear calm. Drakar was going to try and get his hands on that painting. No doubt about that. He was also a stellar adversary where Dani was concerned. He had seen the way they had looked at each other. She had not looked at *him* that way, by god. He was beside himself, wondering what he should do. If he warned her about Drakar and his reputation with women, she might be offended and tell him to mind his own business. That would drive her away. He did not want that. True, he wanted the painting, wanted to find the secret himself, but, ultimately, if Drakar *did* get his hands on it first, well, Dani could hardly be called the spoils of war! He would get something he wanted desperately.

But he wanted both . . . and he was not going to give up easily!

He decided to approach her gently, cautiously. They were walking about the gardens, having finished their dinner, nodding and speaking with guests at random. Soon, all festivities would center around the dancing. He liked the way they had paired off together, as though they *were* together. Perhaps Drakar would see, and realize, that he was butting in. Quietly, he began, "The Russian, how did you find him?"

Dani was lost in her own thoughts—about Drakar—and she glanced up sharply and replied, "He was nice. Why?"

Cyril sensed her defensiveness. His suspicions were correct, dammit. She was smitten by the voluptuous Russian. He reminded himself once more to choose his words carefully.

"I was just wondering. I have met him a few times at openings, showings, and such. He's somewhat of an enigma. No one seems to know where his money comes from. No one seems to know what he does . . . he just seems to flit about with a pretty, and usually quite rich, woman on his arm."

Dani could not help laughing. "Cyril, you sound jealous!"

He felt his cheeks redden. "I most certainly am not. Why would I be jealous of a man who is without respect by his peers?"

Dani frowned. She really did not want to discuss Drakar with Cyril. Besides, for the moment, she was merely intrigued by him, certainly not involved, and there was no need to make a fuss. "I think this conversation is a waste of our time," she said pointedly, "and not how I want to spend my time at my own party. Do you mind?"

Cyril sucked in his breath, held it. Damn, damn, damn, he had really done it. He let his breath out slowly, felt his tight lips spread into a smile he did not truly feel. "You are absolutely right. I sound like a gossiping old woman."

Dani was quick to quip, "A gossiping old *man*, sir. Do not single out women as the only sex to enjoy spreading rumors."

Cyril struggled to keep smiling. She had done it again—put him in his place. Dani Coltrane was truly unlike any woman he had ever encountered in his life . . . and he thought he had seen all kinds. He decided to quickly broach another subject. "I know you probably have a lot to do tomorrow to get ready for Monday," he began cheerily, "so I will just come by and get you in my carriage, and we will go together to Montmartre."

"No!" Dani said quickly, *too* quickly . . . and sharply, for she saw that he was looking at her oddly. She hastened to explain. "Not that I don't appreciate your offer, Cyril, but my plans are made. Kitty is going to help me," she lied. In truth, Kitty and Travis had a government social to attend that would keep them busy into the evening.

Cyril was not to be easily put off. "I am sure you could use more help," he stated evenly, wondering why she was behaving so strangely. "I have no plans. I would be happy to help," he persisted.

Dani groaned inwardly. She did not want to hurt his feelings, but she was not going to allow him to manipulate her. "No, Cyril," she said firmly, "I want to do things my way. I appreciate your offer to help, but I do not need it."

Their eyes met and held. Cyril knew it was useless to argue. He also knew that something was going on . . . something probably concerning Drakar, whom he could see approaching from the corner of his eye. "Very well," he said finally, somehow able to keep that infernal false smile on his lips, "but if you change your mind, you can send word by messenger."

"Of course." She breathed a sigh of relief.

Drakar walked up, nodded curtly to Cyril, as though his presence were acknowledged, then dismissed. He held out his hand to Dani and warmly whispered, "I believe you promised me another dance."

Dani murmured a barely audible "You will excuse me, won't you?" to Cyril, then allowed the most handsome and exciting man she had ever met to lead her to the pavilion.

Cyril ground his teeth together until his jaw ached. He could not, he vowed, allow it to happen. Drakar was only interested in Dani because of the painting. He was going to make a fool of her as he had all the other women in his past, but Cyril was not going to allow it to happen. He had heard the story about *her* past, how she had been in a convent, then left before taking her final vows. She was not used to men in general, much less worldly, sophisticated *womanizers* like that damned Russian. She might be angry now, for his interfering, but later she would be grateful.

His mind was made up. Tomorrow afternoon, he would go to the shop in Montmartre and tell her everything he knew, everything she needed to know, about Drakar.

Chapter Ten

IT was after one in the afternoon when Dani, Kitty, and Travis left their mansion. They had all slept late, for it had been almost dawn when the party had finally ended.

Kitty admitted sleepily she would still be in bed were it not for the embassy function she and Travis were expected to attend. "Of all times for an ambassador to arrive," she had groaned as the Coltrane carriage pulled away from the gates. "I don't exactly need another party right now."

Travis had just smiled; he knew she really did not mind. She loved going anywhere with him, for business or social reasons, and that was one of the myriad of reasons he adored her so.

As they rode through the streets of Paris in the warmth of the golden afternoon, they talked happily of the events of the night before. Never, they were in agreement, had there been a more successful gala in Paris. People would be talking about it for months . . . maybe longer.

Kitty could not resist teasing Dani about Drakar. "You two really had the gossips buzzing. You also had poor Cyril fuming, I'm afraid," she added.

Dani gave her what she hoped was a bewildered look. "Really? Then they must have been starving for something to talk about. We merely shared a few dances." She was glad she did not have to go to the ambassador's reception with them, would only be riding as far as the bridge across the Seine to the Right Bank. The rest of the way was a pleasant walk to Montmartre, and she was looking forward to it, for she had many thoughts to ponder before seeing Drake again.

She suppressed a smile, covered her lips with her fingertips, and turned her head as she remembered the incident when she had called him Drake for the first time. After they had danced, they had walked once more down to the river's edge in unspoken yearning to be alone.

"Drake?" he had echoed, wondering if he had heard her correctly.

"Yes," she was quick to inform him. "I like that better. Drakar sounds like a . . . a *vampire*!" she had said with a laugh.

He had been delighted. "I think I like that better, and you're right. I suppose my name does evoke thoughts of vampires." He made a growling sound, deep in his throat, lowered his lips to her neck and murmured, "Aren't you afraid to be alone with me, my dear?"

She laughed, pulled away from his embrace and teased, "Yes, but not because I fear you're a vampire."

He knew what she meant, and they exchanged a warm look filled with hidden meanings, and stirrings, and as Dani thought about it now, she was almost sure that had another couple not come walking by at that precise moment, he would have kissed her. Had she wanted him to? When they were still strangers to each other? Yes, she silently, firmly, avowed. She had wanted his kiss, and she was not ashamed to admit it . . . at least not to herself. She knew Kitty and her father would probably be appalled.

Travis brought her out of her reverie with the question "How did you like Drakar? I find him to be very nice, a quite learned gentleman, but somewhat of an enigma. No one seems to know very much about him."

Dani made her tone casual. "As I said, we shared a few dances. We talked. He's very interesting."

"Cyril calls him a sybarite," Kitty could not resist interjecting.

"That would certainly be a paradox, when Cyril Arpel has probably visited every bordello in Europe," Travis scoffed.

"Now Travis," Kitty admonished, "you don't know that to be true!"

Travis gave her a lazy, knowing smile. "Unlike you women, I never make a statement unless I know it to be true. And so what if Drakar is a pleasure-seeker? I consider that his business."

Kitty was at once indignant. "Not if he is trifling with your daughter."

Dani looked from one to the other and groaned. How she wished sometimes she had her own apartment, could live by herself and truly be independent in every phase of her life.

"Dani is a big girl," Travis said quietly. "I think she can take care of herself."

"Maybe," Kitty said with a wink, "but I worry because Drakar reminds me of you when I first met you."

Travis pretended to be shocked, shook his head and cried, "God help Drakar if Dani is anything like *you* were! His heart is lost."

It was time for the carriage to turn from the Rue de Rivoli and head for the Place Vendôme. Designed for Louis XIV by the brilliant Mansart at the end of the seventeenth century, it was the location for the reception for the new ambassador from Morocco, and it was considered one of the architectural beauty spots of Paris.

The carriage rolled to a stop, and Travis helped Dani alight to the cobblestone street. "I wish you were coming with us. What time would you like me to send the carriage for you?"

She told him she would make her own way home, not to worry about her. "I have much to do, and I'm looking forward to it. I don't want to be tied to a schedule."

Travis frowned but said nothing. He would have preferred her to not be so independent but was determined to let his daughter spread her wings and fly, if that was what she wanted. Life with Alaina must have been hell on earth. Dani deserved some freedom . . . and happiness.

Dani could see the spiraling white towers of the Sacré-Coeur peeking from behind the corners of the narrow streets. She hesitated, pursed her lips thoughtfully. It was such a gloriously beautiful day that she just had to yield to the temptation of a bit of sightseeing before continuing on to the shop.

She went to the Sacré-Coeur, the "Church of the Sacred Heart," and drew in her breath in awe at the sight of the impressively massive interior, said to be able to hold nine thousand people. There were ornate mosaics, but she was not, at the moment, interested in the decor. Instead, she climbed the steep stairs to the top of the dome where the view offered a miraculous panorama of Paris and a distance of thirty miles or more in any direction.

Dani loved Paris, and France, and seeing the glorious splendor spread out before her only made her appreciate even more her newfound freedom. Yet, she knew she wanted more.

She thought of Drake, the way he made her feel. Yes, he was a womanizer, no doubt about that, but she liked him, and felt confident that he would not manipulate her as he did his other women. She would make sure of that.

So why, she asked herself with a touch of trepidation, was she filled with such anxiety at the thought of being with him again?

The answer was quite simple.

Never had she known anyone like him; therefore, there was no precedent, no comparison, no experience to rely on. Truly she was on her own and would be forced to deal with each and every moment of their time together on sheer instinct alone.

Suddenly, Dani laughed aloud, and it was a good feeling, there on the terrace of the Sacré-Coeur, with Paris sprawled before her in all its glory. She was not, she acknowledged firmly, afraid of this dashingly handsome Russian. In reality, she was looking forward to what was surely to be an exciting time in her life . . . no matter the outcome!

The shop was located on Place du Tertre, and Dani was quite proud of the building she had purchased. The space she would be occupying was not very large, but she would expand as her business grew. Young painters lived in the rooms on the floors above, and she looked forward to making friends with them.

She unlocked the front door, and after taking off her shawl, she began an inspection of her inventory. With Kitty's help and expertise, they had located another antique shop in another section of Paris that was being sold. Not interested in the store's location, Dani had been able to acquire its contents, for the owner had died, and the heirs were interested in liquidating everything as quickly as possible.

She lovingly viewed her favorite pieces from the purchase: a yellow-flowered pearwood table with intricate carvings; luscious linen hangings from Belgium; Flemish paintings dating back to the 1520s; an 1806 portrait of someone unknown by Sir Henry Raeburn.

There were Japanese cloisonné pieces that several people had heard about and told her at last night's social that they were interested in buying. It was amazing, she reflected, how the same pieces had probably been for sale for years in the other shop, in another location, but because of her social position, the fact that she was wealthy in her own right, people wanted to buy from her.

Dani walked to where the Monaco paintings were displayed on one wall, which she had delicately covered in pale blue silk to give them the most elegant background. As always, she became transfixed by the crude rendering of the famed Alexandrovsky Palace. There was just something about it, something she could not explain, that held her fascinated. At first, she thought perhaps it was its frame. Roughly made of some kind of woven twigs, it had been rubbed smooth, as though someone had whiled away many hours long after the painting was completed. But why? She shook her head in response to her own question, knew it was not merely the frame. There was just something sad and haunting about the work. The palace was, no doubt, dazzling in reality, but the artist, obviously an amateur, had somehow managed to capture its architectural splendor while at the same time enveloping it in a melancholy aura.

Dani sighed, shuddered, thought how there was something almost frightening there. Yet she adored it, had no intentions of selling it, no matter how high the offer. Soon, she would be going to Austria and would, no doubt, purchase many other paintings to stock her gallery. After the grand opening, the Alexandrovsky Palace painting would be stored away for the future as part of her own personal collection.

She turned at the melodic sound of the bell as the front door opened.

Drake stepped inside, smiling fondly at the sight of her walking toward him. "As beautiful as I remembered," he murmured. "I was afraid you were only a dream."

Dani fleetingly wondered how many other women had heard such a greeting from the stunning Russian, then said, "Welcome to my shop and gallery."

"Thank you for allowing me a private showing."

"You may not be so appreciative when you have seen my modest offerings. I'm not fully stocked yet, as you can see, but I think there are some interesting pieces."

He followed her around as she showed him what was being offered for sale, and all the while he was burning silently with the anticipation of viewing the Monaco discoveries. So long, he had searched. Each time he heard there was a painting of a landscape in Russia, he tried, when viewing it, to display as little interest as possible, lest he arouse suspicion. But this was the first time anyone had discovered a painting of the palace . . . and that, according to what he had managed to find out, was what he was seeking.

"And here," Dani was saying with a flourish, for she had deliberately saved the gallery for the last, knowing these were the most intriguing offerings of her modest little shop, "we have the great discovery from the wine cellar of Count deBonnett's château in Monaco!" She gave him a sweeping bow, then stepped to one side.

Drake moved forward, quietly drawing in his breath and pretending absolute nonchalance. He went from left to right, slowly, studying each painting carefully, trying to hold back, to appear in no hurry whatsoever. He knew, instinctively, that the palace painting would be the very last one displayed.

Then, he was before it and *he knew*.

A quick, sweeping look told him what he had prepared himself for—that if, indeed, this was the painting he had been seeking for over a decade, the answer would not leap out at him. The puzzle would not be solved in the blinking of an eye. Meticulous examination would be required . . . just as the pseudoartist had intended.

Dani spoke. He heard the sound, not the words. He tore his gaze from the painting, forced a smile, muttered, "Excuse me, what did you say?"

"I don't know why everyone finds this painting so fascinating," she repeated.

A chill of foreboding danced over him, but he managed to hold rein on his composure. "Everyone?" he echoed mildly, then feigned disappointment. "I thought I was being given a privileged showing."

Dani was quick to explain. "Oh, I shouldn't make such a broad statement. There was only Cyril Arpel. He and Kitty have known each other for a while, and when he asked her for a private viewing, I saw no harm. But I was really surprised when he said he'd like to buy this one. After all, it's not even a good effort by an amateur, but . . ." She paused to study the painting once more, then declared, "There's just something inexplicably captivating about it."

Drake frowned, turned away lest she see, for it was becoming increasingly difficult to appear complacent when there was a great, nagging roar building within. Why would a renowned connoisseur such as Cyril Arpel be interested in buying a dilettantish offering such as this?

Why, indeed!

He knew that, somehow, Cyril had discovered the secret. How he found out was not as important as whether others knew as well. Then he decided that was not really a factor. Cyril would tell no one, had probably heard by accident. The Czar would keep his word, Drake was sure.

Lost in thought, he did not hear the sound of the bell as the front door of the shop opened and closed, nor was he aware that Dani hurried to respond . . . nor did he hear her speak when she returned to where he stood, transfixed, before the painting.

"Drake!" She tugged at his sleeve, slightly agitated, for she had called his name several times without response. "Drake, I'm speaking to you . . ."

He turned, looked down at her without really seeing her, then gave himself a mental shake as he silently cursed for allowing his mind to drift. "I was absorbed in the art, I'm afraid. Forgive me."

She smiled tolerantly, then offered an apology of her own as she explained she would have to leave him for a few moments. One of the tenants wished to show her something he wanted repaired. Would he mind her going?

He shook his head, eager to be alone, to scrutinize each detail of the Alexandrovsky Palace as closely as possible.

Then, once more, he allowed himself to drift . . . back in time . . . back to the painful memories that would haunt him until the day he returned honor to his family's name.

* * *

Dolskoi Mikhailonov enjoyed a few drops of royal blood flowing through his veins. Two hundred years before him, from 1645 to 1676, a Mikhailonov ancestor had served Russia as Czar Alexei I. Due to the family blood—and money—Dolskoi had been brought up in the Imperial Russian Court amid a life of luxury and devotion to the reigning Czar and his family.

Dolskoi's father, Serge Mikhailonov, had faithfully served Alexander I during the waning years of his rule, then went on to devote himself to his successor, Nicholas I. Serge was killed in the Crimean War with England, France, and Turkey. But, during the time Serge served his Czar, Dolskoi was growing up looking to the Czar's son, Alexander II, as an older brother. Despite the thirteen years' difference in their ages, the two were inseparable, and Dolskoi called the Winter and Summer Palaces of the royal family home.

The Czar ruled Russia from the Baltic city of Saint Petersburg, situated on a river marsh in a northernmost corner of his empire. So great was the imperium that dawn came to the Pacific coast while the sun set on the western borders. Scattered throughout one sixth of the land surface of the globe were the Czar's thirty million subjects—Slavs, Balts, Georgians, Jews, Germans, Uzbeks, Tartars, and Armenians.

The Czar, it was said, could do no wrong. He was called the *Batiushka-Tsar*, the Father of the Russian people, and a Russian proverb decreed: "It is very high up to God! It is very far to the Tsar!" The Czar was considered to live in a place nearer heaven than earth.

The royal family favored Saint Petersburg, called the Venice of the North. It was considered European not Russian. The architecture, morals, and styles were thought to be of Western influence. Italian architects, brought over by Peter the Great over a hundred years before, had left their mark in huge baroque palaces, situating them between sweeping and broad boulevards.

Saint Petersburg was a northern city where Arctic latitudes played tricks with light and time. Over baroque spires and frozen canals in winter the strange fires of the aurora borealis danced. Summers were as light as winters were dark, with nearly twenty-two hours of daylight.

But it was not in Saint Petersburg that young Dolskoi Serge Mikhailonov and the next Czar of Russia, dreamed of spending their time. The Alexandrovsky Palace was where they loved to be. Built by Quarenghi in the years 1792 to 1796 by Catherine II for her grandson, Alexander I, Dolskoi and his mentor spent every moment possible there.

Alexander II ascended to the throne in 1855, upon the death of his father, Nicholas I. He was then thirty-seven; the man considered his closest confidant, Dolskoi Serge Mikhailonov, was only twenty-four.

It was six years later, in 1861, that Czar Alexander earned the title of Liberator when he emancipated the serfs. Freedom, however, did not produce food, and when the black earth cracked and burst open with drought, and famine came with the withering of grain while still on the stalk, the peasants grumbled and unrest began in the kingdom.

Meanwhile, Dolskoi was enjoying his position of prestigious servitude to his Czar and found himself eagerly pursued by eligible young ladies of court. However, it was not blue blood that won his heart . . . but blue eyes.

Annine Beaumonde was a seventeen-year-old ballerina who had come from France to study at the Imperial Ballet School in Saint Petersburg. She was small, vivacious, with a full bosom, arched neck, supple body, silky-dark hair . . . and the bluest eyes Dolskoi had ever seen.

One look, and he fell hopelessly in love.

Annine could not help but be impressed to have the attention of one of the handsomest and most famous of Russian bachelors. When he proposed, she put aside her dreams of becoming one of the greatest prima ballerinas the world had ever seen.

But only for a short while.

Once the excitement of a wedding so large and lavish as to be the social event of the season faded, Annine quickly became bored. She was an orphan, had been raised in poverty, working her way through the ranks of ballet through sheer drive and God-given talent. One might think that she would have loved the luxury of being married to so wealthy a man as Dolskoi Mikhailonov. She had servants to answer to her every whim. The best dressmakers came to make for her the finest of gowns. She had furs and jewels. She could sleep until noon, receive her hairdresser, then languish all afternoon sipping tea, vodka, or doing anything she pleased. She could attend the Imperial Ballet at the magnificent blue-and-gold Maryinsky Theater every night, then bundle herself in furs and ride in bright red sleighs noiselessly through the glistening white snow to the Restaurant Cuba for refreshment and dancing.

Yet, Annine was miserable. She felt that such an ostentatious lifestyle was sinful in light of so many starving peasants. Restless, bored, she complained constantly to Dolskoi, who became concerned that her nagging tongue would wag at royal functions, within hearing of his Czar. He begged her to watch what she said and did, not to make statements in public that were critical of the Czar and his government.

Headstrong, willful, Annine did as she pleased. She delighted in shocking those she considered despotic. The years passed slowly. Dolskoi continued to love Annine fiercely, but she turned him from their bed, refusing any intimacy. She swore she would never bear a child to be brought up in such an environment. Eventually, he began having affairs, but they were empty, meaningless, for it was to his precious Annine that he longed to give his love.

Annine, meanwhile, discovered the world of Russian folk dancing. There were few parts for a woman, but she was young, energetic, vivacious, and the village people adored her. She joined a troupe that traveled rural Russia, much to Dolskoi's distress, and the gossips wagged voraciously about her gypsy lifestyle, the way she had unofficially abandoned her husband and marriage.

An accident brought her home. During a frenzied dance routine, she had slipped, fallen, and broken her arm. Secretly, Dolskoi was delighted, for he wanted to take advantage of her convalescence at home to attempt to revive their marriage. Despite their problems, she was, to Dolskoi, the most ravishingly beautiful woman he had ever known, and he adored her to a fault.

Annine reluctantly gave in to a single night of lovemaking, more out of boredom than any other reason. She was insanely furious later to discover that she was pregnant!

Dolskoi was delighted. Now his wife would have to stay at home and give up her ridiculous lifestyle of flitting about the country dancing with a band of gypsies. The baby would change everything. They would be a real family, have a real home. There would, no doubt, be other babies, as well, once Annine experienced such a joy.

Annine spent the duration of her pregnancy hating her husband, his Czar, the Imperial Court of Russia, and the baby growing inside her. She would leave, she vowed, and join her beloved friends and say good-bye forever to such a despised patrician lifestyle.

Annine suffered a difficult delivery, however, and was left weakened and ill for over a year afterward. By then, despite her displeasure with her marriage, she grew to love her son, who was christened in the Russian way with three names—his Christian name; the name of his father, with *vich* added, which meant *son of;* and his family name. Thus he was called Drakar Dolskoivich Mikhailonov.

Annine truly endeavored to be a good mother. She was always kind and loving to little Drakar but remained restless and unhappy with her life. She found no joy in the pomp and circumstance of the royal circle, had to be cajoled by her husband to attend any function.

Annine attempted to keep Drakar away from the world of the Imperial Court. More and more, she was resenting the Czar, Alexander II, said to be the most liberal of all rulers of Russia. She shared the thoughts of the restless peasants who rebuked the theory that a czar who did not rule as an undisputed autocrat was shirking his duty to God. Dolskoi accused her of sounding like one of the revolutionaries who were causing so many grumbles and rumbles of late.

When Dolskoi insisted that Drakar be taken to the palace at Gatchina to study with the Czar's grandson, Nicholas, Annine went into a rage. No matter that there was a difference of six years between the two boys; he wanted his son raised as he had been, close to royalty, to grow into the same coveted position as he had. Further, he wanted to exemplify to his Czar that he did not condone his wife's increasingly revolutionary leanings.

Annine was beside herself. Dolskoi pointed out that there would be the finest of tutors, and then later, he would study at Oxford, in England.

Infuriated, Annine left her husband. Fired by her hatred for the Czar and his policies, she became a part of the "University Youth," who were influenced by a variety of socialist ideas taken from Europe but adapted to conditions in Russia. These radical intellectuals saw in the restless peasantry the potential for revolution. They gathered forces and went out into the countryside to stir people up with speeches they did not understand.

Annine joined them, and Dolskoi knew untold shame and humiliation. When Russia declared war on Turkey, he went off to battle, not caring whether he returned or not. Death, he was beginning to feel, was better than life married to a woman he worshipped, who obviously did not return the emotion . . . and seemed to be doing everything she could to cause him to suffer the vilest of debasements.

Drakar heard the rumors about his mother and was hurt and embarrassed. When she would come to the palace to visit him, he would beg her to keep away from her radical friends, to go home to his father and behave as a wife should. She would merely shake her head sadly and tell him he did not understand. He would persist, and finally she would become angry and leave in a huff.

The Czar, of course, knew of Annine Mikhailonov's sympathy with the revolutionaries, and his heart went out to his lifelong friend Dolskoi. To reward him for his courageous service in the war with Turkey, and also in an attempt to lift his spirits in general, Czar Alexander II summoned a young goldsmith named Peter Carl Fabergé and commissioned him to design something suitable for presentation.

To Peter Carl Fabergé, gold was never just gold—it could be green or red or white, and he could fashion delightful effects by contrasting the colors. He knew how to transform exquisitely even the humblest pieces of hardstone—agate, chalcedony, and quartz. And when he used glittering precious stones in his stunning creations, he knew how to use them for the decorative quality, and not for their value alone.

The Czar's only direction to Fabergé was that the piece be exquisite and have something to do with the Alexandrovsky Palace, where he and Dolskoi had shared so many good times.

The result was the creation of the Alexandrovsky Palace Egg. Surmounted by a beautifully cut triangular diamond, the Siberian nephrite egg was decorated with yellow and green gold mounts with a setting of cabochon rubies and diamonds. There were three miniature portraits in a pearl-crusted belt around the egg—one depicted Dolskoi as a boy of twelve, another, Alexander at the same age, and the last was of the two together.

There were also four oyster-enameled roses among foliage, set with rose diamonds and hung with pearl swags.

Concealed within was a colored gold model of the Palace, its roof enameled in pale translucent green, the grounds decorated with bushes of spun green gold wire. The palace sat upon a miniature gold table with five legs.

The Czar gasped aloud when he saw it; his hands trembled when he grasped it. He had pronounced in a voice husky with emotion: "Never have my eyes feasted on anything more beautiful or precious!"

There was an emotional ceremony of presentation to Dolskoi. Drakar, then a student at Oxford University, journeyed from England to attend. He, like his father, tried to ignore the fact that Annine was not present. She had, in the past year, refused to attend any function of state or court.

Meanwhile, the militant party officially organized itself and took the title of Land and Freedom. However, within two years, in 1878, the party had split due to dissension within. One faction advocated assassination of government officials in reprisal for maltreatment of their comrades—hundreds had been sentenced to prison, countless numbers deported to Siberia. Breaking away, the terrorist wing took the name People's Will.

When Dolskoi heard that his wife had joined the new radical terrorist wing, he went into a rage, forbidding her to have anything to do with her comrades. He threatened to tie her, gag her, lock her in a closet. The Czar was promising severe punishment to anyone found to have ties with the group.

Annine herself exploded and declared she was leaving him permanently, ending their marriage. Further, she admitted to being in love with one of the radical leaders, a painter named Zigmont Koryatovich. Dolskoi had suspected something like that for a long time. But apprehension was one thing—he could hide from that; reality, he could not deal with. He was shattered.

When Annine officially left Dolskoi, ending their marriage, the Czar called him in and berated him for not being able to control his wife. Long ago, he thundered,

Dolskoi should have reined her in, taken any measures necessary to stop her. Now it was too late, and the Czar felt that his best friend and confidant had caused him embarrassment.

Dolskoi sank to even lower depths of despair.

The climax came when the assassins of the People's Will made an attempt on the Czar's life . . . and went to extraordinary lengths to do so. In Moscow, they bought a building near the railway track, then dug a tunnel from the building directly under the track, where they planted a mine. The Czar was saved when his train took a different direction upon leaving Moscow. However, some of the would-be assassins were captured, among them, Zigmont Koryatovich . . . and Annine Mikhailonov!

Czar Alexander, in one last effort to restore some semblance of honor and respectability to the man he had loved as a brother, had Annine and her family brought before him. In front of Dolskoi and Drakar, the Czar informed Annine that if she would renounce her radical, revolutionary beliefs, and her lover, and return home to her husband and family, all would be forgiven. Otherwise, she would be deported to Siberia, where Zigmont had already been taken.

Annine spat in his face.

She was taken to Siberia, and, infuriated beyond reason, Alexander demanded that Dolskoi resign from his position in his government. Then, in an attempt to prove to everyone that he wished to completely remove himself from any ties to the Mikhailonov family, he ordered the return of the Alexandrovsky Palace Egg.

Dolskoi, a broken man, said he would comply, but when he went to get the treasured egg, he was horrified to discover that Annine had taken it and given it to Zigmont to be sold to help finance the revolution.

Drakar saw his world blow apart in bits and pieces. Zigmont was hanged, apparently taking his knowledge of the whereabouts of the valuable egg to his grave. His father was killed by one of the Czar's staunch supporters.

Drakar believed his father wanted to die that way. Then, his mother escaped, and he was never to see her again.

Drakar's friendship with Alexander III deteriorated. The revolutionaries successfully killed the Czar in a bomb blast, and, overcome with grief, Alexander, as the new Czar, called Drakar before him and proclaimed that as far as he and the Russian government were concerned, Annine Mikhailonov was a whore and a traitor. His father was without honor, because he refused to return the Alexandrovsky Palace Egg. No one, the new Czar declared, had believed Dolskoi's story that he could not find the egg.

Czar Alexander III stripped Drakar of his family name, his honor, and banished him from Russia.

Drakar was angry but grateful that although the Czar might have stripped his father of all honor, they could not touch his wealth. With inherited holdings in many countries, Drakar could leave his homeland to make his own life.

But then, only a half year after leaving, he was called back to Russia by divine summons of the Czar. He went, more out of curiosity than any sense of duty.

Alexander told him that because of their own once-treasured friendship, he would confide to him a rumor that his mother had, indeed, stolen the egg and given it to her revolutionary lover. There were stories from Siberia that told of Zigmont secretly painting a scene of the Alexandrovsky Palace. Somewhere within the painting was a clue to where the egg was actually hidden. Drakar's mother was said to have taken the painting away with her when she escaped.

The young Czar further went on to inform Drakar that his mother had died in Paris only a few months before. No one knew the whereabouts of the painting.

The Czar also promised Drakar that no one else would be told, that everything would be kept confidential. If he could find the painting and, ultimately, the coveted Fabergé egg, then his father's honor would be restored. ''As long as the egg is missing, no one will ever believe that it was not sold to help finance the revolutionaries," Czar Alexander III tersely informed Drakar. "It must be returned to the Imperial Court, as was the wish of my father."

Drakar agreed . . . and thus his quest began.

Chapter Eleven

By the time Dani returned, Drake was pretending to be browsing about the shop, not wanting to arouse her curiosity by staring at the painting. However, he was still very much in deep thought. He knew it had to be the painting he had been searching for, but he needed closer scrutiny. Zigmont Koryatovich, amateur artist though he might have been, had evidently known what he was doing when he created a mystery on canvas. From what Drake had seen thus far, there was not an inkling of a clue to tell him where the egg might be hidden.

At the sound of Dani entering the shop, he complimented her on her selection of goods.

It was she who mentioned the painting. "Did it make you homesick for your native land?" she inquired pleasantly.

He hesitated before answering, as though he had really not thought about it, then shrugged. "I suppose. It does have a uniqueness about it that I find intriguing." Then, offhandedly, he said, "I might want to buy it from you."

Dani shook her head, cinnamon eyes narrowing slightly. Lord, what was it about that painting? "I'm sorry, Drake, it isn't for sale."

"Why not? It doesn't exactly complement the masters you discovered."

110

"No," she admitted simply, "but obviously you find it appealing. So did Cyril Arpel, and so do I. I intend to keep it for myself."

He shrugged as though it were not important, turned his attention to an exquisite temple lion of jade and pearls. All the while, his mind was whirling. Possession of the painting for only a short time was not going to be enough. Hours of meticulous study and scrutiny would be needed. He had to have it.

For almost ten years, he had been aimlessly wandering about, searching for the painting in a desperate effort to restore the family honor. Only then did he feel his father could rest in peace. It was not his fault, by damn, that his wife had brought such shame and degradation upon the family name. Through the years, Drake had tried to feel pity for his mother, make excuses for her, call her insane . . . anything except what she was. But reality was harsh and cold; she had been a revolutionary, betraying her husband and her son. She had been selfish, willful, not to be trusted—as so many women were.

"I enjoy talking with you, Drake," Dani said, interrupting his thoughts, "but there are some things I need to do if I'm going to be ready to open tomorrow morning."

"I'll be glad to lend a hand," he offered.

There was a small alcove at the very rear of the shop where Dani had had shelves built to display the books she had bought from the other antique shop. Proud of her collection, she still had the top row to arrange in alphabetical order. Drake offered to do it, but she declined, gesturing toward the small wooden ladder. "Just hold this for me. It won't take but a moment."

She clamored up, faster than he had anticipated, and before he could step into position to steady the ladder, it tipped. He held out his arms, and she fell right into them. With a knowing smile, he accused, "You did that on purpose," and then his lips claimed hers in a hungry, soul-searing kiss.

For an instant, Dani was stunned, then, slowly, liquid fire began to consume her. Her arms went about his neck to hold him tightly, and she returned his kiss, pressing her body closer against him.

At long last, he raised his mouth from hers, set her gently on her feet, but his arms remained about her.

Dizzily, Dani swayed in his embrace, and her voice was not convincing even to her own ears when she proclaimed shakily, "That should not have happened—"

Drake threw back his head and laughed. "Oh, Dani, Dani, don't play demure with me. You wanted it as much as I did, and you know it." His eyes met hers hungrily, and his voice was tremulous with desire. "And you want more . . . now . . . like this—"

He crushed her against him, and their lips met, and held, and then his tongue touched hers in a melding delight of sensation that sent both their pulses soaring. His hands moved down her back to clutch her tiny waist, then slipped lower to cup her firm, rounded buttocks beneath her thick skirt, pulling her close . . . so close she could feel the swell of his desire. Her own needs cried out within her, and she fought the impulse to press yet closer. With reluctance, she forced herself to pull from his embrace.

"Too much, too soon, monsieur," she stated more calmly than she felt.

"As you wish, mademoiselle. I have all the time in the world."

Dani turned away, and bit back a sarcastic retort. Why bandy innuendoes when it was apparent they both desired the same thing? She could not deny that she wanted this charmingly handsome, enigmatic man in a way she had never wanted another. True, there had been embraces, caresses, kisses, but dear Lord, she had never before felt the physical evidence of her own body's desire for a man.

She began to walk toward the front of the store. "I have some things to do."

He was right behind her. "I see there's a loose shelf on one of the display cases. If you have the tools, I'd be glad to fix it. Later, perhaps we can have dinner somewhere."

Quickly, she said, "Oh, I don't think so. There's so much I have to do before tomorrow that it will probably be late when I leave, and—"

He spun her around, taking her in his arms once more. Nostrils flaring, eyes blazing, he cried, "Dammit, woman, stop acting like a little girl. You know what we both want."

He kissed her once more, and Dani could not make herself pull away. It *was* happening too soon, and she would not allow it to go any further, not yet, perhaps not ever. He was a womanizer, and she had no intention of being added to his collection. But there was also another factor to be considered: She had never met a man like Drake, whose very nearness aroused her. Love? Lord, it could not be happening, and she was not about to let it happen. Love meant giving herself over to manipulation, subservience, and never again, God, would she allow that to happen, no matter how much he stirred her. . . .

She tried to pull away, but he held her tightly, and then she was yielding once more. She would face her feelings, enjoy them, and when, *if,* the time came and she *wanted* to succumb, then, by god, she would!

Lost in their fevered embrace, neither heard the tinkling of the little bell as the front door of the shop opened and closed. They did not realize they were no longer alone until the irate voice of Cyril Arpel pierced their senses back to the reality of the world about them.

"Excuse me!"

They sprang apart, stunned. Dani was flustered, but only momentarily. After all, she reminded herself, what did she have to feel embarrassed about? She had a right to kiss a man if she wanted to. Her voice frigid, she de-

manded, "What are you doing here, Cyril? You were not
expected."

"Obviously," he said with a sneer, eyes flicking over
Drakar contemptuously.

Jealousy bored Drake. Besides, he needed time alone
to think through his course of action. He wanted the
painting; he wanted Dani. He intended to have both. All
he needed to do was figure out how to go about it. "I
think I will be going," he said, addressing himself to
Dani. "Perhaps I could take you to dinner later."

If Dani had not been so infuriated with the insolent way
Cyril was glaring at her, she would probably have refused the invitation, wanting private time of her own to
get her thoughts together. The man had thrown her into
a whirlwind of emotions. Ignoring Cyril, she placed her
hand on Drake's arm, walked with him to the front door,
then said loudly enough to be overheard, "That would be
lovely. You may call for me at seven. I should be home
by then."

He paused at the door, gazed down at her hungrily.
Then, in a tone so low as to be barely audible, he said,
"I look forward to knowing you better, Dani. What little
I do know, I find utterly fascinating."

He kissed her hand and walked out, closing the door
soundly behind him.

The instant he was gone, Dani turned on Cyril in a
fury. "How dare you walk in here, uninvited and look at
me like that? What I do is none of your business, Cyril
Arpel. Do you understand?" She faced him, hands on
hips, eyes blazing.

Cyril swallowed . . . hard. Had he gone too far? If he
was going to get his hands on that painting, alienating her
was not the way to do it. Quickly he proclaimed, "I'm
sorry. Truly I am. The bell sounded when I opened the
door, and obviously you didn't hear it. What was I to
do?"

Dani sucked in her breath, let it out slowly. Oh, she
was angry! "You could have done the gentlemanly thing,

Cyril, which was to leave as quietly as you came. You had no right to just—just stand there and watch!''

He defended himself. ''I made my presence known. I spoke. Again, I apologize. I should have left, I know, but—'' He shook his head, not knowing what else to say.

She picked up a feather duster, turned and began to vehemently attack a stack of books waiting to be carried up the ladder. ''Please go,'' she said irritably. ''I find your company disconcerting for the moment.''

Cyril watched her with narrowed, thoughtful eyes. He had no intention of merely walking out and leaving things as they were.

She turned, glared at him, anxious for him to leave.

He plunged right in, throwing his arms up in the air in a gesture of defeat. ''All right, all right, be angry if you will, but the least you can do is hear me out. I'm your friend, Dani. I can't let you be taken in by that rogue.''

He began to pace about as she stared in cold indignation. ''You haven't been out in the world as long as I have. I know you led a sheltered life. I would not be much of a friend if I allowed you to go on blindly—''

''I am not blind!'' she snapped. ''Now go, please, before you ruin our friendship!'' she warned.

Stubbornly, he shook his head. ''No. No, I won't. Think me rude if you will, but one day you will thank me for telling you about that man.''

He stopped pacing and stood before her, reached out to clamp firm hands on her shoulders and look straight into her fiery eyes. ''Drakar was banished from the Imperial Court of Russia by the Czar. There was a terrible scandal. I do not have all the details, but I know there is much shame on his family. That is the reason he roams Europe like a gypsy. He fancies himself a connoisseur of women the same as I consider myself a connoisseur of art. He *collects* them, for god's sake!'' he finished with a disgusted sigh.

Dani laughed harshly. ''So what? Perhaps I will start my own collection of men!''

"You don't mean that!"

"If I do, it is none of your business!"

Their eyes met, each challenging the other.

Cyril decided he would go one step further. "They say his mother is responsible for the assassination of Czar Alexander."

Dani raised an eyebrow. "What are you talking about?"

He suppressed a smile. Good. He had caught her interest, at last. "She was a revolutionary."

Again, Dani laughed mockingly. "So what? So am I! I think it's time all women revolted. Far too long have we been treated as serfs!"

Cyril almost laughed himself. She looked so adorable talking of revolutions. Yet he managed to maintain his severe expression and continued: "You don't understand. She was a revolutionary against the Czar."

"Revolutionary or dissident?"

"It doesn't matter. She was having an affair with one of the leaders of a terrorist group committed to assassinating the Czar. She walked out on her marriage . . . her son . . . to live in sin with a man ten years younger than she—a radical. When he was caught trying to blow up the train the Czar and his family were traveling on, she was sent to Siberia right along with him."

He stood back and waited smugly for her reaction. Surely she would run from a man with such a sordid background.

His complacency quickly vanished when she gasped, "Oh, poor Drake! What a terrible thing." Silently, privately, she was starting to understand why he regarded women in such a callous way. Unknowingly, he probably felt aversion toward all women because of his mother's behavior.

Cyril could not believe his ears. "You feel sorry for him?"

Dani regarded him coolly. "Of course. It must have been a terrible thing for him to live through. And," she added condemningly, "it must be even worse to have people like you gossiping about him behind his back."

Cyril groaned and decided to try another ploy. "I must confess, Dani, that I am terribly jealous of the man. Too many times I have seen him sweep women off their feet, make them fall helplessly in love with him. His power over women is legend, for god's sake. I don't want that to happen to you."

He dared to reach out and clasp her hands. Imploringly, he gazed down at her and, in a tremulous voice, whispered, "I don't want to lose you, Dani, before I even have a chance to win your heart for myself."

Dani was momentarily caught off guard by his unexpected avowal. She had to admit that though she was quite annoyed at his intrusion, and his gossiping about Drake, she did like him. She wanted him for a friend.

He continued to hold her hands, a beseeching look on his face. "Tell me I haven't lost you, Dani. Tell me there is still a chance for me."

"You are still my friend, Cyril. Let that be enough for now." She pulled her hands gently from his.

He nodded and sighed. There would be a chance to smooth things over. "If I promise not to say another word about your personal life, may I stay and help you?" he cajoled.

She could not help but laugh, for he looked like a little boy, eyes hopeful, wanting desperately to be forgiven. "Oh, all right, but no more gossiping. I don't like it."

He nodded, then went to work without being told what to do. He began to carry the books up the ladder, changing the topic of conversation to the next day's grand opening. But all the while he was thinking of how he would do everything in his power to stop the relationship between her and Drakar before it truly got started. He was also trying to conjure a way to get the Alexandrovsky painting into his possession.

* * *

Lillian Deauneve stared at the French landscape whizzing by as the train sped from Le Havre en route to Paris. She was not truly looking at the scenery; she was too caught up in thoughts about her unbelievable good fortune. When she had booked passage from London, then across the English Channel, and finally, on the Nord Railway into Paris, she had spent almost her last pounds. She had just enough left to pay for a few nights' lodging at a cheap hotel while she looked for work. This morning, when she had left London, she had felt as though the world were collapsing about her. Now, in the span of just a few hours, everything had changed . . . for the better.

She could make out her reflection in the window; acknowledged, without apology to conceit, that she was still a ravishingly beautiful woman. Hair as brilliant as the finest gold fell softly about her face. Her skin was as pure and soft as alabaster. Smoky purple eyes were fringed with thick, dusty lashes. Her nose was perfectly shaped, with a gentle, saucy tip. Her lips seemed forever curved in a sultry pout.

She wore a traveling day dress of dusty green velvet. The jacket, edged in yellow cording, was opened to reveal a scooped neckline. Endowed with large, firm breasts, she had much cleavage on display. She was blessed with an incredibly tiny waist. Her hips were slim, curvaceous; legs, long and shapely. Even her ankles were lovely.

She smiled at the image before her, the passing French countryside for a background. Lillian knew she was everything a man could want.

Then, suddenly, the smile faded, and the face staring back at her was frowning, pensive as she was struck with the burning reality: For the moment, her beauty was all she possessed in this world!

She sighed in her misery to think how once she had been heiress to the fortune of her uncle Vinsandt Deauneve, a shipping and railroad magnate. When her parents had been killed in a wagon accident while she was still an infant, her unmarried uncle had taken her into his home and raised her as the child he'd never had. Subsequently, she lived in luxury, wanting for nothing. She adorned herself with diamonds and emeralds as casually as gypsies wore beads. She attended an exclusive, expensive finishing school in Switzerland. When she turned eighteen, her uncle gave her a tidy sum to bank away, and she decided to travel about Europe with her nanny, and experience all life had to offer.

Men flocked after her, and why not? She was beautiful and rich. But she did not need a husband, so she enjoyed suitors that appealed to her, then cast them aside. She had everything she needed, and had not a care in the world.

Then things began to change. Uncle Vinsandt began to nag her about the careless way she was spending money, saying she should be more prudent. She ignored him. After all, he was fantastically rich. Each time she drained her bank account, he replenished it.

One day, however, there came a rude awakening. Uncle Vinsandt regretfully informed his beloved niece that he was bankrupt due to mismanagement of funds by an unscrupulous accountant, and his own error in judgment on several costly investment ventures. Lillian was appalled to realize he did not seem too distraught. After all, he had explained, almost cheerily, all was not lost. There was a rainbow at the end of the storm. Since he had had to liquidate almost everything to pay the debts, including the magnificent house in prestigious St. James Park, he was delighted that they would still have the mellow stone manor house in Dorset, and enough money to live comfortably. They would not starve, and Vinsandt loved the peace and quiet of old rural England, with its winding country lanes leading from one steep little valley to the next, set with thatched cottages and cider apple orchards.

Lillian was horrified. She had always hated the time they spent in Dorset, found the atmosphere boring and depressing.

Uncle Vinsandt was quite perturbed over her attitude. He admitted, as he approached his fiftieth birthday, he was grateful to retire from the pressures of the business world with what he did have. She should, he felt, be equally grateful for all he had been able to do for her.

Champagne to ale, Lillian had grumbled furiously.

She made up her mind that she would not be relegated to the life of a country peasant. She did not want to give up the luxury and lavishness she had come to know, enjoy, and love. Consequently, she turned her back on her uncle and a deaf ear to his raging protests. She used her beauty and charm to ensnare an elderly, wealthy duke and become his mistress. By the time she discovered such a reclusive lifestyle was not to her liking, for she yearned to have an exciting social life in addition to opulence, she had managed to get her hands on enough of the Duke's money that she could walk out on him with enough to live comfortably until she found what she was looking for—a fantastically rich husband.

She was sure that marriage to money would insure a future of happiness. After all, she had no intention of settling down and becoming a dreary housewife and—god forbid!—a mother. All she wanted was money, lots of it—to travel and do as she pleased. She knew she could pacify a man by pleasing him in bed, and wangle her way, have her independence. So what if there were those who would condemn her? If she had never enjoyed luxury and wealth, she might have been content with less. But she had sipped champagne . . . and would rather die than be relegated to guzzling ale!

She settled back in her seat, and smiled. Now, thanks to fate, luck, whatever it was called, the gods had smiled upon her. For, little did she know when she opted to pay a higher price for a seat in one of the luxurious compartments, rather than herd with the peasants like cattle in the cheaper sections, that she would find herself sequestered with a handsome young man who was apparently quite wealthy. After all, she could *smell* money the way bees sniffed out a source for honey.

Alone for the moment, while her new friend had a brandy in the smoker car, she could savor the enjoyable moments they had shared during a delicious brunch he'd had brought to the compartment. It had all been absolutely delightful . . . and so had he.

He was, she mused, somewhat reticent when it came to discussing himself. All she knew thus far was that he was American, this was not his first visit to Europe, and he had family here.

The Nord Railway train was speeding southward toward Paris, and they would be arriving within the hour. Although the handsome American had said nothing about continuing their friendship once they reached their destination, Lillian was confident she would have no problem there. She knew he found her attractive and desirable. She could sense things like that in men, especially since every one she came in contact with reacted in the same way.

She had told him she was visiting an aunt in Paris whom she had not seen, or heard from, in a long, long time. Her uncle, she'd fabricated, was worried about his sister, and, because he was too ill to travel, she was making the journey to learn of her condition. She mentioned a rich neighborhood, said enough to give the impression the family was extremely wealthy.

In actuality, Lillian had just enough money left, after purchasing a lavish, fancy wardrobe, to keep her in a modest hotel for a few days, if she ate only enough to stay alive. In that time, she knew she would either have to find a husband or become someone's mistress until she could get on her feet financially. She cursed herself for spending so much of the Duke's money to outfit herself, but then, if she wanted to marry money, she had to dress the part, didn't she?

A shiver of anticipation went through her at the sound of the door clicking open. She smiled up at the sight of John Travis Coltrane entering the compartment.

The way he looked at her told her she was right—he did like her . . . and he wanted her.

He sat down beside her, rather than across, and mentioned that the conductor had just informed him they were running on time, would be in Paris within the hour.

Her hand fluttered to her throat, and she made herself sway ever so slightly, and display what she hoped was a look of utter desperation.

He noticed. "Is anything wrong?" he inquired solicitously.

She shook her head, gave him an apologetic little smile. "Oh, I don't want to burden you with my problems, but I am a bit worried about being able to find my way around in Paris." She went on to tell him that she only had her aunt's address, had no idea what she would do if she had moved away.

"And," she continued, "I speak very little French." She nearly choked on the lie, for she spoke the language fluently, as well as several others. Uncle Vinsandt had made sure she was well educated.

Colt was quick to offer his assistance. "After I've spent a bit of time with my family, I'll go with you to find your aunt."

She pretended embarrassment. "Oh, no, I couldn't impose like that, really . . ." She allowed her voice to trail off softly.

He dismissed her protests with a wave of his hand. "I insist. You get some rest, and in a day or so, we'll go and find your aunt."

She demurely thanked him and settled back in her seat with a small smile.

All the while, the wheels were turning. As soon as he left her at a hotel, she would find a taxi to take her to the neighborhood she had mentioned. There she would find someone willing, for a few francs, to say that her "aunt" had died.

She would also have to report to the Paris police that her purse had been stolen. She could not have John Travis Coltrane wondering why she was almost destitute.

Chapter Twelve

D<small>ANI</small> sat impatiently at her dressing table while Simone, her hairdresser, meticulously wound strands of pearls in her coppery tresses. She had always hated having her hair done, preferred to wear it loose and flowing, but tonight's dinner was formal.

She turned to look once again at the new gown that had been delivered only that day. Of mocha satin, it was sleek, smooth, glamorous. Drop pearl earrings would be her only adornment.

Simone administered finishing touches to her coiffure, smiled with satisfaction and declared, "*Splendide!* Mademoiselle is gorgeous!"

Unconcerned for the moment with humility, Dani agreed, then dismissed her with a warm thank you and a generous pourboire.

Alone, she stared solemnly at her reflection in the onyx-framed mirror over her skirted dressing table. Lovely hair style. Lovely dress. Yet, she was dreading the evening before her. Oh, not everything. She was certainly looking forward to being with Drake as she had been every night since they had met at her party over two weeks ago.

She closed her eyes and allowed the warm rush of pleasant memories to take her away . . . back in time to the moon-kissed evenings spent dancing in Drake's arms . . . afternoons sipping tea at sidewalk cafés . . . picnics on the bank of the river Seine, laughing like children as they sipped wine and munched crisp, fresh-baked bread, nibbled cheese and apples, ruining their appetite for sumptuous candlelit dinners later . . . and not caring.

A special day stood out in Dani's happy reflections. Drake had procured two horses, and they had ridden out into the rolling green countryside, savoring the warmth of the mellow sunlight upon their faces. On they rode, into the hallowed greenery of a dense and fragrant forest. Hand in hand, side by side, they feasted on the consecrated purity of the magnificence of nature unblemished, untouched.

Finally, overcome by the awesome beauty, they had stopped beside a gurgling stream, and there, on a mossy riverbank, surrounded by the gently waving fronds of a weeping willow tree, they had embraced and shared a kiss that left them both shaken.

Dani knew something wonderful was happening between them, and the awareness filled her with an unfamiliar, yet pleasant glow of warmth.

Since they were seen together constantly, Dani knew they were being whispered about in Paris social circles. Some even predicted theirs was the romance of the season and would culminate in the wedding of the decade. Others, mostly young, jealous girls, were portending Dani was merely another of Drakar's short-lived romances, and she would wind up a spurned woman like all the rest of his "collection."

Dani dismissed such gossip. Besides, it was not Drake who concerned her for the moment, for they were enjoying each other and the growth of their relationship immensely.

It was Colt.

Two days before, she had just returned from the shop and was about to bathe and change for dinner when she heard Kitty squeal with joy from all the way downstairs. She had wrapped her robe around her and run to the land-

ing above the stairs to stare down in disbelief at the sight
of her stepbrother embracing Kitty.

She had rushed downstairs to greet him also, ecstatic
to have him in Paris, looking forward to having the opportunity to at last really get to know the brother who
seemed like a stranger.

That first evening, she and Drake had declined to attend a concert to be with Colt. All seemed pleasant . . .
then. It was only when she found herself alone with him
the next morning that the tension surfaced.

She had gone downstairs to have a quick cup of tea before leaving for the shop, only to find Colt already in the
breakfast room—alone. The conversation began amiably,
but then he began to ask her questions about her shop,
and when she happily recounted all that had led up to her
independent business venture, which included the "Monaco find," it was as though she had suddenly, unwit-
tingly, ignited flames of resentment within him.

A shadow had crossed his steel-gray eyes just before
they narrowed in a veil of anger. In a curt, frosty voice,
he had remarked testily, "Well, it's nice someone managed to reap some rewards from the deBonnett château,
Dani. It damn well nearly cost us Coltranes our entire
fortune."

Dani had stared at him incredulously for a brief instant
as she reeled under the full implication of his remark.
Then, indignation overcame shock as she sharply challenged, "Do you blame me for what happened, Colt?"

His eyes flicked bitterly over her. "Yes," he admitted
with candor. "I think I do blame you. After all, if you
hadn't been such a brat, you'd have stayed at home with
us, where you belonged, instead of going to live with that
bitch, Alaina Barbeau . . . and none of it would've happened."

Dani stiffened. She couldn't undo what happened when
she was a child, by god, and it wasn't fair for him to
blame her for his mistakes. "I resent that," she snapped.

"I don't give a damn what you resent, Dani. It's true."

She had then walked out of the room, lest the tears stinging her eyes start flowing. This wasn't the way she wanted things between them. Given time, she hoped they could talk out the tension, become close, but bickering was not the way to peace.

A frown creased her forehead as she thought of another obstacle in their path to a new relationship.

Lillian Deauneve . . . or "Lily" as she said she preferred to be called.

A few days after his arrival in Paris, Colt had gone out and returned with her.

Dani shook her head to think how deceiving looks could be. God, Lily Deauneve was an unpleasant creature. How Colt could stand her was beyond comprehension. True, she was beautiful—but also a conceited, arrogant little snob, and when she wasn't hanging on to Colt's arm and gazing up at him adoringly, she was bragging about her wealthy uncle in England who had sent her to Paris to find his sister. Now she said she dreaded returning to tell him his beloved sister was dead. A few days after his arrival, Colt said he'd taken her to the address where her aunt had lived, was with her when she heard the crushing news. That was also the day her purse, containing all her money, had been stolen and it was then Colt had insisted on bringing her to the mansion, where she had been ensconced in a guest suite and displayed no inclination to leave any time soon.

At first, Dani had felt sorry for her, but not for long. All too soon, when Colt was not around, it became obvious that her grief was not as devastating as she pretended in his presence.

Kitty, with her characteristic candor, didn't wait very long before bluntly asking Colt why Lily didn't just send a message to her uncle about her financial loss and have him post the money to return to England.

Colt was quick to confide he liked Lily and didn't want her to leave so soon. Further, he pointed out, Lily was dreading having to break the news to her uncle about his sister's death since he had a weak heart and she did not want to upset him.

When Kitty had relayed this information to Dani, she had also confided her suspicions that Colt's past experiences with women left much to be desired. He had been taken in by beauty and charm too many times to suit her, and she wanted him to be more cautious with his latest interest. There was just something about Lily Deauneve, she said, that made her leery.

Dani truly was not looking forward to the evening ahead when Drake would be meeting their houseguest, yet she was interested in hearing his reaction, since he was supposed to be so "experienced" with women.

Cyril had met Lily and seemed to adore her, but then he was oozing with charm these days. Dani frowned once more. He was nice, and she liked him, but more and more he found an excuse to come by the shop, or by the mansion, and she suspected he was terribly jealous of her friendship with Drake.

Forcing herself from her wool-gathering, Dani finished dressing and was just giving herself a final inspection in the mirror when Lily suddenly walked in without bothering to knock.

"I'm bored!" she announced petulantly, dropping to the chair nearest the door. "I'm ready for dinner, and I'm dying to go downstairs and have a drink, but I can't find Colt. I suppose he's out making arrangements for our holiday in Spain, but I wish he'd come back. It's lonesome without him. Nobody around here seems to want my company," she added tartly.

Dani, ignoring her barb, casually remarked, "I didn't know Colt was planning a holiday."

Lily was quick to excitedly inform her: "Oh, yes! Didn't he tell you? We're going to Madrid and Barcelona. It's beautiful there. Haven't you ever been?" she asked with feigned surprise.

Dani disregarded the question in favor of one of her own. "Who will be your chaperone?"

Lily responded with a mocking laugh. "Oh, really, Dani! I took you for a sophisticate. Surely you'll agree that financially independent women like us don't have to answer to hypocritical rules of decorum."

Dani shrugged. She agreed but wasn't going to give her the satisfaction of assent. Besides, traveling alone was one thing; traveling with a man, another. "I thought it might show some respect for the family," she said, biting back a reminder that, for the moment, Lily was anything but financially independent.

Again, Lily snickered. "I must've been wrong about you, my dear. It seems you've got a lot of growing up to do." She got up and began to prowl aimlessly around the room, picking up little decorator pieces to scrutinize, then setting them back down and moving on.

Dani said nothing, watching her frostily.

"I understand that your guest for this evening is Drakar," Lily suddenly declared.

Dani raised an eyebrow. "You know Drake?"

"Drake?" Lily repeated. "So, the two of you are already into pet names. How divine." She pretended to become suddenly very grave. "But you must remember the man's reputation. Surely you're aware of his history with women and won't be so stupid as to join all the other fools in his past."

She paused to sigh dramatically, then flashed a taunting grin. "But then again, you still believe in chaperones!"

Dani's expression did not change. Cool, unmoved, she challenged, "You seem to know a lot about him, Lily. Tell me, could you be one of the fools you're talking about?"

Lily's eyes narrowed, darkened with indignation. When she became Mrs. John Travis Coltrane, everyone in this haughty family would have to treat her with respect. No longer would she be subjected to such hostility. With a defiant lift of her chin, she snapped, "Everyone knows about that man, the way he makes women fall at his feet, then kicks them aside so callously when he sees another he likes better. I've never met him, but I certainly know his reputation."

Dani sighed in a display of boredom with the conversation. "Well, thanks for your concern, but I can handle my own affairs . . . and prefer to do so." She turned toward the window. The girl was insufferable. Colt could not be so stupid as to become seriously involved with her . . . or fall in love, God forbid.

Then she spotted Drake coming up the walk and, moving quickly, went to the door. With feigned regret, she said, "Sorry I can't entertain you any longer, Lily, but my guest has arrived. I suppose you and Colt will be joining us for drinks later?"

"Of course," Lily said, and, with a swish, moved past her and down the hall to her own suite. She did not stay there. She waited until Dani had had time to start down the stairs, then scurried to stand in the shadows of the second-floor landing and watch.

Dani waved Cletus away to admit Drake herself. Lily observed their warm embrace, saw him give her a bouquet of roses, watched her kiss him in gratitude.

Lily decided she had yet another reason to hate Dani Coltrane. She was pretty, rich, had everything in the world she wanted, and now it seemed from the way she and Drakar were looking at each other that she had him as well.

She bristled at the sight, knew that if she weren't in such dire financial straits, she could change all that. Colt was extremely handsome in his own right, and she found him charming, enjoyable, but Drakar, the strikingly good-looking, enigmatic Russian, was legend. The woman who became his wife would be envied by all.

She watched them go into the parlor, and she opened and closed her fists in frustration. Returning to her room, she tossed aside the sweet blue dress she'd chosen earlier with a desire to look demure and innocent. Instead she put on a seductive gown of black velvet. It dipped low, displaying the creamy whiteness of her perfectly sculptured breasts. Clinging tightly to her small waist, it dropped straight to the floor. She adored the daring slit she'd had fashioned on the side, which gave a glimpse of her long, shapely legs. Lily would try to win over Drakar tonight. Maybe he would be so captivated he would just whisk her away from Colt and want her for himself . . . on a permanent basis. A fantasy, perhaps, but she could afford to indulge herself for one evening, at least. A prize like Drakar was certainly worth entering the contest.

She generously applied the expensive perfume she'd wheedled the old Duke into buying for her. If something didn't happen soon, such luxuries would be a thing of the past.

She took one last look in the mirror, then, with a complacent smile, decided she was her usual ravishingly beautiful self.

It was going to be a very interesting evening.

And this thought made her happy.

Everyone was gathered in what Travis proudly referred to as "his" parlor. He much preferred it to the delicate pink and white "tea" room which Kitty used for her lady friends.

A cozy fire crackled in the grate of the marble-tiled fireplace. A Russian mahogany and ormolu sofa table dominated the room, around which a suite of Adamesque sofas and chairs were situated, each upholstered in the finest of imported Italian leathers. A Chinese scroll painting on silk complemented a pair of seventeenth-century Chinese lacquered sweetmeat boxes with mother-of-pearl inlay. A reproduction of Girardon's bronze sculpture of Louis XIV perched on a glass pedestal, and a pair of bronze figures flanked the arched doors leading to a terrace beyond.

A butler stood by a glass and wrought-iron cart, ready to fulfill any drink request. Kitty and Travis had opted for champagne, and when Dani and Drake joined them, they requested the same.

Just as Lily approached the doorway leading into the parlor, Colt came rushing down the stairs behind her. Without a word, he drew her to one side, folded his arms around her, and kissed her long and deeply.

Lily responded, but only briefly. She did not want to be mussed. Pulling away, she mockingly chided, "Colt, whatever am I going to do with you? You seem to have only one thing on your mind."

He laughed softly, continuing to hold her as he gazed down at her hungrily. "With a woman like you, what do you expect a man to do?"

She twisted away, truly agitated now as she smoothed her dress. "I expect him to behave himself when he's about to take me in to socialize with his parents. Now come along."

Colt caught her arm, pulled her close once more to fervently declare, "Later, we're going to find time to be alone together."

He was, Lily acknowledged smugly, becoming increasingly difficult to control. She would take him a little further in their lovemaking each time they were alone, only to withdraw and leave him gasping. Soon, it would be time to demurely point out that their relationship had reached a point of no return. To have what he wanted, he would have to marry her. "I want your kisses and caresses more than you know, Colt . . ." She allowed her voice to trail off promisingly as her fingertips danced down his arm.

Quite confident of her charm and power over men, Lily held her head high and walked into the parlor to meet the notorious swain—Drakar.

Travis and Drake rose when Lily entered, then Travis made the introductions. Lily acknowledged silently that the handsome Russian found her lovely, for his eyes held the same look every other man had for her. She accepted a glass of champagne, sat down primly next to Colt, who had followed her in.

After a few minutes of polite small talk, the topic of conversation turned to the subject all of France, and Europe as well, was talking about.

General Georges Boulanger had committed suicide.

Boulanger had once been France's minister of war. A political figure, he had led a brief, but influential, authoritarian movement that threatened to topple the Third Republic in the 1880s.

"I knew the man well. He was quite controversial," Travis remarked.

Drake nodded. He knew how Boulanger had headed the "revanche" movement against German occupation of Alsace-Lorraine, after the fall of Freycinet in December of 1886. Fearing a new war, the government of Maurice Rouvier had expelled Boulanger as war minister. However, Boulanger's clandestine relations with leftists, monarchists, and Bonapartists won him the election to the Chamber of Deputies in 1888. He was then regarded as a threat to the government and was ousted from the army. Eventually, in April of 1889, he had left quietly for Brussels, was tried in absentia for treason, banished in August of the same year. Consequently, his popularity plummeted. Elections were catastrophic for his followers. The next year, 1890, saw him abandoned totally by the royalists and by year's end, he had been deserted by his friends.

"I understand it was the final blow when his mistress, Marguerite, vicomtesse de Bonnemain, died two months ago. He killed himself beside her grave," Drake said.

Lily cooed, "Oh, how romantic. That meant he really and truly loved her. It's a shame they never married . . ."

Drake pressed his tongue in his cheek to suppress the desire to burst out laughing. He would have expected such a melodramatic remark from the fortune-hunting Lily Deauneve. He had recognized her the instant she walked into the room, for she had been wearing the same provocative gown the last time he'd seen her—swishing

across the ballroom of a London hotel, long, shapely legs
displayed as she clung adoringly to the arm of the pompous old reprobate, the Duke of Seville. Someone had told
him that night that Lily was the niece of Vinsandt Deauneve, who had recently lost almost his entire fortune. His
niece, not about to be relegated to the life of the have-
nots after being one of the "haves," had promptly latched
on to the rich, lecherous Duke, who did not care what it
cost to have the self-exultation of being with a beautiful
young woman. It had been a short while later when Drake
heard some gents laughing about how the Duke's latest
fille de joie had walked out on him, taking some of his
money with her.

Travis continued to talk about Boulanger's suicide, and
Drake pretended to listen but all the while he was studying Lily. She might not remember him being at the ribald
party, for he had not tarried long. But he remembered her,
and it was not hard to figure out what she was doing here.
Dani had related to him her tale of woe, and he was convinced it was a lie, designed to engender sympathy. From
the way Colt was looking at her, her scheme was obviously working.

But was any of it his business? His top priority was
supposed to be getting his hands on that painting. Bad
enough Dani had become such an obstacle, provoking
feelings and emotions he'd vowed never to experience for
any woman. Certainly, he had enough concerns of his
own for the moment without becoming involved with
anyone else's affairs.

Finally, they adjourned to the dining room. Two walls
were covered in mirrors, while upon the others there were
finely painted panels, each depicting a month, with the
corresponding sign of the zodiac at the top and an allegorical figure of a god in the center. These were then surrounded by symbols of the stars and sciences and
associated animals.

Dominating the room was a crystal and gold chandelier
with over two thousand hand-carved prisms. Beneath was

an imposing Belgian Régence table of carved marble, with
Portuguese rococo armchairs placed around it.

Kitty noticed Lily admiring the table setting and could
not resist proudly explaining that the silverware had been
crafted out of ore from their silver mine back in Nevada.

They enjoyed a delicious meal of roast suckling pig, a
fricassée of squid, peppers, and mushrooms, and finished
with a strawberry sorbet.

Champagne flowed freely, along with red and white
wine. Conversation was pleasant, unstrained, until Dani's
planned trip to Austria came up and she announced that
she intended to travel alone.

Travis raised an eyebrow, exchanged a thunderous look
with Kitty, then quietly echoed, "Alone?"

Dani did not glance up, merely continued to twirl her
spoon in the bowl of sorbet. "There's no one to go with
me. Besides, I prefer to travel alone."

"It's unthinkable that you'd even want to go by yourself, Dani," Travis stated. "I'll hire someone to accom-
pany you."

She felt mortified. In front of Drake, he was treating
her like a child, and when she looked up to see that Lily
was grinning maliciously, something snapped. "Father, I
am a grown woman," she cried indignantly, "and I have
my own business to look after. I'll not have you hire a
. . . a nanny for me!"

Travis's eyes were stormy. "As long as you put your
feet under my table, Daniella, you'll do as I say!"

She glared at him. Oh, she loved him so very, very
much, regretted each and every day they'd ever been apart
all those precious growing-up years, but the time had
come for her to spread her wings. It was far too late for
him to play the role of guiding father, and she, dutiful
daughter. "I'm sorry," she said evenly, tightly, "I don't
mean to hurt you, but I intend to live my own life the
way I choose. Perhaps it's best," she added, lower lip
quivering slightly, "that I get my own table . . ."

She rose, faced him defiantly.

Colt shifted uncomfortably in his chair, silently fuming. Why did this have to happen tonight? He'd wanted everything nice and pleasant for Lily's sake. She had enough problems of her own without being witness to family tension.

Drake sat in stony silence, also regretting the dispute.

Lily was enjoying the whole thing, eyes glittering as she looked from Travis to Dani, waiting for further explosion.

Kitty bit her lip thoughtfully. She feared Travis's temper, hated what was happening at the dinner table, in front of guests, but decided against interfering. The two were going to have to resolve the problem between them, but dear god, she prayed they would wait and do so in private.

Slowly, Travis rose from his chair, squeezing his napkin into a tight ball and flinging it upon his plate. With gray eyes the color of cold steel, he stared at his daughter. "We will," he promised frostily, "discuss this later."

Dani nodded her head in quick, conciliatory jerks, then, taking a deep breath, murmured, "Please excuse me . . ." and hurried from the table.

Travis started to call after her, but Kitty stopped him with a pleading look. It was best Dani have some time alone, and she called softly after her, "We'll have brandy and coffee in the parlor later. Please join us."

Dani kept on going, heading straight for the hallway that would take her to the rear of the house and the sanctity of the gardens and the night beyond.

Abruptly, Drake stood, mumbled his own excuses, and hurried after Dani.

Lily shook her head in mock sympathy, turned to Travis and declared, "I'm sorry all this happened, Mr. Coltrane, but poor Dani, I guess I know how she feels. My own nanny took sick just before I was to leave London to come here, and there was nothing I could do but go on alone. Still, I felt there was truly nothing wrong with it. I mean . . .'' She paused, smiled at Kitty, then Colt. "We are living in modern times now. It isn't like it used to be."

Colt groaned inwardly. Lily was, he'd discovered, not one to keep her opinions to herself, but now was not the time for her to interfere. He reached out and touched her arm gently, whispered, "Lily."

She shrugged him away. "I see nothing wrong with her going to Austria alone, just like I see nothing wrong with Colt and I going to Spain."

All eyes were upon her, and she knew at once she might have gone too far in making such an announcement. The Coltranes were frozen in shock, and Colt looked both embarrassed and angry. Well, so what? Lily thought defiantly. They would have to be told sooner or later. Maybe her pronouncement would hurry along Colt's proposal. He could just tell his parents they were engaged, and there was nothing so scandalous about engaged couples traveling together. Maybe he would even want to marry her right away and take her to Spain on their honeymoon.

"I think you and I will have our brandy in my study, Colt," Travis said and left the room.

Colt followed without a glance in Lily's direction.

Lily gave her golden curls a toss, shrugged, and said, "Well, Mrs. Coltrane, I suppose we can just have our coffee right here," she suggested brightly.

Kitty got to her feet. She'd had enough of the arrogant young woman for one night. Not caring whether she seemed rude, she coldly declared, "I think the evening has ended. Good night."

And suddenly Lily found herself in a most unexpected and unwanted position: she was all alone.

Chapter Thirteen

"ARE you having a private tantrum, or can anyone join in?"

Out in the garden, Drake sat down beside Dani on a stone bench. Without waiting for her answer, he went on. "It's unfortunate things blew up back there, but don't be too angry with your father. He was just playing the role of concerned parent. It isn't that safe for young women to travel around by themselves, especially beautiful and rich young women," he added pointedly.

Dani laughed brittly. "What am I supposed to do? Hide behind locked doors the rest of my life, never go anywhere? Never have the freedom to live my life the way I choose? No thank you. I'll take my chances. I'll start by carrying a pistol in my purse, and—"

His sudden burst of laughter caused her to fall into an angry silence, then she said, "I don't see anything so funny about protecting myself."

He reached to clasp her hand, but she jerked away. "Oh, Dani, I'm sorry. I really don't mean to make you angrier than you already are. It's just that the thought of a woman like you toting a gun in her purse strikes me as funny."

She glared at him. "Well, it won't be so funny when I take it out and shoot somebody who tries to harm me."

He was suddenly grim. "No, I suppose not. But why not just hire a bodyguard? That's what rich women nor-

mally do. Then you can come and go as you please, and
your family won't worry.''

She thought a moment. That was an idea to be considered, but she had other concerns now. Her remark made
in anger about getting a place of her own struck her as
quite appealing. It would be fun, decorating it the way
she wanted, having her own socials, having absolute privacy and freedom of choice.

''You can hire me, pretty lady,'' Drake said, intruding
on her thoughts.

Dani looked at him, so handsome, so charming, and
the sound of his warm, husky voice, the way he was gazing at her, made delicious tremors ripple through her
body.

''Hire you?'' she whispered, sensing that he was about
to take her in his arms. ''But then who would protect me
from you?''

He did take her in his arms, gathering her so close she
could feel his breath upon her face. As he spoke, he lowered his lips to brush against hers ever so lightly, ever so
tantalizingly. ''No one can protect you,'' he gently
warned. ''I want to devour you . . . I want to take you
to places you've never been before. I want to strip you
naked and cover your flesh with kisses, and I want to hear
you pray that no one will rescue you.''

He kissed her, his tongue exploring her own, tantaliz-
ing, teasing. He moved a hand to trail down her face
gently and cupped her chin to hold her immobile against
his attack upon her mouth. Then nimble fingers danced
down her throat, at last moving to her breasts, to squeeze
and knead each between exploring fingers.

Dani stirred, moaned, knew she should resist, pull
away, but admittedly did not want to. She was enjoying
each second of the sheer ecstacy he was evoking within
her. She relished the rolling, rumbling, of emotions gone
wild, thrilled to the way thunder seemed to be exploding
in her belly as secret, struggling undulations birthed in her

loins. She could feel her nipples becoming cherry-pit taut beneath his eager fingertips.

Her back was arching in silent command to become yet closer to this attempt to devour her soul and spirit. God, she wanted him . . . wanted to explore, and taste, and feel, and experience, and savor . . . all the promised joys.

Her arms clung to him, and he lowered her effortlessly, gently, to the ground and stretched out beside her.

Dani could feel the velvet tickle of the moss and grass against her legs as he shoved her dress upward about her hips.

Placing his knee between, he parted her thighs, rendering her vulnerable to his touch. Dani knew that soon there would be no turning back. She could feel the rigidly pulsating hardness against her, knew what it was . . . what it meant. Soon, he would be tearing away her silk and lace undergarments, and then, though a virgin, she knew he would enter her, take her to places she'd never been before . . . and that was what she wanted . . . to be taken on a journey of joy and ecstacy.

But suddenly, she realized that she wanted to go there at a time of *her* choosing, not his. This was seduction, manipulation at its worst. Damned be the luscious pleasure of desire if it was not fired by her own will, her own decision that it should happen. Never would she allow a man, even a man as appealing as Drake, to command and control her body through deft fingers and hungry, seeking lips.

She pulled away from him.

Drake was stunned. He had felt her succumbing to the cravings and urgings of her own body. Now she was pulling away. He stared down at her in wonder. "Dani, what is it? What's wrong?"

She shook her head, cinnamon eyes meeting blue, and tried quickly to choose the right things to say so as not to hurt or damage the new and wondrous feelings growing between them, to somehow make him understand the way she felt. "Not here. Not now. Not like this."

Drake believed he understood her hesitation. "I have a suite at Le Palais, near the Tuileries, a short ride by carriage."

She shook her head adamantly, but regretfully.

In a calm, even voice, Drake went on. "We'll go back inside, tell your parents that we're going for a ride. Under the circumstances, I'm sure they'll understand."

Tightly, she bit out her next words: "Not until I say."

This time Drake really did understand. He knew Daniella Coltrane was going to be a real challenge to his expertise. She was unlike so many others of her sex who wanted only to feel they had been seduced in order to yield to that which they wanted so desperately, yet had been indoctrinated to believe was sinful to enjoy. Dani could never be manipulated into doing anything she did not wish to do of her own volition . . . and that included making love to him.

Drake gazed at her, not giving away the turmoil of his thoughts. He was experiencing feelings for her that were not of the sort he usually experienced with his women. True, she was beautiful, intensely sensuous, and he desired her fiercely, but there was something else, the appreciation for her as an individual, a woman in her own right, whose opinions and ideals and thoughts and beliefs he respected. He did, by god, enjoy her company. She was more than just another woman to bed, and it was these thoughts and this awareness that directed him to quietly capitulate. "I understand."

He stood, then helped her to her feet.

"Are you angry?"

"Angry?" He laughed at the thought. "I have no right, no reason, to be angry. I wouldn't want you to do something unless you're sure it's what you want to do."

Dani knew that she might be sending him straight to the arms of another woman . . . but that was a thought she would have to push aside.

* * *

After Kitty left the dining room, Lily sulkily requested more wine. She was furious at the turn of events. Everything was ruined.

She brooded intensely and began to think that since Dani was in trouble with her parents, and they would be occupied with her behavior, this might be a good time to convince Colt to marry her. Time was rushing by. How much longer could she remain a guest in the house . . . or linger in Paris, for that matter? Already it was apparent that everyone was becoming concerned about why she did not send word to her uncle about his sister's death and ask for money to replace what had been stolen from her. She was afraid that even Colt would want her to get in touch with him before they went on holiday in Spain, and what could she do? How much longer could she stall?

She chewed a fingernail in perplexity. Colt was fond of her. That much, she was sure of. He also desired her fiercely, but she doubted that he would marry her just to have sex. No, there had to be another motivation.

Her eyes narrowed, and had she been standing before a mirror at that precise moment, when the perfect scheme was born within her mind, she would have viewed herself as almost diabolical.

She rose from the table and made her way quietly to the closed doors of Mr. Coltrane's study. No one saw her as she pressed her ear to the smooth, polished mahogany to eavesdrop.

"I won't have it, Colt!"

"I'm a grown man."

"First your sister wants to prove how independent she is by traipsing all over Europe alone, and now you want to take a holiday in Spain with a young woman, unchaperoned."

"Don't tell me you never went anywhere with a woman alone!"

"We aren't talking about me. We're talking about you—son of an American diplomat in Paris. Because of your social position, everyone watches everything you do. If you take Lily to Spain, you'll be talked about . . . and not in a nice way. Do you want that?''

"I want to live my life the way I choose, without interference from you or anyone else."

Lily smiled, brightened. Colt was standing up to his father, for her!

There was a long silence after Colt's cold, blunt declaration. Lily could not imagine the reason, for she did not truly know Travis Coltrane so she could not know that when his patience was being sorely tried, he would become coldly silent as he struggled inwardly for self-control.

Nor could she see, for the moment, how the two men were glaring at each other.

Finally, Travis sighed, as though he'd been holding his breath for a long, long time. "Son," he said quietly, almost regretfully, "did I interfere when you were living your own life and almost lost the entire family fortune?"

"How long have you been holding that back?" Colt shot back. "I suppose you've just been waiting for the right opportunity to throw it all up to me. No matter that everything turned out all right, and I got back almost every dollar Mason swindled me out of."

"Wait a minute. I was only pointing out to you that you haven't exactly demonstrated the ability to run your own life . . . yet."

Lily decided to go to her room, not wanting to press her luck in escaping detection. What had Mr. Coltrane been talking about? How had Colt almost lost all their money? Her curiosity was piqued, but she told herself it wasn't important. Obviously, Colt had *not* lost anything, and that's all that mattered to her.

Lily removed her elegant dress and lacy undergarments. She took another bath, long, luxurious, lavished herself with perfume. She took out the expensive negligee she had persuaded the lecherous old Duke to buy for her . . . then refused to wear for him. Why should she waste something so immensely sensuous on a dirty old man who didn't need enticing, anyway? She sniffed with disdain to think of all those repulsive evenings in his arms. No, she was not meant to be a mistress. It was going to be much nicer married to a handsome, charming man like Colt and be the epitome of ladylike elegance, welcomed in every circle of society and respected by all. And, she mused with a wicked little grin as she slipped on the white gossamer creation, she could still have little affairs and flings now and then, to ward off the boredom and doldrums of domestication.

She brushed her long golden hair down about her face, decided she liked the effect—childlike and innocent.

Innocent!

Suddenly, she felt a stab of sheer terror coursing up and down her spine. Innocent she was not! Colt was going to realize she wasn't a virgin, and if she weren't, then why would he feel obligated to marry her after he "seduced" her?

She began pacing up and down the room.

Well, she reminded herself, she was a good little actress. She could play the role of innocent virgin to the hilt and even an absence of evidence of her virginity she would make convincing.

Midway down the hall, between her quarters and Colt's, there was a little alcove with a white velvet bench and an arched window that looked out on the gardens to the rear of the estate. During the day, it was a lovely place to sit, and at night, it was shadowy and dark—a perfect spot for her to keep an eye out for Colt.

Finally dressed in what she decided was her most enticing best, Lily stepped from her suite, and peered up and down the mellow-lighted hallway. There was no one about. Scurrying quickly, lest she run into someone, she went to the alcove and blended with the darkness and potted ferns to wait.

It was perhaps a half hour before Colt finally came up the stairs. Lily could tell by the expression on his face, as she spied him through the fern fronds, that he appeared to be quite vexed and a wee bit tipsy, as he stumbled a few times on the stairs.

She waited ten minutes longer, then, after checking to see that the way was clear, went to his door. She did not knock, merely turned the knob, breathed a sigh of relief that it was not locked, and stepped into the shadowed room.

The drapes were opened, and moonlight spilled through the windows. Colt had never invited her to his room, so she needed to familiarize herself lest she bump into anything.

She saw the bed—empty. Where was he? Then she heard a sound from another part of the room, so shadowed she could not make out anything there.

A figure emerged from the abyss of darkness, stepping into the moonlight, naked flesh bathed in silver.

Lily saw and gasped then, realizing he'd heard her, immediately went into her act and pretended to be sobbing as she covered her face with her hands. "Oh, Colt, where are you?" she moaned in abject misery. "I can't see . . . it's so dark . . . I knocked, you didn't hear me . . . please—"

"Lily? What the hell!" He turned on his heel abruptly, returned to his dressing room for a robe, then rushed to where she stood and folded her solicitously in his arms. "What are you doing here? Why are you crying?"

In a feathery, whimpering voice, she said, "Oh, I feel just awful. I know I've caused you so much trouble, and I'm terribly sorry. Your mother is angry with me . . . she just got up and walked out and left me all alone at the table, and I felt like such a fool, and your daddy has been fussing at you all evening. I feel so dreadful. I'm leaving first thing in the morning. I know your parents think I'm terrible, and there's nothing for me to do but leave—"

"Nonsense! Stop crying, Lily, you're just tired. Get a good night's sleep, and—"

"No!" She pushed herself against him, made herself shudder from head to toe as though the idea of being alone this night was terrifying. "I had this awful, awful nightmare. I dreamed I went back to London, and when I got home, I had to tell my uncle about my aunt, and he just . . ."

She paused for effect, then released the words in a hysterical torrent. "He just dropped dead. Right in front of me. I tried to grab him, to keep him from falling, but I couldn't, and he reached out for me, and he was crying, calling my name, and I couldn't hold him up, and both of us fell, and there I was, sprawled on the floor with my dead uncle squashing me. Oh, Colt, it was horrible!" She began to weep uncontrollably as though she could not go on.

He patted her comfortingly, felt somewhat awkward with the situation—she in a flimsy next-to-nothing negligee, and he in a clinging silk robe that did nothing to hide the fact that her nearness was arousing him. "It was just a nightmare, Lily. A bad dream. Your uncle isn't going to die when you tell him about his sister, and you aren't leaving in the morning. So calm down, and—"

"No!" She flung her arms around his neck and clung tightly. "Don't send me away, Colt. Please. I feel so terrible . . . so frightened. Let me sit here with you a while, please. A glass of sherry, perhaps. I'll be all right soon."

He sighed, went to turn on lights, but she asked that he not. "The moonlight is soothing."

There was light enough that he could make his way easily to the liquor cabinet, where he took out a bottle of sherry and two glasses. When he turned, he saw that she had moved across the room and was sitting on the side of his bed, still sniffling, shoulders shuddering with threatened sobs.

They each had a glass of sherry, then Lily pressed her head against his shoulder and pretended to be sleepy. "If you'll just hold me for a moment and tell me you aren't angry with me, I think I'll be fine and can go back to my own room.''

"You know I'm not angry with you, Lily. And neither are my parents. They just don't think like we do. A bit old-fashioned, I'm afraid. But everything will smooth out. It didn't help that Dani had to blow up like she did, but she always was headstrong, hell-bent on having her own way. Now then . . ." He kissed her forehead. "Feel better?" he asked with a hopeful smile.

Lily twined her arm around his neck, brought his face down close to her waiting lips.

He did not hesitate.

With a groan from deep within, Colt's mouth closed over hers, and they fell backward onto the bed.

Lily pulled back from the embrace long enough to whisper innocently, "I know it's all right to be here with you, Colt. I know you'd never do anything to besmirch my honor—"

But Colt was not hearing her words as he moved on top of her.

He was not thinking of honor or any of those damned things.

He was merely a man.

An aroused man.

With a strong hunger.

And . . . for the moment, nothing else mattered.

Chapter Fourteen

DANI was talking with a customer when Drake entered the shop. At once, a warm thrill rippled through her, and she wondered if her cheeks were flushing. He smiled that lazy grin that set her heart to pounding, winked intimately, and indicated with a nod that she should just continue with her business. She noticed that he was carrying a large wicker basket and wore a very pleased-with-himself expression.

She turned to the woman beside her. "Excuse me. What were you saying, Madame Letoye?"

The woman, fiftyish, as rich as she was fat, stared almost transfixed at the painting displayed on the wall before them. Plump jowls jiggling as she talked, she explained that she was quite taken with the art piece, wanted to purchase it, but woefully added, "My dear, I am afraid you are just asking far too much for this one." She gave her a nod of censure. "As a matter of fact, I should tell you that talk is going around that you are overpricing everything in your shop.

"Perhaps," Madame Letoye went on to point out with a condescending little smile, "you are just too young and inexperienced to consider yourself a connoisseur . . ."

Dani felt the muscles along her jaw tense. With great effort, she made herself calmly respond: "I do not claim to be a connoisseur, madame, but I am a businesswoman. I do add to what I pay for my merchandise in order to make a profit. If I did not, then I would not stay in business very long, now would I?''

"Tut, tut!" Madame Letoye wagged a finger under her nose, the flesh hanging from her fat arms rippling in waves. Her mouth was turned up at the corners, but her eyes were narrowed little squints of indignation. "I've been around the world of art much longer than you, my dear, and I know pricing . . . and so should you . . . *if you plan to stay in business,*" she added pointedly.

"Mademoiselle." Drake approached Dani, setting the wicker basket aside. "How much are you asking for that painting?''

Both women turned, and it was Madame Letoye who spoke first, waspishly declaring, "Far too much, I can tell you that."

He ignored the pompous woman, looked to Dani for a reply to his question.

"Sixty thousand francs."

At once, Madame Letoye hooted. "You see? Sixty thousand francs for a Boucher! She must be out of her mind, or else she thinks because a Coltrane is selling it, that makes it worth more.''

Dani sucked in her breath, held it. She was seething. The woman was going too far!

"Perhaps," Drake told the woman, "you do not appreciate François Boucher's talent for female nudity. Take this offering, for example . . .''

He gestured to the painting admiringly. "Young and blond . . . and *quite nude.* An intense vision of female sensuality.'' He paused for effect.

Fat Madame Letoye sniffed with disdain.

Dani pressed her fingertips to her lips to suppress a giggle.

Drake continued. "When Boucher began painting his series of nude girls around 1751 or so, it was said that he was actually painting Louise O'Murphy, who, at that time, was a teenage prostitute kept by King Louis XIV when he became worried about contracting syphilis from a woman any older.''

He turned to Dani for confirmation. "You have no doubt seen his three interiors, "*La marchande de modes,*" "*Le déjeuner,*" and "Woman Fastening Her Garter, With Her Maid.'' Superb examples of the genre."

Dani had not seen the paintings of which he spoke, but nodded that she had, enjoying the moment. Madame Letoye's annoyance and vexation was mirrored on her jowly, fat face. She had encountered someone who obviously knew much more than she, and she did not like it . . . one little bit.

Drake emitted a mock-dramatic sigh, closed his eyes momentarily, then said, almost reverently, "Is there anything in all art quite like his gartered courtesan with her knees spread far apart, and a kitten playing beneath her ankles?''

Madame was taken aback, her eyes widening.

"He was known for painting Madame de Pompadour, the King's *Maîtresse en titre*. Oh, not that she discovered him, by any means. He had been receiving royal commissions for some years. It was merely that she offered a wider scope to his talents. It is said La Pompadour was a woman of strong character, well-formed tastes, and under her sponsorship, he was commissioned to paint panels and decorative elements for rooms in places such as Versailles, La Muette, Choisy, Fontainebleau, and Crécy."

Madame was sputtering. "I—I still say . . .''

Drake was enjoying himself immensely, and did not allow interruption. "Boucher's paintings were the opposite of insipid. They had sparkle. Bite.'' He laughed. "Think how people must have responded in those days to a little Boucher shepherdess in satins and silks, with a powdered chignon, going *barefoot*. Back then, no well-bred female ever walked out of her bedchamber without her shoes . . . t'would have been sexually provocative."

Suddenly, he whirled on Madame Letoye and demanded reproachfully, "And you consider sixty thousand francs exorbitant to pay for a Boucher?'' He quickly drew his wallet from inside his coat, turning to Dani once more. "I will buy the painting, mademoiselle. If this— this *dilettante* . . ."

He paused to give Madame a withering glare before continuing. "If she ever learns anything about the world of art, she just might want to buy it, and I've taken a fancy to it myself."

He counted out sixty thousand francs.

Madame Letoye's eyes grew wide as she furiously searched for words with which to defend herself. None came. She had been put in her place . . . soundly.

With as much dignity as she could muster, she turned on her heel and marched out of the store, wide hips swinging from side to side.

Once the door slammed behind her, Drake and Dani convulsed with laughter. After several moments, Dani proclaimed, "You don't have to buy the painting," and held out the money to him.

He waved it away. "No. I want it. Really. I'll send someone for it later."

"But you don't have to," she persisted. "If you hadn't come to my rescue, I would have lost my temper with that—that puffed-up old bag!"

"I want the painting and that's final."

She held up both hands in a gesture of defeat. "All right, I'll take your money. Are you satisfied?" she asked, feigning annoyance.

"No!" Drake said, grabbing her around her waist and jerking her against him. "I won't be satisfied until I've had this . . ." His lips closed upon hers.

Dani responded, wrapping her arms about him. Oh, how wonderful it felt to be so close to him, to feel the heat of his body melding with her own. With just one kiss, the juices of desire were flowing, and she acknowledged, once more, that never, ever, had a man affected her this way.

Reluctantly, she broke from his embrace. "And what if someone walks in, sir?"

"We're going to take care of that right now."

While Dani watched, mystified, he went to the front door and locked it. Then, after turning the little painted sign from "OPEN" to proclaim "CLOSED," he drew down the shade, retrieved the wicker basket he'd brought with him, and returned to where Dani stood. He held out his hand to her.

"Come along. You've got a beautiful spot for a picnic in that tiny courtyard out back, and Paris will not be blessed with such beautiful autumn days much longer."

Delighted, Dani squeezed his hand and allowed him to lead her to the rear door. There was a tiny patch of grass beyond, perhaps only ten feet square, surrounded by rock walls to separate it from other yards, but it was enough for a picnic in the warm fall sunshine.

From the basket, Drake took a tablecloth of blue and white gingham, which he spread in the center of the grassy court, then gestured for Dani to sit down, which she did, primly tucking her skirts under her. Then he brought forth an assortment of delights: Brie cheese, fresh bread, black sausage, grapes, plums, and a bottle of white wine and two glasses.

Dani could not resist clapping her hands together in delight.

Drake was pleased with her response. "So! You like picnics. I'll remember that, and next time, I'll spirit you away to somewhere . . . *private!*"

He nodded to an old woman staring from an open window in the building next door. When Dani turned to follow his gaze, the woman flashed them a look of disgust, withdrew her head, and slammed the window with a loud thud.

Then, with a shadow of chagrin, Dani admitted quietly, "I've never been on a picnic before. Life with my aunt did not include such frivolities, I'm afraid."

Drake had heard a tale about her having been brought up by a relative and not her father, by way of explanation as to the finding of the paintings in a château she'd inherited. "Sounds as though you had an unpleasant childhood, Dani. I'm sorry. How old were you when you went to live with your aunt?" He was thinking that perhaps she might inadvertently tell him something that would give a clue as to how the Alexandrovsky painting wound up in the hands of Count deBonnett in Monaco.

Dani intended to share only a little of her past with Drake, for, although their relationship was growing intensely, she did not want to divulge all the nightmares and anguish of the past. Yet, the more she talked, the more she revealed, for he was an easy listener, and his eyes reflected that he truly cared, truly wanted to share her pain in order to know everything possible about her. He continued to pour wine into her glass each time it was empty, and with the warmth of the sun above, and the nectar within, she began to feel mellow . . . and the words flowed easily.

As Drake listened to her mention, though briefly, her time in the convent and the incident with Colt and Briana, he found himself wondering whether young Coltrane had been scorched enough by women in the past that he would not be susceptible to someone as cunning and crafty as Lily. Too, he was starting to understand what made Dani strive so hard to be independent, to associate relationships with relinquishment of her own will.

And, he acknowledged silently, grimly, he was going to pay hell getting his hands on that painting if her mind was truly set against selling it. Further, he knew it was time that he put aside the emotions he was feeling for her and think about doing just that . . . ultimately restoring the family honor. Until he achieved that, his life, as far as he was concerned, was in a state of limbo.

"And you?"

Drake blinked himself back to the present.

Dani was prodding. "What about you, Drake? You're such an enigma."

Drake shrugged. "There's nothing to tell, really. My family is dead. There's only me."

"And you roam Europe, never Russia," she pointed out. "Why?"

"When I find what I'm looking for, then I'll stop roaming." He gave her a teasing smile.

"And what is it you seek?"

He set his empty glass aside, took hers away also. Then, not caring that others might be watching, he pulled her into his arms. Caressing her with his eyes, his tone was husky, thick with desire.

"I'm looking for the perfect woman who can give me everything I need and want in this life."

Dani fought the tremors erupting within, did not want him to know how he was affecting her. Struggling to sound playful, she said, "And what will you do with her when you find her?"

He bent his head, so that his lips, warm, seeking, could brush ever so lightly against hers. "Attempt to make her as happy as she makes me . . . forever and always."

Dani knew that if she did not end the tense moment then, she would not find the strength, or will, to do so again. Pressing her palms firmly against his shoulders, she pushed herself away, then scrambled to stand on shaking legs.

"I've really got to get back inside and reopen the shop," she said quickly, too quickly perhaps, for he was watching her with amusement twinkling in his dark eyes, fully aware of the desire he had ignited within her.

"I'm expecting Madame Francia Mebane," she went on, gathering the picnic items and placing them in the basket in a near-frenzy. "I'd completely forgotten about her. I'm sorry, Drake. Forgive me for rushing, but she's coming by to look at a pair of ivory doves I purchased last week."

Drake had slowly gotten to his feet, then suddenly reached out to grab her roughly and hold her tightly, possessively, for a smoldering kiss before gravely pronouncing, "The time is going to come sooner than you think, milady, when you can no longer talk your way around the one thing we both have on our minds . . . the one thing we both genuinely want."

Dani gave him a slightly scathing look. "You presume too much," she snapped waspishly, then swished by him.

She was not truly angry, and they both knew it. They were each biding their time, waiting for what might happen, if fate so decreed it, neither wanting to rush, for both had their reasons for not wanting to be committed to an individual . . . or a situation.

Inside, Dani hung up the "OPEN" sign, unlocked the door, then turned to see Drake again admiring the painting of the Russian palace. "You really find that interesting, don't you?" She went to stand beside him.

Drake nodded thoughtfully, decided it should not make her suspicious to merely talk about the painting. "Aren't you ever curious as to how such a crude and amateurish effort came into the possession of Count deBonnett . . . or why he would want to hide it with his valuable possessions?"

"I haven't really thought about it, to be perfectly honest. The Count was a rather strange person, and I kept my distance as much as possible."

Drake pressed on. "Tell me about him. What was he like?"

"He kept to himself, more to avoid Aunt Alaina than anything else, I think. They never got along well. I can remember them arguing much of the time. He was also a compulsive gambler, and they fought about that." She paused, stared off into the distance as though her mind had gone way, way back in time, then murmured, "I'm really surprised they ever lived together. It was as though they despised each other."

Bitterly, for he was reminded of his own parents' miserable marriage, Drake said, "When it's that bad, I think people should go their separate ways instead of living in hell . . . which is what it must be like to have that kind of marriage."

"They did separate . . . for a time. I was around ten years old, I think," she recalled. "Anyway, it wasn't Uncle Claude's gambling that was a problem. It just seemed that he and Aunt Alaina quarreled all the time. Finally, he said he couldn't take it anymore, and he moved out and went to Paris to live. Aunt Alaina said she didn't care, because she had the château, and plenty of his money. Then she heard gossip that he was having a torrid affair, and she started worrying that he would fall in love with another woman and want a divorce, and not being a citizen of France, she wasn't sure where that would leave her. She didn't want to go back to America. She was really in a dither."

Drake's interest was piqued, and he quickly figured out that if Dani were ten at the time Claude deBonnett left his wife and moved to Paris, it would have been around the same time his mother was supposedly living there, also. Was that how the Count came into possession of the painting? "Do go on," he urged.

"There really isn't much more to tell," she said with a shrug. "Aunt Alaina went to Paris, intending to persuade Uncle Claude to go home with her and mend their marriage, but as it turned out, she had no difficulty in getting him to return. She arrived around the time his lady love died, and he was so grief-stricken that he didn't care what happened to him. That is the time, I remember, that he began to drink and gamble heavily, staying away from the château for days and nights on end. From that point on, I'm sure theirs was a marriage in name only."

Drake tensed, felt the nerves in his jaws tighten. Could it be . . . or was it a mere coincidence? "Tell me," he pressed. "What did your aunt say about your uncle's ladyfriend? Was she wealthy? Of the noble class?"

Dani shook her head and laughed, "Oh, no. Far from it, according to Aunt Alaina. I overheard her screaming at Uncle Claude about her, calling her all sorts of nasty names . . . but making marked references to her social and political stature—names like anarchist, revolutionary."

Dani went on to confide that back then, it had been a game with her and Briana to find out as much as possible about the Count's romance. Briana overheard him babbling to himself in a drunken stupor about his love, about how beautiful she was. With flourish, Dani dramatically quoted, " 'Her eyes were as blue as the robin's egg—' "

She fell silent, placing a hand over her mouth, then exclaimed shamefully, "Oh, I'm sorry. I have no right to make fun. He loved her, or thought he did, and now they're both dead, and I'm wrong to ridicule. It's just that, at the time, Briana and I were just curious little girls, playing a game of spying on grown-ups."

Drake ignored her confession. "Did he ever mention her name?"

Dani thought a moment. "No, not that I recall."

He did not realize he had been holding his breath until it came out in a sudden rush. Then, gesturing toward the painting, he quietly stated, "I want to buy that painting, Dani. Name your price, I'll pay it."

Dani frowned. "It's not for sale." Then, "Why do you want it so badly?"

"Memories of Russia," he said, smiling. "Good memories. I should think it would hold bad memories for you."

She shook her head. "I'm putting the past behind me. To sell something I'm fond of because it might remind me of something unpleasant would be hiding from the past . . . and that's wrong."

Above the front door, the little silver bell jingled.

They turned, then Dani whispered, "It's Madame Mebane," and left him to walk toward her customer, softly calling a cheery greeting.

Drake turned his attention to the painting of the Alexandrovsky Palace once more, allowing his consciousness to be attacked and besieged with provoking contemplations.

Paris, circa 1881.

The time his mother had reportedly lived in Paris.

Count deBonnett had had an affair with a woman who died, in Paris, around 1881.

The time his mother had died . . . in Paris.

The Count's paramour was said to have had eyes as blue as a robin's egg.

The same could be said about the color of his mother's eyes.

The Countess deBonnett had referred to her husband's love as an anarchist . . . a revolutionary.

A fair, accurate description of his mother's political doctrine.

It was becoming clear why the Count had in his possession the painting of the Alexandrovsky Palace and why he had hidden it along with his other valuable works. In all probability, he had not known the secret, or the significance—only that it had been entrusted to his care by the woman he had loved . . .

Who had to be Annine Mikhailonov . . . his mother.

His hands clenched and unclenched at his sides, eyes narrowing with the immensity of his determination.

He had to have that painting!

The sound of Dani's voice penetrated his concentration as she spoke with her customer about the grouse minaudières.

He acknowledged that he found Dani to be the loveliest and most exciting woman he had ever met. With her zest for life, it was exhilarating just to be around her. Never did they seem to be at a loss for something to talk about, which was certainly a pleasant change from the giggling, empty-headed fluffs he normally encountered. Dani was refreshing, invigorating. He cared for her as a person and as a friend, did not regard her as someone to bed, to savor and enjoy until satiated before moving on to yet another. She was different, and he knew, somehow, that they would never be bored with each other.

Perhaps, he mused with a mixture of bitterness and sadness, when the mystery was solved, the Fabergé egg returned to the reigning Czar, Alexander III, to prove his father's innocence of revolutionary activities, then, and only then, could he deal with his distrust of women . . . and be freed from the bitter memories of his mother's deceit and abandonment.

But until that time came, Drake knew he could not commit himself to Dani or any woman. Nothing was more important to him than the painting, and nothing—or no one—must stand in his way of getting it.

Chapter Fifteen

M ADAME Mebane bought the doves, then requested to see the much talked-about "Monaco find." Drake stood aside as Dani obliged. Madame was properly impressed but not really interested in paintings. A Meissen teapot, in the Japanese Imari style, caught her fancy. This time, there was a friendly discussion over price, but Madame made the purchase and finally left, pleased with the results of her afternoon shopping jaunt.

When the door closed behind her, Dani sighed, but with happiness. "Sorry about the interruption, but I am running a business, you know."

"And doing quite well," Drake amiably pointed out. Then he stepped forward to place his hands upon her shoulders. "I want to be alone with you, Dani. Truly alone. Come to my apartment tonight and have dinner with me. I know a wonderful chef who'll cook for us and then send his waiters over to serve us. How does that sound?"

"Lovely," she admitted, "but have you already forgotten that unpleasant little scene with my father? If he found out I went alone to your apartment, he'd be furious."

"Must you tell him? If he asks, say we're going out for dinner."

She did not like lying but reminded herself that her father's old-fashioned values left her no choice. "I would love to have dinner with you," she told him brightly.

"Wonderful," he murmured, gathering her close against him, then lowering his lips to hers.

Cyril had seen enough. He had stood outside the shop for almost two hours, waiting for Drakar to leave. He had seen him arrive and enter only seconds before him, so he had decided to spy rather than burst in and risk annoying Dani as he had once before.

Then, when she had hung the "CLOSED" sign on her door, he had crept forward to peer in the window just in time to see them disappear out the back way. He had already suspected Drakar's basket contained food for a picnic. So he had hurried to the rear of the building and crouched behind stacks of garbage cans to peer through a tiny hole in the brick wall.

And he had seen more than enough!

Cyril decided he would just have to risk Dani's ire, because, by god, he could stand back no longer. He knew Drakar was after the painting, and he knew why, and he would be damned if that Russian scamp was going to beat him out on both counts—the painting *and* Dani!

Cyril opened the door and walked in. "Good day!" he announced coldly, loudly. "Far be it from me to be accused of spying again."

Dani and Drake had sprung apart at the sound of the bell above the door, and Drake regarded Cyril with controlled rage. "Are you a customer, Arpel?"

"A connoisseur, monsieur," Cyril fired back acidly. "I purchase art for my patrons. I understand you are a collector of a different sort." He raised his head ever so slightly, sniffed with disdain as his gaze swept over Drake contemptuously.

Drake stiffened but, with an amused smile, said, "Perhaps since you seem so interested in my business, we should arrange to discuss it at a time when there is not a lady present.''

Cyril raised an eyebrow, emitted a nervous laugh of incredulity. ''Sir, are you alluding to an *affaire d'honneur?*''

Drake shrugged. ''Who can say what the future holds?''

Dani stepped between them. ''Stop it, the two of you. There's no need for this.''

Cyril glared at Drake but spoke to Dani. ''*I* came here to inspect your shop merchandise. Can *he* claim to have had the same purpose?''

Drake shook his head, as though confronted by a fool not worthy of his time or attention. ''Dani, I bid you good day. I'll call for you at seven.''

Then, without so much as a glance in Cyril's direction, he turned and walked out of the shop.

At once, Dani whirled on Cyril, who promptly threw up his hands in surrender and cried in defense, ''I'm a customer! I walked into your shop and announced my presence so I'd not be accused of spying like last time. It's not my fault if Drakar resents customers coming into your shop!''

Dani sighed. What was the use? He was being childish . . . and also jealous, but there was no point in accusing him of that. ''All right, all right. We'll just forget it. Now,'' she said with exaggerated cheer, ''how may I help you?''

Cyril was relieved. She was going to let it pass. Quickly, he began to recite the story he'd made up. ''I have a patron who has heard about the paintings you found in Monaco, and he's interested in purchasing the entire group so he can display them in his private collection as the Monaco Find.

''After all,'' he rushed to point out, ''all of Paris, and perhaps much of France, has heard about the discovery of those paintings. Interest is keen. It would be quite advantageous to possess *all* the paintings you found in one, complete collection."

Dani nodded. That certainly made sense. She turned to where the paintings were displayed, pursed her lips thoughtfully. Then her eyes fell upon the unrefined painting of the Russian palace. "I don't want to sell that one."

Cyril moaned inwardly. Why was she being so stubborn about one crude little painting? She did not know the secret behind it, and he doubted Drakar had told her but maybe he was working on her emotionally, telling her that the painting reminded him of his boyhood home, or some such nostalgic melodramatics intended to engender her compassion and sympathy.

"But my patron insists on purchasing the *entire* collection," he repeated emphatically.

"Well, that's just too bad. He can't have the entire collection. I don't want to sell the little one.

"Besides," she added, somewhat wistfully as she looked at the painting once more, "it's overshadowed by the others, and I find that rather pathetic."

Cyril slapped his forehead in frustration. "You don't understand. By itself, that wretched little painting is worthless. With the others, as part of a *collection*, it becomes valuable. And," he pointed out accusingly, "you're going to cheat me out of a handsome commission."

Dani was unmoved. "Your profits aren't my concern, Cyril, and need I remind you I didn't open this shop merely for personal gain? It's a hobby, and if I don't make any money, I won't starve, so I can afford to keep anything that strikes my fancy, and that little painting, *wretched* though you call it, happens to strike my fancy. I won't sell it."

Cyril saw the way her brown eyes began to flash with sparkles of topaz and knew he was pressing; he decided, for the moment, to back away. "Very well," he sighed. "It's your prerogative."

Dani thought that perhaps she was being foolish to keep the painting when its value was only as part of the whole collection. Yet, there was still that strange, nagging little feeling that made her *want* to keep it—or, she reluctantly acknowledged to herself, maybe Drake had something to do with it. He did seem to have an affinity for the work. Perhaps, subconsciously, she was keeping it for him, and *that*, most certainly, was a supposition she would dwell upon in depth in the future.

Exasperated, she repeated, "It just isn't for sale, Cyril. I can't understand all the furor over it, anyway. I can understand Drake wanting it, for sentimental reasons, but a collector? It seems strange." She shook her head.

So, Cyril silently fumed, Drakar *was* using pathos. Well, by god and everything holy, so could he!

Stepping closer to the painting, he chuckled softly. "I suppose this would evoke some memories for him. After all, it must be a terrible thing to be banished from your homeland . . ." He hesitated only long enough for his words to be absorbed, but not long enough for Dani to question. "It brings back memories for me, too, like the first time I saw Mathilde Kschessinskaya dance."

Dani was properly impressed. "You saw her? Oh, I'm envious. Drake says he's seen her dance too."

Again, a sardonic chuckle. "Of course he has. He was once a close friend of the Czar's son, Nicholas, and they went many times together to see the Imperial Ballet in Saint Petersburg. Did he also tell you that Nicholas is said to be madly in love with the prima ballerina?"

Dani was at once ignited with interest. "No, he didn't, and please tell me everything you know about her." She sat down on a velvet settee, patted the place beside her.

Cyril was pleased with himself; he knew Dani liked being treated to intimate tidbits concerning her idol. He proceeded to relate the gossip of the Russian court but did not admit it had come to him by way of some of his patrons. Let her believe he was a privileged insider.

He told how Nicholas had first met Mathilde Kschessinskaya in the spring of 1890 when the entire imperial family attended the graduation performance of the Imperial Ballet School, and, afterward, the supper. "That summer she was selected to join the troupe which danced for the officers at Krasnoe Selo, where Nicholas was on duty with the Guards. He saw her every day, and it's said they've been having a romance ever since."

He lowered his voice conspiratorially. "It's rumored they have secret rendezvous on the banks of the Neva, and not long ago, it's said he gave her a gold bracelet set with diamonds and sapphires."

Dani sighed. "A French prima ballerina and the next Czar of Russia. It's like a fairy tale, isn't it?"

"Not really." Cyril was quick to disagree. "They say the younger sister of Grand Duchess Elizabeth, the wife of Nicholas's uncle, Grand Duke Serge, is interested in him. She's a German princess, Alexandra Feodorovna of Hesse, and he is also seeing her."

"Well, it all seems terribly romantic, and I think you're very fortunate to enjoy a career that lets you travel and meet such interesting people."

Cyril beamed, pushed on, pointed toward the painting with relish. "That reminds me of some wonderful times."

Dani was once more impressed. "You've been inside the palace?" she asked, awed.

"Oh, of course." He laughed, as though it were ludicrous to assume he had not. No harm in stretching the truth. After all, he had been inside the palace, once, to deliver a painting, but she did not have to know it was not a social visit.

"Yes," he continued. "I remember well the terraces, statutes, gardens, and, inside, the long hallways and the magnificent gold and crystal chandeliers."

Dani yearned to go there one day. "You have a gallery in Russia, don't you?" she probed thoughtfully.

He explained it was actually only a small office and showroom. "When I have something of particular interest or value to several patrons, I go there to set up and receive their bids, and, eventually, sell the piece. Should you venture to Russia on your own buying excursions, let me know and I'll gladly make my facilities available to you."

Dani said she might just take him up on his kind offer. Just then the door opened with a loud, almost rude jangling of the bell. Dani was surprised to see her half brother striding purposefully toward her. From the tight, set expression on his face, it was obvious he was angry.

He addressed himself to Cyril in a curt, almost rude voice. "I'd like to speak to my sister in private, if you don't mind."

Cyril silently cursed the interruption, but on the surface he was the epitome of understanding. "Of course. I was just leaving anyway." He kissed Dani's hand and walked out of the shop, all the while thinking how he would find an excuse to return later.

When Colt and Dani were alone, Dani at once worriedly asked, "Whatever is wrong? You seem terribly upset. Has something happened at home?"

"No, no. Nothing like that." He ran his fingers through thick waves of dark hair, glanced absently about the shop, took a deep breath, let it out slowly.

Dani felt she would surely go mad if he kept her in suspense any longer and was about to tell him so when the words seemed to explode from his lips.

"I'm getting married."

She stared at him, too shocked to speak.

Colt at once stiffened. "Well? Don't you have anything to say?"

She was taken aback by his belligerence. Apparently, he was not happy about his announcement, but why take it out on her? Testily, she demanded, "What do you want me to say?"

"You might try 'Congratulations.' "

"Are congratulations in order?"

"That's normally what people say when someone tells them they're going to get married."

"Of course, when they're happy about it. You obviously aren't."

"What makes you say that?"

"Go look in a mirror. You aren't exactly the image of a happy groom-to-be."

Colt allowed the remark to pass. "You haven't even asked who I'm marrying."

Dani shrugged. "That's no mystery. The only woman you've been seeing in Paris is Lily."

"And you don't like her!" he said accusingly.

"I never said that."

"You didn't have to. It's obvious you and Mother both don't like her."

"What difference does it make whether we do or don't? We aren't the ones who'll have to live with her. But isn't this all a bit sudden? You've only known her a short while, Colt. And have you told our parents?"

"Tonight. I'm telling them tonight. That's why I came here to see you first."

Dani raised an eyebrow. "Why?"

"So you can find somewhere else to go tonight," he tersely informed her. "Things will be tense enough without you starting another fight like last night, which, by the way, ruined the whole goddamn evening for everybody. I don't want a repeat performance tonight."

Dani felt a wave of fury moving violently from head to toe. How dare he march in to her shop and speak to her this way? What if there had been customers? Obviously, it would not have mattered, the state he was in. "Don't worry," she told him stiffly. "I won't be home for dinner. This is one party I want to be sure and miss."

His nostrils flared with the intensity of his ire as he met her furious gaze with his own eyes. "Fine! That's all I wanted."

He turned on his heel and strode angrily toward the door.

Dani watched him and, despite the way he had made her so angry, could not help but experience a twinge of compassion. What evil spell had that nasty little Lily Deauneve cast over him to make him want to marry her? It was obvious he was terribly upset. She hurried after him. "Colt . . . wait, please . . ."

His hand was on the doorknob, but he hesitated, did not turn around, back stiff, rigid. "What is it? I'm in a hurry."

Hesitantly, she placed her fingertips on his shoulder in a gesture she hoped he would interpret as one of love, caring, and compassion. "Colt, listen," she said softly. "I know we've had problems in the past, and since you came to Paris we haven't become close, as I would've liked. I've just been busy with the shop, and Drake, and you've had Lily, and there just hasn't been time for us to really get to know each other. But I want you to know that I do love you and care about you, and I'm worried now, because I just can't help feeling that this marriage isn't what *you* want."

Colt shrugged away her caress but did not turn around, his voice as frigid as his pose. "Mind your own business, Dani. I didn't ask for your approval or your opinion. I just asked you to stay away tonight and give us all some peace."

Dani held her anger in check, managed to keep her voice warm, even. "Believe me, I'm not trying to meddle, but please talk with Poppa, or Kitty, before you get too deeply committed to this."

Suddenly, he whirled around and pointed an accusing finger beneath her nose. "Stay out of it, Dani," he cried harshly. "If it hadn't been for you being such a spoiled brat and letting Alaina Barbeau spirit you away from our family, none of this would've happened. You'd have been where you were supposed to be, and I wouldn't have made a fool of myself and damn near lost the entire family fortune."

He yanked the door open with a vengeance, started out, then hesitated.

Dani stared after him, eyes misting with stinging tears. How could he blame her for everything? She shook her head slowly from side to side, shocked and hurt.

Then, in a voice choked with his own anguish, Colt spoke over his shoulder. "Besides, it doesn't make a damn difference what *I* want. I don't intend to make the same mistake twice."

Then he hurried out, down the cobbled street, and Dani could only stand in the doorway and stare helplessly after him.

Chapter Sixteen

D ANI decided to close the shop earlier than usual. All had been quiet since Colt's disturbing visit, so she locked the doors at three o'clock and went home, thinking how nice it would be to have some time to herself before Drake arrived. A leisurely bath and a glass of wine would do wonders to dispel the agitation Colt had incited.

At quarter past three, Cyril arrived at the shop. He stared at the "CLOSED" sign in the window, and his eyes at once narrowed with rising anger. So, he fumed, Dani was so excited over her coming tryst with Drakar that she could not wait to get home to start readying herself for it. Well, that was just fine, because he knew where Drakar lived, had made it his business to learn everything he could about the man once he realized they were both after the same things—the painting *and* Dani Coltrane. He had overheard their conversation earlier, knew they were planning a cozy little dinner together at Drakar's apartment, and he would just arrange to be outside to keep his eye on things. Drakar did not know it yet, he fumed, but he had a fight on his hands. This was one war Cyril did not intend to lose, no matter the cost or consequences.

Dani was relieved to arrive at the mansion and find no one about downstairs. She hurried up to the sanctity of her room, but her peace was short-lived. She had not yet had time to ring for her maid to draw her bath before there was a loud, insistent knock on her door. With a sigh of dread, she opened it—and there stood Lily.

She was grinning triumphantly, head held high. "I know you know. Colt said he was going to your shop to tell you."

Dani nodded curtly, felt her teeth grinding together instinctively as she fought to quell the resentment bubbling within. She did not like this snitty girl, hated the thought of having her for a sister-in-law, but was damned if she would make a scene. After all, it was Colt's life, and she could certainly defend his right to live it as he chose.

"Congratulations, Lily," she finally said in a voice void of emotion or enthusiasm. "I hope you'll both be very happy. Now if you'll excuse me, I have things to do."

Lily ignored her request and breezed into the room and sat herself down on the divan next to the window and demurely folded her hands in her lap. Then, with a deeply beseeching expression on her face—acquired after too many hours of practice before a mirror—she looked at Dani and said imploringly, "Can you forgive me for my rudeness yesterday? I had no business saying what I said about Drakar."

Dani had not moved away from the door. She knew, instinctively, that Lily was up to something. But what? And why? Apparently, she had what she wanted—a proposal from Colt. Finally, she responded. "That's quite all right, Lily, don't worry about it. Now if you don't mind, as I said, I do have some things to tend to."

Lily made no move to get up, merely continued to look at her in that pleading way. "I want us to be friends, Dani. Good friends."

Unable to hide the tension in her voice, Dani tightly murmured, "We have no problems, Lily . . . if you will just allow me to get on with what I was doing," she added pointedly.

Lily flashed a bright smile. "Colt and I want to be married as soon as possible. Since I have no family to speak of, my poor uncle is too ill to travel and all, we thought it best we just go ahead and get married and skip much of the prewedding formalities, but we do want a beautiful wedding, and we want you to help us plan it."

Dani blinked, astonished. Under the circumstances, she did not want to be involved. With a shake of her head, she declined. "That's out of the question. I'm going to be quite busy with my travel plans, and—"

"You don't understand!" Lily leaped to her feet and hurried to stand before her. "I must have your help . . . and Kitty's. Between the two of you, you can put something together almost as lavish as that party you had when you opened your shop. You and she know lots of people. Colt *is* your brother, and whether you truly like me or not, you owe it to him, and—"

"Lily, stop it!" Dani snapped, holding up a hand for silence. No way was she going to be manipulated into helping plan a wedding she quite frankly thought was a terrible mistake. "I don't have time, and that's final, now please accept my congratulations and best wishes for your happiness and again I ask you to leave me."

Lily took a step away from her, felt her cheeks growing warm with humiliation. "I came here to apologize if I angered you last night; I offered my hand to you in friendship, and this is what I get. A slap in the face."

Dani was not about to be intimidated. "I merely tried to explain that I don't have time to help with your wedding, Lily. I'm sorry if my refusal offends you."

Lily's eyes narrowed ominously. "When I'm Mrs. John Travis Coltrane, you won't treat me like this. You'll give me the respect I'm due."

Dani suppressed a snicker. "I'll treat you as I treat anyone else, Lily, which is as you deserve to be treated. Now"—she took a deep breath, let it out slowly as she pointed to the door with an unwavering finger—"if you don't leave, I'm afraid I'm just going to have to help you out, as you leave me no choice.''

At that, Lily exploded, losing all traces of composure. ''Why, why . . . you conceited little bitch,'' she sputtered, then cried, ''Colt told me how you've never thought of anyone but yourself your whole life, never gave a damn how you hurt people as long as you got what you wanted. Well, I'll tell you one thing, Miss High-and-Mighty Dani Coltrane, you're going to get what's coming to you when you find out your precious Russian lover is nothing but a whore-hopping scamp. He'll bed any woman who spreads her thighs for him, and if I wanted to, I could take him away from you like that . . .'' She snapped her fingers beneath Dani's nose.

Dani was having an extremely difficult time holding her temper in check. She desperately wanted to slap Lily's face until her teeth rattled, but she was determined to hang on to her self-control as long as humanly possible. She closed her eyes for an instant, then took a deep breath and reached out and clamped her hands on Lily's shoulders and shoved her with all her might toward the door.

Lily began to scream and struggle against her, but Dani, though smaller in size, was quicker, and she was able to fling her through the door with a mighty thrust and then leap back to slam the door in her face and lock it.

Lily promptly yelled, ''I'll get you for this, Dani. I swear I will. You had your chance. I'm going to marry your brother whether you like it or not, and I'll take over this house, and I'll make your life hell, and you'll have to get out and go live with your whoremonger Russian as long as he'll have you . . .''

Dani leaned back against the door, trembling from head to toe. My god, where was everyone? The servants could not help but hear and were, no doubt, discreetly ignoring what was going on. Of course, the family was out, or they would have come running. She felt so sorry for Colt. There was just no way he could fancy himself in love with Lily if he could see her as she was now. It made her want to cry to think of him married to such a little witch, but what could she do to prevent it? He would never believe her if she told him about this dreadful scene.

Lily kicked the door repeatedly as she continued to rant and rave. Dani shook her head in disgust, and wondered how long the tirade would continue. Then, suddenly, Lily screamed something that caught her attention.

"Colt told me how your mother tried to break up Travis and Kitty. No wonder Drakar appeals to you. He's a whoremonger like your father, and no doubt you're just like your mother!"

That did it!

Dani's eyes fell upon the vase of late summer roses beside her bed. She walked over, removed the roses, took the vase of water and returned to the door. With one swift movement, she yanked open the door and flung the water in Lily's face, then slammed it quickly against the sight of water dripping down her astonished face.

With a loud shriek, Lily turned and fled down the long hallway toward her room, the sound of her furious cries echoing and then fading along with the sound of her clattering footsteps.

Dani methodically refilled the vase, rearranged the roses, wondered what lies Lily would tell Colt . . . and decided she just didn't care. How she yearned, now more than ever, to just move out of the house and have a place of her own, free of judgment and interference from others. Only then would she start to feel she was truly in control of her life.

She rang for Lurline and could tell from the nervous way she acted when she walked in that she had heard the commotion. Deciding to ease the tension, Dani declared, "I'm truly sorry everyone had to hear all that."

At once, Lurline seized the opportunity to broach the subject the entire household staff was buzzing about. "Mademoiselle, what was wrong with Mademoiselle Lillian? Never have I heard such screaming. She was like a woman gone mad!''

Dani went to her wardrobe, began to look through her vast and lovely selection of gowns. ''I really don't like talking about my family's personal life, Lurline, but if you haven't already heard enough to know what's going on, you soon will, so I see no harm in telling you that my brother has asked Lily to marry him. She asked me to help her plan a wedding, I told her I just didn't have time, and she exploded.''

She selected a dress of mauve velvet with a slightly provocative neckline and straight skirt. Simple, yet elegant. Her marten fur cape would complement the gown, and the evening would certainly be chilly enough for such a warm wrap.

Suddenly, she realized Lurline had not made any comment about her confiding such news. Turning to look at her, she was surprised to see how upset she looked, but Dani knew the household staff had no affection for the spoiled and unpleasant guest, either. ''I know, it's a shock,'' Dani told her as she headed for the alcove where her bath awaited. ''It's hard to believe that Colt can't see through her and realize what she's really like.''

Lurline followed her into the alcove, still not speaking. Dani settled down into the warm water and, when she noticed how Lurline's hands shook as she poured fragrant bath oil into the tub, could not help asking, ''What on earth is wrong with you? You're shaking like a leaf, and look at your face! You're so pale.''

Lurline shook her head, backed away, murmured an apology for her behavior, and started from the alcove.

Dani sat straight up, water sloshing over the rim of the tub. ''Lurline, come back here!'' she ordered. ''I want to know what's wrong with you . . . why are you acting so strange?''

Suddenly, Lurline turned, and the look of fright was gone from her face and in its place one of indignant anger. ''All right,'' she all but screamed, ''I'll tell you. It's

none of my business, and you'll probably report me to
Madame Coltrane and I'll be fired, but I just think someone should know what I saw last night and early this
morning.''

"I think," Dani said coolly, "you'd better explain
yourself, Lurline.''

Lurline sat down on a nearby stool. "I'm going to tell
you everything, and I swear to you I haven't told this to
another soul, and the only reason I'm telling you, mademoiselle, is because I think someone in your family
should try to do something to stop Monsieur Colt from
making what could be the biggest mistake of his whole
life.''

Dani nodded, urged, "Go on, please.''

"Someone," Lurline declared haughtily, "should make
him see that just because he bedded the devil doesn't
mean he has to marry her.''

Dani was beginning to understand what she was getting
at, nodded once more for her to continue.

Lurline explained how the night before, she had been
working upstairs late, because Mademoiselle Lillian had
complained that her suite was not being properly cleaned.
Afraid that she might lose her job if the complaints continued, Lurline took advantage of the family dinner and
went into Mademoiselle's quarters to freshen things up a
bit. "The truth is, I fell asleep," she admitted a bit sheep-
ishly. "I was so tired from working extra hard, and I lay
down on the divan in one of the alcoves and fell asleep.
Mademoiselle did not see me when she came in, and I
awoke only when she dropped something.

"I wasn't about to make my presence known then,"
she hurried on defensively, "She would have really been
furious to find I'd been sleeping in her quarters, so I just
lay there and tried to be as quiet as possible. I was scared
to death, I assure you, because the only hope I had was
to slip out once she fell asleep, but she didn't go to bed.
I could peek around the end of the divan and see into the

bedroom, and I saw her change into a negligee and then she went out again."

Lurline paused to allow Dani to absorb that. "She went to Monsieur Colt's bedroom."

Dani raised an eyebrow but said nothing.

"I know," Lurline went on confidently, "because once she left the room, I naturally hurried to leave myself, only when I eased the door open, I was just in time to see her go into that little alcove down the hall. She must have hidden in the shadows a half hour or so before Monsieur Colt came upstairs. Then she waited a little longer after he went to his room before she just went to his door and opened it and walked in."

Dani knew that Colt would not be cajoled into marrying a woman merely because she sneaked into his bed and invited him to seduce her . . . or she seduced *him*. Oh, no, there had to be more than that. Lurline was watching her to see what her reaction would be, and, impatiently, she motioned for her to please continue.

"Be angry with me if you wish, mademoiselle," she flippantly invited, "but I despise that woman, and I wanted to know what she was up to, because it was obvious your brother didn't invite her to his bedroom. Why would she have been hiding in the shadows waiting for him if he had? Why didn't she just go on into his room and be there when he got there?"

Lurline smiled with malicious delight. "I tiptoed right up to that door and pressed my ear against it and heard her crying about how terrible she felt over what had happened at dinner and how she was going to leave and go back to London, and Monsieur Colt was telling her everything would be all right, and then things became very quiet . . ." She allowed her voice to trail off meaningfully, letting Dani draw her own conclusions as to what happened next.

"And," she rushed to say, "when I went to clean her room the next morning, it was quite early, around seven, I think, and her bed hadn't been slept in, but when I returned later, the covers were pulled back and the sheets mussed to make it appear she'd been there all night.''

Dani gritted her teeth. Lurline had gone too far in her snooping. Reaching for a towel, she wrapped it around her, stepped from the tub, and faced the servant girl with angry, condemning eyes. "You should be ashamed of yourself. If I hear that you've told anyone else about this, I swear I'll see to it you're fired, and I'll also do everything I can to see that no prominent family in Paris hires you.

"You've no right to pry into other people's lives," she continued, mind whirling with all she'd just been told and wishing, despite the possible *need* to know such gossip, that she did *not* know.

Lurline stared at her incredulously, horrified to be chastised. She hurried to defend herself. "But mademoiselle, I told you how I came to be in her quarters in the first place. I wasn't prying. True, I became curious when I saw the strange way Mademoiselle Deauneve was acting, but aren't you glad I followed her? Surely you and your family have a right to know Monsieur Colt is involved with a—a *demimondaine!*" She shuddered with exaggerated loathing.

"How dare you say such a thing?" Dani demanded. "Regardless of your personal feelings and observations, let me remind you that you're a servant in this house and you will keep your opinions to yourself. You are impudent and disrespectful!"

At once, Lurline lowered her head contritely and whispered, "Oh, I'm truly sorry if you're angry, mademoiselle. I just thought you should know. Forgive me, please, and I won't say a word to anyone. I swear it on my mother's grave . . ." Her voice wavered, caught on a sob.

Dani waved her away, not wanting to listen any longer. "Leave me, please. Just go."

Lurline backed to the door, then turned and ran out.

Dani's mind was whirling furiously as she finished dressing. What to do? What was there *to* do? It was none of her business if Lily slipped into Colt's room at night. And how did she know Lurline had not made up the whole story? It was certainly no secret that the servants despised Lily, because she was so unpleasant . . . always screaming at them, complaining and criticizing. Yet, it was doubtful that Lurline or any of the others would go so far as to invent vicious lies to attempt to dishonor her.

So what did it all mean?

Colt was obviously not happy about the thought of getting married, so how had Lily managed to manipulate him into announcing their engagement? Did last night have anything to do with it?

In that moment, Dani could be sure of only one thing—that it was best she stay out of it.

Dani had earlier sent word to the kitchen staff that she would not be at dinner. Promptly at seven o'clock, she saw Drake arrive. At the sight of him, a smile touched her lips. Handsome and appealing though he was, he was also her friend and confidant . . . something she had never experienced with a man before.

She grabbed her fur cape, started downstairs, wanting to leave the house as quickly as possible to avoid any kind of confrontation with Colt or Lily, or her parents. Then, halfway down the stairs, she saw her father crossing the foyer in the direction of his study. She prayed he would not see her.

Her prayer went unanswered.

Travis glanced up, paused. "Daniella. Good evening." There was tension in his voice.

She nodded, politely acknowledged his greeting.

A shadow crossed his steel-gray eyes as memories of the unpleasant scene of the night before came flooding back. "Would you come into my study, please? I think we need to have a little chat before dinner."

Dani stiffened but managed to sound apologetic as she started to explain. "I really don't have time. Drake and I—"

The door chimes sounded. She fell silent.

Travis raised a questioning eyebrow, looked from her to the door, then waved away an approaching servant and admitted Drake himself. Dani hurried on down the stairs as the two men exchanged pleasantries, slipped her hand around Drake's arm and murmured she was ready to leave.

Travis's eyes narrowed ever so slightly. "You two won't be here for dinner?"

"No," Dani said quickly, too quickly, wishing she did not sound so nervous. "We're dining out."

"Then perhaps you have time for a drink before you go?"

Drake was about to speak, to accept her father's invitation, Dani knew, and she couldn't help thinking how nice it would be to have just one drink to perhaps ease the tension, but suddenly she glanced up to see Colt making his way down the stairs. "No." Her voice was sharp, and she did not miss the odd way they watched her. Giving Drake what she hoped was a pleading look, she rushed on. "Didn't you say you had made our reservations for seven-thirty?"

Hesitantly, he nodded.

"Then we'd best be on our way." She gave his arm a tug and feigned regrets to Travis. "Another time, thank you."

Travis opened the door for them. "Of course. Have a nice evening."

As soon as they were outside, Drake laughingly asked what was going on. "You were practically dragging us out of there."

"Later," Dani murmured, relieved they'd gotten out without further to-do. "I'll tell you all about it later."

Drake was warmed by the expression on her beautiful face as she smiled up at him almost adoringly. He pulled her close to kiss her forehead and whisper, "You know that if you have problems, my darling, you can always come to me."

With a happy glow, Dani knew that was true.

Chapter Seventeen

A CARRIAGE ride through Paris by night was far too enchanting an experience to be wasted discussing unpleasant subjects. Dani and Drake soon reached their destination—the small but elegant Le Palais Hotel situated with a view of the Tuileries Gardens. A concierge dressed in an impressive suit of black velvet with gold epaulets was waiting beside a bubbling fountain to help them alight from the carriage. He bowed graciously, greeted Drake with unusual familiarity, Dani noted, then moved swiftly to hold open one of two ornately carved mahogany doors.

Inside, Dani was immediately impressed by the foyer, a small stepped aithrion. She knew from her studies of interior design that the inner court was of Greek origin, and that the Pentelic marble, the marble used in the Parthenon, had also been used here for the four columns supporting the glass roof above. The pattern of the floor was derived from that of the Greek temples, and the proportions of the columns no doubt derived from those of the Doric order of the Parthenon. Tall urns stood beside each and held thick bouquets of fragrant roses and carnations.

Drake led her down the three steps and on across the gleaming floor. The aithrion was bordered on each side by small reception rooms, unfurnished yet impressive, for the walls of each were different. One was of mother-of-pearl, another done in mirrors and crystal, then white lacquer, and, finally, on the side from which they had entered, white silk. "Amazing," Dani gasped, awed. "Every kind of sheen has been used to catch all the light and pass it on. My compliments to their designers, whoever they were."

She heard Drake's light chuckle and whispered "*Merci,*" but had little time to dwell on whether she'd heard exactly right, for he was explaining about the beautiful gardens in the rear that he would show her sometime in daylight. "Small but spectacular. Large chunks of the marble that was brought in from Greece were left outside to use in making a little waterfall. Wild flowers, lavender, and rosemary have been planted all over the ground, so that when the leaves are crushed underfoot, the scents fill the air."

Suddenly it occurred to Dani that she'd not seen a lobby for registration, nor had there been any sign of hotel employees, other than the concierge. When she asked why, he explained, "There are people available if you need anything, but the concept here was to provide a cozy atmosphere amid quiet opulence as opposed to the usual starkness of hotels."

She saw the ornate wrought-iron lift and was quite impressed to realize, when Drake touched a small switch, that it was electric, not steam-driven. She said nothing as he opened the gate to the interior compartment, but as they stepped inside she could not help feeling a bit nervous. "I have to admit I've never been on one of these things when they're operated by electricity. Are you quite sure it's safe?"

Amused, he assured her it was. "The mechanism for this, an electric motor to drive a winding drum down in the basement, was shipped over from New York. It's just like the first one that was put in operation in the Demarest Building over there two years ago. It's still running fine . . ."

Dani leaned back against a wall, her gaze beneath lowered lashes moving over him. All the while she was aware of how his nearness was making her senses quicken. "I thought you told me you lived in an apartment. You seem to know an awful lot about the hotel."

He was leaning against the wall opposite, arms folded across his chest. There was a space of only two feet or so between them, for the lift was small, would comfortably accommodate only four people.

Without raising his hand, he merely lifted a finger to point upward, the play of a smile on his lips as he said, "I've lived in an apartment on the top floor for almost a year."

"Before that?"

"London for a spell. Before that, Madrid. A few months in Amsterdam. I spent some time in Algiers." He shrugged, the look in his eyes almost hypnotic as he met her stare. "I can't remember dates, or all the places. I suppose I'm nomadic . . . can't seem to settle down in one place for very long."

Sardonically Dani wondered if his nomadism extended to his relationships with women . . . but dared not ask. She told herself it did not matter because she would not let it matter and went on to say, "As much time as we've spent together, we've never talked about what makes you such a gypsy . . .

". . . or such an enigma," she added with a mischievous gleam, "as I've gathered from having fortuitously overheard young ladies' talk from time to time."

Drake threw back his head and laughed heartily. Then the lift came to a slightly jerking halt, and, caught off balance, Dani lurched against him, and he reached out to steady her. As their eyes met and held, the mirth faded, and Drake pulled her against his chest, holding her closely, tightly, as his lips tenderly claimed hers.

They stood, locked in embrace, and time seemed to stand still as they savored the stirring moment.

From somewhere below in the dark cavity of the shaft, a bell sounded impatiently to pierce the magic spell.

Reluctantly, they parted. Drake attempted to lighten the moment. "Should've known not to expect privacy in an elevator," he said with a grin, pulling open the gate to reveal large, shining brass doors.

Dani realized they had not reached an ordinary hotel floor, with doors lining each side of a hallway. Instead, she stepped across a marble threshold into a small room illumined by the glow of a regal crystal and coral chandelier.

"I call this my Silver Room," Drake said as he closed the lift and sent it downward. Locking the heavy brass doors behind them, he held out his hand to her. "The chef said he'd have our dinner served promptly at nine. Meanwhile, I've got some delicious beluga caviar and a tasty carraway vodka I had sent all the way from Russia that I think you'll like. But would you like to see my apartment first?"

"I'd love to." Dani paused to admire a mother-of-pearl table which held a group of silver decorative pieces. To one side, a mirrored table held a collection of rose-quartz figurines. A Venetian mirror, heavily edged in silver, hung above a marble-topped side table.

"I use this as an entrance foyer," Drake explained. "I didn't want people stepping off the elevator directly into the parlor."

Dani was impressed. "But I didn't know they had apartments in hotels like this."

Drake nodded. "Ordinarily they don't, but since I liked Paris and thought I might be spending a lot of time here, I just had this designed and renovated especially for me."

Dani's interest was piqued, and she followed him eagerly into the next room, anxious to see more of his decorating skill.

In the dining room, one wall was dominated by a painting of a Roman gladiator and horses, done in gold leaf on canvas. The table was set with silver-gilt and crystal appointments, glimmering beneath a sparkling gold and crystal chandelier.

"I had that brought in from Russia." Drake gestured to the fixture. "It belonged to my uncle. I wanted it here, since I'll probably always keep this place, no matter where I settle down permanently . . . if that ever happens," he added with a wry grin.

There was an octagonal drawing room, a small parlor, a tea kitchen, all lovely and elegantly furnished, but it was Drake's study that made Dani gasp aloud. The curving sofas were covered in alligator skin, and she declared incredulously, "Don't tell me you find that soft!"

"Actually, I do." Drake laughed. "Try it, and so will you. I had the hides shipped in from Africa, and I knew a man who really has a knack for tanning in Madrid, so he did them up for me. The actual sofas were made in London."

Gingerly, Dani touched the rough-appearing surface, then marveled that it felt as smooth and soft as the finest leathers.

"Sit down," Drake said. "I'll go and get the vodka and caviar." He walked out of the room, pleased with her reactions to his decor.

Dani chose one of the small chairs in the room, which was covered in actual leather, as she could not so soon relish the thought of sitting on an alligator's hide, however comfortable. Glancing around the fairly large room, she observed other mementos from Africa—the angry face of a tiger stared down at her menacingly from its place on the wall next to a rhino's indifferent gaze. She shivered in revulsion, turned her attention to the rows and rows of books on the shelves and marveled at the selections in so many different languages.

Drake returned with a tray containing a bottle of colorless liquor, glasses, a bowl filled with bright red caviar, and a plate of tiny crackers and squares of bread. "I see you've been admiring my 'museum,' " he said jovially. "I'm afraid I haven't been as lucky on safari as some of my colleagues."

"Thank goodness," Dani cried with exaggerated approval. "I don't like to see animals killed merely for sport." She gestured to the books. "How many different languages do you know?"

Drake pursed his lips thoughtfully as he sat down and filled the glasses with vodka. "Let's see," he mused. "Fluently, I speak Russian, of course, and English, as you know . . . French, Spanish, German, and the Scandinavian languages, which are basically alike—Norwegian, Swedish, Danish.

"And . . ." he went on thoughtfully after a moment, "I can communicate a little in maybe four or five other languages, enough to ask for directions if I get lost in, say, Morocco, Algeria, or Egypt." He laughingly added, "Enough Swahili to tell the cannibals they'd have to boil me for a week before I'd be tender enough to eat."

Dani could not help giggling at that. "Cannibals don't speak Swahili!"

"Of course they don't," Drake said with a chuckle, "but I like to tease you. Here. To us!" He held up his glass in toast, and Dani joined him.

She took a sip, wrinkled her nose slightly at the unfamiliar taste, then declared, "I rather like it."

"I thought you would." Drake leaned back on the alligator-skin sofa, crossed his legs, took a deep breath, then softly urged, "So. Now that we're relaxed, would you like to tell me why you were so upset when I called for you?"

Dani took several more sips, liked the warm tickling all the way from her mouth, throat, and down to her stomach. "It's Colt. He came by the shop after you left and told me he and Lily are going to be married."

Drake leaned forward, refilled their glasses, then sat back and gave her his full attention as she recounted the entire conversation and the subsequent scene with Lily.

She finished with an apologetic shrug. "I wasn't trying to be rude when I rushed us out of the house. I just didn't want a scene with Colt over the dispute between Lily and me, nor did I relish being around when he announced he plans to marry her. I thought it best we leave.''

She did not see any point in relating Lurline's tale of having spied on Lily and thereby concluding how the engagement might have come about. No need to drag out family skeletons that might not even exist.

Drake was disgusted to think of Colt marrying a woman like Lily—a conniving little golddigger who could smell money the same way alligators sniffed out bait hounds tied to trees. He loathed hypocritical women like that, for, as much as he hated admitting it, if only to himself, they reminded him of his mother . . . and the way she'd ruined his father's life with her selfishness and deceit.

Dani shook her head and said, ''Colt has a right to make his own decisions.''

Drake silently, bitterly contradicted her: *Not when those decisions are manipulated by someone else!*

Dani reached out, touched his arm in a gesture of friendship and gratitude. ''Thank you for listening. I'm sorry to burden you with my family problems, but I want you to know I appreciate your kindness and tolerance.''

''What are friends for?'' he reminded softly, then a shadow crossed his eyes, and he stared at her quietly before confiding, ''I have some bad memories where my own family is concerned, Dani. One day, I'll share them with you. Until then, I want you to know that I understand what you're going through and how it hurts.''

He reached out to pull her tightly against his chest, so close she could feel the sweet warmth of his breath upon her face. He claimed her mouth in a kiss that ignited fires to sweep over them as wildly as a blaze in the wind.

Dani responded with unabashed yearning, twining her arms around his neck to press close against him. She could feel her nipples grow taut as desire swelled within her breasts.

They clung together for long, ardent moments, then, ever so reluctantly, Dani withdrew from the embrace, and their eyes met and held in wonder over the deep, swirling emotions that surged through their veins.

Softly, Drake commanded, "Tell me you've never felt this way before."

"I haven't," she replied honestly, then challenged him with a saucy smile. "Can you say the same, *Drakar*, renowned collector of hearts?"

He laughed and gave her a gentle shake of reprimand. "Yes, I can, you little vixen, but you wouldn't believe me." Then he became somber. "I'm aware of my reputation but not for the reasons you might think. Frankly, I've never met a woman I could trust . . . or maybe I just didn't care enough to try."

Dani knew she might have felt his admission strange, were it not for Cyril having told her about Drake's mother, and her subsequent supposition that his past made him mistrustful of women in general; so she understood . . . or felt she did. "I'm glad," she told him, "that you care enough about *me* to try."

"I do care. More than I want to admit for the moment, even to myself. But trust me, Dani. I'll never hurt you."

How she hoped, with all her heart, that it was so, because, for the first time, she was letting her guard down, and she was all too aware that doing so made her vulnerable. Yet, it was what she wanted—to take a chance on love . . . with Drake. And because it was her decision alone to make, she accepted the risk . . . along with the ultimate outcome, whatever it might be.

Dinner was delectable: fresh duck foie gras with a chicory salad, roasted Mediterranean sea bream complemented by a casserole of prawns and fresh artichokes. There was also the best of white wines and red, champagne, coffee with cognac.

Yet, Drake and Dani hardly touched their food or barely tasted their beverages, for their appetite was only for each other.

A waiter hovered nearby and fretted that perhaps they might find the menu unappetizing. Drake finally grew weary of his frenetic concern and curtly dismissed him.

When they were once more alone, Dani asked, "Aren't you worried that the waiter may have gotten his feelings hurt because you dismissed him? The hotel might think it was his fault, or the restaurant owner might blame the chef and think the food wasn't good."

Drake slowly shook his head. "You see, I own the hotel and the restaurant."

Dani was impressed . . . but not by his wealth, for she was used to associating with people of fortune. What awed her was the realization that he was also, no doubt, responsible for the entire decor of the building, which now explained his whispered *"Merci"* when she was making comments of praise earlier.

Drake stood, moved to pull out her chair so she could also rise. Their eyes devoured each other as he ran his fingertips down her arms and softly asked, "Would you care for dessert in the parlor?"

With a mysterious smile, she said nothing, merely walked into the next room.

Dani knew what she wanted, had known that when the right time came—with the right man—she would have no reservations. There would be no holding back, and hopefully, no regrets.

Facing him, voice steady, gaze unwavering, she reached with deft fingers to slowly unfasten her gown, then allowed it to fall to the floor. Opening her arms to him as she stood in intimate lace and satin undergarments, she announced, "My darling, *we* are the dessert this evening."

With a deep moan of delight and pleasure, Drake quickly lifted her in his arms and tersely avowed, "I've never wanted a woman more, Dani, and I'm going to prove it to you . . . all night long."

Chapter Eighteen

DRAKE stood staring down at Dani thoughtfully. She was asleep in his bed, lying on her side. Her naked body was bathed in the luminous glow of moonlight spilling through the window, presenting her as a flawless sculpture of the finest alabaster.

Beautiful.

He had never known a woman like her.

Not only did she possess all the physical attributes a man could want but she was also keenly intelligent, high-spirited, and extremely good company.

She had been a virgin.

That did not surprise him.

What he did find astonishing was her ability to please him and take him to heights of passion and delight that he'd never found in the arms of another woman. She seemed to know how to excite him, how to give pleasure, as well as take. It was as though, by giving, she was actually receiving . . . and he liked that rare concept.

Drake also knew that Dani was sophisticated enough not to feel he owed her any kind of commitment for having taken her virginity. She was not that kind. She had let him know she wanted him, and if there had been seduction, then it was mutual.

Yet, he could not help feeling a bond to her now and wished his life were not so complicated. He had vowed to let nothing stand in the way of restoring honor to his family's name but knew now he would have to be on guard lest a honey-eyed beauty become an obstacle.

He needed access to the Alexandrovsky Palace painting to study and search for clues that would lead him to the Fabergé egg. Perhaps the time had come to confide in Dani; then she would surely give him that access. What harm would it do, he reasoned, for her to know about his past, particularly when he was experiencing feelings for her he'd never had for any other woman . . . feelings that he wanted to pursue.

He went into the study, drained the last dregs from the vodka bottle as he paced about the room. He thought of Colt again, marveled at how such musings kept coming to mind despite so many personal concerns in his own life. God, how he hated to think of him being inveigled into marrying a fortune hunter like Lily. No telling how many beds she'd romped through in England in her quest to ensnare a rich man.

He wondered what trick she'd used to get Colt to propose. A baby? Too soon for that—even for a schemer like Lily. She would have used a more sophisticated ploy, probably made him believe he'd seduced her, that she was a virgin, so she could moan that unless he married her and made a "decent" woman of her, her life would be ruined now that she was "soiled."

Drake chuckled with bitterness. It was a woman's oldest ploy and had probably worked for Lily since she had the distinct advantage of being a guest in the Coltrane mansion. How terrible it would look for a prominent, important man like Travis Coltrane to have it said that his son had seduced a houseguest, taken her virginity, then refused to marry her.

Well, he figured he'd just have to step in and save Colt's neck . . . maybe even, ultimately, his life, because he imagined a life married to someone like Lily would, in itself, be a kind of death.

He thought about the night he'd had dinner with the Coltranes and how Lily had brushed against him intimately on several occasions, letting him know with secret smiles and fluttering lashes that it was no accident. Without egotism, he knew the signs, knew he could get her into his bed with little effort. The difficulty would be in devising a way to have Colt find them there. He was convinced that the quickest solution would be for Colt to see for himself just what she was before it was too late. Of course, Dani must not know about it. But he intended for Colt to come along before anything actually happened, and once he realized it was all set up, he would never tell. Neither would Lily. She'd be so embarrassed and humiliated she would head for England as quickly as she could book passage out of France.

Drake smiled to himself. It would work. Of course, Colt would be very angry at first, but later he would be grateful.

He glanced at a clock, saw it was the ebb of midnight. Returning to the bedroom, he gazed down at Dani once more, thought how beautiful she was, felt his desire rising again and reminded himself it was late. He needed to be getting her home, where young women of gentility should be at such an hour. Yet, as a slow warmth began to creep over him, he knew he had to hold her close just one more time to savor the memories of ecstacy shared. He lay down beside her and wrapped his arms around her, and in her slumber, Dani sighed, snuggled yet closer in his embrace.

Drake savored her sweetness. The time had come, he knew, to tell her everything, and he would do so at first opportunity, perhaps tomorrow. Then he could continue his quest, ultimately putting his life in order . . . a life he now acknowledged wishing Dani to be a part of.

Cyril Arpel stood in the shadows across the street and stared up at the dark hotel. He could not remember ever being so angry. He was shaking from head to toe, clenching and unclenching his fists at his side, grinding his teeth together so tightly that his jaws were aching.

Enough was enough! Drakar thought he had everything he wanted—the conquest of Dani, and, soon, possession of the painting. Well, Cyril fumed, he'd find out differently. He had tarried long enough. Now was the time to make his move.

He needed sleep, but that could come later . . . after he finalized his plans for stealing the painting . . . and making it appear as though Drakar were responsible. Dani would, no doubt, be so furious she would turn to him for comfort, and Cyril figured he just might wind up winning both prizes after all.

Such a ploy, Cyril contemplated, would not be difficult. After all, stealing the painting was the easy part. All he had to do was break into Dani's shop one night and take it. As for implicating Drakar, well, when he disappeared at the same time as the painting, without explanation, it would certainly look suspicious and incriminating enough for him to be blamed. Cyril knew he would have no difficulty arranging for Drakar to receive an urgent message from Russia demanding his presence before the Imperial Court. Thanks to an unscrupulous worker at the telegraph office, who would do anything for a few thousand francs, Cyril could have such a dispatch sent. He had done so on past occasions when it was feasible to have a rival dealer called away just before an important sale or auction was to take place. And, should Drakar try to send a message to Dani, informing her of his sudden departure from France, well, Cyril acknowledged with a satisfied grin, he could take care of that little item, also.

Cyril took one last look upward at the apartment, then turned away. It was, he vowed, as good as done.

Dani awoke with a start. Sunlight was streaming across her face. She blinked furiously against the sudden intrusion, then a dagger of awareness struck. She was naked. She sat up straight to stare about wildly. This was not her bed. Not her room. Where was she? Then hysteria began to bubble in her dry, tight throat as she realized there was a man lying beside her and recognized Drake at the same instant everything came rushing back to awaken her to harsh reality.

Dear god, it was morning!

She gave Drake a frantic shake as she cried, "Drake, wake up. We fell asleep. Oh, Poppa is going to kill both of us."

She sprang from the bed, began to search about frantically for her clothes, which were nowhere to be seen. Then she remembered her uninhibited disrobing of the night before and ran into the room where she had carelessly discarded her things.

Drake was instantly awake and groping for his own clothes. He glanced at a clock. "Goddammit, it's eight o'clock! How could we have slept so late? How could I have been so irresponsible?" He jerked on his shirt, headed for the door. "I'll have the carriage brought around—"

"No!" Dani almost screamed her protest. "I'll go alone. If Poppa sees you, it'll make it that much worse. There's no telling what he might do."

"No, I won't send you home in a carriage by yourself like a woman of the night, Dani, paid for your services and sent to your door. No. We'll face him together."

He forced a smile he did not feel and kissed the tip of her nose, and Dani blinked back tears of gratitude. "Drake, you really don't have to. He's going to be mad, but I stand a better chance of trying to reason with him than you do. I'll just tell him we had too much wine and fell asleep. He doesn't have to know anything else happened . . ." Her voice trailed off, and she demurely lowered her lashes as memories flooded back of the wonderful lovemaking they had shared. It had been like a dream . . . a dream she knew she wanted to relive over and over again, and no matter what her father did, that dream could not be taken away.

Drake gripped her shoulders tightly, and with eyes steady, unwavering, he tersely declared, "Dani, I've never felt this way about a woman before. I care for you. A great deal. Maybe it's love. Maybe not. Time will tell. A lot of time. I'm not ready to commit myself to marriage just yet, but if that's what your father demands, if he wants me to marry you to protect your good name, then I will."

Dani stiffened ever so slightly, knew he was merely being honest and acknowledged she should be grateful, yet could not help feeling she was being patronized. "Thank you, Drake," she responded coolly, a defined edge to her voice, "but I want more out of life than a husband who considers marrying me a favor!"

She turned away angrily, but Drake caught her, spun her around. "Dani, you're taking it the wrong way—"

"Just take me home, if you insist on being so gallant," she snapped, jerking from his grasp. "I don't think this is the time for you to propose marriage, do you?

"And besides"—she glared up at him, red dots of rage sparkling in cinnamon eyes—"I want you to remember you don't owe me anything. Last night happened because we both wanted it to. You didn't seduce me, or cajole me. It was mutual. It was good, and it was nice, and we enjoyed it, but that's as far as it goes, because it doesn't mean that we now share the almighty, grandiose, once-in-a-lifetime kind of love for each other that the poets write about, that leads to marriage, and children, and a lifetime together. We don't owe each other a damn thing just because we fell asleep afterward and now everyone will know we spent a night together. It does not mean that you are obligated to marry me, and it damn sure doesn't mean I have to marry you!"

She paused, took a deep breath and let it out with disgust. "Have I made myself clear?"

Drake, by then, was also angry. "Yes, I'd say you've made yourself perfectly clear, Dani. Now will you allow me the dignity of being a gentleman and escort you home?''

"Of course.'' She turned away to finish dressing.

Drake slammed out of the apartment, swearing beneath his breath. Any other woman would have been screaming for a wedding ring by now, but not Dani. She was being as casual about the whole thing as a man might be, as though it were nothing to be upset about. Had she not been a virgin and instead a sophisticated woman of the world with many lovers in her past, he might have better understood her attitude. As it was, he was completely baffled. Dani was young and inexperienced. They were both in a great deal of trouble because of what had happened. The Coltranes were highly respected people. To have their daughter stay out all night with a man was unthinkable, and they were, understandably, probably crazy with worry by now. The thing to do was face them, deal with whatever awaited, and later hope there would be time to mend things with Dani.

Suddenly, Drake's world had turned upside down, and he was certain of only one thing for the moment—he did not want to lose Dani because, he mused with a grin despite the tension of the situation, they just might actually share that "almighty, grandiose, once-in-a-lifetime" kind of love she had been talking about.

He was damn well going to find out!

Chapter Nineteen

IN the nearly twenty-nine years she had known Travis Coltrane, Kitty had seen him quite angry on occasion. She had seen men quake in their boots and turn and run at just a threatening glare from those steel-gray eyes. She had also seen his rage erupt and propel him to kill. She had witnessed him stomping to death the traitorous Nathan Wright, who had just murdered her father in cold blood, had heard how Travis also coldly killed that fiend Luke Tate, who had caused so much anguish in their lives.

Yes, Kitty acknowledged as she stared quietly at Travis from the doorway of his study, he could be provoked to mayhem, for his temper and spirit were legend.

But, with a tremble of dread, she knew without a doubt she had never seen him this mad.

Travis stood behind his massive oak desk, staring out the window toward the street in front of the mansion. He had, she speculated, probably been alternating his present vigil with pacing the floor ever since two A.M.—the hour he had gotten out of bed after lying awake since midnight, anxiously waiting for Dani to come home.

The clock above the mantel chimed to announce the time was three-quarters past the hour . . . almost nine o'clock. Travis glanced up at the clock irritably, then slammed his fist against the windowsill. "Goddammit, where is she?" He whirled around to face Kitty and raged, "Enough of this! I'm either going after that Russian womanizer or you'd better notify the gendarmes to lock him up to keep me from killing him when I do get my hands on him!"

Kitty did not wither before his fury and never had. Calmly she told him, "You'll do neither, Travis. If you go looking for Dani, she'll be humiliated and never forgive you. If you notify the police, it will be all over Paris by noon."

He looked at her incredulously and threw up his arms. "Well, just what do you propose to do, woman? She's been out all night long, for god's sake, with a man who's got a reputation for being a goddamn wolf, and you think we're supposed to just sit here and wait for her to come strolling in as if nothing has happened?"

"Maybe nothing has."

Travis yelped at that. "Are you crazy? Do you really believe that?"

Kitty could not help smiling. "Don't judge every man by yourself, dear. We all know in your wilder days no girl came home pure and innocent after a night with you."

Travis grunted. "That's not funny, Kitty, and I'm in no mood for your sarcasm." He turned back to his vigil at the window. "If she isn't here by nine, either I go looking for her, or we call the police. And believe me," he added ominously, "Drakar better pray the gendarmes get to him before I do."

Kitty sighed, walked to the sideboard, and poured another cup of coffee from the silver service. "Travis, I agree with you that Dani shouldn't have stayed out all night like this. I'm not defending her, but I do think we have to remember she's a grown woman, and—"

"And she's my daughter and lives under my goddamn roof!" Travis yelled, turning to stare at her with eyes bulging, the veins standing out on his forehead and neck. He was starting to shake.

Kitty saw the way he looked so flushed and at once put down her coffee and rushed to his side. "Now you listen to me," she ordered, placing her hands on his trembling shoulders. Reluctantly, he allowed her to guide him to sit down behind his desk.

"Travis Coltrane," she scolded, "you're not a young man anymore, and that temper of yours could bring on a heart attack. You've no business letting yourself lose control and get upset this way. Now I'm plenty angry myself, because there's no excuse for Dani doing something like this and worrying us to death, not to mention what this will do to her reputation if it gets out, but there's not a thing we can do about it for the moment. If there was a possibility Dani was hurt, I'd have agreed to search for her hours ago, but we both know if anything like that had happened, Drakar would have notified us, and he hasn't, so we know he's with her and that she's all right. We just have to wait."

"Not much longer, dammit," Travis warned. He pointed to the liquor cabinet. "I need a brandy."

Kitty did not argue that it was an early hour for a drink, because she felt she could use one herself. She handed him a bottle and two glasses.

Pouring them each a hefty drink, he grumbled, "Hell, we didn't need this on top of Colt's thunderbolt last night."

Kitty once more fought back the tears that had been just below the surface ever since Colt had announced he and Lily were going to get married. "I still can't believe it," she whispered brokenly. "I know he's a grown man, and it's probably time he married and settled down, but there's just something about that girl I don't like. I keep telling myself it's none of my business. He certainly has the right to live his life the way he wants and to choose who he wants to marry, but I just have this sick feeling that something about it isn't right."

Travis downed his drink in one gulp, then gave a disgruntled snort. "He doesn't know a damn thing about her.

Neither do we. That boy ought to know by now that he's capable of pulling some pretty damn stupid stunts and making some ridiculous decisions. Hell, it's only been a little over a year that he almost lost his fortune and Dani's by falling for that disgusting scheme of Gavin Mason's.

"And what about that Bowden girl back home?" he raved on as bitter memories came rushing back. "Some old busybody finally wrote to you about that little scandal, how that girl came home after spending the night with Colt, and her family was as upset about that as we are right now, only that girl was in such a daze she walked right into the middle of a bank robbery and got herself shot, and then Colt went out and nearly got himself killed tracking down and shooting the bastards responsible."

Kitty quickly came to Colt's defense. "That's not exactly fair, Travis. I talked to Colt about it and heard his side of the story. Charlene showed up at the ranch that night without him knowing she was coming. He tried to get her to leave, but she didn't, and. . . . " Her voice trailed off momentarily, but then anger took over and she vehemently declared, "It wasn't fair for Colt to be made to look like a scoundrel just because he didn't want to marry her after she'd set him up like that. That was her plan—to get him to take her to bed, keep her out all night, so he'd have no choice but to marry her so she wouldn't be disgraced. He wouldn't be tricked like that. I'm sorry that poor girl is dead, but it wasn't Colt's fault. Any of it."

Travis had been staring at her thoughtfully as she spoke, and when she had finished, he quietly asked, "Do you think that's what Dani has done? Arranged to stay out all night with Drakar so he'll feel obligated to marry her?"

Emerald eyes flashed with fire. "Certainly not! And don't you dare suggest such a thing."

Travis smiled. Kitty was even more beautiful when she
was angry, and if it weren't for the turmoil of the moment, young man or not, he knew he'd whisk her away
upstairs for the love and splendor he could never get
enough of in her arms. Instead, he said, "All right. I
suppose I agree with that. But what about Colt? What
kind of trick do you think Lily has used to get him to
agree to marry her? He tried to sound enthusiastic about
it, but I know my son, and he was about as happy about
the idea of marrying that woman as we are. Maybe she
slipped into his bedroom and tried to use the same scheme
as Charlene Bowden."

Kitty shook her head worriedly. "We don't dare suggest such a thing."

Travis emitted another grunt. "You might not dare, but
I damn well do, and as soon as this mess with Dani is
resolved, you can bet I *will* have a little talk with that
young man, and I don't care how grown up he is. . . ."
His eyes suddenly locked with Kitty's at the sound of the
front door opening.

At once, he was on his feet and starting around the
desk, but Kitty moved quickly to block his way. Placing
her hands against his heaving chest, she pleaded, "Travis,
don't lose your temper. Please give her a chance to explain."

Travis did not reply but gently pushed her aside. He
rushed across the room and out the door with her following close behind.

Dani and Drake were standing in the foyer. Dani's eyes
were wide with apprehension and also defiance, while
Drake stood rigidly by her side, face expressionless but
with the defensive demeanor of one who expects the worst
to happen at any second.

Travis halted several feet away, felt Kitty's cautioning
hand on his arm and acknowledged silently it was best
not to get too close, too soon. He stared from one to the
other in condemnation and anger.

Dani, cheeks slightly pale, cleared her throat, lifted her chin with all the dignity she could muster for the moment and began. "Poppa, Kitty. I'm sorry I've caused you to worry, I really am, but it was all an accident. We had a nice dinner, but we just ate too much and drank too much, and then fell asleep." She forced a helpless little shrug, beseechingly added, "Can you forgive us?"

Travis's teeth ground together so tightly his jaw ached with the same intensity he was feeling in his fists, which were knotted and held against his side as he struggled to keep from lunging forward and pounding them into Drakar's insolent face. Struggling to speak around the constricting anger in his throat, he growled, "And just where did you fall asleep, young lady? In the restaurant you said you had to rush to get to because you had reservations?"

Dani's lips moved wordlessly, nervously. She hated lying this way, but knew she had to for the truth could result in disaster.

"Go ahead!" Travis roared, feeling what self-control he had left slipping away. "Tell me some more lies."

Kitty stepped forward, fearful of what Travis might do. "Please . . ." she whispered nervously.

Drake knew he could remain silent no longer, had to at least attempt to bring the matter under control. "Mr. Coltrane, we were at my apartment," he admitted tonelessly. "I'm sorry Dani lied to you, but she knew if she told you we were going there, you wouldn't like it. All we wanted was to have a quiet little dinner, the two of us. We didn't intend for any of this to happen."

"Then she shouldn't have gone, should she?" Travis challenged. "If she had to lie, then she knew it was wrong, and she shouldn't have gone. Now look what's happened! Her reputation is ruined. You've brought shame on this household."

At that, Dani cried indignantly, "You've no right to make judgments like that, Poppa. Just because I stayed out all night doesn't shame the name of Coltrane. You can believe what you want to about what did or didn't happen last night. And so can all the others who hear about it and choose to gossip. I don't care!''

Father's and daughter's eyes met in blazing fury.

"It seems I have to keep reminding you that as long as you put your feet under my table, you will do as I say, and I won't stand for your impudence and shameful, wanton behavior bringing disgrace on this family.''

"Sir, please!'' Drake dared to interrupt, not knowing exactly what to say but knowing he had to do something besides stand idly by. He decided maybe the only way out was to lie. "Nothing happened. Believe me. It happened just as Dani said. I agree that it looks bad, but no one has to know.''

"Get out! Get out of my house!'' Travis shouted.

Drake was as tall as Travis, and as big, and he had yet to wither before any man, whether right or wrong. He did not flinch and stood his ground, willing to take the consequences of doing so. "Sir, I wish you'd listen to reason. There's no need for all this.''

"I told you to get out, Drakar, before I kill you with my bare hands!''

Drake met Travis's threatening glare. "Very well, sir. As you wish. But I want you to know I have the utmost respect for your daughter, and I am truly sorry for all of this. Neither Dani nor I intended to upset you or Mrs. Coltrane.''

Kitty interceded to plead, "Just go, Drakar. Now. Please.''

Drake backed toward the door, looked at Dani with pain and longing, murmured, "I'll be in touch—''

"Goddammit, man!'' Travis roared as Kitty and Dani struggled to hold him back. He shook his fists and yelled, "You try to see my daughter again, and so help me, I'll have you run out of Paris on a rail. . . . ''

As soon as the door closed, Dani raced for the stairs. Travis shouted after her, demanding that she come right back.

Halfway up, she turned to look at him in abject misery, tears streaming down her cheeks. "No, Poppa, I won't . . . because there's no point in our trying to talk about this. I love you more than you'll ever know, and I'm truly sorry that I hurt you. But it's time you realized that I've got to live my own life. I can't be concerned with other people's opinions and judgments. I'm sorry I lied to you, but you gave me no choice."

She turned and ran on up the stairs and disappeared, heart-wrenching sobs echoing in the stillness.

When Dani reached her room, she quickly closed the door and locked it, then threw herself across the bed. She commanded herself to stop crying as she lay with face pressed against the pillow. She was determined not to react like the child her father thought she was. She was a woman, by god, a grown woman. To hell with the moralists and busybodies so eager to judge. What she and Drake had done was not a sin so dastardly as to mark her as a wanton trollop. They had desired each other, had responded to that desire by making beautiful love, and it was no one else's business.

She sat up. There was only one thing to do: move out of the house. There was a tiny two-room apartment directly over the shop that had become vacant only a few days before. The starving young artist who had lived there had moved out to journey to the south of France in hopes of nurturing his creativity there. No matter that he departed owing rent and leaving a mess. It could easily be cleaned, and she would enjoy decorating it to her own taste. Poppa wasn't going to like it, but there was nothing he could do. Maybe, she reflected sadly, he was trying to treat her like a little girl in subconscious hope of going back in time to those tender years when she was a little girl . . . and he had not been with her to enjoy them as a father should. It was sad, but it was too late, and Dani knew he would have to bear the regrets of the past along with her. Nothing could undo what was done, and it was time to get on with both their lives.

She got up and began to walk about the room, looking at the furnishings and deciding she would take nothing except her clothes. It would be no problem to find furniture for the small apartment.

She passed the window, glanced out, and angrily saw that Lily was running down the sidewalk after Drake.

Drake reached to open the gate just as Lily caught up with him. Lost in his own misery, he had not heard her call out as she ran after him down the walk. Now he looked at her in annoyance and impatiently demanded, "What do you want?" He didn't feel like talking to anyone.

Lily made her voice thickly sympathetic. "I couldn't help hearing Mr. Coltrane shouting. I'm so sorry, Drakar. I don't think you were treated fairly at all. It's an unfortunate situation, but—"

He raised an eyebrow, brusquely informed her, "It isn't your problem, Miss Deauneve."

He moved to open the gate, but she reached out to boldly clutch his arm. "Wait, please . . . "

"I appreciate your concern, but I think it's best I be on my way. If you overheard Mr. Coltrane, you undoubtedly heard him order me to leave."

"He's a snob. Just like his wife. They think nobody is good enough for their precious son and daughter."

Drake raised an eyebrow. "Oh, really? And what makes you say that? I don't think their anger with me has anything to do with snobbery."

Lily turned to glance back toward the house, as though fearful they would be seen together. Then she gave him a warm look and whispered, "Perhaps we could go somewhere for tea and I could tell you all about it. I think we both need to share our thoughts about this miserable family."

Drake felt his lips twitching with the impulse to laugh. It was going to be easier than he thought, but right now he had other things on his mind. "I'd like that, Miss

Deauneve, but I'm afraid I have plans for the moment. I'll be in touch with you, I promise." He caressed her fingertips in a suggestive gesture that she understood quite clearly.

She stepped back, smiled triumphantly. "Of course. I'll be waiting."

She watched him get in his carriage and move on down the street, then turned back to the house and frowned. Damn snobs. How dare they treat her like they did last night when Colt raised his champagne glass after dinner and asked that they toast their betrothal? They had just looked at each other like they'd had water thrown in their faces. Kitty had made a little choking sound and Colt had looked like a shameful little boy. Then Mr. Coltrane, that imperious bastard, had said it was a shock, and they needed time to think about it.

Lily stopped in the middle of the walkway to stamp her feet in exasperation. Colt hadn't said a word, had not spoken up to his father and told him it didn't matter whether it was a shock or not. Oh, no, he just nodded his head and said he understood. Understood what, by god? That his parents had every right to act so rude? Just who in the hell did they think they were, treating her like that?

She turned her head to stare down the street pensively in the direction Drakar had gone. How she wished she had seen him before Colt. The way he'd just looked at her let her know all she needed to know—that he found her desirable. True, he had a reputation with women, but so what? She was different from the others, would know how to manipulate him into marriage like a black widow spider coaxing a new lover into her web.

She pursed her lips thoughtfully. Maybe it wasn't too late, after all. It had been sheer luck that she'd even found out what was going on this morning. She had been sneaking around, hoping to learn what the Coltranes planned to do to try and stop her marriage from taking place. Instead, she'd learned that Dani had not come home last night. She had heard everything, knew that Drakar had been banned from the Coltrane household forever.

Lily also acknowledged the possibility that her own scheme might be in jeopardy. Colt had yielded to his parents last night, said he should have known they would be surprised by such a sudden announcement and they could celebrate later. Then when she'd gotten him alone and told him how humiliated she felt, he defended his parents. Obviously he was just a mamma's boy, and now she feared that if Kitty Coltrane tried hard enough, she could talk her son out of getting married.

It was one thing, Lily fretted, to make Colt feel obligated to marry her after waking to find her in his bed . . . and another to expect those feelings of guilt to carry over into the harsh reality of an actual wedding.

Especially, she bitterly realized, when it looked as though Dani could spend the night with a man and not feel she had to marry him in order to preserve her honor. Dammit, Colt just might look at his sister and have second thoughts about his own predicament.

Lily knew she had to have a backup plan . . . and the answer just might be Drakar.

Maybe Drakar was even richer than Colt.

Maybe, she thought as a warmth spread through her loins, he would be as good a lover as Colt.

She intended to find out . . . on both counts.

Chapter Twenty

DANI took one last look around the room. She had taken only a few of her personal belongings, and most of her clothes. Space was going to be limited in her new home. Two large trunks stood by the door. She only hoped there would be room for what she had packed in those. She took a deep breath, smiled bravely to herself. It was going to be *her* home, no matter how tiny and cramped. The feeling of impending freedom and independence was exhilarating. She couldn't wait to start really living for what she felt was truly the first time in her life.

Lurline had brought her tea and soup at noon, relating what was going on in the rest of the household. Monsieur Coltrane, she confided, had only just left for his office at the embassy, after spending most of the morning behind the closed doors of his study talking with Madame Coltrane. Lurline did not know what they had been talking about, but, with her usual candor, said it had to have something to do with either Dani staying out all night or Colt announcing his engagement to Mademoiselle Lily. Either way, Lurline said tension was spread over the entire house like a giant umbrella, and she, for one, would be glad when it passed. Colt, she reported, had left the house sometime before daylight, one of the coachmen had told her, and had only just returned. Her eyes glittered excitedly as she told how he had passed right by Mademoiselle Lily, not stopping to talk to her.

"She's fit to be tied, she is, stamping her feet and cursing like a hooligan. She's been a little hellcat all day, anyway, storming about and complaining because he wasn't home and that it looked to her like everyone else was avoiding her."

Listening to Lurline had only served to make Dani all the more anxious to leave. A glance at the mantel clock told her she had to be leaving if she wanted to be even a little bit settled in her new home by bedtime.

She rang for Lurline, then asked that one of the coachmen bring a carriage around to the front and to send someone up for her trunks.

Lurline nodded but hung back to express her feelings once more about Dani's decision to move out. "I'm going to worry about you, mademoiselle, living off by yourself, and you know your father isn't going to like it one little bit."

Dani assured her once again that she would be fine, and, yes, she knew Poppa wouldn't approve, and that was another reason she wanted to be on her way before he returned—to avoid another scene. "Now will you please hurry and do as I ask, Lurline? I really want to leave now."

Lurline obeyed, shaking her head worriedly.

Dani went to where she'd laid out her cape, then groaned aloud at the sound of Colt's voice calling to her through the closed door.

"Come on, Dani, open up. I know you're in there, and we've got to talk."

She realized he did not sound angry, merely impatient. She opened the door and promptly informed him, "I don't want to argue with you, Colt. I've got enough problems of my own without fussing with you." She did not invite him in.

"I don't want to argue either, Dani. I just want to talk to you for a minute." He ran his fingers through his hair absently, as though stalling to get his thoughts, his words, in order. Then he saw her trunks and exclaimed, "What's all this? Where are you going?"

She told him, and his reaction was to laugh. "You know Poppa won't allow that."

Dani did not intend to waste time justifying herself. "He has no choice! Now please," she urged impatiently, "tell me what you want. I want to be out of here before he comes home. I'm tired of confrontations."

He looked at her for a few seconds in contemplative silence, then shrugged. "I don't know, really. Things are just turned upside down all of a sudden. I guess you've heard by now that they didn't exactly jump with joy when I told them about me and Lily getting married."

"I didn't expect them to. You hardly know her. Besides," she dared to add, "they probably feel as I do— that you aren't going to be happy with her, and that you're making a mistake."

His eyes narrowed. "I think that's my business."

Dani was exasperated. This was all a waste of time— for both of them. "I agree with you," she conceded, "so please don't involve me in it. If you came here seeking my approval, you won't get it, Colt. I don't see any point in our talking further."

She moved to close the door, but he slammed his hand against it. "Well, I do. Lily says she tried to talk to you yesterday, to ask for your blessings and help with planning a wedding and that you blew up at her and even threw water in her face. I'd like to hear your side of the story."

"Why? You won't believe anything I have to say."

"You never did like her, did you?"

"I tried," Dani replied honestly. "I really tried, but quite frankly, Colt, Lily is one of the most unpleasant people I've ever met."

"Is that why you threw water in her face? That was pretty low of you, Dani. After all, she *is* a guest in this house, and she's also going to be a member of the family soon."

"I threw water in her face because she was standing right where you are, having a tantrum for the whole world to hear. It got her away from my door," she pointed out, then said icily, "Is that what it's going to take to get rid of you?"

Colt sucked in his breath, let it out slowly, waging a battle within himself to control the rage that was about to erupt at any second. "Don't try it with me, Dani." Then, with a contemptuous sneer, he said, "You haven't changed a bit. You're still a spoiled brat and don't give a damn about anybody but yourself."

She knew he was only taking out his own frustrations on her, but dear Lord, she was losing all patience. "It'd really be best if you'd leave, Colt. You're making me very angry."

"What are you going to do?" He pointed to the tiny scar at the corner of his angrily bulging eyes. "Claw my face like the last time you had one of your little fits? Grow up, Dani. Stop acting like a little bitch!"

Dani gasped, lifted her hand to slap him as fury washed over her in a tidal wave, but her arm froze in midair as she saw the despair in his eyes, mirrored amid the rage. He was her brother, she reminded herself, and she loved him, and if inflicting his pain upon her somehow softened his own, then so be it. Nothing would be accomplished by inflicting a scar on his heart to go with the one she regretted putting on his face as a child.

"Please," she whispered raggedly, blinking back the tears. "Let me pass, Colt. I think we've both said things we'll regret later."

He stared down at her, his own eyes becoming moist as the anger began to quickly fade in the wake of her surrender.

Colt stepped aside, head down. Goddammit, why did it have to be this way, he cursed himself. Why had he even come here to talk to her in the first place? But he knew the answer to that. Lily had insisted. She'd said it was bad enough he hadn't stood up to his parents the

night before. The least he could do, she said, was to reprimand his sister for assaulting her. He'd promised to
talk to Dani, to see if he could smooth things over, because he didn't like the way so much friction was devel-
oping in the family.

"Dani! Colt! What's going on here?"

They both looked up from their respective states of despair as Kitty rushed into the room, emerald eyes steaming, cheeks red. "Everyone in the house can hear you
yelling at each other."

Her gaze fell on the trunks by the door, and she raised
her eyes slowly, suspiciously, to challenge Dani. "What
is all this about? Where do you think you're going?"

Dani wondered if the nightmare was ever going to end.
"I'm moving out, Kitty. To an apartment over my shop.
I think you have to agree that I'll never be able to live
my life the way I want to as long as I stay here."

Kitty was horrified. "How can you hurt your father this
way after what you did last night? You aren't thinking of
anyone but yourself!"

Dani met her icy, accusing stare. "I don't want to in-
tentionally hurt anyone."

"You hurt your father last night," Kitty repeated.

"That's right," Dani conceded, "I did . . . but I
never meant to. It was an accident, as I tried to explain."

"You're going to hurt him worse by doing this," Kitty
warned.

"Wait a minute," Colt suddenly interrupted, looking
from one to the other in confusion. "What's all this
about? What are you two talking about?"

Dani and Kitty looked at each other, neither knowing
what to say for the moment.

Colt prodded impatiently, "Well?"

Dani decided there was no point in evading the issue.
Colt would hear about it sooner or later. She started to
speak, then saw the servant coming after her trunks,
waited until he removed them while Kitty watched re-

provingly. When he was gone, she repeated her side of the story.

When she had finished, Colt tersely asked, "And now what happens?"

Dani was puzzled. "I don't know what you mean. It's unfortunate, and I'm sorry everyone got upset, but what's done is done."

Colt spoke as though he were communicating with a child. "Little sister, you stayed out all night with a man. Now I think the decent, honorable thing for him to do is marry you and salvage what's left of your good name, because when this gets out, as it no doubt will, no man from a decent family is going to want you for his wife."

Dani could not help laughing at what she considered nonsense. "Oh, Colt, really! I never thought I'd hear you make such a priggish statement. Do you really think I'd marry solely in hopes people would think me less disreputable for staying out all night with a man?" She swung her head briskly from side to side. "No, big brother, I'll not toss aside all my plans for the future just to satisfy the puritans!"

Kitty waved her arms, demanded silence. "Enough! This isn't doing anyone any good, and I'm sure the servants have heard enough to give them fodder for gossip for the next six months."

Colt said nothing, merely stared at Dani thoughtfully, eyes narrowed, lips pressed tightly together.

Suddenly Dani embraced him, then stood back to softly plead, "Don't think me awful, Colt. I'm only doing what I think is best for me."

He nodded, turned, and walked away. He had many thoughts to sort out within himself, for many questions were burning in his brain . . . questions about his own future which had been provoked by Dani's dogmatic little speech.

Dani and Kitty watched him go, and when he was far enough away so as not to hear, Kitty quietly confided, "He told us last night he wants to marry Lily."

"I know."

Kitty looked at her curiously.

Dani quickly related everything about Colt's visit to her shop and then, later, the unpleasant scene with Lily . . . but once again she kept silent about what Lurline had divulged.

Kitty shuddered with misery and sadly predicted, "He'll never be happy with that girl."

Dani was quick to agree. "I'm afraid not, but, as he said, it's his business." She walked back into the room, picked up her handbag, and announced, "I really have to go now. The carriage is waiting."

She started out the door, but Kitty cried, "Wait."

Reluctantly, but respectfully, she turned, wondering if she would ever be able to get away.

Kitty's green eyes were like a misty sea at ebb tide, painful reflections of blighted hopes. "Remember, Dani, this is your home, and you're welcome anytime."

Dani bit down on her lip, then, with a surge of love, threw herself into Kitty's arms. They embraced tightly, emotionally. "Believe me," she repeated emphatically, "I really didn't mean to hurt anyone."

Kitty nodded, forced what she hoped was a reassuring smile to her trembling lips. "I know you didn't, Dani, and you probably won't believe me, but I do know what you're going through. You're like me when I was your age, wanting only to be myself but condemned each time I didn't conform to what was expected of young ladies in those days."

"Then tell me, Kitty," Dani dared to ask. "Do you think I'm terrible not to expect, or want, Drake to marry me just because of last night?"

Kitty smiled. "I agree with you that you must do what you feel is right for you."

Dani felt a wave of love and gratitude. "Will you try to make Poppa understand how it is?"

Kitty nodded reassuringly, gave her a gentle push. "You'd better run along. He'll be home soon, and I've had all the scenes I can stand for one day."

* * *

Lily was cramped and sore from being in the same position for so long, kneeling in her favorite spying place behind the plants in the alcove. She had hurried there after Colt had stalked into his room, slamming and locking the door behind him, suspecting that he would confront Dani as soon as he collected his thoughts.

Her hunch was right, and now she knew she had to move fast or she'd never be able to manipulate Colt into marriage . . . not after he had time to think about how his sister was in a similar situation but felt no obligation to marry for honor's sake. It was even more thought-provoking because the family, and probably the servants, and no doubt, soon, all of Paris's elite, would hear about Dani's indiscretion. So far, no one was aware of hers.

She waited until Kitty walked away, then moved from concealment and hurried to knock softly on Colt's door.

"Go away. I don't want to talk to anybody," he responded irritably.

"It's me," she called petulantly. "The least you can do is talk to me when it seems no one else in this house wants to."

She heard an exaggerated sigh, the sound of unspirited footsteps, then he opened the door and wearily greeted her. "Lily, quite frankly I'm sick of your nagging . . ."

Her lips parted to speak, but he shook his head, waved his hands in protest. "No more. I mean it. I apologize if my family has hurt your feelings, but I'm not responsible for their actions, and I don't want to hear any more about it. Now please let me get some rest before dinner. We'll talk later."

Not about to be dismissed, she quickly brushed by him to go and position herself in the middle of the room. With arms folded across her bosom, she defiantly declared, "We're going to talk now, Colt, and decide on a wedding date. I don't intend to go on like this, not after the scandal your sister has caused."

He was not surprised that she'd heard. How could it be avoided? He closed the door, walked over and sat down in the leather chair by the window. With no warmth or enthusiasm whatsoever, he said, "Go ahead. Talk."

Lily could not help thinking how handsome he was— so appealing with his white silk shirt partially unbuttoned to reveal a thick, curling mass of dark hair upon his broad, rock-hard chest. When he was smiling, which she had not seen him do of late, his gray eyes sparkled with flecks of blue, crinkling at the corners to give him almost a little-boy look.

Colt was, without a doubt, every bit as good-looking as Drakar, and while she'd never had the pleasure of making love with the attractive Russian, she knew it would be difficult to surpass the pleasure she had known with Colt. Comparatively speaking, however, she would be willing to settle for either but was smart enough to know it was best to go with what she already had.

Hesitantly, she began. "I know all about how Dani stayed out with Drakar last night, ruined her good name. I won't let that happen to me, Colt."

He frowned, bluntly pointed out, "No one knows about you spending the night with me, Lily."

Lily managed to retain her composure but inside she was becoming frightened that her scheme might be failing. "I realize that," she admitted, "but what will happen to me if you don't marry me? Am I supposed to trick a man into thinking I'm a virgin, only to find out differently on our wedding night? Do you think he'd still want me for his wife after he realized I'd deceived him?"

Colt leaned his head on the back of the chair, closed his eyes as though by so doing he could wish away all the misery that had suddenly assailed his life.

With no warmth, she said almost accusingly, "I love you, Colt. I thought you loved me."

"I never said I loved you."

She made her lower lip tremble. "You made me think you did. You made me think you cared."

"I did, and I do, but I sure as hell never gave you any cause to think I was of a notion to get married anytime soon." He paused, watching the tears spill from her eyes and thinking once more how he'd caused a lot of trouble by not keeping his pants on.

"I just can't help wondering if maybe we're making a mistake, Lily. We don't really know each other, and I don't think I'm ready to settle down with one woman."

Her heart flip-flopped with fear. "But what about me and my future?" Her voice bordered on hysteria. "What decent man will want me?"

Colt dreaded her reaction but dared to speak his mind. "Dani doesn't seem too worried about that situation. Maybe times are changing, Lily. Maybe it no longer matters to a man what the woman he loves did in her past." Gently, he added, "I know if I truly loved you the way I hope one day to love the woman I want to marry, it wouldn't make a difference whether you were a virgin or not."

Lily knew in that instant that it was going to be difficult, if not impossible, to maneuver Colt to the altar purely out of a sense of duty. Crossing to where he sat, Lily leaned close enough for him to feel her furious breath upon his face.

"Well, let me tell you something, Mr. High-and-Mighty, I'm not about to have my future ruined because of you. You seduced me and you'll marry me!"

Colt laughed, gently pushed her back as he stood. "That's a lie, and you know it. You wanted it as much as I did."

"That's not what your mommy and daddy will believe when I get through talking to them."

He blinked in disbelief as he saw the evil, sneering look on her face. "What did you say?" he hoarsely demanded.

She stood, hands on hips, as she eyed him haughtily. "You heard me. I'll go to your parents and tell them how you brought me in here and seduced me in your own bed, practically right under their noses. How do you think they'll like hearing that about their baby boy?''

Colt promptly snarled, ''Not a goddamn bit, and you know it.''

''Well, maybe they won't have to know about it. I should think they'd be happier having a wedding than a lawsuit—which will happen when my uncle hears about this.''

Colt had never wanted to hit anyone so damn bad in his whole life, man or woman. ''That's blackmail, Lily.''

Flippantly, she cooed, ''So? You leave me no choice. I'm not a wanton little whore like your sister. I have pride. She's probably moving out to start her own bordello, anyway,'' she added with a nasty giggle.

Colt took a menacing step forward. ''Don't push me, Lily. I won't listen to you talk about my sister that way.''

She decided it was time to change her approach and ran to fling her arms about his neck and press close. ''Please don't hate me, Colt,'' she said tearfully. ''I just love you and want to be your wife. We're going to be so happy. I promise. You'll see that this was all for the best . . . '' She lifted her lips for an expected kiss.

Colt roughly unfastened her arms, disgust mingling with fury as he flung her away from him. ''Dani was right when she said you were the most unpleasant person she'd ever met. I wish I'd seen through you long ago.''

Lily stumbled, fell backward to sprawl into a chair. She began to cry—genuine tears. ''I'll go to your parents. I swear I will.''

''No you won't.'' He struggled to keep his voice down, because, by god, he felt like screaming out at her for all the heavens to hear. ''I won't hurt them any more. I'll marry you, goddammit, but we'll do it quickly, with no fanfare, no frills. Then we're moving back to America and live on the ranch, where you'll try to learn how to be a decent wife.''

Lily suppressed a triumphant cry. Instead, she made herself sound quite plaintive and sincere. ''Colt, you might be angry with me now, darling, but you know it's not fair for you to insinuate I'd ever be anything but a decent wife for you.''

Colt sucked in his breath, cursed himself for nearly losing control. After all, up to this point, he had been crazy about her. They'd enjoyed some good times together, in bed and out, and he had to admit he'd been toying with the idea of a future with her somewhere down the road. ''All right, I'm sorry,'' he said contritely.

She lowered her face to hands which she made quiver, murmured brokenly, ''Maybe I should just leave and go back home.'' She paused to sniff, choke a bit on a sob. ''I love you, but if you don't love me, and you don't want to marry me, then I'll just get out of your life.''

When he did not immediately respond, she dared to peer fearfully up at him between her fingers, and by then the quivering was not false. Was he going to take her up on her mock-offer? Had she sounded *that* convincing?

Colt was staring out the window, shoulders slumped in defeat, eyes miserable and downcast. With all the finality of a coffin lid closing, he whispered, ''I'll marry you, Lily. And we'll make the best of it. I don't love you,'' he bluntly said, turning to stare at her to hopefully make her somehow see that he truly meant every word, ''but I'll try to do everything I can to make you happy.''

Lily leaped to her feet and threw her arms around his neck once more, and this time he did not push her away but neither did he yield.

''Oh, Colt, I'll make you love me. I swear I will.''

Colt held her, his embrace as cold as his heart.

Chapter Twenty-one

DANI awoke with a smile on her lips, for the reality of her dream dawned on her as clearly as the sunlight streaming through the window. She was free!

Happily, she got out of bed to pad about the tiny rooms for the closer inspection she'd been too weary to make the night before. A good cleaning was surely needed, but she could close the shop early if there were no customers and take care of that this afternoon. There was little furniture—a cot and chair in what was supposed to be the bedroom, and a table and chair and small wood stove in the other room.

Well, that would change drastically, she thought. She'd seen a lovely mahogany spool bed in an antique furniture shop last week that would match nicely with a cherry-wood armoire she'd fancied at yet another store. There were some decorative pieces downstairs that would brighten up the place, and, of course, she could make some curtains. The kitchen was another matter. It would take a bit of planning there, but she had time, all the time in the world, and Drake would probably be glad to help.

Drake.

She felt an instant wave of sadness. What should have been beautiful had so needlessly turned into a nightmare. But maybe it was all for the best, because now she had what she'd wanted for a long time—to be on her own. Still, it was regretable that Poppa had to be hurt.

As for Drake, well, that was another matter. Perhaps she'd overreacted yesterday morning when he nobly offered marriage in an attempt to redeem them both. He was being a gentleman, that's all, and she'd become nearly hysterical from shock at their predicament. She would just explain that to him, apologize for being so unpleasant. Maybe inviting him over for a cozy dinner in her apartment would smooth things over.

Then again, maybe it was time to just get away for a while, to travel as Kitty had urged. It would give everyone time to get their thoughts in perspective.

She took a cup of tea, and went downstairs to the shop. Walking around, she gazed thoughtfully at her collection of merchandise. The offering was meager. The truly fine objets d'art had been bought in the first few days after the grand opening. All too soon, it seemed that the only reason people came into the shop was to see the paintings of the renowned Monaco Find, but even interest in those was starting to wane, as she had known it would eventually. She resolved that something had to be done. She would not give people reason to snicker behind her back, to think of her as merely a dilettante who had quickly become bored with the responsibilities of running her own business; Dani was fiercely determined to be a respected businesswoman.

As she stood at the window staring out at the inhabitants of Upper Montmartre as they began their day, she lifted her cup to sip the last of the tea, and that was when the idea came to her. The cup she held was ordinary, but if she could offer truly exquisite china, like the coveted Flora Danica of the Royal Copenhagen factory in Denmark, then her shop would be considered truly unique. It was said that the first dinner service of Flora Danica was made between 1790 and 1802 for Catherine the Great of Russia, consisting of one hundred place settings with 1,802 pieces in all. When the Danish Princess Alexandra married the Prince of Wales in 1864, a second set was given as a wedding present.

Dani had become fascinated with the rare porcelain when she came across a book which told how in 1757, Denmark's King Frederik V commissioned a botany professor to do a magnum opus on *flora danica,* titled *Flora of the Danish Kingdom.* The study eventually grew into seventeen volumes, and finally an illustrator named Johann Christoph Bayer was commissioned to work on the china, and over the next eleven years, he decorated by hand most of the first service, eventually ruining his eyesight.

Dani recalled that only last week a customer had asked whether she had among her merchandise anything particularly exquisite, as she wanted something extraordinary for a favored niece's wedding gift. Flora Danica would certainly have been appropriate, and Dani knew if she could arrange to procure and import the famed porcelain from Denmark, she would be touted as the most successful entrepreneur in Paris.

So, she asked herself excitedly, what was stopping her from going to Denmark on her first shopping excursion?

Filled with enthusiasm as the idea took hold, she unlocked the front door, posted the "OPEN" sign in the window, then began to dust and straighten. She hummed softly as she worked and thought how the timing for the trip would be perfect. Tensions would be forgotten within the family, and maybe she needed time away from Drake to come to terms with her feelings for him.

A warm glow suffused her as she thought of his dear and handsome face, recalling those splendorous moments in his arms. He had carried her so gently along to each and every pinnacle of joy, and when, at last, they had leaped together from the ultimate peak, they had become one.

That was what was so frightening—that single nucleus they had experienced for a few precious seconds. Was that love? Was she really falling in love with the gentle, yet awesomely strong Russian? His wit and charm and keen intelligence . . . the expressive blue eyes fringed

with incredibly long and thick lashes . . . his stirringly
sensuous mouth . . . the appealing accent of his native
tongue . . . these all served to make him the most attractive man she had ever encountered.

She wanted to see him again.

She wanted him to make love to her again.

The sound of the bell at the front door annoyingly
brought her out of her pleasurable reverie. Her vexation
was increased by the sight of Cyril Arpel walking into the
shop. He was wearing a tweed overcoat, a bright red scarf
around his neck, and a gray hat which he promptly removed as he greeted her happily. "My, you look lovely
today. You're almost radiant. Are you *that* glad to see
me?" he added teasingly.

If she were truly glowing, she knew why . . . and
wasn't about to divulge such a secret. She disregarded his
bantering. "Bonjour, Cyril. What brings you out so
early?"

Cyril found it hard to pretend joviality when he was
still steaming inside over what he'd seen last night. With
extreme effort, he lightly replied, "Seems that every time
I come by, we're interrupted, so I thought I'd try to visit
early to ask if you'd like to have dinner with me tonight."

Ironically, the doorbell jangled at that precise moment.
Lurline walked in, obviously straining from the weight of
the tapestry bags she carried. Without fanfare, she told
Dani, "Madame Coltrane sent these over." She set the
bags down and stood back, nodding politely to Cyril.

Dani was puzzled. She'd packed everything she wanted
or needed. As she moved to see what was inside the bags,
Lurline said, "She sent some of your books, mademoiselle. And some of the objets d'art from your room."

Dani was impressed with Kitty's thoughtfulness and
said so, adding, "But you tell her it wasn't necessary. I
could have brought them over myself later."

With her usual candor, Lurline brightly observed, "It was probably her way of saying she's not angry and wants you to be happy here."

Dani frowned, not wanting to discuss personal matters in front of Cyril, and she could see he was eagerly taking in each word. "Well, you run along now, and do relay my appreciation."

Lurline moved to the door. "Yes, I'll do that, and Madame said to tell you to please come for a visit soon."

The moment she left, Cyril could not restrain his curiosity. "What's this all about? It sounds as though you've left home." He laughed at what was surely a ludicrous assumption.

Dani picked up the bags, set them to one side. "That's exactly what I've done. I live here now."

Cyril was stunned, and could not resist expressing disapproval. "It's unheard-of for a young lady of your background and breeding to live alone. People will—"

"People can go to hell if they don't like it," Dani snapped rebelliously. "I'm not going to live according to other people's rules, Cyril, and if you think I'm going to stand here and listen to you criticize me, you're crazy."

Cyril shook his head, sighed. "It seems every time I open my mouth I annoy you, Dani. I'm truly sorry."

She was not about to be manipulated into feeling pity for him. "If you'd mind your own business, we'd get along just fine."

He gritted his teeth. He had not come here to have a fight. Softly, he attempted to smooth the friction. "Back to my purpose in being here—I'd like to take you out to dinner tonight." Stepping closer, he gently touched her arm. "Quite frankly, my dear, I'd like time for us to be alone together, without interruptions, and maybe you'd find out I'm not such a despicable person after all."

Dani wearily assured him she found him quite nice when he was not prying into her business.

"Then you'll have dinner with me?" he asked hopefully.

She shook her head, moved away from him. Her plans were to close early, straighten up her apartment, then surprise Drake with a visit to invite him over for dinner tomorrow night. Oh, it was all she could do to keep from singing aloud at the thought of actually being able to prepare an intimate little dinner for the man she might be falling in love with! How wonderful it was to be free! Her dream was truly a reality, and she intended to live it well.

Cyril was watching her closely, could see her mind was elsewhere. "Why not?" he demanded coolly. "What else do you have to do?"

Exasperated, she cried, "Oh, Cyril, why do you make me say such things to you? It's none of your business what I have to do. Please just accept my regrets."

Petulantly, he said, "Well, the least you can do is give me a reason why you don't want to be in my company."

Wearily, she decided there was no harm in telling him. Maybe he would stop badgering her if he realized once and for all she was interested in another man. "I'm going to visit Drake."

He stiffened at once. Drakar . . . Drake. By any other name the man was still a scamp. Broodingly, he looked over Dani's head and beyond to where the painting of the Alexandrovsky Palace was displayed. An idea was rapidly forming. Now that she was living upstairs, it might prove difficult to break in at night, but since he knew she'd be out this evening, what better time to make his move? If he waited any longer, the Russian would have her eating out of his hand . . . and *his* hands would, no doubt, be on the painting. Cyril couldn't let that happen. Returning his attention to Dani, he acquiesced. "Very well. Maybe we can make it another evening. . . ."

"Of course," Dani murmured, knowing all the time she had no intention of going out with him.

He hastened to add, "But don't make it too long. I'm going to be leaving Paris soon, and I probably won't return till spring."

It was Dani's turn to be curious. "Why will you be away so long?"

"The season. I always go to Saint Petersburg for the season."

Dani blinked, not understanding. "What season?"

"Why, the social season, of course. In Saint Petersburg. Officially, it begins on New Year's Day and lasts until the beginning of Lent, but I like to go over early in November. There's so much going on." A dreamy expression took over as he attempted to describe how the aristocracy spent the long winter nights moving through staggering rounds of concerts, balls, banquets, ballets, operas, midnight suppers, and private parties. "Everyone who is anyone is there, and I wouldn't miss it for the world." He could not help sounding boastful.

Dani was obviously envious. "It sounds so exciting."

"I'd love to take you there with me, but I don't suppose that's possible."

She shrugged, then brightened. "I'm thinking of going to Denmark, to visit the Royal Copenhagen factory to see if they'll let me import their Flora Danica porcelain and offer it in my shop."

He shared her enthusiasm. "That would really be unique, Dani. I hope you can arrange it. But it's a shame that we won't be leaving Paris at the same time. I prefer to go by ship, before the rivers freeze, and we sail right around Denmark to enter the Baltic Sea. In fact, the ships usually stop in Copenhagen. I could go with you to the factory, perhaps help make the arrangements."

Dani readily agreed that would've been nice but explained she didn't know just when she could get away. "You're probably leaving much sooner than I."

"Probably." He smiled to himself, not about to admit he intended to get out of Paris as soon as possible once he had the painting in his possession. Drakar would head for Russia the fastest way available, and Cyril hoped Drakar would be gone by the time he got there so he would be free to search for the egg without worrying about the Russian's presence.

A customer wandered in, and Cyril left. He had a lot to do in preparation for the evening, and first on the agenda was a visit to the telegraph office to arrange the bogus message for Drakar. He had toyed with the idea of having it appear to come from Czar Alexander but rejected that plan. As soon as Drakar found out the Czar hadn't sent for him, he'd realize someone wanted him out of Paris, especially when he returned to hear the painting had been stolen. No need to risk that, not when it was easy to conjure up a message from a nonexistent relative, a distant cousin of Drakar's father, that Drakar would never have heard of, who was also interested in restoring honor to the Mikhailonov name. The message would be worded so as to hint that this cousin had information about the Fabergé egg but feared the revolutionaries were on his trail. When Drakar arrived and found no cousin, he could assume his relative was a victim of the radicals still searching for the egg and the money it would bring.

Of course, the telegram would be delivered in the wee, wee hours of the early morning, after Dani would have left his apartment, and if Drakar tried to send a message to her informing her of his sudden call to Russia, Cyril would have a paid ally nearby and ready to sabotage that effort.

He whistled merrily as he made his way to the telegraph office, confident he had thought of everything.

Lily paced about restlessly in her room, chewing on her nails, then yanking them from her mouth angrily, only to repeat the nervous habit a few moments later. She was frightened that Colt was going to renege. Yesterday evening, after promising to go through with their marriage to preserve her honor, he'd resisted her attempts to get him into bed. She had petulantly told him she felt rejected, but he had irritably said that was just too bad . . . he wasn't in the mood. She had left in a huff, but he had not hurried after her as she'd been sure he would. Dinnertime came and she was alone. The elder Coltranes, she was told, were in seclusion for the evening because Monsieur was not feeling well. Lily certainly knew the reason for that, had expected him to have a stroke when he found out his precious baby daughter had moved out of the house. But when she heard that Colt would not be joining her for dinner, she felt her own personal stroke coming on. She hurried up to his room, but he did not respond to her frenzied knocking, and after she lost patience and angrily shouted his name, Kitty had appeared to frostily tell her Colt had gone out for the evening and would she mind not making so much noise? Lily had bit her tongue to keep from sticking it out at the snobby matriarch, and rushed to her room to send for wine and proceeded to get drunk enough to quell the rising fury as she waited up for Colt. But she had fallen asleep, had not heard him come in, and first thing this morning, she had gone to his room only to be told by his maid that he'd already left for the day.

Lily picked up a vase, started to throw it, caught herself and set it back down. She had to get out of that room or she would go crazy. Dammit, what was Colt doing? Where was he spending his time? They needed to talk, to make plans. Most of all, she fumed as she made her way through the quiet house, she needed to get him to an altar before he changed his mind.

There was no one about. Stomach rumbling, she went into the kitchen where Bevette, the day cook, confided that Monsieur and Madame Coltrane had left unexpectedly for a holiday in Chantilly. They had not said when they would be back.

Bevette was happy to have someone to complain to. "No one tells me anything around here till I've already done a day's work. I had lunch ready to go on the table when I found out you were the only one here." She gestured to a sideboard where a cold salmon salad waited. "Do you want to be served in the dining room?" she asked, as though it would be a great imposition.

Lily wrinkled her nose. "I'm not hungry. But tell me, do you know where Monsieur Colt has gone?"

Bevette shook her head.

Lily cursed beneath her breath, started out of the room.

Bevette called out irritably to ask whether they'd be present for dinner. "Maybe I can do for the night chef what no one has had the courtesy to do for me—save him from a lot of unnecessary work if Monsieur Colt isn't going to be here . . . and you aren't going to be hungry," she added testily. She'd never liked the haughty wench anyway.

Lily seized the opportunity to unleash some of her own frustrations. "Don't bother me with your problems, goddammit!" she screamed. "I'm sure you're getting paid for your trouble, you whining old crone."

Bevette's eyes widened, lips parted in hurt and surprise. Monsieur Colt, she thought for the hundredth time since the news had spread through the house, had to be insane to even think about marrying such a shrew.

Just then the back door opened, and Lurline walked in. Looking from one to the other, she hesitantly asked, "Is something wrong?"

"Nothing is wrong, you little twit," Lily snapped, "except that I find myself all alone in this house, and such rudeness doesn't need the added insult of having to listen to the servants griping." With one final glare, she walked out, leaving them staring after her.

Lurline wanted to know what on earth had happened, and Bevette shrugged, said she must be upset about hearing that the Coltranes had left on a holiday after Monsieur Colt had disappeared.

"He hasn't disappeared," Lurline said with a sneer. "He's down at that little bistro on the Rue de Berri, drinking, no doubt, to forget his stupidity in getting mixed up with that little tart. As for the Coltranes leaving, the first I heard about that was when I came back from taking some things to Mademoiselle Dani, but I'm not surprised. I'm afraid Monsieur didn't take Mademoiselle Dani's moving out very well.''

Bevette sighed, said she wasn't going to worry about any of it, and walked over to eat the salmon salad herself.

Lurline decided to help her.

Lily went into Travis's study and helped herself to his liquor cabinet and a bottle of his best brandy, then went into Kitty's elegantly furnished parlor. With a sweeping gaze of envy she knew most of the opulent decor would be hers one day . . . if she became Mrs. John Travis Coltrane, she reminded herself. Oh, where was Colt? And why was he avoiding her? There could only be one reason, and she didn't like thinking about that. A pity, she reflected, that she hadn't made Drakar fall in love with her. He was at a good age to settle down to marriage and probably wouldn't have needed much prodding. After all, she had heard some whispers of scandal about his family, how it was rumored he'd actually been banished from Russia by the Czar. Why, he'd probably be grateful to settle down and have a real home, and of course, Lily mused, none of those simpletons he'd been seeing, Dani included, could even come near her own beauty and social graces.

It was then, while she was lost in deep ruminations over Drakar, that the messenger came. Lily, hoping for word of Colt, went to the door herself, waving away the butler.

A skinny young man in a bright red suit and flat-top hat of black held out an envelope and brightly said, ''Mademoiselle Daniella Coltrane.''

Lily snatched it from him. *''Merci.''*

He continued to hold out his hand expectantly, palm up. The smile on his lips was frozen. ''Is there anything else, mademoiselle?''

She closed the door in his face. Eagerly, she rushed into the parlor to rip open the envelope, knowing it had to be from Drakar.

It was.

Eagerly, she scanned the lines: "Regret everything. Let's make amends. Please come for dinner around eight tonight. I care deeply."

Lily smiled, folded the paper, and tapped it thoughtfully against her chin. She had overheard someone remark at a tea that the rich Russian had his own apartment on the top floor of a hotel he owned. It would be easy to find out which one. This afternoon she was going to drop by, on the pretext of telling him she'd inadvertently received his message for Dani and, regretfully, did not know where she'd moved.

She was trembling with anticipated glee at the thought of how, after she charmed him thoroughly, he'd extend the invitation to her instead, and if things went according to plan—Colt and his family could go to hell!

Lily hurried upstairs to dress and prepare for what was surely to be the greatest performance of her life.

Chapter Twenty-two

DURING the time Antone had worked as concierge at Le Palais, he had become accustomed to the comings and goings of Monsieur Drakar's numerous ladyfriends. Each had been lovely in her own way but none quite so beautiful as his guest of the previous evening. Her hair had gleamed and glittered with the brilliance of roasting chestnuts, and never had he seen such striking eyes—kind and friendly and the color of honey. She was not only Monsieur's loveliest choice thus far but also obviously one of the most refined.

So why, Antone wondered with a sigh of exasperation as he stared after the haughty young woman, did his master now relegate himself to such a churl? He allowed that she was somewhat pretty, but dear Lord, such a disposition. Why, in his fifteen years of service to the public, never had he seen such behavior. Such a tantrum she threw, all because he'd told her she could not go up to Monsieur's apartment unless she were announced. No time for that, she'd screeched, she would announce herself. When he'd protested, she'd really begun to scream like a banshee. Passersby paused to stare. So he had let her go. If Monsieur scolded him, so be it. A small price to pay, he'd tell him, to end Mademoiselle's shocking scene in front of the hotel.

* * *

The lift stopped in front of impressive brass doors. Lily hoped she didn't look as nervous as she felt. Her future security could depend on what she was about to do. At least, she consoled her tremulously pounding heart, she was confident that she looked quite lovely in the yellow velvet dress and matching cape edged in ermine. She loved the way the hood framed her face, giving her an aura of innocence.

She raised the ornate knocker on the door, tapped lightly.

The door opened almost immediately, and Drake stared down at her. His surprised expression quickly changed to one of amusement. "Well, Mademoiselle Deauneve. To what do I owe such a pleasure?"

Lily flashed her most beguiling smile, floated by him as she chided, "You know you can call me Lily." Immediately awed by the lovely decor of the Silver Room, she almost forgot her little speech of explanation but quickly recovered to say, "I have something for you. This"—she held out the envelope—"and my apology."

Not understanding, Drake looked at the envelope, then at her questioningly.

"I'm afraid I opened it by mistake. I was expecting a message myself. When I saw it was for Dani, I was quite embarrassed."

Drake stiffened with instant annoyance. "Then why didn't you go ahead and give it to her . . . along with your apology," he said tartly.

"I didn't know where to send it," she said innocently. "She's moved out of the house."

He asked Lily to tell him everything she knew.

She shrugged, removed her cape and tossed it carelessly onto a chair. "I really don't know very much. It's been a nightmare around there the past two days. Everyone seems to have gone crazy. The Coltranes left unexpectedly to go on holiday somewhere, and Colt is never around. I think he's avoiding me."

She gave him a look of misery and softly accused, "I told you yesterday morning that things weren't going well for me. You said you'd make time for me later."

He crossed the room to stand beside her. "It seems I have time now, Lily, and hearing all this truly distresses me."

She blinked back the practiced tears that always appeared on command. "It's worse than you can imagine, Drakar. Colt is just treating me terribly, and he knows how dependent I am on him. I have no one else but him to lean on, and, oh, I know you don't want to hear about my troubles . . ." She allowed her voice to trail off dramatically, a few tears to spill forth and trickle down her cheeks.

Drake knew what was expected of him. "Please go on, Lily. I'm your friend."

She felt a happy rush within. Dabbing at her eyes with a hanky, she said, "I'm not sure you want to hear the whole story."

"Of course I do."

She then told him the entire fabricated story of how she happened to be in Paris in the first place and the subsequent loss of her purse containing all her money, then of Colt's kind invitation to stay at his parents' home, and, with a little self-conscious blush, how he'd finally proposed to her.

Suddenly, the demure sadness disappeared in a rush of anger as she exclaimed, "Now that snobby family of his is ruining everything. They think I'm not good enough for him, and he's making a fool of me. Maybe"—her voice caught on an angry sob—"it's all for the best. I'm through with Colt. I don't want to marry a wishy-washy mamma's baby, anyhow."

Drake nodded with sympathetic understanding. "I'm sorry things didn't work out for you, Lily, but I really appreciate your coming over to tell me about Dani," he continued. "May I offer you a drink in gratitude for your inconvenience?"

"I'd love that, Drakar. Thank you."

He led the way into his study, and she went on to confide, "You know, Dani is such a spoiled brat that I'm surprised you were able to abide her, but you probably never saw that side to her the way I did."

Drake feigned concern. "Really? Is there something I should know?"

She pretended regret to have to be the one to tell him. "I'm afraid so. Dani is headstrong, selfish, doesn't care who she hurts as long as she gets what she wants. Why, she and Colt had a terrible fight yesterday, and Madame Kitty had to break it up because Dani was about to attack him."

Drake reacted with proper indignation. "You mean to say her temper is that bad? She'd attack someone physically?"

Lily sniffed with disdain. "She would . . . and has. She threw water in my face."

"No!" Drake was having difficulty keeping a straight face.

Lily recited the same story she'd told Colt, finished with the observation, "She's a hellion, Drake. You just don't know her."

He filled two glasses with vodka. "Well, it seems I don't, and I'm grateful you came over here today, really. Oh, not that I was even close to being serious about her, but it's best to find out these things so I can stop wasting my time with her."

"That's how I feel about Colt," she primly agreed, taking the glass he offered.

He gestured for her to sit down on the sofa, and she exclaimed over the alligator skin, thought it marvelous. In fact, she cooed, she loved everything in the room, declared that he had marvelous taste.

He sat beside her, and she maneuvered to provocatively afford him a better view of her bosom, which she noticed he was appreciating. The vodka was going to make things so much easier, for she would be able to say later that she wasn't used to drinking the Russian liquor, had been intoxicated and not in control. She drained her glass, and he politely refilled it.

Drake urged her to tell him more about this unpleasant side of Dani. Lily enjoyed her lies, all the while moving closer to him till their thighs touched.

He noticed how her voice was becoming slurred, thought it was part of the act to pretend to be so intoxicated she lost control and offered herself for easy seduction. He knew he could have her anytime he wanted . . . only he didn't want her. He merely wanted Colt to be able to see how easily she could be had by any man with money and how he'd be making the biggest mistake of his life if he allowed himself to be tricked into marrying her by whatever devious scheme she concocted. But Colt wasn't here, and Drake needed time to set up his own chicanery.

He slipped an arm around her shoulders, drew her close and whispered, "I'd really hate to see you return to England just now, when we're getting to know each other."

Lily obligingly melted against him. This part was easy. She needed no pretense, for she found him extremely desirable. "Yes, that's true, and we've got so much in common, because we've both been used by Coltranes, haven't we?"

His lips brushed against hers tantalizingly. "But no more, my sweet. No more. Promise me you won't leave Paris till we've had a chance to really get to know each other."

She shook her head slowly, eyes glowing with the heat that was rapidly spreading over her body in response to his nearness. "No, no, I won't. We'll have all the time we need, but—"

He silenced her with a kiss, deep, hungry, searching. His free hand moved swiftly to pull down the teasing bodice of her gown, exposing firm and luscious breasts that served to arouse him despite his resolve that his contempt for this shrew would thwart any true desire. Her

nipples grew taut and hard beneath the gently pinching
caress of his thumb and forefinger.

"Yes," she moaned, arching her back to press yet
closer to him.

Drake lowered his lips to gently suckle each nipple,
feeling the swelling of his desire. It couldn't happen now,
he reminded the pounding within. It couldn't happen at
all, and he was only torturing himself but had to go far
enough to make her believe he truly wanted her. He felt
no guilt over plans to expose her for the money-hungry
little bitch she was. After all, what she wanted to do to
Colt was much worse. She'd get over this, move on to
someone else until she finally succeeded in marrying a
man for his money.

Lily was sliding back to lie down, pulling him along
with her. With pretended shyness, she maneuvered to
touch him between his legs and gasp at the swelling there.
"Oh, Drakar," she cooed with exaggerated awe. "You
are wonderful. I can't wait . . ."

She pushed him away gently and then with unbelievable speed was out of her gown and undergarments to lie
before him naked. She parted her thighs, rendering herself vulnerable to his assault. "Take me, darling," she
begged. "Oh, Drakar, take me, please. Fill me with your
love . . ."

He felt his heat rising to boiling, knew he'd reached
the point of no return. Quickly, he undressed, then easily
entered her with one mighty thrust. He could not help
smiling to himself at the way she remembered to squirm
a bit, gasp as though pained by the unfamiliar violation.

She lifted her legs to lock about his waist in a viselike
grip and bring herself to a rapid climax. Drake afforded
himself the same quick release.

They lay together for a few moments in silence. Then,
taking a deep breath, Drake resigned himself to the fact
that he'd been weak, but hell, he'd never apologized for
being a man. He sat up, straightened himself while Lily

quickly did the same. Any fear of having ruined his plans was dissipated by her next words.

"I can't wait for you to love me again." She laid her head on his shoulder, looked at him with adoring eyes. "I'll admit I was deeply hurt by Colt in the beginning. I felt so humiliated that he'd renege on his proposal to me, but I see now that it was fate taking over because you and I are destined to be together . . . and I'm so glad I saved myself for you."

He was momentarily stunned by her performance. God, she was good. No wonder Colt had been fooled.

"But it's sad we'll have to part soon," she went on to say, sounding as though she were about to cry. "I'll have to leave the Coltrane mansion, and I have nowhere to go except home to England . . ." Her voice trailed off meaningfully.

Drake caught his cue, brusquely commanded, "No, you can't. We need time to see if this is real, Lily. I know you don't want to rush into anything any more than I do, but surely you agree we need to give it a chance to see if it's real."

Quickly, she agreed. "Yes, yes, of course I do, my darling." She sat up to face him eagerly. "But what do we do? How can I face Colt after this . . ." She lowered her lashes in false shame.

Drake pretended to ponder the situation gravely. "As I said, neither of us wants to rush into anything. Meanwhile, I'm going to check with my hotel manager. I'm sure he can find an available suite for you—no charge, of course."

She felt like shouting with joy but exhibited humility. "No, no, I couldn't let you do that."

"Why not? It's my hotel."

Shyly she asked, "Do you think it'd be proper?"

"I see no other alternative. It's certainly not your fault your purse was stolen."

He stood, sounding genuinely apologetic as he told her, "I've got a business appointment this afternoon, and I have to be leaving soon. Suppose you just go back to the Coltrane mansion, pretend nothing has changed, and tonight come over here and we'll talk again.''

She slipped her arms around his neck. ''Try and stop me, my darling.''

He kissed her with great effort, for the fire was out and resentment and contempt had extinguished even the embers. Now he only wanted to go through with his plan to expose her.

Once she'd left, he wrote a short note to Colt requesting his presence at his apartment at half past nine to discuss important personal family business. Colt, no doubt, would think it concerned his sister.

He rang for a servant, gave him precise orders to give to the courier, then sat back to pour himself a brandy. He was not happy over what he had to do but consoled himself by thinking that one day Colt would be grateful he'd spared him a life of misery married to a gold-digging shrew.

Chapter Twenty-three

ARNALD Twigby stared at the envelope in his hand as he stood outside the back door of the Coltrane mansion. It was starting to rain, and he wasn't very happy about the prospect of getting wet. Neither was he thrilled over returning to the same house where he'd been treated so rudely earlier in the day. He hadn't received the usual gratuity, and, adding insult to injury, he'd had a door slammed in his face. This visit, he'd gone to the rear in hopes of not encountering the same woman who'd been so uncivil to him earlier.

He had already knocked several times, so he began to pound loudly, an apprehensive eye on the dark, threatening clouds overhead. In the distance could be heard the rumble of thunder and there was an occasional slash of lightning to brighten the dimness of the late afternoon sky.

Inside, Hugeley Metalberne sat at the kitchen work table, guzzling from a bottle of sherry. He frowned as the knocking continued insistently. He rose from his chair, stumbled to the back door.

He jerked it open to irritably demand, "Well, what is it? What do you want?"

Arnald groaned softly. No gratuity from this drunken slob. "I've a message for Monsieur Coltrane."

Hugeley belched. "He isn't here."

Arnald had explicit orders to give the message to the name on the envelope and no one else. If he couldn't make his delivery now, he'd have to make yet another trip to this primitive place.

"Then could you tell me where to find him?" he pressed. "I have orders to deliver to him only."

Hugeley shook his head, started to close the door.

Arnald threw up his hand to block it. "Please. It's getting dark, and there's a storm brewing, and I'll just have to keep coming back until Monsieur is available. Won't you save both of us a lot of trouble and tell me where I can find him?"

"I'll see he gets it." Hugeley snatched the envelope from Arnald's hand, gave him a shove backward, then quickly slammed the door.

Arnald immediately began to beat on the door with both fists, protesting loudly. "Wait! Come back. Open this door. You can't do this. I've got my orders."

"I'll save us both some bother," Hugeley shouted through the door. "Now go away."

Arnald felt the first splattering drops of rain. He stood there a moment, washed in anger and frustration, then decided what the hell? Who was going to know? As far as he was concerned that old drunk could have been Coltrane. In fact, if anything was ever said, if there was any trouble, he'd just say the old drunk *said* he was Coltrane. How was he to know? Besides, it served everybody right, because he hadn't been tipped for his trouble.

He hurried away to escape the impending storm.

Hugeley shuffled back to the table, sat down and took another drink. He stared at the envelope a moment, then began to worry that he might be getting himself in a peck of trouble for taking it. He decided he'd better see what was going on so he'd know whether he'd truly erred. With shaking fingers, he tore open the envelope. Then, as he read the few short lines, his eyes grew wide with fear at the realization that he'd interfered in something that sounded terribly important. He'd heard of the man who signed it—Drakar, a very wealthy and powerful Russian who would not be happy over such interference.

Frantically, Hugeley tore the note to pieces and reached for the bottle of sherry. If anyone asked, he'd swear he didn't know anything about any message, that no one had come to the door all evening. Let the courier get fired. He had to look after himself; he had a wife and two children to feed. Couldn't afford to lose his job over a silly mistake. As far as he was concerned, none of it had happened.

It was late, almost eight-thirty. Dani had meant to leave the shop for Le Palais over an hour ago, but it seemed everything had conspired to make for a busy day. There had been more customers than usual, most of them browsing to while away the afternoon. Finally she was able to begin her cleaning chores, but in the midst of all that two of her tenants had gotten into a loud argument, and she'd had to calm them down by threatening eviction. Artists, she was discovering, could be quite temperamental.

As a result of the hectic day, she was quite frustrated and dropped the basket she was carrying. The bottle of champagne she had planned to share with Drake shattered.

With a mild curse, she cleaned up the mess. There was no more champagne as good as what she'd intended to bring, but anything would have to do.

In a little alley between buildings across the street, Cyril impatiently watched from the shadows. Unconsciously, he popped his knuckles, an annoying habit whenever he was nervous. Everything was all set. A courier would take the bogus telegram from Russia to Drakar at exactly three in the morning. Dani would, no doubt, have left his apartment long before that ungodly hour.

Breaking into the shop would be no problem. On his earlier visit he'd unlatched a window when Dani wasn't looking. All he had to do was step inside once the neighborhood was sleeping, take the painting, and leave. He'd made arrangements to have someone watching in readiness to abort any attempt by Drakar to tell Dani he had been called away—even to the point of becoming physical if the Russian himself appeared. It would be made to look like a robbery; he would knock Drakar unconscious, steal his wallet, drag him down to the railroad depot, and leave him there. If that happened, Cyril was prepared to concoct a scheme to spirit Dani quickly away so she'd not be there later, should Drakar make yet another attempt to see her.

He frowned to think it would be nearly a week before he could leave Paris, but because of the season, ships were not leaving from Cherbourg as often as in the summer. Well, he'd just conceal the painting, act normally. Everything would be fine.

He smiled complacently. Everything was going according to plan. Soon, the painting would be in his possession . . . and who could say how Dani would react when Drakar disappeared so suddenly and she believed he was a thief?

Colt prowled angrily through the house. Almost nine o'clock, dammit. Where was everybody? His parents weren't there. The servants had retired for the night. Even Lily was not to be found, and he particularly wanted to see her.

After two days of drinking, he'd finally passed out, only to wake up with a terrific headache and the resolution that he'd have to go through with marrying her. No matter that Dani saw things differently regarding her own honor. Lily apparently didn't share such liberal views. She swore she loved him. He believed she did. He felt it was the gentlemanly thing to do to preserve her self-respect. He'd work at making the marriage a good one, and maybe it would be. He didn't love her, never pretended that he had, but he had to live with himself, and by god, he'd gone through two experiences with women where he'd felt guilt and self-loathing afterward, and dammit, enough was enough.

So where was Lily now? He wanted to tell her of his ultimate decision, and set the wedding date. Then they'd go together to talk to his parents and he'd stand up to them and let them know he expected their blessings. He was a grown man; they were treating him like a little boy, and he wasn't going to stand for it.

His head throbbed as he pushed open the kitchen door. A small light illuminated the empty room. Suddenly, he felt a wave of hunger and walked over to where some covered dishes sat on a counter.

The torn bits of paper caught his eye.

He picked up a large piece, could make out only a few words . . . but it was enough.

Goddamn Drakar!

He tore out of the kitchen, out of the house. Rain slashed down in torrents. The rumble of thunder that shook the ground beneath him was in unison with the angry thudding of his pulse.

It was not difficult to figure out what had happened. In her heartache over thinking she'd been rejected, Lily had turned to the eagerly waiting arms of that wolf, Drakar. Who else would he send a message to at the mansion? Dani no longer lived there and, from what he'd gathered, was no longer under his spell.

He hailed a carriage for hire, leaped inside, and commanded, "Le Palais. Hurry."

No matter that he did not love Lily. She was his betrothed, a guest in his home, and, subsequently, under his protection. He'd be goddamned if Drakar was going to make her another of his conquests.

Drakar had trifled with his sister, and now he thought he could add Lily to his harem.

Colt's teeth ground together so tightly his jaw ached.

Who the hell did the bastard think he was?

He was shaking from head to toe in his fury.

God, he hoped he was wrong . . . hoped it was all a mistake and that he'd find Drakar alone, that there'd be a simple explanation for the fragments of the note he'd read, as well as Lily's mysterious absence at this hour.

Colt drew in his breath so sharply, so deeply, his chest ached.

Yes, he hoped he was wrong, all right, because if he wasn't, he knew he was probably going to kill the son of a bitch with his bare hands.

Antone stared thoughtfully after the young lady he thought so beautiful as she made her way into the hotel. A blessing for the eyes, he reflected. Not many so lovely passed his vision.

He pulled a cheroot from his coat pocket, stepped into the shadows and lit it. No harm in smoking, Monsieur Drakar had told him, so long as the guests did not see him. Well, he supposed it was all right to take a break. This was the slow time of the evening.

An hour or so ago, the snitty miss who'd made such a disgusting scene earlier returned to enter the hotel without so much as a word or a glance in his direction.

Then, just a few moments ago, an agitated young man arrived and seemed upset as he asked the way to Monsieur's apartment, said he did not need to be announced.

Now the beautiful lady had arrived.

Antone drew on the cheroot thoughtfully, decided he had a right to be annoyed.

After all, if Monsieur was having a party, the least he could have done was tell him about it.

Chapter Twenty-four

DRAKE pretended he'd had too much to drink, thinking that could excuse him for resisting Lily's efforts to get him into bed without offending her.

Since she had arrived, around eight o'clock, she had made it obvious she would prefer to forget the sumptuous dinner he had ordered and make love instead.

Drake wasn't about to let that happen. Not again. He planned for them to be settled on the sofa directly in the line of vision from the Silver Room, at approximately nine-fifteen. By nine-thirty, when he expected Colt, he would make sure they were in the midst of a very passionate embrace so Colt would see them immediately.

But dammit, it was not yet nine and Lily was making it difficult to keep on schedule.

"I'm not hungry," she whined, leaning against him so he could feel her breast pressing. "Not for food, anyway," she cooed suggestively.

"Not for food," Drake drunkenly sang, waving his wine glass, "but for spirits! Who needs food when we have the nectar of the gods!"

He pretended to try to stand, deliberately lurching forward as he slurringly complained, "Where's that wine steward? I told him to bring vodka! I want a man's drink, not a lady's tea!"

He fell clumsily into his chair once more, banged his glass on the table irritably.

Lily continued to smile, but her eyes were cold with annoyance. How could she convince him she was the only woman in the world who could satisfy him in bed if she could not get him there? A long, formal dinner was a waste of time. Reaching out to caress his arm, she leaned to kiss his ear and blow gently, warmly, then coaxed, "We've had enough to drink, love. We have other, more enjoyable courses on the menu for tonight . . ." Boldly, she placed a hand on his thigh, gently squeezed, then began to trail anxious fingertips toward his crotch.

Inwardly, Drake moaned. Things could not get out of hand. Colt had to see them kissing—nothing more, because, after the initial shock, he knew all hell was going to break loose. Colt would be furious, Lily would be contrite . . . probably say she'd been lured there, plied with drink, forced to submit. He knew he was going to have to be in a position to tell Colt it was a setup. If he and Lily were caught in the very act, Colt would never believe it was anything except what it looked like.

He pushed Lily away and this time got to his feet without pretense. Wagging a finger, he feigned admonishment. "No, no, young lady. You will not cheat me of my man's drink this night. How else can I satisfy a little minx like you? I need all my energy!"

He made his way to the liquor cabinet, effectively stumbling, while Lily stared after him, mildly annoyed but also flattered that he found her passion such a challenge.

Drake was pouring a drink when he felt Lily's arms go around him.

"I want you, Drakar. Now . . ." She pressed close.

He could feel the cherry-pit hardness of her nipples through the fabric of his shirt . . . could subsequently feel his own arousal.

He sucked in his breath as her hands lowered to caress him.

Triumphantly, she cried, "You want me, too, Drakar."

He twisted away from her clutching hands, forced a laugh as he looked down at her. "My dear, allow me one drink, please, and I promise to love you all night long." He kissed the tip of her nose, turned once more, heard her sigh with agitation at being put off.

Stealing a look at the clock, he saw it was not quite nine. Damn, how was he going to be able to keep her at bay for over half an hour? Slow and easy lovemaking was the only answer, but as eager as she was, that was going to be a difficult ploy.

He downed the glass of vodka in one gulp, did not mind the familiar burning collision in his stomach. Normally, he preferred to sip the strong Russian drink, but the moment called for quick dullness to his senses.

"Drakar . . ." she whined, stamping her foot impatiently.

Again, he turned, this time sharply sucking in his breath at the sight of her exposed breasts. She had scooped them from the bodice of her gown, held them cupped in her hands in bold offering. "Take me!" she commanded hoarsely, fiercely. "Now!"

He groaned once more and reached for her, knowing he was in for the most god-awful thirty minutes in his whole life. He was going to have to muster restraint as never before, because no way was he going to give in again.

Lifting her in his arms, he carried her to the sofa and held her across his lap. Obligingly, as their lips met and held in a tongue-scorching kiss, he began to gently squeeze her breasts.

This, he reflected miserably, was not precisely the way he had wanted Colt to step off the elevator and find them.

Suddenly, time ran out.

The elevator doors opened.

Drake froze.

With a loud bellow of rage, Colt burst into the room. "You son of a bitch!"

Drake released Lily so quickly that he dropped her right on the floor, where she landed with an indignant screech followed by a frightened scream as she realized who was there.

She said the first thing that popped into her shocked mind: "Colt, it's not what you think—"

Drake stood, prepared for the worst.

Colt's face was red with rage, gray eyes bulging and sparked with fury. His fists clenched and unclenched at his sides as he struggled against the sudden fierce desire to kill them both.

Lily frantically yanked up the bodice of her dress, as she quickly picked herself up off the floor.

Drake eased himself around to stand so that the sofa was between him and Colt. "Let's talk about this, Colt," Drake said with more ease than he felt. "I was expecting you, so you know it was a setup . . ."

"A setup?" Colt bellowed, indignant to realize the bastard would dare to insult his intelligence with such a ridiculous lie. "I just happened to find the note you sent her. Otherwise, I'd probably have gone on being fooled, wouldn't I?"

Lily was hit with the realization that Drakar had suddenly turned against her and now she stood to lose both of them. Quickly defending herself the fastest way she knew how, she cried, "Oh, Colt, thank God you're here. He invited me here, said he wanted to talk about your sister, then he put something in my drink, because everything went hazy, and he was pushing me down on the sofa, doing terrible things . . ."

She began to cry hysterically, attempted to throw herself against Colt for expected comfort, but he roughly slung her away.

Once more Lily found herself sprawled on the floor.

Colt pointed a finger of warning, eyes narrowed menacingly, voice a harsh rasp as he trembled from head to toe with boiling rage. "Stay away from me with your lies,

Lily. I know what I saw, and you aren't drugged and you weren't being forced."

"Calm down and listen, Colt," Drake urged. "I set this up so you'd see her for what she is. Everything she's told you is a lie. She never came to Paris looking for her aunt."

Colt lifted his loathing gaze from Lily cringing beneath him to look at the Russian with equal malice.

"It's true," Drake went on quietly, matter-of-factly. "She came here to find a rich man to take care of her, because she's destitute. I heard all about her in London, when she was an old man's mistress, till he tired of her."

Lily beat at the air with her fists, lips curled back in a hating snarl. "You bastard! You goddamn, no-good bastard! You're lying. You tell him you're lying, or I'll claw your eyes out—"

She had gotten to her knees, ready to attack Drake with fingers arched, but Colt quickly moved to place one foot against her shoulder and shove her back down. "Best thing you can do is get out of my sight," he snarled.

Drake seized the opportunity to continue. "I knew who she was that night we all had dinner together. Dani had told me the story about how she came to be at your house, and I knew right away what she was up to."

Lily screamed, tried to get up again, and Colt once more pushed her back.

"I only wanted to help you, Colt. When Dani told me you were planning to marry her, I knew I had to do something to make sure that never happened."

Colt had a gut feeling that the other man was telling the truth, yet he felt no gratitude. In that stark moment of cruel and painful awareness, he knew only that once more he had been taken in by a woman. He was flooded with utter and complete humiliation.

The man responsible for this awareness was standing there looking at him in pity.

Colt never liked to be pitied, and with a savage roar, he sprang for him.

Just then, Dani stepped off the elevator. For a second, she merely stood there, eyes sweeping over the scene before her as she attempted to comprehend. What were Colt and Lily doing here, and why was Lily on the floor screaming? Why was Drake standing behind the sofa?

That was the precise moment when Colt lost all his control, dove across the room to grab Drake around the throat with his outstretched hands, and sent them both crashing to the floor along with a nearby table and lamp.

Dani screamed, rushed forward to command, "Stop it, both of you! Have you gone crazy?"

Drake clutched Colt's choking hands as his head was banged painfully up and down on the floor. He didn't want to hit him but neither did he intend to take a beating. He kneed him between his legs, rolled away as Colt released his hold to double over in pain.

It was then Drake realized Dani was there and he felt as though he were the one who'd just been smashed. "It isn't what you think—"

"Yes it is." Lily cut him off. "He sent me a note, asked me to come here, then attacked me, and now he's trying to lie his way out of it. Ask Colt. He found the note and that's why he's here."

Colt was coming out of the sea of pain slowly, but was aware of all that was going on and nodded in agreement.

Drake was unflustered, surely Dani would listen to reason. "I sent a note, but not to Lily. It was to Colt, asking him to come here tonight. It was my intention that he find her here and then realize she didn't care anything about him and was only after a rich husband." He shook his head. "I can't understand how he could have misinterpreted my note."

Colt sneered, struggled to stand. "You never intended for me to read it at all, you goddamn bastard. Neither did Lily. She thought she tore it up, but I could make out just enough to know who it was from and where she'd gone."

Drake slammed his hand against his forehead. So! Colt never received the note. Someone else had intercepted it, tried to destroy it. Who and why could be determined later. The important thing at the moment was to do something to smooth over this mess. He did not like the way Dani was looking at him with such pain-filled eyes. He held out a hand to her. "Will you believe me?"

Her voice was so cold, it seemed like an echo from a tomb. "I think I knew all along just what you are but my heart kept arguing with my mind. No more," she finished quietly, then turned and walked back to the elevator.

"Wait!" Colt hurried to follow, the elevator doors closed.

Drake felt his own anger rising. Was this all he meant to Dani? Was she yet further proof that all women were selfish and willful . . . just like his mother?

Lily stood, started toward him with a lust for vengeance glittering in blue eyes suddenly black with rage.

Drake regarded her coolly. "The best thing for you to do now, Lily, is to have the elevator sent right back up."

He turned and walked out of the room.

Despite herself and the rage within, Lily knew he was right.

Cyril eased the window open with little effort or noise. He stepped inside. Dani's shop was dimly illuminated from the light of a street lamp filtering through the front windows, but he did not need to see to find his way, for he had memorized the interior.

He went directly to the wall where the paintings of the Monaco Find were displayed. He found the one he was after, removed it, stepped back outside the window, the precious painting held tightly against his chest. He did not bother to reclose the window. After all, he wanted to make sure that the burglary looked exactly like what it was—an "inside" conspiracy . . . only the finger of suspicion would be pointed at Drakar, for he was the one who would be disappearing so suddenly, so mysteriously—not he!

He hurried down the alley, pausing in the shadows only long enough to make sure no one was around, then happily went on his way.

Drake frowned with irritation at the sound of someone knocking. He stood before the door. "Yes, who is it?" Lord, it was after three in the morning.

"Telegram, sir."

Drake was at once apprehensive. News of his mother's arrest, then her later escape from Siberia, had come in the night at such an hour.

And he had received the painful news of his father's death at a similar time.

He took a deep breath of dread, held it, let it out slowly.

"Monsieur Drakar," the voice said, quietly insistent. "Please, monsieur, I have a telegram for you."

Drake opened the door and took it, fished in his pocket for a few francs, then closed himself away from the world as he tore open the crisp envelope.

His heart began to pound faster with each word. He'd never heard of the cousin who had sent the message, but that did not matter. No doubt, every kin of Mikhailonov blood and heritage would want to see the honor of the family name restored, and this one, whoever he was, thought he knew where the Fabergé egg was hidden.

Drake was ecstatic and at once began rushing to get his things together. The cousin had intimated he was in danger—the revolutionaries suspected he had important information—and so no time could be lost in enlisting Drake's help.

He paused, needled with thoughts of Dani.

How he wished there had been time to confide in her, then she could share his joy at this first hope in ten years.

But she hadn't wanted to share his life . . . had not cared enough about him to hear him out. And now it was too late.

Another willful, selfish woman. He hated them all!

With a sneer, he resumed his packing . . . all the while knowing that he hated far less than he dared to admit.

Chapter Twenty-five

DANI was awake but reluctant to rise and face the day. She wondered whether she had even been asleep, for the night was a misty blur of misery.

Drake and Lily.

She squeezed her eyes shut in an attempt to blot out the painful image of them together.

Why?

She had felt she had come to know and understand Drake, she had believed him not to be as the gossips whispered.

Until last night.

She swiped furiously at a tear with the back of her hand. She would not cry. There was nothing to cry over. She was still herself, her own person, independent and free. Nothing else was of consequence. If he tried to explain, to make peace, she would turn a deaf ear. It was over. Of course, it was actually none of her business whether he saw other women, but she had no intention of wasting her time with a man who could not be trusted. After all, Lily was engaged to her brother, and for Drake to see her was unforgivable.

Finally, she convinced herself that nothing was being accomplished by lying in bed in mortifying reminiscence; life had to continue despite the undeniable aching within.

She bathed, dressed, and went downstairs to her shop to make coffee, determined to stay busy. She was having her second cup of coffee when Colt walked in, looking as though he had not been to bed. Brow furrowed, eyes puffy and shadowed, he approached her to grimly murmur, "What can I say except that I'm sorry?"

Her heart went out to him but she knew he did not need, or want, her sympathy. "There's no need to say anything. Coffee?"

"Please." They went into her little office, and he slumped into a chair.

"Have you been to bed at all, Colt?"

He shook his head. "Afraid not. I went back to the house and I may have dozed some during the night from sheer exhaustion. "Mostly," he admitted with chagrin, "I was thinking about what a fool I was."

Wryly, Dani corrected, "What fools *we* are."

"Yeah, I guess you could say that. We were both taken in."

He went on to confide that he reasoned Lily had become desperate. No doubt she thought that if she couldn't drag me to the altar, Drake was a viable option." Looking at his sister thoughtfully, he wondered just how much of his personal life to reveal, then decided maybe he could ease her own pain a bit and bluntly admitted she was the reason he'd had second thoughts about marrying Lily.

She blinked in confusion. "Whatever makes you say that?"

He had no choice but to remind her of her indiscretion. "You stayed out all night with Drakar but didn't want to marry him to smooth things over."

Dani was at once defensive. "Of course I didn't. That's certainly nothing to base a marriage on, regardless of what others might think. I have to live my own life."

"So do I."

She wondered what on earth he was talking about, then it all came flooding back at the same time he offered revelation.

"Lily came to my room one night. I'd had too much to drink, I'm afraid. I didn't make her leave."

He waited for her reaction.

Dani merely shrugged.

Colt wondered if he'd not been explicit enough. Surely she was sophisticated enough to know what he was talking about. Patience ebbing, he went on to bluntly admit, "I know now she was lying, but at the time she pretended I was the first man she'd ever had and declared that no decent man would want her for a wife, and it was all my fault, because I seduced her . . ." He paused, shook his head from side to side in self-admonishment. "What a crock of bullshit! And I was stupid enough to believe it."

Dani's heart went out to him. "I know all about that night, Colt."

He stared at her, amazed. "How?"

She related Lurline's story.

Colt's reaction was to laugh. "Seems everyone knew the truth about Lily but me. If Drakar hadn't run like a scalded dog, I might be inclined to believe he did set it all up for my benefit."

Dani had turned to refill her cup but whirled around sharply. "What did you say?"

"I said I might've been inclined to believe—"

"No, no." She shook her head, long hair flying. Something was needling within, a strange feeling she did not like. "What do you mean—Drake ran?"

Colt hated being the one to have to tell her, for he had no way of knowing how far their relationship had gone, how deeply she had been hurt by all of this, but saw no other way now except to inform her Drakar had left suddenly and mysteriously sometime during the night.

"I went to the hotel this morning to get some answers. I wanted to get it straight in my mind whether or not he was telling the truth, but when I got there, the concierge said he'd left during the night and wasn't expected back anytime soon. That makes me think maybe he *was* guilty and didn't want any more trouble and decided to just get out of Paris till things had a chance to cool down.''

"Strange," Dani whispered, more to herself than to Colt, then mused aloud, "Drake isn't the type to run from trouble. It doesn't make sense that he'd run away in the middle of the night like a coward when he was more than ready to face you last night, when you were in a rage. "And," she added in a pained voice, "I would have thought he'd make some attempt to speak with me.''

Colt got up to place his hand on her shoulder in a gesture of love and comfort. "I'm sorry, Dani. I really am. I guess you just had him figured all wrong. I know how you feel, because I was taken in the same way by Lily.''

Dani admitted to being hurt, but more than that she was confused. "Are you sure he didn't tell anyone where he was going?''

"The concierge said he'd probably gone back to Russia.''

Dani bit back tears of regret for what might have been, for what she had thought there *was*.

"Yes, I suppose he would return there if he wanted to get away for a while." She turned and gestured. "He seemed to love his country, said this painting reminded him—''

She gasped, fell silent, hands flying to her face as she stared at the empty wall.

Colt followed her gaze, did not understand anything except that her face was suddenly drained of color and she looked horrified. "Dani, for god's sake, what's wrong?''

She pointed a trembling finger to the blank space on the wall where the painting of the Alexandrovsky Palace should have been hanging. "It's gone.''

"What's gone?" he echoed, alarmed.

"The painting Drake liked so much . . . one of the ones I found in Monaco and refused to sell to him. It's been stolen.''

"Are you sure? Maybe you set it aside to dust it or something—"

"No, no!" She was almost screaming. "It's been stolen. But how—"

Her gaze fell on the open window she had not noticed before.

"There! That's how he got in! Drake must've slipped in here last night while I was sleeping upstairs."

"Why would he want it?" Colt asked.

"The bastard!" she fumed. "The arrogant bastard! So used to having his own way that he takes what isn't given to him."

Colt was mystified by the intensity of her reaction. "Was it valuable?"

"That's not the point! Don't you see? *He wanted it!* I told him he couldn't have it. He *stole* it from me. And I'll be goddamned if anyone uses me that way!"

Colt started for the door, his own ire rising. "I'm going to report this to the authorities."

"No. Don't."

He turned to stare questioningly. Surely she couldn't be so infatuated with the rogue that she was going to let him get away with burglary.

"I'm going to deal with it myself. In my own way."

He walked back to where she stood. "What are you talking about? What do you think you can do? Let the police handle this and do a complete investigation. Something else might be missing that you haven't noticed yet. Besides, you can't prove Drakar did it."

"I know he did it. Who else would want just that one painting?" She sighed with exasperation, then repeated, "I told you he wanted to buy it, and I told him it wasn't for sale. I remember noticing the way he looked at it, almost in a trance. It was strange, but I never thought much about it at the time, only that maybe it made him homesick, because it was a painting of a palace where he had spent a lot of time when he was a boy."

Colt was fast growing impatient. "Dani, you're being ridiculous. A man isn't going to commit a theft just to take some worthless piece of art that reminds him of a boyhood home."

She eyed him coldly. "Drake would. I told you, he's used to getting anything he wants. He did this to show me that once and for all."

Colt shook his head, threw up his hands in surrender to such mad theory. "If you don't want it back and you don't want to have him punished, fine. Don't report it."

Stubbornly, coldly, she announced, "I'm going to get it back."

He laughed uneasily. His sister sounded too sure of herself. "And how do you propose to do that? He's far, far away from here by now."

"I'm going to Russia," she quietly replied.

"You are *what*?" he said, stunned, then quickly recovered. "You'll do no such thing."

"You can't stop me!"

"You just watch me." He was glaring down at her with steely eyes. "If I have to tie you to a post, I'll be damned if you're going to go traipsing off to Russia after a worthless painting."

"It isn't worthless. It's part of a collection that the Paris art world has talked about for months. And it belongs to *me*. I'll be damned if I'm going to sit back and do nothing and let that bastard just walk off with it. He knows I know he took it. He's probably laughing right now to think how naïve I was."

"Dani, I won't let you. I'll go to Pa and—"

"Shhh!" She cut him off, waving her hands frantically at the sound of the bell above the door and the sight of Cyril walking in. Her lips slowly curved in a secret smile as the devious plan began to form. Leaning closer to Colt, she confidingly whispered, "You don't have to worry. I won't be going to Russia alone. Here comes my traveling companion now."

Colt followed her gaze, shook his head in disgust. "If you think I'm letting you travel with him by yourself, you're crazy."

Dani was assailed with yet another interesting thought. "Then come with us, Colt. It would do you good to get away."

She started toward Cyril, calling out a warm greeting.

Colt looked on and slowly began to nod his head in agreement as he thought over her invitation, deciding that maybe a trip to Russia was the very thing to help him forget that once again he had been deceived by a woman.

Cyril was momentarily stunned by Dani's warm welcome and her overall ebullient mood. He had dropped by on the pretext of inviting her out to dinner again, all the while anxious to see her reaction to the theft of the Alexandrovsky Palace painting. Certainly he had not expected to find her so happy.

She greeted him genially, reaching out to squeeze both his hands in welcome, and gushed, "Cyril, I'm so glad you came. I was just telling Colt how bad I feel about turning down your invitations to dinner. I've neglected you terribly, I'm afraid. Let me make it up to you by preparing a cozy dinner for you at your place tonight."

Cyril was really baffled then. "I—I don't have a *nice* place, Dani," he attempted to explain, disappointed to have to do so. "I live in a small room above my office, and—"

"That's all right." She waved away his excuses, then steered him to where the coffeepot waited. "Poppa and Kitty have gone on a holiday, so we'll just go to their house, and I'll dismiss the servants and make dinner for you myself."

Cyril was flabbergasted, could not fathom what was happening but was nonetheless pleased. "Well, I'd love to, Dani."

Colt and Cyril exchanged cool greetings, and Colt, sensing that Dani wanted him to leave, politely did so.

"I'm afraid you were right about Drakar, Cyril," Dani said after a while. "He's everything you said he was."

Cyril's eyebrows rose. Things were working out just as he'd hoped. "Oh? What caused such a revelation, my dear?"

She shrugged, hated having to bring up the subject but knew it was important for him to know Drakar was no longer a part of her life. If not, he might be reluctant to take her to Russia with him. "Suffice it to say you were right. I really don't care to discuss it."

Politely, he obliged. "I certainly don't want you to talk about anything that upsets you, Dani. Just remember that I'm your friend, and I'm always ready to help any way I can."

"And I'm your friend, too, Cyril." She felt no guilt at the adoring way he was looking at her. Forcing enthusiasm, she said, "I'll have dinner ready at eight, and we'll have a nice evening, all right?"

"Wonderful." He wanted to crush her in his arms but did not dare.

After he left the shop, Cyril paused outside to ponder. She had said nothing about the painting or blaming Drakar for its theft . . . and she had to have noticed. Probably that was the reason her brother was present so early in the day. She'd sent for him first thing.

But, he mused, it was no surprise that she hadn't said anything to him. After all, she had her pride, and it had probably been hard for her to even admit he'd been right, without the pain of confiding everything. She probably felt like a terrible fool, which was certainly understandable.

Cyril felt so good inside, and the smile that touched his lips transcended all the way to his very soul. Everything was working just the way he'd planned. Dani, so beautiful and desirable, was turning to him in her frustration, and that was wonderful!

Whistling merrily, he continued on his way . . . very much looking forward to the evening ahead.

Chapter Twenty-six

"WHY do you need Cyril Arpel? If you want to go to Russia to try and find Drakar, *I'll* go with you. Besides, you don't even know for sure that's where he went, and if he did, how in the hell would you know where to even start looking for him?"

Colt paused to draw a ragged, exasperated breath before continuing his diatribe, shaking his head in disgust. "It's a wild-goose chase, Dani. Why don't you just call the police and report the theft and let them take it from there? Why do you have to be so damn stubborn?"

She wondered for the hundredth time why he couldn't understand something so utterly simple and struggled for patience as she attempted once more to make him understand. "It's a personal vendetta, Colt, if you want to call it that. I'm just not going to let him get away with it. Besides, I need Cyril—he has the necessary social connections to take me places I need and want to go. As for not knowing where to look for Drake," she added with determination, "if he's in Russia, believe me, I'll find him. He'll be where the glitter and excitement is, and that's where I intend to be."

Colt threw up his hands in resignation. "So be it. We'll go, but I think you're crazy."

He left then, not wanting to be around when Cyril arrived.

Dani hurried to put the finishing touches on the dinner she had carefully prepared. She had set a cozy table for two on the balcony outside the upstairs parlor, which overlooked Kitty's rose garden, still fragrantly lovely with meager late-season offerings. The moon was at its fullest, and the air was not terribly cool, so the setting would be lovely.

She had selected a simple but elegant gown of black velvet with long sleeves that tapered to points at her wrists. The neckline, demurely heart-shaped, was exquisitely edged in a thin band encrusted with tiny blood opals. Her hair was brushed back from her face and cascaded down to hang full and loose around her shoulders, and she wore a headband across her forehead identical to the opal trim of her gown.

A last glance in the mirror as the doorbell sounded assured her of the look she had sought to achieve—delicate refinement.

Cyril took one look at her and gasped aloud. "My god, Dani, you are beautiful!"

Dani curtsied playfully. "Why, thank you, kind sir." Then she beckoned him to follow her upstairs.

As they made their way, he curiously asked why the house seemed so deserted. "I know you said your parents were on a holiday, but didn't your brother have a houseguest?"

She stiffened at the allusion to Lily. "Mademoiselle Deauneve left for England unexpectedly."

Cyril noted the chill in her voice, opted not to pursue what was obviously an unpleasant subject that did not interest him anyway.

Upstairs, Dani served an aperitif of champagne with *crème de cassis* and an appetizer of thin Lyonnais sausage, and Cyril was delighted. "If this is a sample of your culinary talents, Dani," he said, "I'll propose before the second course!"

Before the first course had ended, Cyril inquired as to whether she had finalized her plans to travel to Denmark.

She seized the opening at once. "I've decided to take you up on your kind offer!" she stated.

He blinked, pretending not to know what she was talking about . . . all the while feeling cold apprehension descend. Surely she did not mean what he feared she meant.

Then, with her next words, he was forced to realize his suspicions were sadly correct.

"I'm going to Russia with you."

He swallowed hard, reached for his glass of wine and took a quick sip, wanting precious time to react properly. Finally, when he trusted himself to speak, he asked, "Are you quite sure, my dear? I plan to stay until spring, and you'd have to travel back alone, because you certainly couldn't stay away for that long."

She agreed but was not about to tell him she would not be returning alone, because he might not be pleased about Colt joining them. That would have to come as a surprise.

"We'll worry about that when the time comes," she said dismissively.

"Why do you want to go? And isn't this rather sudden?"

Dani shook her head. She'd been prepared for his surprise and his questions. "I need a change. I'm rather tired of Paris, and you've whetted my appetite for Russia with your wonderful tales of the season there. Besides, you know all the right people, and you can show me around . . . if you still want me to come," she added, deliberately sounding as though she were on the verge of being terribly hurt and disappointed should he renege on his invitation.

Cyril could do nothing except be reassuring and hope he appeared sincere. "Yes, yes, of course I do."

Dani grinned and sat back in her chair, folded her hands in her lap as she looked at him in happy anticipation. "Then when do we leave?"

Dammit, he knew he'd be happy to have her with him as far as Denmark, but once they were in Russia she could prove to be a problem when he started searching for the Fabergé egg. He told her he had already booked passage. "You might not be able to make a reservation on the same ship. The agent told me they were terribly crowded."

She was undaunted. "Nonsense. First class is never fully booked."

He looked at her a moment, hidden longings surfacing, doubts and fears submerging. "I think we can arrange things, Dani," he whispered, "and I think the two of us can have a trip we'll always remember." He reached out to cover her hand with his.

She gently withdrew from his touch, thinking how grateful she was that Colt had decided to go too. No doubt, Cyril would probably be making advances at every turn, and the last thing she wanted for a long, long time was that kind of relationship with a man.

They finished dinner and had coffee inside, then Dani pointedly looked at the mantel clock and said she hoped he'd not think her rude but felt it time they ended the evening.

"Remember, I gave the servants the night off, Cyril. It isn't proper that we be here alone together so late."

It was the moment he had been waiting for. Setting his coffee aside, he lunged for her, wrapping his arms around her and crushing her against him as he heatedly declared, "Yes, I know we're here alone, Dani, and you just don't know how long I've waited to do this . . ."

His lips came down on hers bruisingly, and he held her so tightly she feared she could not breathe. She struggled out of his grip. "Cyril, no!" she protested vehemently.

At once he let her go. He forced himself to quell the resentment bubbling inside as he recalled how she'd stayed so late in Drakar's apartment unchaperoned. Well, there would be many opportunities for them to be alone together once they were on the ship, and he was confident that sooner or later he would be able to break down her reserves and have her the way he wanted.

When Dani and Colt arrived in the resort town of Chantilly, twenty-five miles outside Paris, they were instantly impressed by the sight of the massively elegant château where their parents were staying during their holiday. Perched high on a hill rising out of a lake, it was surrounded by beautiful gardens and a deep, mysterious forest, giving the impression of an enchanted palace found only in fairy tales.

The château, Dani was later informed by Kitty, had been the Renaissance country home of the noble and illustrious Condé family, and when the last descendant, the Duc d'Aumale, built an additional building to house his immense collection of paintings, it turned out to be even larger than the original dwelling.

They had arrived unannounced, and Kitty and Travis somehow felt the surprise visit had nothing to do with the situation concerning Dani's indiscretion with Drakar, or their disapproval of Colt's engagement to Lily.

Later, during dinner, they learned their suspicions were justified.

Colt announced he'd broken his engagement to Lily, without explaining why, and that he and Dani were going on a holiday to Russia and had no idea how long they would be away.

Dani enthusiastically described plans to stop in Denmark on a buying jaunt for her shop.

The elder Coltranes exchanged glances, eyebrows raised, intuitively acknowledging there was another reason for the trip that was not being divulged.

Early the next morning, Travis invited Dani to go with him to view the famed racing stables of Chantilly, knowing she would enjoy seeing the magnificent eighteenth-century stone structure, with stalls for 250 horses and and 400 hounds, along with rooms for huntsmen and grooms.

He also wanted an opportunity for the two of them to be alone together.

Dani was properly impressed with the surroundings, said it seemed more like a palace than a stable.

Travis, comfortably attired in a riding habit of red velvet coat and white satin pants, chewed on a cheroot as he reminded her that Chantilly had been a racing center for a long time, but added it wasn't exactly his idea of a place for a holiday. With a wry grin, he added, "You can guess there's some art involved."

Dani laughed. "I've heard. The Duc d'Aumale left his magnificent collection to France on the condition that the paintings never be removed from Chantilly or lent for any exhibition. I imagine Kitty is in heaven living with the fifteenth- and sixteenth-century drawings."

Suddenly, he got to the point. "Why are you and Colt going to Russia?"

She blanched, floundered for an explanation he would believe. "I told you—"

"You told me what you wanted me to know," he contradicted. "I want the real reason."

A slow smile touched her lips. "I guess I can't fool you, can I?"

"No." Gray eyes twinkled with just a hint of amusement, for he was quite serious. "Tell me everything."

And she did, from start to finish, including her innermost feelings about Drake, and how humiliated she felt.

Finally, when her heart was emptied, she stood before him to touch trembling fingertips to his cheek. "Poppa, I'm truly sorry I hurt you with all of this. I know how I shamed you, but I have to make my own decisions, my own way in the world. Can you understand?"

Travis wrapped his arms around her, pressed her close against his chest. How he loved this beautiful young woman, so like her mother who'd died in his arms. She was his daughter, flesh of his flesh, a part of his heart, and he never wanted to cause her a moment of pain. "Yes, honey, I do understand," he whispered huskily.

"You're that much like me, aren't you? You've got to go where life takes you and heaven help anyone who gets in your way."

Dani gazed up at him, eyes misted by tears of adoration. "I love you, Poppa," she whispered tremulously.

Travis felt the moisture of the ages in his own vision as he responded tenderly, "I love you, too, Dani . . ."

Chapter Twenty-seven

Dani found the sea voyage fascinating, exciting . . . and fun. Along with Cyril, she and Colt had been among those fortunate to book first-class passage on a special sailing of the luxurious White Star *Britannic*. Not only was the food, wine, and service superb, their cabins were large and lavishly furnished, containing private bathrooms with hot and cold running water. There was even the brilliance of electric lighting derived from four generators. The sea was surprisingly smooth; no one experienced even a twinge of seasickness and all marveled that they might as well have been staying in first-class hotels. There were many activities onboard to while away the days, and all in all, the trip was a joy.

Dani fell in love with Copenhagen—a metropolis of fine old buildings and beautiful spires rising from the copper roofs of churches.

The ship was in port in Copenhagen overnight, so there was ample time for Dani to visit the Royal Copenhagen factory where she was delighted to be granted a commission to sell selected pieces of Flora Danica in her shop. There was even a hint that if all went well she might even be able to acquire an entire set in the future.

Delighted with her success, Dani took Colt and Cyril sightseeing during their remaining time in port. They visited the Amalienborg Palace Square to view the Royal Guardsmen on duty for the Royal House of Glücksborg, with their striking tall bearskin caps. Then they strolled along the lovely promenade "Langelinie" and along the sound to gaze at the beautiful Renaissance palace of Rosenborg, with its beautiful flower beds, majestic trees, and pleasant walks lined with sculpture.

They enjoyed a lunch of Danish *smørrebrød*—open-faced sandwiches of buttered bread topped with a variety of garnishes, such as sliced ham, roast beef, or cheese. For dinner, they opted not to eat onboard the ship but instead sampled the seafood in a restaurant in the Tivoli Gardens, then spent the evening at the Royal Theater enjoying a performance of the Royal Danish Ballet.

When, at last, it was time for the *Britannic* to steam from the Nyhavn waterfront, Dani stood at the ship's railing and made a silent promise to return one day to experience more of the lovely charm of the wonderful country of Denmark.

Upon their arrival in Saint Petersburg, thanks to Travis having sent messages to influential acquaintances advising that his daughter and son were arriving for a visit and requesting that any courtesies granted them be considered a personal favor, Dani and Colt found themselves in a social whirl from the moment they came down the gangplank of their ship. They were also not neglected by Cyril, who was being extremely polite despite his disappointment over Colt's presence which had, of course, thwarted plans for seducing Dani.

Dani marveled at Saint Petersburg, capital of the Russian empire. She was fascinated at the way the city was built on water, spreading across nineteen islands which were chained by arching bridges and laced by winding canals.

Carefully planned under the personal direction of Peter I, the city named for him was molded of huge baroque palaces in red and yellow, blue and white, or pale green. All buildings were painted, no matter how small, and were plastered and ornamented in colors and styles of the south.

Dani loved being there for the winter season, when arctic latitudes played tricks with time and light. Nights began early in the afternoon, lasting till the middle of the next morning. Whirling snowstorms and icy winds swept across the flat plain surrounding the city to lash windows and walls of the Renaissance palaces, freezing solid the Neva River, she had been told, from mid-November to April.

Yet, despite the gloomy monotony of winter gray, there were days when the sky would glow silver-blue and turn the snowy world to one of sparkling crystal. Dani then would blink against the dazzling glare of the sun.

Despite the mystical, magical beauty of winter, it was said that the loveliest time in Russia was May through June, the time of the poets' paradise called "White Nights," when only about forty minutes of semidarkness occurred within a twenty-four-hour period. By eleven in the evening, the day would fade to a milky haze of pearl and silver, mysteriously veiling the landscape in iridescence.

Dani learned that in addition to the charm and gloss, Saint Petersburg was considered to be the center of Russian life, with great opera, ballet, symphonies, and chamber orchestras playing the music of Tchaikovsky, Glinka, and Mussorgsky.

The official language was French, not Russian, and the best furniture and clothing came from Paris.

It was truly an exciting world of glitter and glamour. Dani had lost count of the receptions she attended where officers in blazing decorations on their brilliant uniforms escorted elegant ladies in billowing satin dresses of every color in the rainbow. She had sipped champagne in ornate high-ceilinged drawing rooms, nibbling cold sturgeon and caviar.

Kitty had written to an influential patron of the arts she had met in Paris to make sure Dani was invited to the Bal Blanc, a dance where young, unmarried girls in virginal white dresses danced quadrilles with young, unmarried officers, while being watched by cold-eyed chaperones.

Cyril had them invited to the Bals Roses to witness the flashing jewels and blue and green and scarlet uniforms as young marrieds swirled to waltzes and gypsy music.

It was a world where ladies donned their diamonds in the morning, attended a church service, entertained for lunch, walked in the crisp, cold winter air in the early afternoon, then spent the remainder of the day preparing for yet another magnificent ball in the evening.

Yes, in a short period of time, Dani had sampled a large part of the excitement and glamour offered by Saint Petersburg . . . but was all too aware that something had eluded her.

She had not encountered Drake.

And how could she even look for him without appearing obvious?

She had thought he would be among the glitter and excitement, then reminded herself he had been banned from the Imperial Court . . . which meant, of course, that others in high society systematically deleted his name from their invitation lists, as well.

So, if he were in Russia, where was he?

This worry plagued her endlessly, her misery intensified by the inability to share her anxiety with anyone.

Again, due to the esteem of having such an internationally revered father, Dani and Colt were provided with residence in the French Embassy, located on the banks of the Dvortsvotsky Most, with a view of the Neva River and situated only two blocks from the Winter Palace of the Czar.

Though small and modest, their rooms were quite comfortable. Colt had a place to the rear of the first floor, with an outside entrance so he could come and go at will, while Dani was more protected, as intended, in a small suite on the second floor with a balcony overlooking the Neva in one direction, the Moika River visible the other way.

Dani loved to stand on the balcony and look toward the Winter Palace, truly a sight to behold. The grandiose edifice was in the baroque style, easily the largest and most splendid building in Saint Petersburg. Each of the palace's four façades had a character of its own. The eastern had a canopy on pylons, its projecting wings forming the main courtyard which opened into the city toward the shipyard, called the Admiralty. The western, ornate with baroque cupids' heads, lions' faces, and scrolls, looked to the Summer Palace in the distance. The northern, facing the Neva, was quieter in style but had a double tier of white columns to impressively effect light and shade. The southern, and main, façade had three arched entrances with Corinthian columns of pure white Italian marble. On the roof were over 176 sculptural figures interspersed with vases.

Dani had a special reason for standing on her balcony this particular evening, trembling with excitement. In a few hours she would actually enter that majestic place. She and Colt had been invited to a ball given by the Czar himself, Alexander III.

When she had told Cyril of the invitation, he had insisted that she take him along as her escort. "Despite my business and social connections," he bitterly admitted, "I've never been to a royal ball, and after all the invitations I've gotten for you, it's the least you can do for me."

Dani was grateful for his kindness and regretted having to say no to him. "The invitation plainly states Colt and I are invited together, just the two of us. I'm truly sorry, Cyril."

He had become quite indignant. "Well, I don't understand how you managed to get such an invitation. It's probably a mistake. Your father probably doesn't even know the Czar," he added testily.

Now, tonight, Dani was too excited to worry over Cyril's hurt pride.

When the invitation had arrived, personally delivered by a bearded Cossack soldier in scarlet tunic, black fur cap, boots, and shining saber at his side, Dani knew she had to have a very special gown for the occasion. She had gone to Saint Petersburg's reigning fashion dictator, Madame Kerensky, the couturière who designed for the wife of the Czar, the Empress Marie Feodorovna.

The dress subsequently created especially for her was of cream silk, embroidered in blue and silver. Then she had spent a large sum on a blue velvet ribbon adorned with diamonds and pearls, which she had entwined in her reddish-brown hair.

Colt had procured a carriage for the evening, and from three blocks away, they could see the pleasure dome flooded by light. When they arrived at the grand entrance, Dani handed her newly purchased white ermine cape to an attendant, and they then ascended the wide white marble staircases, which were covered with thick carpets of gold and red velvet.

They found themselves amid great columns of malachite and marble and jasper supporting high gilded ceilings, from which hung immense gold and crystal chandeliers that dripped with diamond-cut prisms.

Along the walls were baskets of orchids and palm trees in large pots framing huge gilded mirrors.

At intervals along the corridors were stationed troopers of the Chevaliers Gardes, wearing white uniforms with silver breastplates and silver eagle-crested helmets. There were also Cossack Life Guards standing at attention in scarlet tunics.

Dani and Colt whispered together in speculation that there were probably three thousand guests in attendance. Diamonds and rubies and emeralds glittered in the sparkling lights of the chandeliers. The rooms were awash with a sea of colors of every shade. There were officers everywhere—generals wearing medals from the Turkish wars, young Hussars in full dress with tight elkskin breeches. Then there were the austere court officials, dressed in severe black and gold-laced uniforms.

At precisely 8:30, an expectant hush fell on the room as people stepped back to allow a man carrying an ebony staff, embossed in gold with the double-headed eagle of the Czar, to walk to the center of the grand ballroom. He then tapped the staff three times on the marble floor.

Colt leaned to whisper in Dani's ear, "Makes me wish I was back on the ranch instead of being at a circus."

She held a finger to her lips. "Shhh. That's the Grand Master of Ceremonies. The ball is officially starting."

Suddenly great mahogany doors inlaid with gold swung open, and the Grand Master boomed, "Their Imperial Majesties."

Dresses rustled as ladies sank into a deep curtsy, Dani included.

Then Czar Alexander III appeared, bearded and tall. Next to him was his dark-eyed Danish wife, the Empress Marie.

At once, the orchestra began to play a polonaise, and the festivities began.

Dani was besieged by the unmarried Hussar officers, some of whom remembered her from the Bal Blanc. Happily, she enjoyed quadrilles, chaconnes, mazurkas, and waltzes. Then, suddenly, when she was resting between sets with Colt, her breath caught as she realized the Czar himself was by her side. At six feet four inches tall, he was like a great Russian bear.

He reached for her hand, raising her fingertips to his lips, smiled, and spoke in flawless French. "I was told that when I found the most beautiful woman at my ball, I would find Mademoiselle Coltrane. Welcome to Russia and Saint Petersburg. I trust you are enjoying your visit."

Poised and self-confident, Dani did not become flustered before such an important personage. She gave an obligatory curtsy, however slight, before responding. "Quite enjoyable, sire. Thank you for inviting us to the

Imperial Ball.'' She yielded to Colt, who bowed before the Czar.

Czar Alexander addressed himself once more to Dani. ''It was my pleasure to invite you and your brother, mademoiselle. I hold your father in high regard and wish that his children will have a nice visit to my country.''

Dani was aware that all eyes were upon them as they chatted. Empress Marie was nowhere to be seen, and she wished she could have met her as well.

''Tell me, my dear, is there anything in Russia you would like that has not been made available to you?''

Having vowed to never allow an opportunity to pass her by, Dani quickly said, ''I would love to attend the Imperial Ballet.''

Colt rolled his eyes, wondering how his sister could be so gauche. Didn't she realize the man was just being polite, for god's sake, and certainly had more to do with his time than worry about her social life?

Czar Alexander snapped his fingers, and immediately one of his aides stepped to his side. ''The Imperial Ballet it shall be. Tomorrow night at our beautiful gold and blue Maryinsky Theater. Does that make you happy?'' he asked jovially.

Dani curtsied once more. ''You're very kind.''

''If you and your brother would care to join us afterward, the Empress and I are entertaining some friends here at a midnight supper.''

Dani did not ask Colt's opinion; it did not matter. ''We'd love to, and thank you for inviting us.''

He moved away then, and Colt could not help smiling at her happiness. ''I guess this is the highlight of your trip.''

The sparkle of joy was replaced by one of bitter remembrance. ''No. The highlight will be when I get my painting back. Did you know that Drakar was once close friends with the Czar's son, Nicholas?''

He shook his head, took a glass of champagne from a passing waiter.

Dani might have been tempted to confide more, but just then a dashing Hussar officer claimed her for a quadrille, leading her away from Colt's side.

He leaned back against one of the classic pillars, sipped his champagne and watched, wondering if the evening would ever end.

To one side of the grand ballroom stood a small group of young women, each lithe, lean, and lovely, albeit they were not as richly attired as the other ladies present. They wore modest gowns, very little jewelry. Their coiffures were identical, sleeked back into tight chignons.

They stood quietly watching, a few smiling demurely to catch the eye of young Hussars they fancied. Yet, they did not mingle, did not dance, kept themselves apart from the other guests. They were in attendance merely as decoration on a whim of the Czar's son Nicholas. They were members of the elite Imperial Ballet, and because Nicholas was very much in love with the star ballerina, Mathilde Kschessinskaya, these other young ladies had been invited.

However, it was not Mathilde who discreetly watched Dani's every move, but a green-eyed beauty with fiery red hair who was oblivious to the appreciative looks from the men around her. Neither did she notice the envious glares from women who silently, resentfully, acknowledged that she was easily one of the most beautiful ladies present.

She was not even aware of the way Mathilde herself, the only dancer dripping with expensive jewels and appearing wealthy, fired glowering looks at her now and then.

The young woman was intent on watching every move Dani Coltrane made.

Finally, when heads were turned in the direction of the Czar and his empress as they moved to the center of the ballroom to lead a waltz, the girl quietly backed into the shadows and made her way to a terrace door, where she exited to disappear into the night.

She knew Drakar was waiting to hear what she had seen at the Imperial ball.

Chapter Twenty-eight

PATRICK O'Bannon was a handsome Irish seaman who had captured the heart of a Russian beauty—Natasia, a member of the distinguished Romanov family.

As a Romanov, Natasia, by education, language, and taste, was a member of the cosmopolitan aristocracy of Europe. The Romonovs spoke French better than they spoke Russian, and were considered among the elite of society.

Natasia had been titled a princess by virtue of being a cousin of then reigning Czar Alexander II. It was to him that she made her request to be blessed in marriage to Patrick, whom she had met on a sojourn to Dublin during a particularly boring summer.

The Czar and the entire Imperial family were shocked by Nastasia's wish to marry a man who was not only a commoner but a foreigner as well. The marriage was forbidden, and Natasia then turned her back on her country and family and ran away to Ireland to wed her beloved there.

A year later, she gave birth to the only child she was destined to have. Patrick took one look at his newborn daughter and said, "Irish eyes! By glory, even at birth, you can tell the lass will have Irish eyes."

He had thus named his child Jade, confident she would possess eyes the color of the fine gemstone. His prediction came true, and she further blossomed into a child so beautiful that passersby turned to stare, marveling at her loveliness and the rich, vibrant red of her thick, lush hair.

"A pure-blood colleen if ever there was one, b'gorra!" Patrick would crow ecstatically, while Natasia would beam proudly, not caring one whit that her daughter's Russian heritage was being denied.

Life was happy for the O'Bannon family during those golden years, despite Natasia's periodic bouts of homesickness.

Then, when Jade was eight, tragedy struck—during a storm at sea, Patrick O'Bannon was lost and presumed drowned.

Stricken with grief too deep to bear, Natasia wilted like a flower in the sun.

A year later, Alexander II was assassinated. With renewed sorrow and plagued by a desire to see her homeland, Natasia took her daughter to Russia for the funeral of her distant relative.

Jade, with her rare and special beauty, at once caught the eye of Marie Pavlovna, sister-in-law of the new Czar, Alexander III. Marie and her husband, Vladimir, had three sons . . . but not the daughter Marie yearned for. From the moment she saw Jade for the first time, with her brilliant green eyes and silken hair the color of the cardinal, Marie coveted her fiercely. And it was obvious to everyone that Natasia was not well, certainly not able to raise her daughter alone. Marie began to badger her to allow her to adopt Jade.

Natasia resisted with a mother's love, wished only to return to Ireland and her home there, where Patrick's relatives could help her with Jade until she grew stronger.

But Natasia became weaker, was stricken with a fever. Finally, as she breathed her last, she signed away Jade's care to Marie Pavlovna.

On the surface, at least, her mother's disfavor with the royal family was forgotten through the years as Jade grew up at court, the darling of all who knew her, including

Czar Alexander III. She grew up in the company of his children, was tutored by the same instructors.

The summer she was twelve, Jade's foster mother took her on a holiday to Paris. It was there, while attending a ballet at the Eden Theater, a hall given over to musical extravaganzas, that she fell in love with the dance while watching Virginia Zucchi, a virtuoso ballerina, said to be possessed of genius as a dramatic dance performer.

Jade announced, with all seriousness, that her desire was to become a prima ballerina, and she was willing to make every sacrifice to achieve her goal. Marie was delighted and saw to it that she was properly enrolled in the Imperial School of Ballet in Saint Petersburg.

Jade had been aware, during her youth, of how some of her cousins at court snickered behind her back, called her names because of her mixed blood. Determined to prove herself as a dancer, thereby meriting the respect necessary to overshadow her mixed lineage, she studied and practiced diligently and was heralded by her instructors to be destined for greatness.

Jade never behaved like a spoiled Romanov brat. Witty, industrious, she possessed a kind of pixie humor, sometimes suddenly pretending anger then smiling and exuding charm once again.

She continued to follow the career of her mentor, the Italian Virginia Zucchi, who went to Saint Petersburg at a time when the Maryinsky audience was somewhat apathetic to ballet. Zucchi had danced first at a summer theater in some pleasure gardens, causing such a furor with her intense dramatic acting and a solo danced entirely on *pointes* that all Saint Petersburg rushed to see her. When the Imperial Theater reopened for the winter season, she was offered an engagement which resulted in continuing visits and a strong revival of enthusiastic public attendance.

Jade was thrilled to be named as her understudy in a performance of *The Lily Pond*—and was determined to one day be as great as her idol.

But on this crisp winter night, ballet and her career were the farthest things from Jade's mind as she hurried away from the palace in the snowy night, making her way toward the small hotel on the square. She wrapped her white fox cape tightly around her against the wind. No carriage this night, she vowed. She was too well-known, and no one must discover her destination.

Pulling the hood of her cape down to hide as much of her face as possible, she entered the hotel from a side entrance, opting for the stairs rather than the lift. It was an arduous climb to the fifth floor but she did not care. The dear and beloved friend who awaited was worth every effort and inconvenience.

She had but to knock once before the door was jerked open. She flung herself into Drakar's arms, the two embraced, and Jade blinked back furious tears at the thought of the heartache inflicted upon her companion of so many years. They had known each other well while she was growing up with the children of the Czar, when Drakar had been such a good friend of Nicholas's. All too intimately she knew the tragic story concerning his family and his ensuing banishment from court, which she termed unfair and said as much loudly and clearly, much to the dismay of her foster family.

"She was there."

Drakar nodded grimly. So, his suspicions were correct. When first he'd learned there was no cousin with knowledge of the infamous egg, and subsequently realized the message summoning him to Russia was a fake, the wheels within had begun to turn.

"Was she with Arpel?"

She removed her cape, tossed it aside. "I didn't see him all evening." She went to stand before the fireplace to warm her hands.

Drakar was puzzled once more. He'd finally concluded Cyril Arpel was the only person who'd want him out of Paris, for, since he was knowledgeable about art and had traveled extensively in Russia, it was logical he might have heard about the painting, recognized it. He'd had friends watching his office, was not surprised when he'd heard he was in town. What did stun him, however, was hearing about the beautiful woman who'd traveled with him. Her description fit Dani. More checking proved he was right on that point too. So he'd called on Jade to help, knowing in her position she had access to the most intimate circles of society. But where was Cyril tonight and why was Dani at the Imperial ball alone?

He spoke his thoughts to Jade, who promptly shook her head. "I didn't say she was there alone. I said I didn't see Cyril Arpel around her. She was with her brother."

"Her brother?" he echoed, truly mystified then. "Are you quite sure?"

"I'm positive it was her brother, because when I saw the Czar walking toward her, I positioned myself so I could overhear their conversation, and I heard the introductions."

She continued to tell him all she knew, particularly the part when the Czar invited Dani and Colt to attend the ballet as his guests.

She finished by saucily declaring, "I knew she'd be pretty."

"And what made you think that?" he asked, amused.

"Because it would take the most beautiful woman in the world to win your heart."

He reached to playfully tweak her nose. "*You* have already won my heart. Years ago. And you know it."

"Drakar, be serious," she chided.

The light left his eyes. "I am serious. It doesn't matter now what I ever felt for Dani. She hates me. That's the way it is. But I've got to get my hands on that painting."

Because she cared so deeply for him, wanted him to be happy, Jade said, "Can you really be so sure she hates you?"

"I'm sure," he snapped. "Now let's not talk about it. I'd just like to know what she and her brother are doing

here, why Dani would leave Paris and travel with Arpel.''

He had confided to Jade about the painting, and she
thought for a moment, then suggested, ''Maybe he's told
her the story behind the painting and agreed to divide the
reward for the egg with her if she'll help him find it.''

''Good logic, but you don't know Dani. Granted, she
might go on a treasure hunt for fun, but not money. She
doesn't need it any more than you do.''

Jade's expression did not change. It was common
knowledge that, as a Romanov, she had a generous inheritance. She would never have to worry a day in her
life over money; she even gave her meager earnings as a
dancer to charity, for she did not need it. Material things
had never been important to her, anyway.

She walked over to where Drakar stood staring pensively out the window into the night. Pressing herself
against his back and wrapping her arms around his strong
chest, she gently inquired, ''Can I do anything at all to
help?''

Drakar did not respond at once. He was wondering how
to find a way to see Dani and finally confide everything.
Then, if she were involved with Cyril in any kind of ploy
to recover the egg from its hiding place, he might be able
to change her mind and help him instead.

Slowly a plan began to form. Turning, he drew Jade
over to sit beside him on the sofa. ''I need to get to Dani,
to tell her the truth about everything. Getting her away
from Arpel is no problem. No doubt she's staying at the
French Embassy because of her father's importance, and
Arpel has his own place.

''The problem will be Colt,'' he went on thoughtfully.
''He'll be staying nearby. That's where *you* come in if
you're willing to play a little game.''

''Tell me everything, and then I'll decide.''

He then explained what had happened his last night in
Paris, how he'd tried to help Colt. ''Now it seems from
what you tell me, he's soured on all women. What he

needs is to become interested in a girl who, for all intents and purposes, is not wealthy. A hard-working girl, who would seem to have every reason to want him merely for his money, only," he continued after flashing a mischievous grin, eyes twinkling, "the poor girl turns him down and says she doesn't care how rich he is, she just isn't interested.

"That," he finished with a satisfied nod, "should show Monsieur Coltrane that not all women are alike, and then I won't have to feel so bad about the way my other scheme turned out. It'll also give me a chance to be with Dani. Will you do it?" he asked hopefully.

Jade did not have to ponder for long. It sounded intriguing. No one would get hurt. Colt would be disappointed, of course, when she had to tell him he just wasn't the sort of man she could love, but ultimately he would be happier, have a healthier outlook concerning women. Besides, he seemed nice and was certainly attractive. But would he find her attractive enough for the scheme to work? She revealed her thoughts to Drakar, and he told her she was ridiculous.

"All men find you beautiful. Colt will be no exception, believe me."

So they finalized their plans. Jade recalled that one of the students at the ballet school was having a romance with one of the couriers stationed at the embassy. So she was confident that, through her friendship with the girl, it could be arranged for her to pose as an embassy maid.

"Just leave Colt to me," she finished confidently. "I'll play the role of seductress, yet restore his confidence in women so he won't regard each one he meets as someone out to get his fortune."

"But what about tomorrow night at the ballet?" Drakar was quick to point out. "If he sees you on stage, he might recognize you later."

"No, that's not a problem," she said, waving away his fears. "My hair will be styled as it is now, and I'll look quite different in costume than I will as a *femme de chambre*—starched uniform and cap, hair braided.'' She gave a mock curtsy and winked.

He chuckled. ''Very well. We'll set things up for to-morrow night, when they return to the embassy after the Czar's midnight supper. I'll leave Colt to you, and I'll slip into Dani's room and attempt to make her believe me.''

Chapter Twenty-nine

DANI was enthralled to actually be at the breathtakingly beautiful Maryinsky Theater and see the famed Russian ballet. The fact that she was sitting in the back row of the Imperial box was merely frosting on the cake, for it was grand enough just to be in attendance.

The audience glittered with finery and jewels in complement to the crystal and gold chandeliers sparkling throughout the hall. Dani's own costume was in competition with Empress Marie herself. Fashioned of emerald velvet, the bodice was crusted with hundreds of tiny topazes. Impressed by his sister's beauty, Colt had marveled at how the stones caught the happy glimmer in her cinnamon eyes that night.

The performance was *Coppélia*, which had been created during the Franco-Prussian War. Tears of joy had come to Dani's eyes at watching Mathilde Kschessinskaya perform as the mischievous heroine, Swanilda.

Dani applauded with respectful delight at the introduction of Marius Petipa, the brilliant ballet master and choreographer of the Imperial Ballet.

The colorful costumes, the precision and lightness of the dancers, held her entranced throughout the performance. She could close her eyes, pretend it was actually she on stage so gracefully maneuvering the *battements* and *pirouettes*.

All too soon it was over, and they were at the Winter
Palace once more. Supper was served in a long mirrored
hall, the food displayed on damask-covered tables amid
delicate carvings of ice. They enjoyed *bliny*—small pancakes served with caviar; fish served with melted butter;
pyelmeni—meat dumplings; *borshch*—a beet soup; *stakan
kiselya*—a dessert of thickened cranberry juice; and *ma-
rozhnoye*—Russian ice cream.

There was rich steamed coffee, unbelievably dark in
color, as well as champagne, a variety of wines, and, of
course, vodka. Dani had to stifle a sneeze at the taste of
the *Ghorilka s pertsem* variety, Ukrainian in origin and
seasoned with hot peppers.

Dani was not surprised when the Czar's daughter Princess Xenia attached herself to Colt and made herself his
unofficial hostess for the evening. She was pleased to see
them walk together into an adjoining parlor to view some
of the palace's art collection.

She herself found the company of the Czar's son, Nicholas, to be quite enjoyable. She was tempted to ask him
questions about the dancer she admired, remembering
Cyril's gossip about the future Czar's romance with
Mathilde Kschessinskaya, but did not dare. She did, however, when responding to his polite inquiry as to how
she'd enjoyed the ballet, enthusiastically comment, "All
the dancers were good but none equaled Mademoiselle
Kschessinskaya. She is truly wonderful."

There was no missing the look of pride and affection
in his dark, piercing eyes, as he agreed. "Yes, Mathilde
is an artist Russia can be proud of."

As Nicholas kindly took her on an intimate tour of one
wing of the palace, Dani's mind raced to think of a way
to bring up the subject of Drakar. Just thinking of him
brought bitter bile to her throat. Cyril had told her Drakar
and Nicholas had once been close. Perhaps now that
Drakar was no doubt back in Russia, the two had been
in contact.

Suddenly, a large mural on the wall of a parlor caught her eye, and she cried in recognition, "The Alexandrovsky Palace."

Nicholas was mildly surprised. "You recognize that?"

She mutely nodded, momentarily mesmerized.

A servant appeared with a tray containing glasses of champagne, and Dani absently took the glass Nicholas gave her. He was curious about her strange reaction and asked, "Then you've been to Tsarskoye Selo?"

"No."

He emitted an astonished chuckle. "Then how did you recognize the palace?"

She decided perhaps this was an opportunity to let him know the fabled painting had been found and to learn if he knew Drake was in Saint Petersburg. She related the story of her Monaco Find, how the crude rendering of the Alexandrovsky Palace had subsequently been stolen . . . but did not mention Drake . . . or that she knew the secret of the painting.

The young man destined to be the next czar of Russia listened to her every word. When she had finished, he took a deep breath, feigned a sympathetic expression, and said, "How unfortunate, but you said yourself the painting was obviously worthless, so you really haven't lost anything, have you?"

He did not give her a chance to comment, for he turned and began to talk of other things as he led her out of the room.

Dani did not miss the strange look that had come into his eyes, knew he had been startled by her story. Preoccupied with Nicholas's reaction, Dani did not observe how the servant who had been hovering nearby had nearly dropped his tray when he'd heard her story.

Nor did she notice the way he turned to scurry away in the opposite direction, looking quite pale and shaken.

Colt reluctantly left Dani at the door of her suite. She was very depressed, for the opportunity had not arisen for her to ask Nicholas if he knew anything about his old friend's whereabouts.

"Tomorrow," she said with finality. "I am going to see Nicholas and come right out and ask him if he's heard from Drake. I've got to find him," she went on angrily. "I don't intend to stay in Russia all winter like a frivolous debutante. I want my painting, and then I want to go home. I've a business to run."

Colt kissed her cheek. "I'll go with you if you want. I don't have anything else to do. Now get some sleep."

He left her, went to his own room downstairs at the rear. He liked the way the embassy was arranged. The business offices were situated in the middle of the square building, while a hallway ran entirely around to separate the private residences and guest quarters from the offices. Colt had a bedroom, private toilet facilities, and a tiny parlor. The size suited him fine.

He unlocked his door, stepped inside, realized all the lamps were burning and wondered why. The evening maid usually left on only the night light in the parlor.

"Oh, monsieur. I am so sorry!"

He blinked at the sight of the young girl coming from his bedroom, carrying a bundle of bed linens.

She was almost trembling with her apology. "Please do not report me. I will lose my job. I should have been finished with my duties hours ago, but I was late leaving my other job, and I'd hoped to finish before you returned."

A glance at the clock on a nearby table caught his eye. It was nearly four A.M. He eyed her suspiciously. "Maids don't work this time of the night. I think I'd better call security."

"No, please!" She dropped the bundle of linens and covered her face with trembling hands, peered out at him through her fingers. "No, monsieur. Please do not report me. I would lose my job, and I must have it to live. I have to help with my family, and—" She swung her head wildly from side to side, appeared to be sobbing as bright red hair came undone from pins beneath her white lacy cap to cascade downward and swing loose and free around her face and shoulders.

Even in his surprise, Colt had not missed seeing the rare beauty of this girl. Her green eyes, so wide with fear, looked like crystallized jade. She wore a white uniform, buttoned up the front to beneath her throat, but he could see the way her lush bosom strained against the fabric. The cotton skirt reached to the floor, but he had also noticed the curve of her rounded bottom.

She was gorgeous.

He walked to where she stood, pulled her hands from her face and held her wrists to force her to meet his stern expression. "Tell me the truth, girl," he harshly demanded, "or I'll call security right now. What are you doing in my room this time of night?"

Jade pretended to be terribly frightened, although she found it difficult to keep from laughing to think how good an actress she was. With great effort, she made her voice tremble. "I am telling the truth, sir, you must believe me. There are no jobs in Saint Petersburg for poor, uneducated girls like me. I can only find work as a maid, and I clean a mansion during the day for a countess so miserly she will only pay for one servant, and I must do the work of many before I can leave. I don't make enough money there, so I had to take this one at night, and they've been very understanding about my sometimes coming in late, as long as I don't disturb any of the guests.

"Your room," she rushed on, words tumbling on top of each other as she feigned near-hysteria, "has been last, because you always come in late, but tonight I was much later than usual but dared to think I could finish before you returned. Please, sir, forgive me."

She slumped against him then, laying her head on his shoulder as though completely exhausted, well aware that her breasts pressed against him intimately.

Colt's breath caught in his throat. Damn, she was lovely, and he could feel desire welling . . . and something else . . . an unfamiliar tenderness.

Feeling somewhat embarrassed for having behaved like an ogre when she was obviously telling the truth, he released her wrists and put his arm around her to comfort her. Gathering her close, he walked her to the velvet bench by the window and sat her down. "Let me get you a glass of wine. I've a carafe in the bedroom.

"And stop your crying," he crisply called over his shoulder. "I won't report you."

He disappeared into the other room, and Jade dabbed at her eyes with the corner of her starched blue apron. Such an actress. She'd actually produced a few genuine tears, she marveled.

He returned with a glass of Burgundy.

"I shouldn't," she protested. "I'd be severely chastised for drinking, especially here, with you . . ." She looked up at him through thick, silken lashes.

Colt sucked in his breath involuntarily. God, he'd never seen anyone so magnificently beautiful. Her skin was the color of fine cream, and her hair glowed with a thousand fires. There was an unfamiliar accent to her voice that was melodic, sensuous.

He sat down beside her. "Now what's this about you having to work two jobs?"

She repeated her story between sips of wine, finished by hopefully asking, "Can you understand now why I was so frightened when you came in, monsieur? You truly promise not to report me?"

He smiled. "I never promise anything. My word is good enough. Tell me," he went on, "what's your name?"

She gave him a warm look. He was nice, quite handsome, and she only hoped she could do what Drakar had asked without hurting this very desirable young man. "Jade," she told him.

He looked into the misty depths of her eyes and felt a rush within as he murmured, "Jade," then smiled. "Of course. What else could it be?"

In the salon of her suite, Dani tossed aside her fur and went to stand before the warmth of the marbled fireplace, which was enframed by mahogany. Upon the mantel was an array of German and Swiss silver-gilt pieces before a painting by Ruoppolo.

The suite was charming, but Dani was not thinking of opulence or comfort as she rubbed her arms absently, pensively. Her thoughts were much like the fire, twisting, dancing, finally disappearing into thin streams of smoke without resolution or form.

Where was Drake?

He had to be in Russia.

Where else would he have gone?

And why, dear god, did he have to leave so suddenly and do what he did? To steal the painting, to destroy everything that had been growing between them? How could he want something that badly? Perhaps she might have understood had it been a valuable piece of art, or if he'd even been in dire need of the money it might bring. But he was a very rich man.

She shook her head, bit down on her lower lip to stifle the impulse to cry.

What a fool she had been! The bitter taste of that realization would linger for a long, long time.

With a sigh of disgust, she went into the bedroom. Just inside there was a small dining alcove for intimate teas or late suppers. A French chandelier hung above the Sheraton pedestal breakfast table, surrounded by four Regency chairs. A lovely beige and gold Aubusson rug covered the coldness of the marble floor.

The bed dominated the room; it was a Georgian cherrywood with a canopy covered in flowered chintz. The walls were done in faux-bois paneling, echoed in the painted nightstand. A matched pair of mahogany serpentine china cabinets stood on each side of the draped and arched doorway leading to the balcony.

She was assailed by a chilling draft, noticed irritably that one of the sheer panels covering the glass was gently billowing. A door had not been properly closed. She moved to shut it, then froze as the sound of a familiar voice seemed to reach out to caress with its tenderness.

"Good morning, my darling."

She did not have to see to know it was Drake who spoke. For a moment, she continued to stand perfectly still, drawing in her breath as she commanded her pounding heart to slow. Finally, she went on to close the door, and only then did she turn.

He was standing in the shadows in a far corner of the room. Contempt dripping like venom, she hissed, "You bastard! How dare you sneak into my bedroom . . . but then, sneaking around in my quarters during the night seems to be your forte!"

Drakar stepped from darkness into light and, arrogantly smiling, inquired, "And what is that supposed to mean?"

She saw that he was dressed in black shirt and trousers, cursed herself for the sudden rush of warmth within. Truly he was a handsome devil. "Which?" she fired back acidly. " 'Bastard' . . . or the reference to your nocturnal tendencies?"

He stood before her. "I knew you were angry about what happened that last night in Paris, so I suppose that's where the name-calling comes in, albeit a bit strong for such delicate lips, but what's the reason behind the rest of your sarcasm?"

Dani clenched her fists at her side, aching to slap the insolence from his handsome face. "Wasn't it insult enough that you turned out to be the womanizing scalawag I'd heard you were—without your stooping to the level of a common thief?"

He raised an eyebrow. What in the hell was she talking about? "Explain that remark, Dani."

She waved her arms wildly, unleashing some of the furious energy threatening to explode. "You know damn well what I'm talking about. What you can't have, *you take*!"

He grabbed her arms, pinned them to her sides. How dare she make such an accusation? He'd thought she was a mature, intelligent woman. There had been no seduction. She'd given herself freely.

His own ire erupted. "Are you crazy? You dare to play the role of innocent, indignant virgin? You know you wanted it every bit as much as I did. There were no commitments, and—"

"Damn you!"

He fell silent before the detonation of her fury.

Dani struggled to keep her voice down, lest someone hear, but dear god, she didn't think she'd ever been so mad. "I'm not talking about what happened between us, and you know it. I'm talking about your stealing from me. How could you?"

"Steal?" he echoed, stupefied. "I've never stolen anything in my life."

He released her to stare down in complete bafflement. "I swear I don't know what you're talking about."

Dani regarded him coldly. He sounded sincere but she knew he was the sort who specialized in appearing innocent. Lips curling back contemptuously, she challenged him. "You lie, Drake! You know I'm talking about the painting. You took it the night you ran away from Paris."

Fingers of dread clutched his spine, mentally shaking him to awareness as he asked the question he feared to have answered. "Are you talking about the painting of the Alexandrovsky Palace?"

Her laugh was brittle, taunting. "You amaze me, Drake. Did you think I wouldn't suspect you? Why, you were the first person I thought of before I even heard you'd run away that night—too scared to face my brother.

"God, Dani, I didn't take it. I was even planning to come tell you the next day why I wanted it so badly. But

I received an urgent message calling me to Russia. I had to leave, and there was no time to come and tell you. You wouldn't have listened to anything I had to say that night, anyway.''

She laughed coldly. ''Oh, another of your mixed-up messages? You do seem to have a time with them, don't you?''

''Believe me, I wasn't running away from Colt. Once he'd had time to calm down, I was going to explain everything to him and make him see the whole thing was set up for him to realize Lily was a fake.''

''I don't care about any of that now,'' Dani snapped. ''You probably did me a favor by letting me know what a liar and a cheat you really are before I wasted any more of my time on you. I came here for one reason—to get my painting back. I didn't want any publicity about the theft, but if you don't return it, you leave me no choice but to have you arrested.''

''I didn't take your painting, Dani. If I had, would I have come here tonight?''

She laughed tauntingly. ''I wouldn't put anything past you. You probably came here because you heard I was in Saint Petersburg to have you arrested, so you decided to sneak in here and pretend you didn't know anything about the theft. Well, it won't work, because I don't believe you. Now give me my painting,'' she finished, raising her voice ever so slightly, ''so I can go home and forget I ever knew you!''

Her eyes burned into his, fiery dots of burnt, smoldering cinnamon.

He turned away again, this time walking to the french doors leading to the balcony. Flinging one open, he drank deeply of the crisp air, hoped the frost in his lungs would move on to his brain and awaken him to some way of making her believe him.

But, he reminded himself with painful awareness, if the painting had been stolen then he was right back where he'd started ten years ago when he set out to find it for the Czar and restore honor to the Mikhailonov name. Unless . . .

He snapped his fingers, ignored her scorning glare as he turned and cried, "Arpel!"

"What does Cyril have to do with any of this?" Dani coldly asked.

He took a deep breath, held out his hand to her. "You don't owe me anything, Dani, and I can understand why you're angry and upset, but all I'm asking is for you to hear me out, give me a chance to explain my side."

She looked at his outstretched hand, the beseeching expression on his face, but was not moved.

"Dani, please. Give me a chance."

"Why should I?"

He closed the door behind him, took a step closer to her. "Because I think if you're honest with yourself, you'll admit there just might be a slight chance that I am telling the truth, and if you don't hear me out, you're always going to wonder."

She continued to glare at him, did not yield. "You flatter yourself to think I have that much regard for you, monsieur."

Quietly, he used his last verbal weapon. "Are you afraid?"

"Afraid?" she echoed with a shrill laugh. "Of you? All I have to do is scream once, and the guards will come running. I'm surprised you were even able to sneak in here."

"Not of me," he said, "of *yourself*, your *heart*. Are you afraid to hear me out because you're afraid to admit you care?"

She laughed once more, promptly dropped to the velvet bench at the end of the bed. She gave him a curt nod. "Go ahead. Talk. I'm sure this will be a very interesting lie, but at least you'll see I'm not like your other women. I can be around you and not fall under your spell."

He ignored her sarcasm, began to pace about the room, speaking quietly, in an almost hushed tone, as he proceeded to reveal the secrets of his past.

A half hour later, he finished with a ragged sigh. "That's it, Dani, and I swear every word is true."

He faced her then, for he'd avoided looking at her as he spoke, not wanting to see her contempt or ridicule lest it prevent him from confiding the true depth of agony in his heart.

"Can you believe me?" he asked.

He saw golden-brown eyes brimmed with tears.

Then, at last, she trusted herself to speak and held out her arms to him. "Yes, I can, Drake. Maybe I'm a fool, but I do believe you."

Quickly he lifted her to her feet and drew her against him in a deep embrace that left them both shaken.

Huskily, he declared, "I'm never going to let you go again, Dani. I swear it."

She laughed, softly, tenderly, then stood on tiptoe to kiss each cheek. "No, you won't, because I'm not going to let you."

He continued to hold her, daring to further confide that, because of his mother, he'd mistrusted all women. "That's why it took me so long to tell you about my past, Dani. I had to grow close to you."

"I knew some of it. Cyril told me about your being banished from court due to some scandal with your family." She shivered just to think of his anguish. "But he didn't tell me just how terrible it was."

"Cyril has the painting. I know it. Somehow he knew the story about Zigmont Koryatovich concealing a clue to the whereabouts of that egg somewhere in the painting. He figured I was after it, too, so he sent me that fake telegram to get me out of town in order for him to get his hands on it. He was betting that you'd blame me once you discovered the painting had been stolen, and he was right."

"I'm sorry, Drake," Dani whispered.

"How did you happen to be traveling here with him? I figured he'd show up in Saint Petersburg sooner or later, so I was having his place watched. That's how I heard you were in Russia, but I couldn't understand why."

She explained how it had all come about, how she'd used Cyril to assure her access to society and the world of art in Saint Petersburg. "I knew he'd be in the middle of the social whirl, and even though, thanks to Poppa, Colt and I got invited to the Imperial Palace and the ballet, there's very little else we would've been able to be a part of without Cyril. He's furious with me now because this is the second night I've had an invitation that didn't include him."

Drakar told her not to feel pity. "I'm still having him watched. He's seeing one of his old girlfriends and having a marvelous time."

Dani was amazed that Cyril could stoop so low but conceded it would be quite valuable to his career to be the one to discover the secret of the painting, and, subsequently, the famous missing Fabergé egg.

The nerve in Drakar's jaw tightened as she spoke, then he tersely predicted, "Well, he's going to be very disappointed, because we're going to get it back. Evidently, he hasn't figured out the secret, or he'd have done so by now."

Worriedly, Dani asked if he thought he'd be able to unravel the mystery.

"Given enough time to study the painting, yes. I'm not worried about that. I just have to get my hands on it, that's all."

"I'll help any way I can."

His voice was warm, as caressing as his hands that moved along her back and downward to cup her buttocks and press her closer to him. "It helps just knowing you're on my side, Dani, that you're with me in this."

He kissed her, and this time they gently fell upon the bed, yielding to the rising passion within, the emotions of desire that would not be denied.

Chapter Thirty

Two nights passed before Drake and Dani dared to enter Cyril's shop, located on a busy street facing the Griboyedov Canal. The first night, they had stood outside at dusk long enough to see his guest of the evening entering. Knowing the tall, thin dark-haired woman would, no doubt, stay until dawn in his rooms upstairs, they had turned away in disappointment, their plans for burglary thwarted for the night.

Each day, Cyril had invited Dani to go out with him in the evening, and she had made her excuses. He then made his own plans.

The evenings, however, Dani happily reflected, had not been wasted, for she and Drake had spent the time in his hotel room over intimate dinners, getting to know each other, no longer concealing anything from each other.

There had, however, been a confrontation of sorts between Colt and Drake when Dani had brought them together at breakfast in her suite the morning after her reunion with Drake.

At first, Colt had been belligerent, angry, but she had pleaded with him to listen to everything Drake had to say. Finally, he had grudgingly consented and Drake explained his scheme to expose Lily, then went on to confide his own past, so that Colt would not think him responsible for the theft of the painting.

At first, Colt was dubious, but, as Drake talked, he sensed, as Dani had, that he was telling the truth. Finally, he was able to give his blessings to both in their attempt to recover the painting and to their renewed relationship.

Dani wondered later about how preoccupied Colt had seemed. The past few days he'd suddenly begun to behave mysteriously, making excuses to spend time alone, saying he had some sightseeing to do on his own. Acknowledging that it was of course his business, she was still curious.

Meanwhile, Dani and Drake were growing closer with each hour they spent together, and Dani privately acknowledged that if what she was feeling for him was not love, then never would she understand either the true meaning of the word or the emotion.

She dared to believe, also, from the look in his warm blue eyes when he held her and made love to her, that he was also experiencing the same feelings.

But they needed time, she knew, much time, for each to come to terms with the true depth of their feelings.

Most of all, it was imperative that Drake get the painting into his possession and once and for all unravel the mystery and end the quest that was consuming his life.

But . . . unless they were able to get inside Cyril's shop, that all-important time was standing still.

Finally, on the third night, their vigil was rewarded when Cyril left his shop and hailed a passing carriage. Dressed regally, he was obviously going to an opera or concert, and would be out for many hours.

They watched the carriage disappear into a whirl of snow, then, hand in hand, they ran across the street, boots crunching in the ice and snow.

The door was locked, of course, but Drake was prepared. Reaching into his pocket for the special tool he'd brought, he slipped it into the keyhole and within seconds, the door swung open without evidence of burglary.

Once inside, he locked it once more, lest a policeman come by, routinely checking.

They opened a glass door and entered the wide hallway which served as Cyril's modest gallery. Dani was unimpressed with the art displayed, finding none of any great merit.

There was a door at the end of the gallery, and one on each side. The one on the left opened to a stairway to the rooms upstairs. On the right, there was a small room, empty, which Dani said was a private salon, provided for any patron wishing to be alone for contemplation of a work he was considering buying.

"We'll go upstairs after we check out his office," Drake said, moving through the remaining door.

The room was large and furnished with a desk, several chairs, and a small sofa. Shelves stacked with books and papers covered one wall; two trunks stood against another. In a corner stood empty discarded shipping crates for paintings.

"Check everything," Drake directed crisply. "Even the shipping crates. The painting was small and might be stuck down in one of those. I'll take care of these." He moved to one of the trunks and began to rummage through prints and old canvasses, obviously worthless.

Dani stepped away from the crates, disappointed. "I'm sorry. There's nothing here."

Together, they searched everything else in the room, then Drake glanced around in futility and sighed. "Well, it's obvious he didn't hide it down here. It's probably upstairs, where he can have more privacy scrutinizing it. Let's go up there."

They started to leave the office, but suddenly Drake reached out to pull Dani against him almost roughly. "Someone's coming," he whispered, then Dani also heard the sound of a woman laughing shrilly. He grabbed her hand, pulling her along with him as he stepped into the gallery. Ahead, through the frosted glass door, they could see two figures stepping into the foyer.

A woman's voice: "I told you it would be much nicer here than at the opera. Wait till you taste the supper I'm going to make for you."

Cyril's voice, thick with lust, echoed, "I'd rather have a taste of you, my pet."

The woman laughed again.

Drake gave Dani a tug. "In here. They won't be going into the private salon."

He closed the door quietly after them, and they stood very still in the darkness, scarcely daring to breathe as they listened to the sounds of Cyril and his ladyfriend making their way through the narrow gallery, finally disappearing up the stairway to his rooms.

Somewhere above a door slammed, and seizing the opportunity, Drake quickly led Dani from the building.

A short distance away, they found a café open. They hurried inside, and when they were settled at a table in a secluded corner and a pot of hot coffee had been served, Dani expressed her crushing disappointment.

"I'll just have to spend an evening with Cyril to give you a chance to search the upstairs," she dismally offered.

Drake concurred. "Have the embassy chef prepare a supper and invite him over," he suggested. "It shouldn't take me long."

"What if you don't find it? What if he's already figured out the clues and found the egg and sold it?"

He had thought of that possibility but not with any great amount of concern. "I don't think that's likely. If he'd already found it, all of Europe would have heard about it by now. It's worth a fortune in gold and diamonds, not to mention the artistic value because it's a Fabergé creation."

"You need to find it as soon as possible," Dani said, "and I'll see to it that you have all the time you need tomorrow night. It's going to be hard to be pleasant to that miserable little sneak after all he's done, but he deserves to be on the receiving end of a little treachery. I'll even try to kidnap Colt from whatever he's doing these evenings," she rushed to add. "He can join us to keep Cyril from getting any romantic notions."

There was the play of a smile on Drake's lips. "I wonder where Colt's spending his time. Surely there's not a woman involved, as sour as he is on the opposite sex."

Dani regretfully concurred. "I'm afraid that's something he'll have to resolve himself. Lily wasn't the first to beguile him, but he's promised himself she'll be the last. He's so afraid they're all after his money."

He struggled to keep a straight face. He felt a bit guilty over not confiding his scheme but was afraid she wouldn't approve. Better, he felt, to never acknowledge he knew anything at all about Colt's short-lived romance with Jade O'Bannon.

It had begun to snow quite hard, the wind whipping the frozen white crystals into cascading sheets that were blinding in intensity. Drake observed the impending danger of being caught away from their quarters in such weather and determined they should leave the café. He took Dani to the front door of the embassy and, after a soul-searing kiss, lustily told her, "We're going to have to find a way to kiss each other good morning instead of good night."

With that, he plunged into the whirling white night of frozen obscurity, and Dani stared after him wistfully—wantonly—for she wanted him with a passion that still awed her with its gnawing hunger.

Too keyed up to go to bed just yet, she went to Colt's door and knocked, thinking how nice it would be for him to join her for hot chocolate and pastries. The embassy chef always left something in the kitchen for a midnight supper of sorts.

Colt opened the door almost at once. He was wearing a robe, and she was at once taken aback by the bright, happy glow in his eyes. She extended her invitation but he politely declined, saying he was tired, had already retired for the night, would see her in the morning. He almost closed the door in her face.

Dani then went to her own rooms, once again puzzled by Colt's mysterious behavior, vowing that as soon as the situation with Drake and Cyril and the painting was resolved, she would find out just what was going on in her brother's secret world.

Drake was surprised to find Jade in his hotel room, curled up in a chair by the window and staring out at the white world beyond, abject misery etched upon her lovely young face.

At once, he crossed the room to kneel before her and take her hands in his. "Jade, what's wrong?" he worriedly asked. He could see the unshed tears glimmering in her awesomely beautiful eyes.

Wretchedly, she shook her head and looked at him with so much pain and despair that his own heart constricted with agony. Swallowing hard, she forced a smile and, with great effort, made her voice calm. "Well, did you find it?"

He shook his head miserably, released her hands and stood as he told what had happened. He saw her disappointment and rushed to explain the plans for the next night. "With Dani keeping Cyril busy, I should have ample time to look in his rooms upstairs. If the painting is there, rest assured I'll find it."

She nodded, turned sad eyes once more toward the window and the crystal-tinged darkness of the world beyond.

Drake was puzzled by her mood. "Jade, has Colt done something to hurt you?"

"No, nothing like that," she was quick to assure him as she stood. Retrieving her cape from where she'd carelessly tossed it across the bed, she said, "I found an understudy who was eager to take my place, after I pretended to sprain my ankle. Now I can spend my evenings with Colt, but in order to keep him believing I'm working as a maid at the embassy, I have to leave him for a few hours, then I go back to have a good-night drink. He's waiting for me now. I just came by to see you and ask how things went tonight.

"It all leaves me quite tired, physically and emotionally," she said with a sigh as Drake took her cape, draped it across her shoulders. "I'll be relieved when it's all over."

He nodded with understanding. "It's logical Colt would be leery of a new relationship, Jade. It may take a little time, but I'm confident that any night now he'll do or say something that will put you in a position to declare that you just can't feel any more for him than friendship, no matter how rich you've heard he is. "Then," he said in finality, kissing her cheeks in turn as he hugged her, "it will be all over, and I will forever be in your debt."

He opened the door for her, and she stepped out into the hall, her parting words barely audible. "That's not what I'm worried about."

Then she was gone.

And Drake was left staring after her, more bewildered than ever.

Chapter Thirty-one

CYRIL stared at the painting lying on his bed, and frowned. Dammit, he had spent hours studying every detail and still had no clue as to where the revolutionary pseudoartist had hidden the Fabergé egg. The painting was merely a crude replica of the palace. No more. No less. How in the hell did Koryatovich intend for anyone to guess where the treasure was hidden within? According to legend, no one, except for the Czar and a few confidants, even knew the subject of the famed painting. Others knew only of the rumor that Koryatovich had done a painting, giving the clues, and that it had been smuggled out of prison by his ladylove, Annine Mikhailonov.

Cyril felt abject frustration to actually possess the painting and not be able to decipher the mystery. There was certainly no one he could ask to help. He turned it over in his hands, shook his head. He'd removed the frame, made of some kind of wood he was unfamiliar with, certainly not from a tree found in Russia, to afford closer scrutiny . . . but to no avail.

Carelessly he bent to shove it under the bed, thinking angrily that the whole thing was probably a hoax.

He took one last look at his reflection in the full-length mirror. Dressed in a jacket of royal-blue velvet, tight elkskin breeches, and an overcoat of black leather, he knew he looked extremely nice. Doubtless Dani would think so too. Perhaps, he mused, it was time to just forget about

the painting, regard it as a myth, and concentrate on winning her heart. Then he could forget about a "find,"
could even forget about seriously pursuing his career, because if he married into the Coltrane millions, he'd never
have to work another day in his life.

He smiled at his reflection. Dani liked him. He was
sure of it. True, she'd been busy on her own a few evenings since they'd arrived in Saint Petersburg, and he'd
been miffed a time or two, but she *was* a Coltrane and it
was only natural she'd be entertained by dignitaries now
and then, and he wouldn't be included. Still, once they
were engaged, it would be a different story. He'd be accepted then.

He sighed with happiness just thinking how his life
would be as the husband of Dani Coltrane. They would
never want for anything, would travel the entire world like
royalty. So, to hell with snobby old rich women nagging
him to find them an exclusive painting to make their
equally snobby friends envious, and to hell with crude little paintings with mysterious legends.

He was going to forget everything except the number-
one priority in his life for the moment—making Dani his
wife.

He picked up the little foil-wrapped box lying on the
table. As soon as he'd received Dani's handwritten note
inviting him to supper in her quarters at the embassy, he'd
visited the House of Fabergé on Bolshaya Morskaya Street
to buy a special gift.

Peter Carl Fabergé himself had waited on Cyril. In
1870, at the age of twenty-four, he'd taken over the prestigious firm established by Gustav Fabergé in 1842. The
House had grown steadily since, having been granted the
Royal Warrant from Alexander III in 1885, after design-
ing the first imperial easter egg for the Empress Marie
Feodorovna. In the same year, another honor was bestowed—a gold medal at the Nuremberg Fine Art exhibition for gold replicas of Scythian treasures. Then, in

1890, the premises in Saint Petersburg doubled in size, and another store was opened in Odessa.

Cyril was awed by the tiny gold brooch, not quite two inches in size, that Fabergé had offered him. In the form of a knotted bow of broad ribbon, it was enameled translucent pink over a moiré background and bordered with rose diamonds set in silver.

There had been no quibbling over price. In the House of Fabergé, one never asked price. The piece was taken "on approval" and either returned within a few days, or payment rendered upon inquiry as to amount.

Cyril knew the piece was expensive, and while he was certainly a man of moderate means, such a gift was not in his budget. However, he considered it an investment in his future. If Dani accepted it, chances were he'd eventually win her hand, and once that happened, money would never again be a problem. He knew he could stall Fabergé for payment by telling him his ladyfriend had not yet made up her mind as to whether she liked the piece. And if she flatly refused to accept it, well, he'd just return it.

Whistling happily, Cyril put the tiny package in his coat pocket and left.

Dani waited impatiently for Cyril, anxious for the evening to be over. She wished Colt could have joined them to help relieve some of the pressure, but he had declined without explanation, merely said, with a mysterious smile, that he had other plans. Dani had not probed, for she respected his privacy, and suspected there was a woman involved. Good. Perhaps he was coming out of his bitter cynicism of females.

There was a soft knock on the door, and she checked her appearance in the gilded mirror. Her dress of mauve satin, the scooped neckline edged in mink, was tastefully alluring.

She swung open the door, and Cyril stood smiling at her, shining eyes becoming glazed with desire as they swept over her.

"Lovely, as always, my dear," he said, kissing her hand. Then, once they were inside, he gave her the present. "For you, because you've come to mean so much to me," he murmured.

Dani groaned inwardly. She didn't want any gifts from him. With effort, she made her voice pleasant. "Cyril, you shouldn't have. It wasn't necessary." She laid the gift on the sideboard next to the door, dismissing it as she gestured to the array of crystal decanters and glasses. "Would you care for a drink before dinner?"

Cyril was bewildered. It was not like Dani to be ungracious. He'd not seen her in several days, not since she'd gone to the Imperial Ball and then to the ballet, but somehow, he sensed a disturbing change.

She was staring at him expectantly, her hand still extended to indicate the offering of liqueurs, whisky, and vodka.

"Ah, yes," he said finally. "Schnapps would be nice. But don't you want to open my gift?" With a wink, he added, "It's from the House of Fabergé."

She did not respond, merely busied herself pouring their drinks.

"Peter Carl Fabergé himself helped pick it out for you," he continued. "You *do* know about the famed goldsmith to the Imperial Court of Russia, don't you?"

Dani's eyes narrowed. Oh, how she yearned to tell him just what she did know about the work of Fabergé!

With a tight smile, she said, "Yes, I do, and you're very kind, Cyril, but I've always been shy about opening presents. Can it wait till after dinner?" She knew by then she would probably throw it in his face, so why go through the charade of pretending to be appreciative now?

Disappointed, he said he supposed that would be all right, then took the small glass of schnapps she offered, downed it in one, burning gulp.

Dani poured a brandy for herself, then indicated they should take a seat in the parlor.

Trying to dissipate the strange, tense mood that had somehow descended, Cyril mustered enthusiasm as he urged, "Tell me about your visit to the Winter Palace, and I'd also like to hear how you enjoyed the ballet."

She was only too glad to oblige, relating every delightful detail.

Cyril pretended to be captivated, but all the while he was thinking about how truly lovely and desirable she was, how his arms ached to hold her, his lips burned to kiss her . . .

"Cyril, are you listening?" Dani asked, annoyed.

He nodded his head jerkily, embarrassed. "Yes, yes, do go on, please."

There was a knock, and she stood, knew it was the waiter to serve the first course. "Never mind. It's time to eat, anyway."

Doggedly, he followed her into the dining alcove, noted with interest that it adjoined the bedroom. That would make it convenient should he be fortunate enough later to make her desire match his.

Dani dawdled with her soup, while Cyril ate his quickly, wanting to have dinner finished as quickly as possible to dispense with the hovering servant. "Don't you like it?" He indicated her nearly full bowl.

"I don't eat as fast as you do, Cyril," she replied tightly.

He blanched but said nothing, merely waited until she finished.

She was equally as slow with the other courses, hardly touching her food. Finally, when he had a second cup of coffee waiting for her to finish her entrée, he could not resist asking, "Is something wrong, my dear? Aren't you enjoying your meal?"

She raised an eyebrow, looked at him as though he'd gone daft, snapped, "Whatever are you talking about?

Just because I don't gulp my food down like you do doesn't mean anything is wrong.''

Cyril had had enough of her foul disposition. He met her fiery stare and demanded, "All right, Dani. Would you mind telling me why you invited me here tonight if you can't be civil? You've been in a bad mood all evening. I brought you an expensive gift, and you don't even show me the courtesy of opening it. Then you bite my head off every few minutes. If I've done something to offend you, tell me, so I can try to make amends. If I haven't, then please stop being so uncivil.''

Dani struggled to keep from exploding. Oh, the nerve of him—looking so smug, so sanctimonious. No matter that he had stolen from her or that he'd attempted to ruin Drake's chances of restoring honor to his family name in order to selfishly gain fame for himself. No matter that he nearly ended her relationship with a man she might love. Oh, no, Cyril thought he'd done nothing wrong, and his only concern for the moment was why she was treating him so coolly.

When Dani did not speak, Cyril began to feel uncomfortable. Icy fingers of apprehension had begun to dance along his spine. She was, he worriedly observed, staring at him with loathing. Why? What had he done? Was there some way she could have found out about his having taken the painting? No. There had to be another reason for her strange behavior—but what?

"Would you like me to leave?" he asked stiffly.

Dani silently acknowledged she would like that very much but could not take a chance on him discovering Drake in his apartment. Once the painting was found and in her possession, he couldn't do anything. Until then, he could accuse Drake of burglarizing. They couldn't risk that.

Finally, she bit out an apology. "I'm sorry. I must be tired. Shall we have dessert served in the parlor?''

Cyril was at once the epitome of concern. He nearly knocked over his chair in his haste to help her with hers.

"Of course, of course. Let's make ourselves comfortable in front of the fire."

His gaze fell on the foil-wrapped box, and he quickly retrieved it and thrust it into her lap as she sat down on the divan before the crackling fire. "Open this, please," he urged, sitting close beside her.

She moved away, hedged. "I told you, Cyril, you didn't have to buy me a gift. I think it best you returned it."

"No. You have to see it, at least. Fabergé would be quite disappointed if he thought you weren't impressed enough with his reputation that you'd not want to at least see his creation."

Anything to pass the time! Dani gritted her teeth and ripped off the ribbon and paper with almost vengeance. But, lifting the lid of the tiny box, she could not help gasping at the sight of the exquisite brooch. "Cyril, it's lovely," she cried, holding it up to the light, fascinated by the way the tiny stones danced in the fire's glow.

But the fascination was short-lived.

Replacing the brooch in the box, she held it out to him. "I can't accept your gift."

Cyril blinked, disappointed and confused. "But why not?"

"It isn't proper."

"Isn't proper?" he echoed, laughing. "Why, my dear, what's wrong with a gift between friends?"

"People might think it precedes a more serious announcement."

He moved closer, slipped his arm around her shoulders, and huskily declared, "I hope so. I want our relationship to grow, Dani. I want to be more than your friend. Surely you know that by now."

He saw the ominous flash in her eyes, felt the way she stiffened at his touch, yet felt compelled to plunge ahead and declare his feelings: "I love you, Dani, and I think you love me too. Why else would you have come on this trip? You wanted us to be together, to get to know each other better . . .''

Dani felt nauseous. Once, she might have entertained thoughts of romance with Cyril, albeit frivolous, for he was handsome, charming, good company. But since the discovery that he was a conniving sneak thief, she regarded him only with contempt, could hardly bear his company.

He tried to kiss her, clasping her face with his hands as she attempted to twist away. "Dani, please, please," he begged, the heat of his desire making his breath ragged, his voice hoarse. "I only want to make you happy, because I love you . . . I've loved you from the first moment I laid eyes on you. You must've known, and you must love me too—''

"I don't love you!" With one mighty thrust, Dani tore from his arms and leaped to her feet to stare down at him, bosom heaving, as she gasped with incredulity. Oh, the arrogance! Did he really think she was so vulnerable? So easily manipulated?

Cyril, astonished by her reaction, also stood. Anger and humiliation began to wash over him as he realized that she could reject him so completely and intensely. "Then why did you invite me here tonight?" he demanded coldly. "I don't appreciate being used, Dani, I—''

"You dare to accuse *me* of using *you?*" she cried, about to explode, then suddenly she commanded herself to be silent. *It was not time!* There had been no signal from Drake that his mission was successfully completed.

Cyril ran agitated fingers through his hair, lifted his chin slightly, attempting to maintain dignity as he tersely suggested, "Perhaps I'd best leave and return when you're not in such a foul mood. Whatever's bothering you, Dani, it's not by my hand. I've never been anything but kind to you." He snatched up the jewel box; if she continued to regard him with apparent contempt, he certainly wasn't about to waste an expensive gift on her.

He started for the door.

Dani's teeth ground together and her fists clenched as she watched him prepare to leave. She knew she could not allow it. Even if it meant enduring his kisses, she had to keep him there until she received word from Drake. Oh, damn Colt, she fumed silently, why couldn't he have been here tonight?

"Cyril, wait—"

He turned, suppressing a smile at the look of desolation on her lovely face. "Have you thought of something else you can say to hurt me?"

"Cyril, I—"

There was a knock on the door.

Relieved, Dani brushed by him quickly, spared, for the moment, from being ingratiating. "That's probably our after-dinner cordials. We'll have one last drink and maybe I'll feel better . . ." Her voice trailed off as she flung the door open to find the waiter standing there looking quite confused.

He was holding a silver tray on which rested a large cream pie. He flashed an apologetic smile, shrugged helplessly. "I realize you've already been served the dessert you ordered, mademoiselle, but a gentleman delivered this to the kitchen and was most emphatic that it be served to you at once. He also said that you'd understand it was of special significance for a very special occasion."

The warmth of happy realization spread through Dani like a great cascading wave. "*Merci!*" she said, laughing, unable to resist a curtsy as she took the tray.

She set it down on a nearby table, kept her back turned to Cyril, who was watching in stony silence.

She heard the waiter close the door behind him.

"More dessert?" Cyril asked lightly, thinking perhaps sweetness might help her mood.

Dani grasped the pie and turned to face him.

He heard her declare him a lying, loathesome son of a bitch . . . just before the cream splattered in his face.

Chapter Thirty-two

In his hotel suite, Drake and Dani sat opposite each other, the painting on a table between them.

Drake sighed, shook his head, ran his fingertips through his hair in frustration. "I don't see it. I can't find a single clue to tell me one damn thing. As far as I can tell, it's nothing but a crude drawing of the palace, and the egg could be hidden anywhere inside, and there are over a hundred rooms! I wouldn't know where to start looking if permission was granted to search!"

Dani shared his gloom but was curious to know why the revolutionaries chose the palace as a hiding place. "Isn't it well guarded?"

"Oh, yes." Drake then described the way he remembered security during his many visits. "There's a permanent garrison of five thousand infantrymen, carefully selected out of all the regiments of the Imperial Guard, and then there are guard detachments at the gates and foot patrols in the park, as well as sentries stationed inside in the vestibules, staircases, corridors, kitchens, and even in the cellars. They've even got plainclothes guards just to keep an eye on the people that work there, and they probably number well into the hundreds—servants, workmen, tradesmen."

"So it wouldn't have been easy to have gotten in there to hide anything," she mused, wondering if it was all a hoax.

He sensed her thoughts. "It would've been difficult, true, but from all I've heard about Zigmont Koryatovich, I'm not surprised he was able to do it. He loved to make the Czar, and his armies, look foolish. For him to have hidden the Fabergé egg inside the palace was a slap in the Czar's face. And there was never any doubt that's where he hid it. He and my mother were captured near the palace.

"In fact," he continued, "they say Koryatovich went to his death bragging about it. That's how the legend of the painting began. On the morning he was executed, he told one of his jailers that when my mother escaped, she took with her the one clue to where the Fabergé egg was hidden. The jailer got word to the Czar who, in turn, told his son Nicholas, and he, because of our past friendship, told me. After that, it was hushed up to keep would-be fortune hunters from trying to sneak inside the palace to look for it."

Dani's heart went out to him, for she knew the agony of being so near . . . yet so far. Ten years he'd searched for the painting, and now he had it . . . but could not find a single clue.

She was struck by another thought. "Did Koryatovich actually admit your mother escaped with a painting that contained the clue to where the egg was hidden? Maybe she actually took something else."

He shook his head. "No. The guards had let Koryatovich have the art supplies he asked for, feeling sorry for him, I suppose, because he was scheduled to die. I guess they saw no harm in a doomed man painting a few pictures to while away what was left of his life."

Dani looked pensive a moment. "I'm going to pay Monsieur Arpel one final visit," she then announced.

Drake raised an eyebrow. "Why? What business do you have with him?"

"He still has something that belongs to me, and I intend to have it."

Drake glanced at the canvas and nodded. "Ah, yes, the frame. I found the canvas under the bed but there was no sign of the frame."

Dani stood, gathered her things, and moved toward the door with Drake following. "To be perfectly honest, I valued the frame more than the painting, because it was so unusual."

Drake had to admit he'd not paid any attention to it. "I was always too busy concentrating on the painting whenever I had the chance."

With a parting kiss, Dani went her way. The night was clear, stars twinkling like ice crystals in a sky of black frost. The world around her glittered white, a million crystal diamonds studding the landscape. The wind was soft, as caressing as a baby's breath, and she clutched her ermine wrap tighter as she moved toward the carriage that would take her to Cyril's shop.

A lamp burned above the door but all was silent. Dani knocked with determination. It was not that the frame was valuable; she merely wanted what was rightfully hers. Cyril had lied, stolen, manipulated. He should be grateful Drake was so concerned with unraveling the mystery that he hadn't sought revenge, for Cyril was no match for the Russian's strength and fury.

She was about to knock once more when Cyril opened the door to look at her in surprise. "Dani!" He almost choked on her name, then leaned out to nervously glance left and right, making sure she was alone before he gestured her inside.

Once they were in the foyer, he asked hesitantly, "What are you doing here? I thought you never wanted to see me again?"

"I don't," she curtly confirmed. "Just give me the rest of what you stole from me, and I'll be on my way."

His expression was blank. He shrugged helplessly. "I'm sorry. I don't know what you're talking about."

"I want the frame," she snapped.

He laughed softly, incredulously. "That unrefined thing? Whatever for?" He put a cajoling hand on her shoulder. "Come on in, my dear, and let's talk about this. I know you're angry, but if you'll just let me explain everything, you'll see it's just a harmless situation, something to laugh about, not get upset over, and—"

"Cyril, don't patronize me!" she cried, slapping his hand from her shoulder and glaring up at him venomously. "Just give me my property so I can get out of here. I find you so despicable it makes me nauseous to even breathe the same air as you!"

He lifted his chin as though slapped. "All right then," he curtly told her. "I'll get your *worthless* frame to go with your *worthless* painting, and then you can run to your *worthless* lover!"

He left her standing in the foyer, returning moments later with the frame. He thrust it at her. "Here. Take it and go. If you can't be open-minded about this thing and see it for just a harmless, amusing situation, then it's best we don't try to be friends any longer."

She tried to feel pity for him, could not. "Cyril, we were never really friends. You don't manipulate your friends!"

She left him staring after her as she hurried out to the waiting carriage.

Dani did not notice the man standing in the shadows across the street . . . just as she'd not seen him following her constantly since the night of the Imperial Ball. She was too anxious to be on her way, for she'd decided to use the retrieved frame as an excuse to see Drake once more that evening.

Drake sipped a brandy as he continued to scrutinize the painting. Lord, he thought, Zigmont Koryatovich might have been many things, but one thing he was not was an artist. A child might have accomplished the same replica with less effort.

But what was the blasted key?

God, to be so close, to actually have the damn thing
in his hands after all these years, when it'd been his only
glimmer of hope that he could restore his father's honor
so the wretched soul could rest in peace. . . . and then
not to be able to decipher any meaning.

It was painfully frustrating.

And it didn't help matters that he now had another reason to resolve what had become a life's quest.

Dani Coltrane.

He *had* to solve the mystery; Dani deserved more than
a man banned from the Imperial Court, a man whose
family honor had been stripped away.

A sound at the door brought him out of his reverie. He
opened the door, then blinked at the sight of Jade standing there, looking cold and miserable, green eyes misted
with sadness.

She stumbled into his arms with a broken sob. He
pushed the door shut, then held her close. "Jade, darling,
what's wrong? What's happened? Has Colt done something to hurt you?" His voice had an apprehensive edge.

"No, no," she assured him quickly, clinging to him
tightly. "Oh, Drakar, help me, please—"

"Anything!" He held her away from him, gave her a
gentle shake for she was near hysteria in her grief. "Just
tell me what's wrong . . ."

"I love him," she said brokenly, miserably, her gaze
meeting his in a silent plea for help. "I know it wasn't
supposed to turn out this way, but I love him . . ."

She crumpled against him, and Drake maneuvered her
to the bed so they could sit down. Then he asked to hear
the rest of the story.

Bitterly, she bit out the account of how Colt had told
her of his feelings, that he felt he could love her, wanted
to pursue those feelings . . . and would she be willing
to come to Paris to live with his family for as long as it
took them to come to terms with their relationship?

"I'm a member of the Imperial Ballet of Saint Petersburg, and this man thinks I'm an uneducated urchin. He

even says he'll help my family out financially so they won't be upset when I leave Russia. Oh, Drakar," she wailed, "what am I going to do? You said yourself Colt's been hurt by women deceiving him. What do you think will happen when he hears how *I've* deceived him?"

Drake could no longer hold back his amusement. "You said you loved him. I don't see a problem."

Her voice rose in furious frustration. "Don't you understand? I've lied to him—"

"But it was a *nice* lie, Jade, with no harm intended, and it's turned out even better than I expected."

She slumped against him, sobbing once more. He lay back across the bed, pulling her down with him to cradle her and hold her close, wanting to soothe, wanting to make her see that her world had not ended, that it was, by a quirk of fate, just beginning . . . and it was going to be wonderful.

Drake did not hear the door open.

He did not know that Dani had entered the room until he heard a gasp and looked up to see her standing there staring down, ashen-faced.

It was, he realized as bitter bile rose in his throat, like going back in time to that night in Paris.

And, just as she had done before, Dani looked at him with loathing before she turned and ran from the room.

Chapter Thirty-three

DRAKE caught up with Dani as she reached the landing of the floor below. He grabbed her and swung her around to face him. "This time," he hoarsely avowed, "you're going to stay around long enough to hear my side, dammit!"

Rage was a snake, twisting and writhing through her body and soul. He had her arms pinned to her sides or she'd have struck him. "You lying bastard! You could never be true to one woman, could you?"

"Dani, listen to me—"

"No, listen to me, please . . ."

They both turned to Jade, who was leaning over the railing above.

"Don't be angry with him. It's all my fault. Come back upstairs and I'll explain everything."

Dani regarded her with contempt. "I don't have any quarrel with you. You're just part of his collection." She struggled against Drake. Oh, how could she have been so blind? So stupid? Once more, she'd fallen into his trap, allowed him to manipulate her.

Jade shook her head vigorously. "No, you can't believe that. You have to listen, Dani—"

"You know me?" Dani interrupted, incredulous and becoming even angrier that Drake could speak of her to one of his "harem."

"Of course I do. He asked me to spy on you at the Imperial Ball and report back to him about everything you said and did." She looked to Drake for approval, saw he appeared quite willing for her to tell all, so she rapidly continued. "I made it possible for him to slip into your suite at the embassy and surprise you."

Dani was even angrier to hear that. What kind of pervert was this strange girl that she'd spy on another woman for her lover?

Jade sensed what she was thinking, rushed to explain. "Drakar and I aren't lovers, Dani. We're very dear friends. I was only helping him to get to you."

Dani gave her head a reckless toss, fingers tightly gripping the frame she still held. "Just leave me alone," she said with a sneer. "I don't want to hear anything either of you has to say!"

"Dani, please listen to her," Drake begged.

"Why should I?"

"Because then you'll know the truth," Jade softly responded. I'm not in love with Drakar. I've been seeing your brother, Colt."

Dani was stunned. She'd suspected Colt was seeing someone—but why all the mystery?

Drake released his hold, moved to put his arms around her as he urged, "Can't we please go back upstairs to my room? We can talk this out without the other hotel guests hearing." Irritably, he nodded to a door just down the hall, slightly ajar, with an eavesdropper obviously hovering on the other side.

Dani allowed him to lead her back upstairs, then sat in stony silence while he related his plan for Jade to pose as a poor girl to ultimately reject Colt so he'd come to a new awareness of women.

"Actually," he finished with a wry grin, "Jade is probably as rich as Colt. She's a member of the Romanov family."

Dani knew of the prestige and wealth of the Romanovs but that was not what impressed her. She looked at Jade in awe and murmured, "You dance with the Imperial Ballet."

Jade frowned, and gave Drake a disconsolate glance. "After this, who knows? I'm supposed to be recuperating from a sprained ankle, not posing as a servant girl at the French Embassy."

Drake looked to Dani hopefully. "Now do you believe me?"

She laughed softly, gently chided that if he didn't have such a notorious reputation with women he would not be suspect.

Jade chimed in to agree.

Drake shook his head in mock disgust, then turned from where they'd sat down on the divan and went to open a bottle of wine.

"So what happened between you and Colt?" Dani asked of Jade. "You look so unhappy."

Jade regretfully told her that Drake's scheme had backfired. "I thought, as Drakar did, that it would all be a lark, that it'd never get very far before I could make my little speech to him about how it didn't matter if his wealth matched the Czar's, I could only love for love's sake.

"But," she went on to dismally admit, "Colt was so wonderful that I found myself becoming more and more interested, and I knew he was sincere when he professed to be falling in love with me."

Dani was listening to every word she spoke but was staring at Drake all the while in wonder. This was a side to him she'd never seen before—his capacity for tenderness and caring for others—and she liked that trait . . . liked it a lot. He walked over and set the wine bottle and glasses down on a table, and she reached out to take his hand, held it lovingly as she attempted to encourage Jade to make amends. "Go to Colt and tell him the whole story, just as you've told me. I don't think he'll be angry."

Jade shuddered at the thought of confessing all to Colt. "I'm afraid he'll be so humiliated he'll hate me."

They both looked at Drake reproachfully. After all, it had been *his* idea.

He threw up his hands. "Well, I'm not going to be the one to tell him. Not after Paris . . . and Lily. I never wanted him to know I had anything to do with this."

"That's true," Jade told Dani. "He didn't want you to know, either, because he was afraid you wouldn't approve, yet he felt it was the only way to get Colt to stop being so cynical about women."

"You didn't say what you actually did when Colt let his feelings be known," Dani said.

Jade blinked away fresh tears. "Nothing. I just ran away. I couldn't go through with it, and I ran out and came here, because I was so miserable and there was no one else I could talk to besides Drakar."

"Tomorrow," Dani said firmly, "you'll talk to Colt and tell him the truth. If you really care about him, that's the only way."

Jade nodded, but not with enthusiasm. "He'll never want to see me again."

Dani sighed, looked from one to the other as she shook her head and declared, "When are you going to learn you can't go around playing with people's lives? Even if you have the best of intentions, things have a way of back-firing."

Drake shrugged. "I see no harm, as long as people are mature enough to realize the intentions were good."

"It's said the road to hell is paved with good intentions," Dani countered.

"Enough!" Jade cut in, trying to sound cheerful. "Let's stop talking about me. You've got enough problems of your own, because you still haven't found the secret of that painting."

For the first time, Drake noticed the frame. "You got it."

Dani gave it to him. "And Cyril was about as pleasant as you said he'd be."

Drake left them to go to a far corner of the room and study the frame. The two young women chatted like old friends, when suddenly, Drake cried, "By god, I think I've got it!"

They leaped to their feet and ran to his side. He pointed excitedly to the frame. "That's it. Russian olive! The wood of this frame is made from Russian olive! An obvious clue," he rushed on, fascinated, "if someone is familiar with the palace. Otherwise, they'd never discover it."

He went on to explain: "The grand staircase in the palace is made of Russian olive. The trees only grow in the southern regions of Europe, but when Catherine the Great commissioned the Italian Quarenghi to build the palace a hundred years ago, she insisted the railing of the grand staircase be made of Russian olive, because the tree doesn't grow in that region, and she wanted something unique, special."

Recounting memories of his childhood, he told how Nicholas's grandfather, Czar Alexander II, had scolded him and Nicholas one day for sliding down the banister. Then he proudly told them about the Russian olivewood, how the trees had been imported from Greece.

Looking happily from one woman to the other, he said, "Russian olive isn't that easy to obtain, and Koryatovich sure as hell didn't find any in Siberia. He must've had time to remove one of the balusters before he was caught. I remember they're so close together you'd hardly notice one missing unless you were looking for it.

"The egg," he predicted with firm conviction, "has to be hidden somewhere around those stairs, because that's the only structure anywhere in the palace made of Russian olive."

Drake reverently looked at the painting. Zigmont Zory-atovich had certainly been clever, but now the nightmare of the past could end . . . and a possible glorious future with Dani could begin.

He turned, took her in his arms, oblivious to Jade's presence. He kissed her, then asked, "Who wants to go with me to the Alexandrovsky Palace?"

Dani laughingly informed him he'd better not even think about leaving her behind, and then they turned to Jade, who declined, explaining that while she'd love to join them, to be there for the ultimate moment, she felt it was more important to see Colt.

"Drakar, you might have some problems getting inside the palace," she reminded him. "Everyone knows you were banished from court, and you can't just walk in there without some kind of permission."

Arctic eyes narrowed in bitter remembrance. "Then I'll just have to go to the Czar and get *his* permission."

Jade was apprehensive. "You're going to have to tell him why you want it, and he might think it's a wild-goose chase and say no."

Dani snapped her fingers as she suddenly remembered something. "No! He won't, because you can go to Nicholas and ask him to help." Quickly she recounted the night at the Winter Palace, when Nicholas was giving her a personal tour, and she'd seen the mural and ultimately confided to him the story of the Monaco Find.

Drake's enthusiasm was strengthened. "Nicholas won't be a bit surprised to hear I'm around. Despite everything, I believe he's still my friend and would be willing to help."

He instructed Dani to return to the embassy. "Dress warmly," he urged. "It's about twenty kilometers to Tsarskoye Selo, and we'll be going by sleigh."

To Jade, he was compassionately encouraging. "I really believe once you explain everything to Colt, he won't be angry, because he obviously cares for you. Just tell him if he wants to vent his rage on anybody, make it me, and I'll try to make amends later." He winked, attempting to brighten her spirits.

They left him and went outside into the twilight glow that did little more than brighten the snow. At such an hour, there were no *izvoschchiks*—carriages for hire—and would not be for some time. Fresh snow had fallen during the night, then frozen, leaving a crusty surface, and they walked cautiously toward the embassy.

Dani offered to go with Jade to talk to Colt but was not surprised when she declined. She wished her well and went to her suite to bathe and change into warm undergarments, a riding habit of wool, and leather boots that reached to her knees. Next, she laid out a thick cape fashioned of wolf pelts and gloves of warm, silky, rabbit fur.

She rang for her maid to bring steaming, spicy Russian tea, bread and butter sandwiches, then settled down to wait for Drake.

She was almost trembling with excitement. To be part of the culmination of something so important to Drake meant almost as much to her as it did to him, for she wanted to share everything in his life.

It had been almost three hours since her return to the embassy when there was a knock on the door. Thinking it had to be Drake, she rushed to answer . . . only to find Cyril Arpel staring at her, shame-faced, nervously twisting a thick fur cape in his hands.

He did not give her a chance to rebuke him. Quickly, he stuck his foot in the door to bar closing, then attempted to touch a nerve of sympathy in Dani. "I had to come and apologize, Dani, to tell you how sorry I am for everything. Can you forgive me?" he begged anxiously, hopefully. "Can we be friends?"

Dani had stiffened at the sight of him, and his woeful plea had not moved her. Firmly, she shook her head. "You've done too much, Cyril . . . gone too far. I just don't see any way we can ever be friends. Now please leave."

"No!" He shoved his weight against the door as she attempted to close it, his words coming out in a frenzied torrent as he made his plea. "You owe me a chance to make amends, Dani. After all, I brought you to Russia with me, showed you around, introduced you to people, did everything I could to make you happy. Again, I'm sorry for what I did, but I never meant to hurt anybody. Now let me try to make amends by helping you and Drakar search for the Fabergé egg. I don't want to keep it. All I want is to be the one to get the credit for finding it, and the painting. Is that too much to ask?"

Dani furiously told him that if he'd been honorable in the beginning and confided in her, she might have been willing to cooperate—then. "Now it's too late. So leave or I'm going to call security," she warned.

Their eyes met and held—his almost tearful with desperation; hers cold with resolution.

Cyril knew she was not going to change her mind and stepped away from the door. Promptly, she slammed it. He turned away dejectedly, head down, shoulders slumped. He'd made a mess of things. Pure and simple. It was over. He'd lost both the painting and Dani, and there seemed to be nothing he could do about it.

He was almost to the end of the corridor, about to open the outer door when, through the leaded-glass window, he saw Drakar getting out of a horse-drawn sleigh in the street.

Quickly, he leaped back to stand in an archway, pressed himself against the wall . . . and waited.

Drake opened the door, hurried toward Dani's suite.

Cyril stayed where he was as everything began to come together: Drakar arriving with a sleigh, and he'd not missed the way Dani was warmly dressed, obviously ready to go out.

They were on their way to Tsarskoe Selo . . . and the palace . . . to look for the egg.

He did not have to wait long, for within minutes the two approached.

He heard Drakar's voice:

". . . it was as we'd hoped. Once you told Nicholas about the painting, he figured something was going on, that I had to be around somewhere, so he was more than willing to go with me to see his father, and he was eager to cooperate. He said he'd be as glad as I would to have all of this over with so both his father and mine could rest in peace . . ."

His voice faded as he and Dani opened the door and closed it behind them.

Cyril stepped out to peer through the glass, waited till they disappeared from sight in the sleigh, then followed. He wasn't exactly sure what he was going to do, did not have a specific plan in mind, but he was certain of one thing: when the coveted Fabergé egg was found, he was going to be there to claim the credit . . . and maybe even the egg, he thought with a resentful sneer.

Chapter Thirty-four

IT was late afternoon when they reached Tsarskoye Selo, and for many hours the world had been a gray sea of snow and ice. There was faint illumination from a moon somewhere beyond the gloomy pall, and they could see the outline of the high fence of the Imperial Park. Cossack horsemen, resplendent in black fur capes, boots, and shining sabers could be seen as they rode on patrol.

"There's always security," Drake explained, "but not as much as when the Czar is in residence. They have to constantly be on guard against the revolutionaries."

They entered the park, and passing Yekaterinsky Palace, Drake pointed out that it contained over two hundred rooms.

Dani was appropriately impressed, but when they reached their ultimate destination—the Alexandrovsky Palace, she gasped. "I can only say Zigmont Koryatovich did not do it justice. It's magnificent."

A wary guard carrying a rifle came out of a stone gatehouse. Unexpected visitors at such an hour were unusual, but after examining the dispatch Drake handed down, he waved them on, not about to argue with the imperial seal of the Czar.

They drew up to the main façade, with its sweeping terrace and marble stairs.

"It looks absolutely deserted," Dani murmured, clinging to Drake's arm as they made their way up the steps.
"There's hardly any light at all from within."

"I told you there'd only be a skeleton staff, and that's
to our advantage. We won't have people breathing down
our necks watching."

The palace regent responded after a time to their
pounding on the doors. He was dressed regally in a red
cape bordered with imperial eagles and wore black patent
shoes, black silk stockings, and white lace garters at his
knees. Like the guard at the gate, he was suspicious, but
after reading the imperial message, he bowed graciously
and offered his services in any way required.

Drake curtly dismissed him. "Just keep the rest of the
servants away. We want this section of the palace to ourselves."

"Oh, there are no other servants on duty at this hour,"
the regent was quick to inform him. "Will you and the
lady be staying the night, sire?"

Drake thought a moment. He'd like nothing better than
to whisk Dani upstairs to one of the royal suites and make
love to her all night long in a celebration of what was
sure to be the end of his quest . . . but such pleasure
would have to wait. He wanted to get that damned egg
back to the Czar as quickly as possible, and then there'd
be time for such joys.

"No," he said finally, "we'll be leaving shortly."

Dani's gaze swept the glittering magnificence of the
grand hall. It was large enough for a ballroom, with marble floors polished to shine brilliantly even in the faint
light of lanterns. She knew it would be a staggering vision beneath the brilliance of the twelve huge crystal and
gold chandeliers which hung in a straight line across the
thirty-foot-high ceiling.

On each side of the foyer were tall mirrors, interspersed with priceless paintings and portraits along the
grand walkway.

A fountain stood in the middle, adorned with cherubs holding pitchers which, no doubt, would freely flow with champagne during gala socials.

But now the fountain was empty and still . . . as was the entire palace. All was silent, as though they had just entered a massive tomb.

Dani followed Drake through the foyer to the wide stairway at the rear. The steps, she noted, were small and narrow, covered in lush red velvet. The balusters, ornately carved, were indeed constructed so close together that it would be difficult to notice if one was missing.

Closer scrutiny proved Drake right—the wood appeared identical to that of the painting's frame.

Drake moved to the newel post on the left, gave it a mighty tug, and it twisted off. "Two chances," he whispered. "If it isn't here, we've got the one on the other side."

He reached inside, and Dani cried aloud with delight, for she could tell by the sudden glow in his eyes, the way his whole face suddenly ignited in triumph—he'd found it.

He withdrew his arm, opened his hand to display a small leather pouch. Tremulously, he whispered, "This is it! I know it!"

They leaped into each other's arms, laughing, almost crying with their joy, clinging together with unsurpassed happiness.

"It's over, Dani. It's finally over. Now my father can rest in peace, and I can hold my head up, and get on with my life, *our* lives, and—"

With a sudden gasp and groan, he slumped in her arms.

Dani did not have time to scream or make a sound as she struggled to hold on to him, to keep him from slipping from her arms and onto the floor.

But then a giant hand came across her neck from behind, and Drake's unconscious body slid downward, and the pouch he'd held in his hand silently rolled across the gleaming floor, back toward the stairway.

Her shriek of horror was muffled by another hand, and she saw the reason for Drake's collapse. A large scruffy man stood grinning at her as she struggled against whoever was holding her from behind and twisting her arms tightly, painfully, in restraint.

He had mean eyes—narrow, squinted black eyes set beneath thick, bushy brows that matched the beard covering the lower part of his face. He was fierce-looking, a deep purple scar running from one temple down to the corner of his mouth.

The man seemed swathed in clothing—a blanket, a cape, rags, whatever means available to secure warmth against the frigid weather. A worn hat of some kind of skin was pulled tightly down on his head, and long strands of greasy black hair hung recklessly around his ears and neck.

Dani was trying to comprehend the meaning of what was happening. These men had to be revolutionaries. Somehow, they'd heard the painting had been found, knew Drake had deciphered the clue, and knew where the Fabergé egg was hidden. Now they'd come to claim it.

The man before her grinned with chipped teeth and spoke in broken French but clearly enough that she could understand what he was saying. "You should not be afraid, mademoiselle. We mean you no harm."

Dani hoped her fury was mirrored in her eyes as she glared at him.

He went on to explain who he was—Vordan, patriot commander of the People's Will Party—and his comrade, who held her, was Miliukov. For a decade, their mission had been to find the coveted Fabergé egg. "As a tribute to our leader, Zigmont Koryatovich, so that he will not have died in vain. We knew that sooner or later you and Drakar would come."

Suddenly Dani closed her eyes, willed herself to be calm, for surely the horror of what was happening had caused her mind to play tricks.

She thought she had seen, from the corner of her eye, someone hiding, peering out from beneath the stairs.

She thought, dear God, that that "someone" was Cyril.

Opening her eyes, without looking toward the stairs, she mustered every ounce of strength she had against her captor to twist in another direction, thereby unconsciously directing the man called Vordan to turn also . . . away from the stairs.

And, just before she gave her mighty lunge, causing whoever held her to also turn his back to the stairway, she had seen something . . . and had flashed her eyes shut once more, lest they give away the startling realization that Cyril Arpel was, indeed, crawling out from beneath the stairs and heading for the pouch that had rolled from Drake's hand when he fell. She knew he had to have followed them to Tsarskoye Selo, no doubt aware of another, quicker way to sneak inside the palace, so he could be secretly waiting when she and Drake came in through normal means.

"So you will now tell us where it is hidden," her captor demanded.

The hand mashing across her face parted fingers just enough that she could speak, ready to bear down once more should she try to scream. She opened her eyes and challenged him venomously. "Do you really think I'd tell you bastards anything?"

He sneered, regarded her with contempt, reached to caress her breast intimately. "If you value your worthless aristocratic life, you'll tell me, and if you are very nice, perhaps I will show you what a real Russian man is like." He nodded toward Drake's still form. "You think it is good with a plutocrat?"

"I'm not afraid of you," she lashed out tartly. "Your kind intimidates, by fear and violence, and I'm not about to let you bully me." Dani dared a fleeting cut of her eyes and saw that the pouch was gone . . . and so was Cyril.

Vordan was tiring of bantering with a mere woman. He began to glance about the foyer, then spotted the newel post on the floor. He turned to Dani with wide eyes, suddenly cognizant of what he'd failed to notice in his haste to sneak up on them and render Drakar unconscious.

The egg had already been found!

He grabbed Dani by her throat and began to choke her, sending her head bobbing to and fro as the other man tried to retain his hold. "Where is it? Do you hide it on you, little bitch? Tell me, or I will rip your clothes from you and throw you into the snow naked to freeze."

Dani struggled to speak, for her throat was being squeezed painfully shut. "I . . . don't have it . . ."

Miliukov angrily twisted her away from Vordan's assault, thundered, "You're going to kill her, and then we will have nothing. Look around for it. Search Drakar. I will search her."

Vordan stepped away, nostrils flaring with rage, eyes glittering ominously. He began to wildly look about, roughly searched Drake. "It isn't here," he cried.

"Then I will search this one . . ."

"No! Someone else was here. He grabbed the pouch we found in the newel post while you were busy with me, and now—"

Miliukov applied the pressure necessary to silence her again. "She may be telling the truth. There might have been someone else, who sneaked away while we were busy with her. We cannot take a chance she is not bluffing. It is too dangerous."

Vordan nodded grimly. "Let's go. We have her, and we will hold her for ransom . . . or trade her for the egg." Taking a rag from inside his cape, he roughly shoved it in Dani's mouth the instant Miliukov removed his hand. Another was quickly wrapped around her wrists to securely bind them together.

As she was abruptly hoisted over the shoulder of her abductor, Dani had one last glimpse of Drake lying so deadly still on the floor, blood seeping from the wound on the back of his head.

With unbearable anguish and a heart on the verge of breaking, she wondered whether she would ever see him again . . . the man she now knew she loved without question.

Chapter Thirty-five

DANI was carried out through a narrow door that led into a passageway designed for servants' use. Entering the shadowy kitchen, she could sense by the stale odors that the facilities had not been used for a long while—probably since the first hint of winter.

Vordan opened a large wooden door, and they entered a storage room. At the end of the rows of barrels and bags of dried beans, flour, salt, sugar, and spices, there was yet another door, this one a mere hatchway, used for delivery wagons and carts. Squeaking hinges swung it up and out, giving exit.

Vordan whispered to Miliukov to wait until he checked for any Cossack patrols, then disappeared only momentarily before returning. "The fools. As long as their precious tyrant isn't in residence, they give us little thought."

Dani was jostled roughly as they ran through the snow, the sound of their footsteps an eery crunch within the white abyss of silence.

They reached a thick clump of snow-covered shrubs, and Vordan quickly pulled out a crude wooden sled. Dani was unceremoniously shoved onto it, felt her breath being crushed from her as Vordan lowered himself to lie on her back, holding her securely in place as he gripped the sides and ordered his partner to hurry.

Miliukov positioned himself directly behind the sled and began to push with all his might to move them across the frozen terrain.

Vordan pressed his lips against her ear and said, "We may not have the Fabergé egg now, but soon we will, because that is the price your plutocratic friends must pay if they want you back . . . alive!"

He threw back his head and laughed maniacally, as Dani shuddered in terror to realize she was truly in the hands of madmen. They were, after all, members of the most radical wing of the revolutionaries, the terrorist faction known as People's Will. They had split from the main party, Land and Freedom, and advocated assassination of prominent officials.

For the first time in her life, Dani knew complete and total fear.

She shrank down into the sled and began to pray . . . for Drake, that he was not seriously injured and would ultimately come for her, and that Cyril had not, as she was starting to bitterly suspect, taken the egg and run for his own glory, without another thought of her well-being or Drake's. She prayed to be wrong about him . . . prayed that he was on his way with the palace guards to save her . . . yet knew with a rumble of nausea that she prayed in vain.

They reached a section of the woods near the end of the Imperial park. Branches, hanging low with the weight of the snow, loomed in their path.

Vordan began to warn Miliukov to be careful, but just as he opened his mouth to speak, a heavy branch, laden with snow, was suddenly released like a catapult, striking Miliukov squarely in his face. With a cry, he fell backward, and Dani whipped her head around to see a hulking shadow leap down from the tree above.

With one deft blow from his attacker, Miliukov was knocked unconscious, his face sinking into the deep snow.

Vordan, momentarily stunned, finally rallied to emit a bellow of rage as he bolted from the sled—only to have a fist slam into his face, and another viciously pound the top of his head and drive him to his knees. He pitched forward, no longer a threat.

Dani strained to see the face of her liberator as he came to her and snatched away the gag from her mouth.

She screamed softly in horror to realize he was just as scruffy and ominous as Vordan and Miliukov.

Another of the revolutionaries. Were they fighting over her?

"Do not fear me," the man said in crisp, clear French. "I am your ally. Others of my party are now at the palace ministering to Drakar. He is not hurt badly," he hastened to inform her, sensing her terror. "I made sure of that before I took a shortcut to lie in wait for you."

He turned the sled around and began to push it back in the direction they'd just traveled, the fresh trail smooth and easy to maneuver.

Dani burned with curiosity. "Who are you? How did you know what was going on?" She could not see him, for she faced the way they were going, and he pushed from behind.

Pride ringing in his voice, he huskily declared, "The People's Will faction are not the only ones who have eyes in high places. We have known for some time that Drakar was back in Russia, so we were sure all we had to do was wait, and sooner or later he would make his move, and when he did, the terrorist faction would be right behind him. They watched him; *we* watched *them.*"

He went on to say that he had heard how Vordan had decreed a decade ago that he would never stop searching for the Fabergé egg, would not rest until it was in the possession of the People's Will, as his comrades thought Zigmont Koryatovich had wanted. "What Vordan refused to believe, however," he told her in a voice filled with remorse, "is that in the end, it was not the intention of Zigmont that the terrorist faction have possession of the egg, because although there might have been others around him he could've confided in, he chose to go to his grave without divulging the secret to any of them.

"I was to have met Annine Mikhailov in Paris, where she was to give me the painting so I could learn the secret and ultimately find the egg, but I was unfortunately detained in prison for a few months, and when I got out and made my way to Paris, she was dead and there was no trace of the painting . . . until you found it in Monaco, as I've heard."

Dani turned to stare at him incredulously in the white night, drank in the sight of him, determined to remember every detail of his face—warm brown eyes; clear skin; a neatly trimmed mustache; white, even teeth. He was truly handsome, despite his scruffy clothes and demeanor.

"You're one of them, a revolutionary," she pointed out tersely. "You also want the egg, so why are you helping me? Are you planning to hold both me and Drakar as hostages until Cyril Arpel turns it over to you as ransom for us? He won't. He—"

Something landed in her lap.

It was the pouch Drake had found inside the newel post . . . and the precious Fabergé egg!

"This should rest your fears. I saw a hysterical little man sneaking out of the palace, and I followed him. All I had to do was snarl at him"—he paused to laugh, remembering—"and he practically threw that at me, fell to his knees begging me to let him go. The last I saw of him, he was running through the park crying like a baby."

She could see the outline of the rear of the Alexandrovsky Palace ahead. Gingerly closing her hands around the pouch, she maneuvered to stare at him once more. "Why?" she asked in wonder. "Why are you doing this?"

Abruptly, he stopped pushing the sled, came around to draw her to her feet. "I will take you no farther. By now, my men have probably taken care of Drakar, and he's waiting for you . . . and the egg. Go now. We'll be nearby to insure your safe return to Saint Petersburg, though I doubt it will be necessary.''

Dani stubbornly shook her head. ''No. I'm not leaving here until you tell me who you are and why you are doing this.'' She dared to reach up and caress his cheek with her fingertips in a gesture of gratitude. ''You may well have saved my life. I have to know whom to thank.''

His eyes narrowed thoughtfully, then, finally, he nodded. ''Very well. Then, you can make sure the Czar and all of Russia know it is a tribute to Zigmont that the egg is returned to prove the innocence of Drakar's father, and also a tribute to his mother, whom I loved like a sister . . . and respected as a comrade. She would never have wanted her son to suffer because of anything she did.

''Neither of them were truly bad,'' he rushed to emphasize, a slight tremor to his voice hinting of the vast emotion he was experiencing to discuss something so painful. ''Remember this—Zigmont Koryatovich was first a member of the Land and Freedom Party, a revolutionary, yes, but a murderer, no, and it was only through the influence of maniacs like Vordan that he became caught up in a web of violence.

''But in the end,'' he rushed on, eyes shining and moist, ''he'd changed his philosophies. I know this to be true.''

He stepped away from her, suddenly gruff as he commanded, ''Now go. Drakar awaits. It is over. Everyone can rest in peace.''

He turned and started walking away, but she ran after him, begging, ''Please. I must know your name.''

He sighed, shoulders slumped, did not turn to face her. ''My name is Serge . . . Serge Koryatovich. Zigmont was my brother.''

She watched him disappear, a white shadow in the night, and then he was gone, and she blinked against the tears that trickled forth to freeze upon her cheeks as she made her way back to the palace.

Drakar was waiting, and when he saw her, he ran to her and lifted her in his arms and swung her around and around before crushing her against him. "I dared to believe they told me the truth," he told her. "I waited here, as they said I should, and dear god, it's true. You're here."

She pulled from his arms to hand him the pouch, and when he gasped, started to ask questions, she pressed her fingertips against his lips and said, "No. Not now. We have many, many tomorrows to talk about yesterday. For now, all I want to talk about is how much I love you . . ."

He groaned. "Oh, god, I love you, too, Dani."

It was the beginning of a new life together . . . a life that would be committed not to regret over past transgressions or mistakes . . . but a future devoted to . . . love and splendor.